The Doppelgangers

The Doppelgangers

The Others

David Ray

iUniverse

THE DOPPELGANGERS
THE OTHERS

iUniverse books may be ordered through booksellers or by contacting:

iUniverse
1663 Liberty Drive
Bloomington, IN 47403
www.iuniverse.com
1-800-Authors (1-800-288-4677)

ISBN: 978-1-4917-9718-1 (sc)
ISBN: 978-1-4917-9717-4 (hc)
ISBN: 978-1-4917-9719-8 (e)

Library of Congress Control Number: 2016908039

Print information available on the last page.

iUniverse rev. date: 05/24/2016

Contents

Oth-ers…

a. different <something other than it seems to be>
b. disturbingly or threateningly different: alien

Preface

David Blue tried to be a good person. He treated everyone with respect, and was a good father to his children. Lovingly and devoted to his girlfriend Deanne Lee Byrd. The best friend anyone could ask for. He said his prayers, paid his taxes, never took anything that wasn't his.

The kind of person that would give you the shirt off of his back if you needed it. In short David Blue was an all-round decent man... but no matter how hard he tried...

'...evil just kept messing with him!'

Dedication

This book is dedicated to my children...
Sarai, Elizabeth, David and Aaron.

My mother, Betty Lou Cuthbertson-Fleming.

My sisters and brothers, Seriata, Mary, Tony and Michael.

Last, but not least...to my very best friend, *Life'*...which has taught me that, if I spend more time understanding that I do not have 'to do' in order to be, then I would discover... that I already am.

Finally, to all those lives I have crossed....

"you all left a little piece of yourselves with me...thanks."

David Ray

Chapter 1

Going Home

Veteran's Psychiatric Hospital
1600 West Broad Street
Columbus Ohio

Eleven forty-five, David Blue was supposed to have been discharged, but who ever heard of being discharged from a hospital on time?

David Blue sat in his room thinking...

"... What is taking so long, the doctor tells you that you are going to be discharged in the morning, and then you wait until its lunch or dinner before you do get to go home...they should've left me with my chili stain!"

Six months ago at his farm in Port Clinton, Ohio. David Blue's experience with seeing evil doubles of himself and his friends, tormented him beyond words.

David devised a scheme to pretend to be one patty shy of a cheeseburger, making everyone believe that he had lost his mind, and doing so he hoped that the Doppelgangers would leave him alone.

It's been a long six months since Deanne; David's girlfriend along with her best friend Kristin drove him from the farm in Port Clinton, Ohio to the Veteran's Psychiatric Hospital in Columbus.

Six months afterwards, David's mental health team felt David's progress and recovery could be best achieved at home around familiar surroundings.

The mental health team felt that with a controlled medication regimen, and familiar surroundings that it would only be a matter of time before David would snap out of the mindless abyss he was in, and return to a mentally stable person.

The evil doubles or Doppelgangers told me when they were tormenting me at the farm that, spirits don't co-mingle.

They told me that multiple spirits would cancel each other out, and that they preyed on the healthy, those of sound mind.

In the beginning when I was admitted to the hospital I saw Doppelgangers hiding in closets, and under my bed, peeping around corners, just waiting for an opportunity to torment me.

I came close to slipping up once, and revealing myself, but had it not been for one constant, insignificant thing...a chili stain which was on the wall of the dining room in the psychiatric hospital...I would have never made it.

I would sit and stare at that chili stain, making it the only thing in my universe...and it worked.

Often times whenever a nurse had their back to me, the Doppelganger of that nurse would emerge from the nurse and stretch its face right in front of my face, in an attempt to test me, to see if I was faking it.

Most nights while I lay in bed and as an attendant left my room after making their nightly bed checks, the Doppelganger of that person would climb in bed with me.

Not taking up any space, or even making a depression in the bed. The Doppelganger would just be there, lying next to me and staring until morning.

Each day and each night I experienced this over and over until one day, The Doppelgangers just stopped appearing.

I think it was about five months after I'd been in the hospital, I had a thought...

"Maybe they're making me feel like they're gone or maybe they're hiding and waiting for me to let my guard down so they can come after me again...I got to keep my cool; the main thing is for me to get out of here."

One of my other concerns was how soon do I expose to Deanne that I'm not a soggy *'fruit loop' which has been sitting in a bowl of milk?*

I knew that I couldn't rush my miraculous faked recovery, it would take time, and it would take planning. I had thought that when the time was right, I would start out slow.... maybe simply looking at Deanne, and then progress to speaking.

I also had to make certain that the Doppelgangers never discovered that I was pretending.

On one of Deanne's visits she told me that my best friends Tim, Mary, Wendi and Steve apologized for not joining them at the farm, for our annual Labor Day get together.

I knew regardless of what Deanne was saying... our friends were there...they were at the farm, and I knew they were there.

The Doppelgangers somehow made them disappear and fixed it so that when someone disappeared everyone else had no recollection that they were even there...but I knew, they didn't trick me.

The Doppelgangers are clever and evil, and made continuous threats that an even greater evil was coming...called the Others.

Deanne was at the nurse's station getting me discharge instructions. I sat motionless in a wheel chair in my room, pretending to stare out of the window when Deanne entered saying...

'Blue...Blue baby, it's time to go...I'm taking you home Blue, you're finally coming home'.

I kept my eyes trained to the exit sign above the door as Deanne pushed the wheel chair, thinking...

'I'm really going to miss that old chili stain on the wall...now I'm going to have to find something else to focus on, until I think it's safe to reveal myself.'

My training as a prisoner of war in Vietnam, taught me how to mentally and emotionally shut down to avoid feeling pain or divulging information, and it was that training which got me through the past six months.

My plan was, as soon as I felt that the Doppelgangers were no longer interested in me, I would slowly show Deanne and my doctors that I was normal, but it had to be planned right.

The drive from the Psychiatric Hospital to the main road was a three-mile stretch on a one lane bumpy gravel road. I sat motionless, with my seat belt on, hands on my lap staring directly ahead wanting to look over at Deanne, but dared not to.

Deanne was and had always been a stunning woman to look at, with the right balance of beauty and grace, and not being able to look at her and show her that I was looking at her was killing me.

I met and fell in love with Deanne at first sight. Very few find a love such as the one I had for Deanne, the kind of love where being in the same room, occupying the same air made it hard to catch your breath.

On this day, Deanne dressed in all of the things that she knew I loved seeing her wear. Deanne wore white Capris, a pink top with a light white sweater and sandals. This was my coming home day, and Deanne wanted to make it special for me...all the way down to what she wore.

I struggled to keep from looking over at Deanne, but every time Deanne had her head turned, my eyes traced her pretty white legs, lovely feet, her light pink toe nail polish, and my nose took in the lovely scent of the berry lotion Deanne had on.

The drive from the hospital to our condo on Pecan drive with all the traffic was about an hour away, but with all the activities in town that day, it was easily turning into a two-hour drive.

It had been six long months since I kissed Deanne or made love to her and I was as hungry as any man could be for a woman.

My plan was to return back to normal quick...but not too quick. I wanted to feel her in my arms, to smell her sweet lovely white skin, to kiss and smell her pretty pinkish white feet.

I admit...I loved everything about Deanne ever since I met her in college thirty years ago. We were one of the three interracial couples at Capital University back in the mid-seventies, before I left college and entered the Army.

Broad & High Street
J.C. Woolwood Building, Tenth Floor

Forty-two-year-old James Hargrove was the youngest CEO and president of the Ohio Atlantic Power & Surge Company.

It was an average Monday afternoon, with all of the headaches you can expect, but James Hargrove has just closed one of the biggest business deals of a lifetime... merging Ohio Atlantic Power with, Europe Biogenetics.

James decided to leave work a couple of hours early, to celebrate with his wife Beverly of twenty years. Everything was set; his two children were staying with his sister and their family for the night.

Since becoming CEO of OAP five years ago, James put everything he had into the company, but unfortunately not the same could be said about his marriage.

James and Beverly met while attending the University of Arizona. James married Beverly shortly after graduation and moved to Ohio for a promising career with Ohio Atlantic Power.

Beverly was a year James' senior, and while she was equally talented if not more so, placed her career on hold so that James could solidify his position within management at OAP.

The story stays the same but the people change...a wife puts her career on hold for the husband, who becomes a financial success and ignores his wife, and later the husband has an affair with someone at work leaving the wife totally devastated.

Such was the case between James and Beverly, but it wasn't James who had the affair...but Beverly.

James truly loved Beverly but there is a truth which says...things you cherish most in your life can be taken if they're left neglected.... this, James would soon learn.

James and Beverly had two great kids, Cassandra, sixteen and Michael James, fourteen. Cassandra was a little rebellious to authority and Michael James was quite the opposite, quiet and reserved, engrossed in art and video games.

It was Friday and Beverly made arrangements for Cassandra and Michael James to stay with her sister and her two kids for the weekend.

Originally James had told Beverly that he was going out of town and would be back Sunday night, but after thinking long and hard about his marriage, thought he would surprise her by staying home this weekend.

Beverly use to hate it when James would go out of town for weekends, and although she had the kids with her she felt alone not having James with her, that was until the day of Kim Weston's graduation ceremony.

James walked as fast as he could, to the south side elevators, which led to the parking deck next to the lobby.

The elevator door opened, and James noticed there were only a few people on the elevator, and he'd have to wait on the second elevator because a man, a very large man in a powered scooter, with a crooked smile, and a foul smell, had taken up most of the space in the elevator.

Once the elevator doors closed, James turned his head to the second elevator watching the arrow slowly descend from the tenth floor to the lobby. James anxiously tapped the elevator bottom repeatedly, and after looking at his watch, decided to take the stairs.

For a man in his early forties, James was in remarkably good health. A nonsmoker and a nondrinker, James exercised twice a day in the company gym once in the morning before work, and again after work.

An avid cyclist, James knew his powerfully strong legs would have him in the lobby, long before the elevator.... so, with one fluent move, he flung his shoulder bag over his shoulder and went down the stairwell.

James made his way from the tenth floor to the fifth floor in no time, when he heard an alarm sounding off on that floor.

James started to ignore the alarm, but stopped midway between the fifth and fourth floor and then headed back to investigate the alarm.

Making his way into the office lobby area, James looked into each cubical and into each office only to discover the suite was completely empty and said to himself...

"This is just my luck.... the first time I decide to be a Good Samaritan...there's no one to rescue."

The alarm stopped as James made his way to the fourth floor landing when the door opened behind him. James turned and saw nothing except the door closing.

Curious, James opened the door and looked in both directions, but there was no one visible in the hall.

As James took a step off the fourth floor landing, he caught a glimpse of something or someone out of the corner of his eye. Nervously looking all around, there was no one there at all.

James backed into the stairwell when something rushed passed him, spinning him completely around.

James walked to the edge of the stairwell and looked down, but saw no one going down the stairwell steps.

Repositioning his shoulder bag James turned suddenly, as something brushed passed him.

All James saw was a glimpse of someone in a coat or jacket as James yelled...

"You could at least say excuse me...asshole!"

James decided to use the elevator on the third floor but when he tried the door handle which led out to the elevators, the door was locked.

Once on the second floor landing and for a brief moment, he felt a sense of relief, and it was then that he heard voices of people who gathered in front of the elevators.

James tried the door again and again but it was locked. He pounded several times on the door, but no one came over to stairwell door.

James stood there looking out the small window on the door and thinking to himself...

"What the hell.... now I know they can hear me."

James pounded on the door louder and started yelling...

"Hey...Somebody!"

James was only one floor from the lobby and walked towards the steps when he heard doors opening and slamming shut in the stairwell above him.

Thinking that someone heard him pounding on the door and was coming to see what was wrong, James started to climb back to the second floor, but froze in mid step thinking...

"C'mon James, think about what you're doing...you're one floor away from the lobby, so why the hell are you going back up?"

James began a slow decent to the first floor trying to look cool calm and collected as he straightened his tie when he suddenly he heard multiple voices in front of him in the darkness.

It sounded like children singing and laughing, with overlapping voices....

"La-la-la-la-la-la-, la-la-la-la-la-la,

Teddy Bear, soda crackers;

Got you on the steps,

Teddy Bear will rope your neck,

Till it's Time to make you dead

La-la-la-la-la-la-, la-la-la-la-la-la."

James turned and began backing up the stairwell towards the slamming of the doors he had heard just a few moments ago above him.

His heart began beating faster and faster as he felt a great sense of anxiety with each step he took.

Wiping the beads of sweat from his brow, James tried the door handle to the second floor only to discover door would not open. As he looked out in the hall area through the small window, he saw that there was no one there.

Feeling more anxious, along with cold chills on his neck James slowly started climbing up the steps to the third floor landing.

With each step he took he could hear the laughter of the children growing louder and louder.

Their singing had an almost high pitched ear piercing eerie tone, almost demonic-like, along with the sound of a loud heartbeat...soft at first, and then louder.

James looked down over the rails as he climbed up, when he saw something that made him move faster.

In the darkness red eyes with a distinguished black ring around the middle of the eye, following him.

There were so many pairs of eyes that James took off running up the steps and trying each door handle.

James remembered passing a security phone in the stairwell on the fifth floor next to a fire extinguisher as he grew closer to the fourth floor.

As James climbed each step he had a sense someone was above him in the stairwell, because he could hear the sound of steps and breathing which mirrored his steps and stopping each time he stopped.

As James made it to the fifth floor he saw the door which led to the fifth floor elevator area closing.

Trying to catch the door before it closed, James yelled and pounded louder on the door, but the door closed, leaving James with a decision to go up to another floor.

Suddenly James turned around throwing his back against the door, remembering the red eyes which were following him up the stairs.

Spotting the red phone box on the stairwell wall, James opened it pressed zero for the building operator.

James pressed for the operator several times before hearing a voice which said...

"James Hargrove you can't get away... why so out of breath?"

James held the phone away from his ear thinking...

"Who the hell is this, and how did they know who I am?"

Suddenly James heard the voice saying...

"Hello Mr. Hargrove, so you're locked in the stairwell he-he-he-he..."

James stood in shock as he was listening to someone on the phone who knew that he was in the stairwell.

James started to respond but he heard a scratching sound like the needle on an old stereo sliding across an album... then the voices coming from below him in the stairwell seemed to be getting closer and louder...

"La-la-la-la-la-la-la-, la-la-la-la-la-la-la,

Teddy Bear, Soda Crackers

Chase you up the steps

Feel our breath on your neck

Teddy going to make you dead

"La-la-la-la-la-la-la-, la-la-la-la-la-la-la."

James let the phone drop from his hand and grabbed the fire extinguisher and tried smashing the small rectangle glass on the door.

The glass was almost busted completely when something grabbed him from behind, dragging him towards the steps.

James cried out for help as he was being dragged by the collar of his jacket down a flight of steps.

Lying on the floor and struggling to get up, all that James could see was a weird darkness on top of him which was so heavy that no matter how hard James fought to get free, he couldn't.

Then James heard the laughing of the children's voices coming at him out of the darkness.

James lifted his head a little looking all around, but all he saw was darkness one moment then multiple pairs of those red creepy eyes.

All of a sudden the laughter and the children's voices were silent, and the darkness which surrounded James was gone, and he was able to move.

Then a small light began illuminating the stairwell where James lay. James grabbed his shoulder bag which was lying in the corner.

James stood and as he looked down in the stairwell realized that going down was out of the question, that he had to make it to the elevator on the floor he was on.

Getting the door open was going to be a struggle because the doors automatically lock and the only way to unlock them was from the inside.

James tried the door knob which was locked, so picking up the fire extinguisher, James began beating the door knob until the knob fell off the door.

James took the bracket which held the extinguisher to the wall and inserted it in through the opening of the door to release the latch.

Just when it seemed useless, James got lucky and heard a clicking sound from the locking mechanism in the door.

James put his right shoulder into the door and with his left hand continued fiddling with the lock until he heard the clicking sound again, when James rammed his right shoulder into the door, causing the door to open.

Falling through the door, James saw the elevator slowly closing as he began crawling towards it and yelling...

"...*Hold the elevator!*"

Felling fear like he has never felt before, James began crawling as fast has he could to the elevator when something grabbed hold of his legs pulling him back towards the door.

James kicked and yelled for help as loud as he could. James mere inches away from the elevator door which was almost closed.

Lying flat on his stomach James was able to sink the tips of his fingers underneath the silver metal transition piece which held the carpet edge down

James continued kicking and yelling not knowing that the tips of his fingers getting close to a chunk of jagged metal.

As James was being pulled away from the elevator and to the door, his fingers got snagged on the jagged metal cutting the first digit off of three of his fingers.

As James was being dragged into the stairwell door, he left a trail of blood on the carpet which would have been visible for anyone to see, had not the color of carpet been red.

Unable to resist any longer James was pulled into the stairwell when the door slammed shut.

Just as James's body was in the stairwell the elevator bell sounded and the elevator door opened as six employees stood talking of their weekend plans, when one of the employees pushed the lobby floor button.

As the elevator door closed...if any of them had been listening closely...they could have heard the muffled screams of James in the stairwell.

As the elevator descended from the fifth floor, kicking sounds could be heard coming from inside the stairwell where James was until there was a blood curdling scream.

In The Lobby

The mass exit of employees and visitors was well underway as Amy Smiles, thirty-six years old, mother of two, and a veteran of the Air Force prepared herself to meet and greet over three hundred employees and guests, as they exited the building.

Amy Smiles worked the building with her partner Reggie Parker. Amy met Reggie while they were both at the Columbus police academy, and became partners and best friends ever since, and like all friends... each with their own secrets.

Reggie's secret was, that several years ago he discovered that Amy was a little more than just his partner.... she was also his sister, who was lost to him when they were infants.

Amy's secret was that she was going to tell Reggie that not only was she pregnant, but she was going to hand in her resignation from the police force in thirty days and move overseas with her husband Jerry Locklear.

Amy's prenatal instructions from her OBGYN were to reduce stress. Amy's pregnancy was also going to be difficult enough due to a gunshot wound to the abdomen she suffered last year.

Amy had resigned herself to her decision, but telling Reggie would prove to be a matter all by itself.

Ever since Reggie found out about Amy's true identity he planned on years of being around Amy to catch up on all they missed growing up.

Amy placed her shoulder bag in the bottom drawer of her desk and looked over at Reggie on the opposite side of the lobby.

Reggie was six feet and six inches tall, and weighed around two hundred and fifty-five lbs.

Reggie was in remarkably good health at forty-seven years old. Reggie, or *"coach"* as everyone called him, had but one physical defect and that was he walked with a slight limp, due to a football injury.

As the crowd began filing down the hallway towards the two checkout counters, standing almost six feet eight it was not hard for Reggie to pick out the Executives from the front line employees.

Reggie married his high school sweetheart and the mother of his three children...Perry McKenzie, who was the captain of the cheerleading squad.

Shortly after high school, both Perry and Reggie went the separate ways until a twist of fate bought them back together.

Reggie had been drafted by the New York Jets and during the fourth game of the regular season suffered an ACL injury which required surgery.

Reggie returned to his home town of Columbus, Ohio to recuperate and it was during this time on one of his doctor's visits, he literally 'bumped' into Perry who worked as an RN for a local physician who specialized in sports injuries and orthopedics.

After a few visits Reggie and Perry continued to have those odd innocent looks at one another until Reggie got up enough courage to ask Perry out for dinner, who gladly accepted.

The more Reggie and Perry saw one another, the closer Reggie was to making up his mind about quitting football altogether, so Reggie applied for and graduated from the Columbus Police Academy.

Reggie became a police officer with the Columbus police department shortly after the dreams of his football career ended.

Because of Reggie's size and height picking out the executives was no hard task because Reggie could see over the tops of just about everyone walking in the lobby.

As Reggie would spot the executives, he would have their keys as well as their parking pass key ready, for easy exiting through the side door, across the street.

Reggie's attention was however drawn for a moment to the direction of his partner who was having a minor disturbance on her side of the lobby.

Reggie positioned himself between his counter and the front door in case Amy needed assistance, but soon returned to his counter as Amy signaled to him that everything was under control.

In the short time that Reggie's attention was drawn from the executives to Amy's counter and back to his counter, Reggie failed to notice that the Top Executive in the building Mr. James Hargrove had exited the building through Amy's side.

One by one the executives exited through the four turnstiles in search for the Transit Agency buses which would take them to the 'Park-N-Ride' lot located ten blocks away, to their cars.

As the lobby emptied of its last employees and guests Reggie noticed one set of keys and one parking pass key remained on the counter.... Mr. James Hargrove, CEO of O.A.P.

Walking over to Amy and waving the car keys and parking key at her Reggie leaned against the counter and said...

'It looks like we're going to have company for a while...'

Removing the hair from her eyes, and pulling it back behind her ear Amy replied...

'Wow.... with it being Friday, a pay day and a four-day weekend who in their right mind....'

Reggie interrupted Amy, before she had an opportunity to finish her statement and said...

'O.P.S.... Mr. Hargrove'

Amy replied while putting both hands on counter.......

'Something is not making sense Coach!"

Reggie glanced down at the car keys and the parking pass key and then turned around to Amy.

Grabbing the keys and the pass key from Reggie and tapping them on the counter Amy said to Reggie worriedly...

'No Coach.... No, something is wrong here.... Mr. Hargrove exited through my turnstile. I'm telling you one of the people who left the building was Mr. Hargrove, I remembered it... because he was limping badly.'

Reggie grabbed the keys from his belt and turned to Amy...

'Look Smiles, you obviously mistaken...I checked Mr. Hargrove in myself this morning and I didn't see any limp.

Why would he check his car in and then walk...I'm going upstairs to see what's what, if Mr. Hargrove comes down call me.'

Reggie disappeared down the hall, and into one of the elevators.

Amy had just picked up her bags when her cell phone began vibrating as she recognized the number...saying.........

"Hello honey biscuit."

Amy put her bags back down on the counter and sat down to a welcomed voice on the other end of the phone, her husband Jerry Locklear...

Amy did not realize that there was a dark shadowy figure standing directly behind her, as she happily talked with Jerry...

"Hey beautiful.... how's things going... you going to come straight to the Shack or do you have to stop on the way?"

Jerry asked as Amy glanced at her watch saying...

"No Baby, the only stop I have is in trying to keep myself from ripping your clothes off tonight... but changing the subject a little... I'll be on the late side, because we have one executive still in the building".

Jerry sighed then replied...

"So what are you telling me that it's going to take you about an hour and a half?"

Amy sat up straight and said...

"Now... there you go tripping again, if I take twenty to six seventy...it's no more than forty minutes' tops.... but just in case... I want a full rack of ribs, a baked potato, Asparagus and a Bay Breeze."

Amy ended her call just about the same time that the elevator alarm sounded and Reggie exited and walked up to Amy...

"Building's empty...I don't get it...I mean why would he leave his car; I mean he lives clear across town.

"Unless..."

Amy said, as she placed her cell phone back in her bag.

Reggie picked up Mr. Hargrove's keys and with a puzzled look, said...

"Unless what, Smiles!"

With a straight face Amy said...

"A secret rendezvous.... back seat freaks.... aww C'mon coach... CEO's do it too... dang, they probably invented "Parking Garage sex."

15

Reggie placed the keys in the lock box and turned to Amy and said...

"You see that's what I'm taking about...if it was some kind of freak-a-whack-a-doo, sex in the back seat...he'd need his car."

Amy grabbed her bags and looked at Reggie saying...

"Maybe it was her car, or his car...I'm just saying coach...this is two thousand –six."

Reggie and Amy exited the building, when Amy looked over at Reggie saying...

"Now don't stand us up tonight besides I got something real important to talk with you about...okay coach?"

Reggie told Amy that Perry was meeting him there so he was going directly there.

Polaris Center
Columbus, Ohio

I wished that Deanne would've just taken me directly to the condo or ran her errands before picking me up. I hated sitting in the car especially out in a busy parking lot with everybody watching.

Deanne put the car in park and said...

"Blue...I hate leaving you in the car...but I promise, I'll be in and out before you know it."

The temperature outside was in the fifties and pretty mild, overcast skies, with threatening rain clouds gathering.

Deanne put my window down a little and locked the doors and headed inside the Farmer's market.

I continued to stare ahead, thinking...

"While I was at Giggle Central, things were so much easier; during the afternoon hours the nurses allowed me time alone.... but now look at me."

With all the people watching me I didn't dare move of course anyone of these people could have a Doppelganger...

When the unthinkable happened!

Just then a fly flew in through the car and landed on my forehead. I tried moving my eyes just enough to make the fly move, but instead of flying away the fly landed on my cheek just under my right eye.

I started blinking my eye hoping that would make him fly off. I quickly scanned my eyes up towards the store looking to see if Deanne was coming but I didn't see her.

Polaris Fashion Place is Columbus' premiere place to shop. It has a lot of everything for everyone, except for one thing...places to park.

Parking at Polaris has always been a chore because of all of the shops and things to do. Deanne was lucky to find a place to park so quickly, as I thought...

"Just a few people are coming this way...now's my chance, I'll just brush my hand in front of my face real fast and get this pesky fly off of me before anyone sees me."

I had no sooner taken my hand off my leg when out of the corner of my eye I noticed a family coming up alongside of the car.

It appeared to be a family of four heading to their car.

From what I could see it looked like a couple, possibly in their late forties with two teenagers, one boy and one girl.

The teenagers trailed their parents with the teenage boy preoccupied with playing a video game.

The teenage girl and the mother both carried shopping bags in each hand, as the Father carried something large in both hands, occasionally stopping to get a better grip.

I sat motionless and carefully watched them and thought...

"As soon as they pass in front of me...this fly is dead bug meat."

The mother and father reached their car first while the son was called to unlock and open the car's trunk for his father.

I was seconds away from dealing with the fly, when daughter caught my eye.

She stopped directly in front of me. The girl stood looking in the direction of her parents when her head slowly turned in my direction.

My stare was up and to the right of the girl so there wasn't direct eye contact at first. Something was extremely odd about this girl as I noticed the girl's face was beginning to become distorted.

The girl was looking straight ahead but another face, a second face emerged from her and turned toward me, when I thought...

"Oh no it can't be...she's a Doppelgänger...and she's coming over here!"

I thought to myself...

"Deanne I hope you're through shopping and on your way to the car because I'm about to approach melt down here, and it's not going to look pretty."

The girl walked up to the front of the car and placed her hands on the hood of the car and bent down looking directly at me.

My eyes spotted the girl's father and brother wrestling with the large package, not noticing that their daughter had stopped two cars away.

The girl took her finger and traced a line from her right cheek to her nose, and that's when the fly which was on David's cheek fly into one of David's nostrils.

Still motionless not moving not twitching, until felt that I wanted to let out a quick snort but did not want this girl to think that I had any control over anything.

The girl then turned her head to the left and then to the right in amazement with a look on her face which said...I must be a vacant shell of what used to be a human being.

The girl was satisfied and turned to walk away when I sneezed.

The girl suddenly appeared next to me at the passenger window pressing her nose through the opening of the car window and sniffing.

I kept my eyes focused directly to the front realizing that he made a mistake, and hoping that the sneeze did not give me away.

The girl stared directly at me and then said as she continued sniff....

'Ooh...ooh...I'm telling!

Wait till the others find out that you've been pretending this whole time.

Twisted and Dread, Twisted and Dread;

Fooled us once, now it's on again

Twisted and Dread!'

Just then the door opened and Deanne placed the bags she had in the back seat saying...

'I'm back, Blue Baby... see there...that wasn't long was it?'.

As Deanne was getting in I slowly cut my eyes to the right, the girl was no longer standing next to me but was with her family.

I began thinking as Deanne reached over and patted him on the leg...

"What I just saw was a Doppelganger... they know that I've been faking.... They know there's nothing wrong with me."

On the way to the condo I wanted so badly to say something to Deanne, I wanted so badly to reach over and touch her silky smooth skin and say something to her...but how would I explain my quick recovery.

Deanne reached and inserted a CD in, and turned up the volume, singing...

"...You got a smile so bright
you know you could have been a candle....
I'm holding you so tight
you know you should've been a handle...."

Until Deanne started singing, I had almost forgot that I was supposed to be pretending to be a vegetable and just about said...

"Gosh Deanne it's .... you could have been a handle"

I've had always corrected Deanne on singing the right words to songs and Deanne knew it irritated me when she sung the wrong words.

Only a few more blocks and then me and Deanne would be on Pecan Drive, when Deanne stopped for the light, singing...

"The way you swept me off my feet, you know you could have been a broom;
The way you smell so sweet, you know you could have been some perfume."

There were a group of people passing in front of the car and I got the feeling they were staring at me.

Deanne waved to be polite...but I knew who and what they were...they were Doppelgangers'.

Seeing the condo, I never imagined how good it looked and how good it was going to be, to be back at home.

The last time I saw the condo was six months ago when we were leaving for the farm for Labor Day weekend with six of their friends.

Deanne left our dog Shone next door with the neighbors while she picked me up from the hospital.

As Deanne pulled into the driveway, their neighbors Clara and Bill stood with Shone...

"Hello you two."

Clara shouted as she hugged Deanne.

Bill reached to open the passenger side door to help me out when Deanne motioned for him not to.

Bill stepped back while Deanne helped me out of the car saying...

"Uh...good to see you Dave, I know you're glad to get back to yard work and Browns football. The talk is Charlie ...uh what's his name is going to start."

Deanne whispered into Bill's ear about my condition, leaving Bill feeling a bit stupid. Deanne handed Bill the shopping bags from the back seat that carried them to the porch and sat them on the porch swing.

Clara walked Shone up the steps behind Deanne who had me by the arm.

Deanne led me inside and came back out and grabbed Shone as Clara and Bill carried the groceries inside and sat them on the counter saying...

"Well...it's good to see both of you back. Deanne call me and we'll set up a lunch or something after you two get settled in."

Clara and Bill started down the steps as Deanne took the mail from the mail box and closed the door.

Bill turned back at me and Deanne's when Clara gave him an elbow to the ribs...

"What did you do that for, I was just...."

"David is our neighbor Bill not some kind of freak."

Clara said as they climbed the steps to their unit.

Chapter 2

Unlocked Doors

1001 East Rich Street

It was an unusually chilly autumn night as Beverly Hargrove thought that instead of riding the COTA bus, she'd walk.

It was still light out so she would make it home long before it would get dark, not to mention Beverly needed time to figure out how she was going to tell her husband James, that she had been carrying on a relationship with another woman.

Beverly was so engrossed in to her thoughts that she did not see the dark shadowy figure lurking in the trees, which had followed her from Broad Street.

Beverly and James' house was about four miles away through some lightly wooded area on the east side of Columbus, and as she was about halfway home she had a feeling that someone was behind her, walking the same direction and gaining on her.

Beverly didn't think all that much about it because the library had just closed, not to mention that she noticed a bus passing her which probably just dropped off a load of passengers.

The leaves began rustling and swirling under the wind as Beverly crossed the street. Beverly turned to check for cars when she noticed something which seemed vaguely sinister.

Several times, Beverly turned around slightly to see if she recognized the man, but she only saw a dark figure; and that seemed very odd, because it was not quite dark out, and she should've been able to the person a little more clearly.

Beverly kept walking at her same pace and then she began walking a little faster, because she could feel something, or someone was right behind her...matching her steps.

Beverly could hear the sound of footsteps overlapping hers and then with every step she took the other footsteps were in sync with hers.

Something or someone was keeping pace with her staying behind her...she had a feeling that something was up... as she said to herself...

"Just four more blocks, to go."

Kim Weston & Beverly Hargrove
3 Months Earlier

It was a Friday afternoon and nearly all of the twenty-three staff members of Duncan-Brown and Brown, where Beverly worked was invited to Kim's graduation commencement, Beverly was the only one who stayed for the after party.

Kim was in her second year as an intern for the law firm and upon receiving her degree was promised a position as one of the staff attorneys.

Kim was originally from Indiana, moved to Columbus three years earlier upon her acceptance in Ohio State's Law program.

Kim was a bubbly and extremely gorgeous young woman standing five-feet seven, and weighing one hundred and thirty pounds.

Kim's dark brown eyes, her naturally shoulder length curly hair could have easily landed her on the cover of any beauty magazine, but Kim valued her razor sharp wit, and her love for the law.

Kim lost her father five years ago to a heart attack. Her father had a reputation as being one of the toughest litigators in Indiana.

The night of Kim's commencement ceremony, would prove to be a life changer, but not just for Kim, but for Beverly as well.

All of the staff from Duncan-Brown and Brown attended the ceremony and afterwards, slowly filed out of the auditorium headed back to the office to prepare for an important case.

Kim was a little disappointed that no one was going to be able to stay for the party, but she knew the office had a very important case coming up the following week.

Beverly had driven Kim to the commencement and told Kim since her husband James was out of town, and she had the day off, not to mention her children were at camp and that she would hand with Kim.

The after party saw Beverly a little uncomfortable at first, with a room full of twenty-twenty-five year olds, and music that Beverly would never listen to...turned up as loud as it could go.

Kim was drinking pretty heavy and Beverly didn't want the embarrassment of her young protégé's partying to get out of hand, landing her out of a job as fast as she was offered it.

Beverly made her way over to Kim after dancing to a song that seemed to play on and no, not to mention dancing with a young twenty-five-year-old, who was trying to prove that he wasn't drunk, just merely acting....'cool'.

Beverly's whispered in to Kim's ear and told her that she was going to head home, and if Kim had a way home.

Kim told Beverly that she wanted to say good night to one of her classmates and that she would be ready to leave.

Beverly went out to her car noticing that someone had her blocked in, when two girls and a guy climbed into the car and sped away, leaving Beverly room to pull out of the parking space she was in.

Beverly and Kim climbed the steps to her apartment which was on the second floor. Kim was visibly intoxicated and needed help maintaining her balance.

Once inside Kim's apartment Kim asked Beverly to stay and have a drink with her. Beverly told Kim that one drink would be all it took and she would be smashed.

Kim reminded Beverly that since no one was going to be home at Beverley's, so she could stay there the night.

Beverly agreed and the two women sit watching television and finishing a large bottle of Chardonnay which someone had given to Kim as a graduation gift.

Suddenly Kim got up and turning the television volume down, turned on the radio and started dancing. She tried to get Beverly to join her, but Beverly explained that dancing was one thing that she definitely could not do without falling and busting her ass.

Beverly sat and watched Kim as Kim danced. Beverly sat thinking that Kim was a very good dancer and at one point Kim stumbled on the rug, and fell towards Beverly who helped steady her.

Beverly was becoming a little uncomfortable sitting there and watching Kim dance.

To take her mind off of feeling the odd feeling of watching Kim dance...Beverly ended up filling her glass several time, and before Beverly knew it, she was watching Kim's every movement.

Kim noticed Beverly's stare and danced closer and closer to where Beverly was sitting until reached out and touched Kim's hand.

Kim stopped dancing and slowly and deliberately leaned in and kissed Beverly.

Beverly and Kim embraced and made passionate love that evening.

Beverly found herself feeling something that she felt in years. Beverly was caught wrestling with feelings of right and wrong and woman with a woman verses a woman with a man.

Once a week for the past three months, whenever Beverly's husband, James was out of town, Beverly spent time with Kim.

Her kids always had a weekend project at school, or were over with Beverly's sister, hanging out with her two children, so getting away to spend time with Kim was not a chore.

Beverly's thoughts were consumed with how Kim made her feel and the fact she was planning a weekend with Kim, and was going to tell her that she was in love with her.

The last three months of passion with Kim was so heavy on Beverly's mind that she did not see that the dark shadowy figure which had crossed the street in her direction. Beverly had just passed a group of people and glanced behind her to check the traffic as she crossed the street, and that's when she saw a dark figure, a shadow, stopping and then following her from a distance.

Beverly felt nervous as the dark figure mirrored her moves. When Beverly stopped the dark figure stopped and when she moved...the dark figure moved.

Feeling a sense of apprehension coupled with fear, Beverly looked back and across the street to a crowd of people which was leaving the local library.

Beverly had several bags in her hands and shifted the bags so that she could reach her cell phone and call James making certain that he was still heading out of town.

Just as Beverly located her cell phone and placed it in her right front pocket, an EMS vehicle passed her... sirens blasting, and turning onto the same street Beverly would be turning on to.

As Beverly approached the corner she could see a swarm of emergency lights a half a block away from where she was standing.

Beverly had friends who lived on that street and if the dark figure was still following her, well.... seeing Beverly's friends...he would turn around and go away and stop following her.

Beverly was within a block from all of the emergency lights and a crowd of people gathered on the street.

Suddenly Beverly was tapped on the shoulder by one of her friends Barbara Hogue, who said...

"Beverly...hi there you're out late, Judy Mason just told me the old couple which lives on the corner... well the old man suffered a heart attack."

Beverly was moving her head from side to side trying to see if she could see anything said...

"Hello Barb.... got off work a little late and decided to pick up dinner, I hope the old man will be alright."

Beverly sat both bags on the ground beside her and pulled her coat together buttoning it, as the evening air began rustling... when Barbara said...

"I think their son and daughter are there, but I'll find out something tomorrow.... look Beverly, are you going with us to the Glühwein Festival Tomorrow?"

Beverly picked up her bags and stepped out onto the street in the direction of the alley which ran into her street and said....

"Yeah I'd like to go, but it depends on James and if he is still going out of town..., I called him several times, but he's not answering... look, I got to go... see ya Barb."

Beverly crossed the street and headed into the alley which was dimly lit not noticing the dark figure, in the bushes keeping pace with her.

Beverly was usually home by five thirty but her all day romance with Kim, caused her to lose track of time and it was going on seven in the evening.

Beverly's focus quickly went from Kim, the emergency vehicles, and the dark figure following her to calling James again, which didn't answer his phone.

Beverly started thinking that James wasn't answering her calls because he was on a plane.

Suddenly, Beverly heard the sound of children laughing.

Initially Beverly thought that there was a party at one of the houses, or maybe one of the neighborhood kids was having a sleep over.

Beverly became increasingly concerned as the voices went from laughing to singing, then to a discerningly distorted demonic tone singing ...

"La-la-la-la-la-la-, la-la-la-la-la-la,

Teddy Bear, Soda Crackers;

Teddy Bear mad,

Teddy Bear chasing' you;

Bet you won't make it home

La-la-la-la-la-la-, la-la-la-la-la-la!"

Beverly's pace picked up from a slow steady walk to a fast walk.

Beverly reached her house at the corner of Rich and Twenty-First Street, when strangely enough... the laughter and singing stopped.

Beverly pulled her house keys from out of her coat pocket and unlocked the door.

Turning around and almost out of breath, Beverly stood looking in both directions, not seeing anything or anyone not even the dark figure which was now in the trees above the front door and slithering from the roof and into her house.

Closing the door behind her and peeping out of the door drapes, Beverly said...

"So... *what the hell just happened ...I know what I just heard?"*

Beverly went into the kitchen and placed the groceries down on the counter and began putting everything away.

Beverly double checked to see if the door was locked and went to the car port expecting to see if James' car was there.

Beverly kicked off her shoes and dialed James' number. Immediately the call went straight to his voice mail.

Beverly poured herself a glass of Chardonnay taking a couple of sips as she went through the mail.

Beverly never drank wine especially Chardonnay, but after that first glass with Kim three months ago... Chardonnay has become Beverly's choice of drink.

The wind outside had picked up and started to blow ferociously, that tree limbs from the neighbor's tree broke off and hit against the side of Beverly's house startling her.

With her nerves already shaken, Beverly poured herself another glass of wine, and walked over to the window unaware that she was not the only one in the house.

Beverly placed pasta in a pot and set it to boil along with broccoli, while she seasoned and sliced several chicken breast and began sautéing them.

Beverly arranged the broccoli, chicken, butter and pasta in a casserole dish and placed it in the oven.

Dinner was thirty to forty minutes away as Beverly went upstairs and ran water for her bath.

Before getting into her bath, Beverly came down stairs and turned the oven to low, poured herself another glass of wine and stood looking out the window sipping her wine and thinking about Kim, when...

Suddenly the lightening flashed and the thunder roared causing Beverly to jump and spill her wine...

"Damn"!

Beverly said as she wiped up the spilled wine on her sweater and off the floor.

Beverly made herself a plate after her bath, and sat in front of the television eating and watching the news.

She checked her cell phone to see if there was a call from James, which there wasn't. Beverly then dialed Kim's number, and when she got a busy signal...ended the call.

Beverly heard the sound of the wind roaring outside and walked over to the window to peep outside...just then her cell phone began vibrating in her pajama bottoms, causing Beverly to jump...

"Damn!"

Beverly shouted as she scrambled for the pocket opening. When Beverly answered the call a familiar wand welcoming voice said...

"Hi there lover."

It was Kim's voice calling Beverly back. Beverly poured herself another glass of wine and after cutting off all the downstairs lights, walked up to her bedroom.

Beverly wasn't worried about James coming home and catching, because she lit a few candles and turned off the bedroom lights, and when and if James pulled into the carport, she would see the headlights.

Beverly lay across the bed excited and happy to be talking to Kim. She told Kim how much she missed her and wished that she had stayed the night with her instead of coming to a dark house alone.

Kim told Beverly that she can always throw a few things in a bag and that she'd come and pick her up.

As tempting as that sounded to Beverly, she told Kim that James hasn't called her, and if she came back out...she'd have to first make sure that James was out of town.

Beverly lay on top of the bed fondling herself as she talked with Kim for hours, until she noticed something passing in front of her bedroom door.

Beverly told Kim she thought James was home, and went out into the hallway to check. With Kim holding on the line, Beverly came back and told her that it must be her nerves, and that James was not home.

Beverly also told Kim about the creepy feeling she that someone had been following her as she walked home.

Kim told Beverly that she should considered leaving James a note, pack a few things and she'd be there in less than thirty minutes.

Beverly finally agreed and told Kim to give her about an hour before coming to pick her up.

Beverly wrote James a note saying that she was having an all girl's night and that dinner was in the fridge and that she'd probably stay over at either Kim's or Donna's for the night.

Thirty minutes had passed as Beverly had packed a few things when she noticed car headlights pulling up to the car port as she looked out of the window saying...

"Damn...Damn, I'm going to have to call Kim and tell her that James just got home."

No sooner had Beverly dialed Kim's number when the door bell sounded.

Wondering why James had not pulled into the car port when she peeped out the window and saw that it was Kim's car and not James' car parked in front of the car port.

Racing to open the door, Kim stood at the door smiling as Beverly let her inside.

After shutting the door, the two stood hugging and kissing when the message light from Beverly's home phone flashed.

The two of them walked over to the phone as Beverly pressed the play back feature on the phone and heard...

"...Hi darling, just wanted to remind you that I think I'm going to fly out to New York Friday night...I'm not sure, but I'll call you if I change my mind."

Kim looked at Beverly and smiled saying...

"...Well he didn't call, so that means he's in New York...right?"

Beverly motioned to Kim to follow her upstairs, so that she could get the bag she packed.

Once Kim and Beverly made it to the bedroom, Beverly picked up her bag and turned and looked at Kim who was dressed in tight jeans, a pull over sweater and a pink baseball cap, revealing her curly brunette hair.

Beverly stood staring at Kim who asked...

"What?"

Beverly sat her bag on the foot of the bed and replied...

"Nothing...you-you just look so damn good."

Kim walked up to Beverly and placed her hand on Beverly's arm, stroking it lightly until they were in a locked embrace.

Beverly had thrown her head back as Kim started kissing her neck line, when Beverly moaned...

"Don't you think we need to take this to your apartment, c'mon let's go babe."

Kim stopped kissing Beverly's neck line and as Beverly grabbed her bag and cut the bed room light out, they both heard a loud thump on the wall, as Kim shouted...

"What was that?"

Beverly reached back and cut the light back on and said...

"I don't know...it was probably the wind."

Kim and Beverly both slowly walked over to the door, and as Beverly put her hand on the knob to open the bedroom door, they heard another loud thump and the extra bedroom door opening and closing...again and again.

Beverly back away from the bedroom door when Kim grabbed hold of Beverly's arm saying...

"Look, let's get out of here!"

No more than a second passed when they heard the same loud thump followed by the pitter patter of children's feet running from room to room laughing and singing...

"La-la-la-la-la-la-, la-la-la-la-la-la,

Teddy Bear Soda Crackers;

Bev & Kim locked inside,

Open the door, go try to run

If you don't you're both going to die

La-la-la-la-la-la-, la-la-la-la-la-la,"

Kim grabbed Beverly's bag which had fallen to the floor from the bed and told Beverly...

"Look we need to go...follow me out the front door and to my car...okay?"

Beverly and Kim reached the bedroom door and just as they tried leaving, the door slammed shut and all the lights went out.

Kim could feel that Beverly was shaking and on the verge of tears when they heard the same voices singing....

"La-la-la-la-la-la-, la-la-la-la-la-la,

Teddy Bear, Soda Crackers

Said run if you dare,

You'll never leave, try it and see
Teddy says...BOO!"
La-la-la-la-la-la-, la-la-la-la-la-la."

Beverly and Kim stood huddled in the dark bedroom, crying and sniffling. Beverly saw a faint street light outside and walked over to the window, hoping to get somebody's attention, when she turned to Kim screaming.

There was a dark shadowy figure climbing on the roof towards her bedroom window. Kim wondered why Beverly was screaming when she caught a glimpse of something at the window scratching and clawing at the glass.

In the dark bedroom Kim and Beverly stood at the bedroom door screaming and trying to get the door opened, when Beverly whispered at Kim...

"Quiet, did you hear that...someone's in the room with us, c'mon let's lock ourselves in the closet. I got my cell phone here, we can call nine one-one."

Kim and Beverly locked themselves in the walk-in closet in Beverly's bedroom, while Kim held the closet door knob as Beverly dialed nine one-one.

The phone continued to ring and ring, when suddenly a voice answered saying...

"...Hello Beverly...what's your emergency other than the fact that you and your pretty lover are going to die!"

Beverly was so scared that she didn't pay attention to what the person on the other end of the phone had said, when Beverly whispered to the operator...

"This is Beverly Hargrove, and I live at one thousand and one east rich street...we need help, somebody's broken into my home."

Again the voice on the other end said...

"Beverly, Beverly...come out, come out wherever you are...Teddy knows you're in the damn closet!"

Beverly dropped the phone after hearing that, and suddenly the other side of the closet door it started violently shaking, while someone was beating of the door.

Kim was holding onto the door with all of her might, as both women began screaming louder and louder.

Kim and Beverly both cried for help as loud as they could when the closet door was yanked open, then there was nothing but a silence.

Pecan Drive

As Deanne walked me through the living room to the steps the look on my face was that of a child discovering new.

Deanne lead me upstairs to the bathroom, but when I got to the door I stopped afraid to go inside. Six months earlier, this whole nightmare started with me seeing this creepy little girl.

When I was being discharged the charge nurse reminded Deanne that when it comes to using the bathroom, that all she had to do was walk me over to the commode and back me up slowly, and gently push down on my shoulders and I'd sit.

Deanne had been a registered nurse for over ten years and was very familiar working with all types of patients, but because I was her boyfriend, Deanne acted as if she was fresh out of nursing school, and dealing with her first patient.

The sweet scent of berries from Deanne's shampoo filled my nose as she bent down to pull my jogging pants down.

I was thinking...

"Hurry up Deanne...hurry up before I go in my pants."

Deanne got finally got me on the commode, and then walked out of the bathroom and took the cell phone from her pants pocket.

As I sat there on the commode and sure that Deanne was out of sight...I lowered my head and said to himself...

"Whew! It's about time... I'm glad Deanne stepped out to give me some privacy."

I wanted to let out a sigh of relief but knew I'd best save that for another time. Slowly lifting my eyes up towards the mirror I noticed that the mirror was completely fogged up.

Just then the fog on the mirror quickly dissipated and the face of the little girl dressed in a white raggedy dress appeared.

At first I thought I was imagining that I was seeing this same creepy girl who approached me in the Polaris parking lot only this girl was older...much older.

This was the same girl I'd seen out at the farm six months earlier, only something about her was different.

Her hair was dark brown and scraggly looking and wet, while her face looked like that of young girl in her teens, care worn, and her eyes...her eyes were solid black with no pupils.

I began hyperventilating and beads of perspiration formed on my forehead and ran down my face.

Looking up and to the right I hoped that Deanne was on her way back in to get me, because I didn't want to be in the bathroom alone with her.

That's when I heard Deanne talking on her cell phone.

Without moving my head, I looked back towards the mirror hoping that the girl was gone and upon not seeing her I quietly let out a sigh of relief and lowered my head.

Just then I smelled the strong scent of vanilla and began thinking...

"Oh no...oh no... this can't be happening again."

When the Doppelgangers first appeared to me six months ago the smelling of that scent was followed by the appearance of a Doppelganger.

Carefully scanning the mirror, I saw something move, and as I turned my eyes, in between me and the shower was this creepy little girl.

I wanted to move but dared not to. I wanted to make some kind of noise so that it would bring Deanne back in the bathroom, but how could I do that with the girl standing there?

I watched as the girl inched closer to me, my heart racing and pulse beating, when she put her finger to her lips and said....

"Twisted and Dread, Twisted and Dread,
Tried to fool us, make us think your mind was dead,
Twisted and Dread, Twisted and Dread...
They're coming after you, but this time we'll get you,
Oh by the way...
BOO!"

Deanne walked in the bathroom just as she said that and began helping me up and then walked me downstairs and sat me on the sofa and went into the kitchen to prepare lunch.

Again I sat motionless staring at the television, which was not on.

Deanne purposely came in and turned the television to the one television show which I hated...John from Cincinnati, hoping that it would help snap me back to reality.

My Doctor at the VA informed Deanne to slowly introduce me to familiar sights and sounds which would trigger emotions from me... and Deanne knew that this show would do it, because I absolutely hated it.

Deanne knew that if the television show that I hated so much would maybe light a small spark in me, but instead of lighting a spark...it was only torturing me.

I wanted to scream...

"Deanne I hate this show and you know it."

Only I couldn't, I had to sit and pretend to be emotionless. Not blinking too much, no facial expressions, no nothing.

If there ever was a time to revisit the saying..." bored to death" ...I was living it.

Deanne came downstairs and walked over to me and put a straw up to his lips and said...

"Here Blue...I know you'd like a sip of wine, and I know you hate drinking good wine from plastic cups...but"

I sipped the entire plastic cup of wine down, thinking how good that taste even if it was in a plastic cup.

My only fear was that I wouldn't get drunk on the wine seeing that it's been six months since I've had anything stronger than ensure and water.

Deanne took the cup from my lips and went into the kitchen.

I slowly turned in Shone's direction who was chewing on her doggy bone toy and alternating between it and licking her paws when I motioned for Shone.

Shone's tail started slapping the floor as she jumped up on me and began licking my face.

Turning to see where Deanne was, and feeling safe that she was in the kitchen, I thought....

"Now, is as good a time as any...while Shone is licking my face, I'll let out a loud scream and Deanne will see it and thinking that Shone's licking bought me to myself."

Little did I know that my plan was only as good as what I had to work with...and you know what they say...

'The best laid plans of mice and men always goes astray."

There are tons of things we'd all like to have a little *'heads up'* on, but then some things just don't fall into that category.

Shone continued to lick face just as I had expected her to, but just as I was ready to open my mouth and scream...something happened!

The television screen came on without the volume turned up and I saw the face of the little girl in the white dress.

Apart from the raggedy dress she was wearing, she had one of those old timey party hats on and a party whistle inside her mouth.

From the kitchen I could hear Deanne calling my name, and it was at that moment when the little girl in the dirty white ragged dress took the whistle from her mouth and wagging her index finger at me as the words appeared on the screen...

"Twisted and Dread, Twisted and Dread
Who's fooling who...Teddy Bear says."

I took a deep breath and exhaled slowly and then opened my mouth to cry out.

"What in the hell is the matter, I'm yelling but nothing, no sound... no nothing, what the hell is going on!"

As Deanne entered the room I tried yelling again, and again, but nothing was coming out of my mouth.

Deanne came over in front of me and saw me panicking to speak... only this time I was not pretending.

If I thought that I was scared earlier...now I'm way past scared. I had everything all planned, and couldn't even make a sound.

Deanne was standing in front of me hugging me, seeing that I was returning back to my self...but I couldn't get anything to come out of my mouth, not words, not even a scream! I sat in the living room massaging my neck and throat, while Deanne ran into the kitchen to get me something to drink.

As I gulped down the orange juice which Deanne handed me, thoughts about giving it totally freaking out were filling my head.

Six months ago I hatched up this plan to pretend to be a vegetable, pretending to be unable to speak ...but it was only a game, it's not supposed to be like this!

All I could think about was that all I had to do was open my mouth and let six months of pinned up words come out.

I could hear the words rolling around in my head...dying to come out, but couldn't understand why I was unable to make a sound?

I thought...

"Is it possible that a person can make himself unable to walk, hear or speak?"

I could feel my heart pounding, and my blood pressure getting all jacked up.

I felt as if I was being put into a casket, and they were lowering me into the ground, all the while my heart was pounding in the casket, with no one to let me out.

I started to panic and stood up too quickly; not seeing the flower pot sitting on the stand, and knocked it over. Just then Deanne came running in, and when she saw me cried...

"Blue...Blue...Oh Blue Baby, you're back...you're alright!'

I stood looking at Deanne and said ...

"Yeah I'm back alright...but something's wrong...I can't talk, why I can't make a sound?"

Deanne was so excited that I was coming out of the catatonic state I'd been in for six months and tried to assure me by calling the hospital, and saying that everything was going to be alright.

Central Barbeque Shack
Reynoldsburg, Ohio

Reggie was sitting outside of Central Barbeque Shack when Jerry walked up. A few minutes later Perry came out with the restaurant pager and said...

"Hi Jerry, where's Amy?"

Jerry put out his cigarette in the ash container and said...

"How you doing Perry, Amy called me right before I got here and said she'd be here in about ten minutes."

Jerry was not one of Reggie's favorite people in the world, but whenever they were around one another Reggie tried to be polite and social.

The restaurant pager began vibrating and the lights started flashing when Reggie said...

"Looks like we're up, you and Amy driving separate cars home tonight?"

Jerry popped a cert in his mouth and said...

"Nope, I parked my semi off of I-seventy-one and hitched a ride to here...I'll have Amy drive me to my rig on Sunday evening."

Jerry held the door open saying...

"You might want to have Amy follow you to the edge of Columbus off of route thirty-three, that way she won't have so far to drive."

Jerry entered the restaurant saying...

"I thought about doing that until the dispatcher called and told me my outgoing load is taking me first to Cleveland and then to Pittsburgh...so you see having the rig parked off I seventy-one is perfect."

Jerry's response to Reggie came with little sarcasm and perhaps a little jealously. Once Jerry told Amy that Reggie was a little too close to her and wondered if there wasn't something more to their relationship other than being partners.

What Jerry didn't know was, Amy and Reggie were brothers and sisters.... something that Reggie only discovered by accident a year earlier and without sharing it, even with Amy.

39

After being seated in the booth, Jerry excused himself and went back outside to wait on Amy, who was just pulling in to a parking space on the side of the restaurant.

Jerry walked over and met Amy and greeted her with a kiss and said...

"There's my baby...Reggie and Perry are already inside waiting on us."

Amy placed her purse in the trunk of her car and said...

"Sorry I'm late sweets...I stopped to get gas and picked up my uniforms out of the cleaners, which someone forgot to do for me."

Amy punched Jerry on the arm and then kissed his cheek, and then they both walked into the restaurant.

By the time Jerry and Amy got to their booth, Perry was snacking on Texas Toast, while Reggie was swallowing the last mouthful of beer in his mug.

Amy and Jerry sat down when the waitress arrived saying...

"Hello, and how are you two doing... can I get you something to drink?"

Amy ordered a double sea breeze, while Jerry ordered a draft Michelob Light.

The conversation at the table was relaxing and festive. Amy and Perry talked about an upcoming baby shower a friend of theirs was having, while Jerry and Reggie tried to make conversation, though neither had anything in common except sports.

Amy and Perry's conversation dominated the entire evening; Reggie had very little say to Jerry but did try to engage him in a variety of subjects, in between eating.

Reggie ordered the full rack of baby back ribs, loaded baked potato, and barbeque beans, while Perry order the combo ribs, chicken and pulled pork with fried okra.

Amy and Jerry both shared the house pork special plate which featured a large portion of, Brisket, Pulled Pork, Baby Back Ribs, Slaw and Beans.

Shortly after eating, Reggie told Amy that he wanted to talk to her about a case and then they stepped outside to talk.

Once outside Amy asked Reggie if he minded if she smoked and Reggie said no. Then Reggie asked Amy...

"I don't mean to get too personal, but what do you see in Jerry...I mean I'm bringing up every subject I can think of that a man would know something about but he knows nothing about nothing."

Blowing the smoked out of her mouth Amy replied...

"Why did you marry Perry; why do people marry who they marry...why do we become partners...coach we're together with who we're together with...I don't know."

Amy sat down on the bench while Reggie joined her saying...

"You don't know?"

"Amy stood up to stretch and said to Reggie...

"He may not have much to say to you, but he loves me and treats me like a queen, but I thought you wanted to talk about a case?"

Reggie started to walk out into the parking lot and away from a small crowd which was beginning to form near them and asked Amy to follow him saying...

"No, we're not going to talk about Jerry all night, the truth is I got something on my mind about those murders that occurred last week, and..."

Before Reggie had a chance to say anything else Amy cut Reggie off as her cell phone started ringing and vibrating, saying...

"Hold on for a sec, this is my sitter...I got to answer this."

Inside the restaurant, Jerry seized the opportunity to ask Perry about Reggie and his connection with Amy, and if it bothered her as much as he was bothered by it.

Perry told Jerry that when Reggie's male partner retired and Amy was assigned to work with him, there were moments when she was bothered, but those feelings slowly disappeared over time.

Perry reminded Jerry that police officers have an unusually close relationship with their partners, and he shouldn't let it bother him.

Perry went on to tell Jerry that while Amy and Reggie are close, they were not having a sexual relationship or an affair.

Thirty minutes passed when Amy and Reggie came back to the table. Without taking her seat Amy signaled to Jerry and said to Perry...

"Guys I really enjoyed myself but we better get on the road, our sitter called and said that she took Jerry Jr. to her house because the storm was pretty nasty in Lancaster right now."

Jerry was getting up from the booth when Reggie looked at both of them and said...

"You guys be safe, with Jerry being a truck driver and all, bad weather on a dark winding road is a no brainer for a trucker...right?"

Jerry nodded as he extended his hand to shake Reggie's hand. Perry looked over at Reggie and said that they too ought to get on the road as well, and besides that, Perry wanted to stop at the store on the way home.

Reggie, Perry, Jerry and Amy, left Barbeque Central after a long Friday, and the threat of severe weather.

Jerry and Amy were headed towards their car when Amy waved goodbye saying to Perry...

"We're going to have to do this again Perry and coach I'll see you Monday, bright and early!"

Jerry and Amy hopped in their car and left the parking lot heading to interstate seventy-one, to connect with state route thirty-three for a long lonely drive to Lancaster.

Outside of Columbus heading to Lancaster, Jerry and Amy would encounter at least a ten-mile stretch of sharp curves and a densely wooded section of highway.

Just as the weather channel forecasted, the lightning was flashing, thunder cracked and lit up the sky and where a few drops of rain once hit the windshield, suddenly gave way to a torrential downpour.

Jerry was no stranger to driving in storms being a semi-truck driver for the past fifteen years, but Jerry noticed there was something strange, almost spooky about this storm.

The dark sky revealed the most eerie threatening ominous black clouds, which rotated and hovered over the entire stretch of route thirty-three.

Each hill that Jerry went up and down on, the clouds seemed so close to the ground that you could stick your hand out of the window and touch them.

Every mile or so, Jerry and Amy kept peeking at one another in disbelief and shock, over the way the storm was developing.

During the daytime the drive to Lancaster posts an incredible breath taking view, something right off of a Jane Sill oil painting, but at night and particularly this night... the sky was telling a much different story.

Jerry slowed the speed of the SUV down, as large amounts of water began collecting on the roads.

Amy said, nervously...

"Jerry, don't you think you'd better slow down, I know you're experienced with driving in this kind of weather and all that, but look... look at the sky and these spooky ass clouds."

Reluctantly Jerry nodded his head in agreement and just as Jerry nodded in agreement the windshield instantly fogged up.

Jerry reached to switch the defogger on when Amy screamed! Jerry slammed on brakes, as the car started to hydroplane.

Jerry and Amy plunged off the road smashing through the steel barrier and slid thirty feet down the steep embankment.

Their car almost flipped over but a combination of quick thinking on Jerry's part plus the muddy embankment allowed the SUV to remain upright as it came to rest on four wheels.

Pale, bloody and shaking, Jerry quickly turned to see if Amy was all right. Amy moaned and nodded that she was okay.

Straining his eyes as he looked through the muddy rain soaked windows, Jerry said to Amy...

"Amy...are you alright babe....do you have your cell phone, I don't know where mine is, but we're going to have to call for help."

Amy reached for her green clutch which Jerry bought her as a Christmas gift, which was lying on the passenger floor board with all of the contents sprawled across the floor and said...

"Oh my head...here, here's my phone, you calling a tow truck?"

Jerry grabbed Amy's cell phone pretending not to hear Amy, and said...

"Not unless we plan on walking all the way to Lancaster in this mess...

Jerry was about to finish his statement when the operator of the tow truck company answered and Jerry began to explained where they were and what happened.

Jerry told her where and they needed at tow truck when the phone went dead.

David Ray

Looking bewildered, Amy asked Jerry...

"Well, did they say they were sending someone to help us?"

Jerry sat speechless for a moment and said to Amy...

"That was odd...I never had a chance to dial."

Taking her cell phone from Jerry, Amy and said...

"What do you mean you never had a chance to dial...weren't you just talking to someone about getting us a tow truck?"

Jerry lowered his head and placed his hands across his fore head and said...

"Amy, what I said was I never dialed the operator or anyone...the number started ringing and then the lady from the tow truck company was talking to me."

Amy glanced down at her phone and then back to Jerry saying...

"Honey, we just slid off the road and you were probably in shock from almost flipping over or being killed, you dialed the number... just forgot you did."

Jerry looked over at Amy and said angrily...

"They said they would send a truck, but since we're off the road and down an embankment, one of us is going to have to stand out on the highway so the driver can spot us."

Looking puzzled Amy said...

"What's wrong with that...I mean it makes sense."

Jerry tried to start the car and when it failed to turn over he rolled the window down let out a scream and then rolled it back up again.

Jerry looked over at Amy saying...

"Amy this 'is all messed up! I never told the lady we were down an embankment...how did she know that?"

Amy blurted out...

"Maybe they know this area...besides all of that, the only thing that matters is...we have help on the way...right?"

Jerry unlocked the doors and turned to Amy and said...

"You see all this rain...the dispatcher said one of us was going to have to stand on the road so that the tow truck doesn't drive past us, and I'm not about to try and take my big ass up a muddy hill...which has got to be slicker than shit!"

Amy put her head down in her hands and said...

"Did you have to say it like that, Jerry what are we going to do when the tow truck passes us by because they can't see us...how are we supposed to get out of here"?

Amy started to open her door when Jerry said...

"Okay babe, I'm going... I'm just trying to time it. The dispatcher said it'll be about an hour before a truck gets here, besides I'm not going to stand out in the rain for an hour waiting."

Jerry took the keys out of the ignition and was about to tell Amy he was going to look in the trunk for something to drape over his head when they felt a loud bang against the rear passenger side of the car.

Amy screamed and said...

"What the fuck was that...did something just hit us?"

Amy tried to open the glove compartment for her gun, when Jerry said...

"Calm down baby it's probably a deer or something that couldn't see through all of this rain and ran into the car."

Taking the keys from Jerry, to unlock the glove compartment, Amy said...

"Look Jerry a deer's eyesight is a hundred times better than ours, now if you want to be Dr. Doolittle's assistant fine but a deer isn't going to run into things....no matter what the weather."

While Amy struggled with the lock of the glove compartment suddenly a blurry figure crossed in front of their headlights and walked around the front of the car, towards the driver side.

Amy took her hand and cleared the windshield and then screamed. Jerry had the door partially open when the door slammed shut, nearly catching Jerry's leg.

Jerry tried to turn to see could react, when something smashed the driver's side window.

Someone or something had shattered the driver's side window and was dragging Jerry through the shattered window.

Jerry's hands attempted to grab the steering wheel but it was too late.

Although Jerry was a large man whoever or whatever attacked Jerry, had to have been considerably larger.

Amy beat against the glove compartment and then started to scream as she saw Jerry being pulled through the shattered window.

Amy tried to grab onto Jerry's legs to pull him back into the car, but whoever had Jerry was enormously strong, because while Amy was holding onto Jerry's legs she was being pulled from the passenger side into the console.

Jerry's legs were thrashing around and kicking as he was being pulled through the window, cutting his legs on the broken glass which was embedding itself into Jerry's legs and ankles.

The rain poured into the opening, washing Jerry's blood down onto Amy's hands and arms.

Amy tried looking out through the shattered glass to see exactly who it was that had Jerry, but the rain was coming down so hard that all Amy saw was darkness.

Frantically Amy began grabbing at her door handle trying to open the car but the door would not bulge.

So many things were racing through Amy's mind as she heard the muffled screams of Jerry which suddenly went silent.

Whether through fear or panic or a little bit of both, Amy's police instincts and fortitude shrank, and all that was left was a woman crying...crying because she knew she was about to die and there was nothing she could do except cry...

"Help...help me...help meeee!"

Amy sat in silence for a while shivering and shaking, she had just watched her husband drug out of the window by some lunatic, and knew she would be next.

Then she heard a sound growing louder and louder...bump...Bump... BUMP! Amy screamed as all four car locks popped up and down, over and over again, and then car horn began blowing.

Amy panicked and began kicking the door trying to get out, and with each kick she heard the voices of the creepy children singing that same sadistic tune over and over...

"La-la-la-la-la-la, la-la-la-la-la-la-la

Teddy Bear soda crackers,

Amy's in the car

Better get out... hurry up

The big man's on his way.
La-la-la-la-la-la, la-la-la-la-la-la."

Suddenly as the singing ended, the door locks popped up and that's when Amy saw a light coming towards her through the rear view mirror.

Amy turned thinking that it was the tow truck, when suddenly she saw faces...the faces of little children sitting in the back seat laughing and singing...

"La-la-la-la-la-la-, la-la-la-la-la-la,

Teddy Bear Soda Crackers locked you in the car,

Teddy Bear having fun, there's no place to run

"La-la-la-la-la-la-, la-la-la-la-la-la,

The children began laughing louder and louder, and singing the same tune over and over, until Amy began violently pulling on the door handle and screaming uncontrollably.

Several times Amy tried her door and then slid over to the driver's side and tried opening the driver's side door, but it to...would not open.

In desperation Amy tried starting the car until finally after the third or fourth time, the car started.

Amy put the gear shift in drive, and tried going forward but the mud was so deep that the car tires simply spun in their tracks.

Amy began alternating between drive and reverse all the time gunning the engine until suddenly, the car started sliding sideways and then began moving forward.

Amy was still screaming when the car slid and crashed into something before hitting a tree jolting Amy's head back and forth.

Dazed and scared Amy reached to wipe away the blood from a cut on her forehead, when the front door locks mysteriously popped up.

Amy saw in front of her a light in the distance...it was not like the light which she had seen coming behind her, but this light was not only coming closer, but it swayed left to right, as if it were being carried by someone.

Amy turned and looked through the rearview mirror expecting to see the faces of the children, but there was no one in the back seat.

Peering through the windshield with the rain beating down on the window Amy could see that it was a man, and said…

"Thank you…thank you…thank you…halleluiah, thank you Jesus."

Unable to open the door Amy kicked the remaining glass out of the window and climbed out, feet first.

The rain was coming down so hard and it was so dark out, that Amy didn't know where or what was on the ground below her.

All Amy knew was that she had to get out, she had to get away and find out what happened to Jerry.

Amy's feet touched ground as she wiped the rain from her face and tried looking all around her softly crying out…

"Jerry, Jerry, Jerry."

With her hands stretched out in front of her, Amy tripped and fell face first over something. Amy reached up to wipe the rain from her face, not realizing that her hands were not only covered in mud…but something else.

With no street lights in the area and the black clouds shielding any light from the moon…Amy held her head back to allow the rain to rinse the mud from her face.

All around Amy was mud and cold wet grass, as Amy stretched out her hands and pushed down, trying to get her balance in order to stand up, when she felt something unusual…something warm.

With her attention off of the light in front of her Amy began feeling clothes, and then a leg and next a face and began crying to herself…

"Oh no…….. not my baby, it's not you Jerry!

Just as the clouds were shifting, they gave way to enough moonlight and that's when Amy saw what her hands had felt, and she screamed in horror as she saw it was Jerry.

Amy's hands were feeling all over Jerry's face when a man appeared out of the darkness with a lantern.

Amy cried as she looked up into the light unable to make out who was standing there, because whoever it was held the lantern down besides his waist.

Suddenly the man bent over and held the lantern over Jerry and Amy could not believe what she was looking at, Jerry's throat had been cut from his left ear to his right ear so deep that his head was nearly decapitated, causing Amy to vomit.

Then Amy began screaming and crying...and begging the mysterious man to help her, but he just stood there in the rain, saying nothing and doing nothing.

Amy looked down at Jerry and then turned up towards the mysterious man, when he shinned the lantern in his own face, and Amy screamed.

Confused and in shock, Amy didn't know what she was going to do, but when she got a good look at the man standing over her...her cries and pleas for help stopped.

Standing over her was a very large man about six feet eight or nine inches tall and about three hundred pounds, dressed in a pink ballerina's tutu, white tights, muddy black sneakers and wearing a clown's face.

The shock of seeing this man dressed like this caused Amy to fall backwards. Amy turned over on her knees crawling until she was finally able to stand up.

Amy turned in the directions of the man in the Ballerina's tutu begging and pleading for him not to hurt her when she slipped and fell in the mud.

She saw that this man in the ballerina's tutu had a wheel barrel beside him and a rope around his shoulders.

Amy tried scooting away on her behind, and then turned over and began crawling away as fast as she could, digging in the mud and grabbing the wet grass for traction.

Amy wanted to cry for help when she noticed something odd... all around her it was raining cats and dogs, but where the man in the ballerina's tutu stood there was no rain, no nothing except a strange thick milky white fog surrounding him and engulfing him.

When Amy turned back around and tried to crawl away from the man in the ballerina's tutu she felt the weight of something heavy on the back of her head, mashing her face into the mud.

The man in a ballerina's tutu had his right foot on Amy's head, mashing her face into the mud with such force until Amy's body no longer kicked and moved, but lay lifeless.

When Amy came to and opened her eyes, she could barely see because of the mud in her eyes. Amy could tell that she was bound by the wrist and ankles with a rope and she inside of the wheel barrel.

Amy started to cough and gag from the amount of leaves and mud in her eyes and nose, when the man in the ballerina's tutu held out his hands and motion for her to be quiet.

Amy finally saw the outline of trees and through the trees, a clearing and in this clearing there was a house, an old abandoned two story wooden house.

Amy saw that it was an old two story wooden white house, with large dead trees on either side.

Amy struggled in the wheel barrel to get free when the man in the ballerina's tutu stopped pushing the wheel barrel and let it slam to the ground.

The man in a ballerina's tutu again walked over in front of Amy and cautioned for her to keep quiet and to stop trying to get away.

As Amy flinched in fear and lay still in the wheel barrel, the man continued pushing the wheel barrel as it bounced over a fallen tree log causing Amy to bounce up and down inside the wheel barrel until Amy landed on her left side.

Amy started to cry thinking about Jerry when all of a sudden the man wearing the ballerina's tutu suddenly stopped.

Amy was experiencing more fear than she had ever felt in her life, not knowing what was going to happen to her, except that was she was going to die some unimaginable death.

Her mind went from thinking of Jerry to the baby inside her and the fact that she'd never see her baby or all people she loved.

Amy dropped to her knees and then lay on her back crying when all of a sudden the man in the ballerina's tutu bent down and picked Amy up out of the mud by her hair.

Amy began screaming as her legs were kicking the air as she was being lifted higher into the air.

The Man in the ballerina's tutu held Amy up to his face and looked at her helplessly struggling to move, struggling to escape.

As Amy's eyes focused she first saw his eyes which were milky white with no Iris, and then she saw that where there should have been a mouth...there was nothing, no lips no nothing.

Amy started crying and begging for the man in the ballerina's tutu not to hurt her or her baby.

Amy's cries were quickly silenced as the man reached down and scooped up a handful of mud and leaves and shoved it all in her mouth, making Amy gag.

As Amy was gagging the man in the ballerina's tutu kept wiping the mud from Amy's lips and shoving it back into her mouth, and then he let her body drop to the ground.

Bending over Amy the man in the ballerina's tutu scooped up two handfuls of mud and filled Amy's mouth until Amy began chocking.

Then he quickly sat down in the mud beside the wheel barrel, and placing both hands on the sides of his face, rocked his head from side to side mocking Amy as she gagged.

Amy tried spitting out the mud and leaves and was on the verge of passing out when the man in a ballerina's tutu with one hand, squeezed Amy's cheeks together and shook her face, making her open her mouth wider.

Amy knew that she was about to die and if there was any hope in anyone coming to her rescue she would have to let out the loudest ear piercing scream that she could.

In an act of desperation Amy spit out the mud and leaves from her mouth and let out the loudest scream of her life.

It wasn't a high pitched scream but a hoarse scream of horror and agony.

The man in the ballerina's tutu again squeezed Amy's cheeks and reached down and scooped a big pile of mud and leaves, and shoved it in Amy's mouth.

Amy began choking and gagging, as the man in the ballerina's tutu shoved more and more mud and leaves into her mouth.

Amy then realized that she had to make a horrible decision... swallow as much of the mud and leaves as she could or choke to death and die.

In a last ditch effort to breathe, she closed her eyes, and started to swallow as the man in the ballerina's tutu continued scooping up large handfuls of wet mud, leaves and God knows what into Amy's mouth.

With no choice but to either swallow or choke to death, Amy began to let the mud and leaves slide down her throat, that's when she felt something wiggling against the tip of her nose, and moving in her mouth!

Not only was Amy swallowing mud and leaves, but she was also swallowing worms, slugs and all sorts of bugs.

The time had come and gone for Amy to try to stop swallowing and even though she wanted to spit everything out...she couldn't because the man in the ballerina's tutu was squeezing her mouth closed.

Just when Amy thought that the man in a ballerina's tutu was through torturing her, he shoved a final huge handful into her mouth and then placed one hand on Amy's head and the other under her chin...forcing her mouth closed.

Amy gagged and gulped and as she did the man in the ballerina's tutu watched Amy's throat began to bulge and stretch.

The amount of mud, bugs, and worms was so repulsing to Amy that she began vomiting, but because her mouth was being forced closed; the vomit began spewing out of her nose.

Amy's body started jerking violently until her head slumped down into the wheel barrel.

The man in the ballerina's tutu grabbed the handles of the wheel barrel and after lifting them up, pushed Amy around the back of the house.

The man in the ballerina's tutu reached underneath Amy's legs and grabbed the excess end of the rope which dangled from Amy's ankles and lifted her out of the wheel barrel and dragged Amy's lifeless body through the mud and up the steps, her head banging against the ground, hitting logs and embedded rocks.

The man in the ballerina's tutu climbed the steps of the house and kicked open the door, dragging Amy behind him, her head crashing on each of the wooden steps.

As the man in the ballerina's tutu entered in through the door, a clump of Amy's wet hair was caught in one of the broken wooden steps.

The man in the ballerina's tutu, with one hand grabbed Amy's ankles and yanked Amy so hard until a large section of her hair and scalp was snatched from her hair and lodged in the broken steps.

As he dragged Amy with her head bleeding profusely, Amy began coming to...moaning with her hands grasping for whatever she could grab a hold to, her fingers caught into the small slithers of the steps.

The man in ballerina's tutu paid no mind to Amy and with a mighty tug, snatched her until one of fingers broke off in the steps.

As he entered the house he watched as Amy's head hit the last few steps, causing Amy to moan as he slammed the door shut!

Pecan Drive
8:15 a.m.

After a restless night's sleep of watching David toss and turn, Deanne went down stairs and made a cup of coffee and called Wendi saying...

"Hey Wend...I'm sorry for calling so early in the a.m. but I was hoping that you were up, I wanted to catch you, before you made plans for today."

Wendi hadn't gotten much sleep herself because Steve was away all weekend, with a couple of friends hunting, and said...

"Aww girlfriend you didn't wake me, there's no way I can sleep when Steve's not here...so, what's up...you alright?"

Deanne didn't want to come off sounding like a drama queen, so she took a big sip of her coffee and said...

"Blue's almost his normal self...he's-he's going to be alright, the only thing is...for the past six months he hasn't said a word, and yesterday he tried to speak...but nothing came out."

Wendi was glad to hear the news that I was returning to his normal self. She owed David a lot, after all it was I who got Wendi and Steve together.

Wendi was on the verge of asking Deanne a question when Deanne interrupted her...

"I got to take Blue to the VA this morning at nine thirty but when I get back home, I really need you to come over, I need to talk to you."

Wendi sighed, and answered Deanne softly...

"Dee, is this what I think it is?"

Deanne was pacing the floor and nervously looking up the steps to make sure That David wasn't coming out of the bedroom and said...

"Remember when I told you that he cheated on me with Mary...?"

Wendi was one of the last romantics, a person who believes in love at first sight and all of that, who also knew how much David truly adored and worshipped Deanne, saying...

"Deanne we talked about this month's ago, you can't just throw it at him right now...I mean you told me you were going to wait... look, just call me when you guys get home, and I'll head over, okay?"

Deanne heard David moving around in the bathroom and said...

"Okay look, Blue's up, so I'll call you later."

Wendi was about to end her call when she looked down at her phone and saw that Steve was calling and said...

"Ok Deanne, Steve's calling so I'll just get myself ready to head that way in about a few hours... C'ya...bye."

Once Wendi ended her call with Deanne, she tried to switch over to catch Steve's call but Steve had already hung up.

Not sure if Steve was in a tree stand or in the middle of the woods or something, Wendi decided to take a chance on calling Steve... maybe something was wrong.

Wendi headed upstairs and after leaving the bathroom went into her bedroom and sat down on the bed and dialed Steve's number.

The number rang and rang, and then went straight to Steve's voice mail. Just as Wendi was about to lay her phone down, it rang...

"Hello, Steve..."?

It was Steve, but Wendi could hardly hear him, so she pressed the volume control on her phone but his voice was still cutting in and out, when she heard....

"Hey Wen...Hey babe sorry for calling so early, we're moving our tree stands to another spot, some kids spooked away the deer we almost had, so I decided to buzz ya, to see how you were doing."

With a puzzled tone in her voice, Wendi said...,

"Kids... kids are out hunting too?"

Sounding a little out of breath, Steve replied...

"Can you hear me babe? No...there are no kids hunting, but an hour ago right when this big ass 'ten-pointer' came out of the brush we heard some kids' singing, and naturally...the deer heard them too, and ran back into the woods."

Wendi sat her cup of coffee down on the nightstand and said...

"Well, maybe there was a cabin of boy scouts or girl scouts or something; you know how voices can carry in the woods."

Re-adjusting his blue tooth Steve said...

"Yeah, we kind of thought that too only there are no cabins anywhere near this area, plus boy scouts and girl scouts don't have outings in this area when it's hunting season."

Wendi sat down by the computer to see what the weather was going to be in Columbus and said...

"Well babe, before you go I got a call from Deanne and she told me that Dave's home. I'm going to head over that way in about three or four hours, I'll tell him you said hello."

Steve was just about to end his call with Wendi when he heard something coming out of the woods down below him, and in a whisper said right before switching off his blue tooth...

"Dave's home...good, I'm going to have to...uh oh, looks like I got action...love you babe."

Within a few minutes Steve called Wendi back...

"Damn babe...I thought a deer was moving in the woods down below me, and right when I was all set to shoot...a bunch of damn kids were walking through the woods.

Wendi's voice became more concerned...

"Well babe if there are kids in the area...don't you think you ought to just pack it up try again tomorrow morning, in a different area?"

Steve put the gun's safety on, and as he poured some coffee out of his thermos, he said...

"Well todays definitely shot...first we saw them last night and now twice this morning...!"

Wendi said...

"What about last night Steve, you know I hate it when you start to say something and then leave me hanging...so what happened?"

Steve, realizing that he just gave Wendi a reason to launch a *full scale investigation* into last night's events...emptied the remaining coffee from his thermos and said to himself...

"Damn...I had to open my big fat mouth!"

Tapping his blue tooth, he said...

"You still there babe, signal's going in and out...I lost what you said."

The tone in Wendi's voice went from concern to a sign post which read....

"You're about to piss me off."

In a conversation that Wendi had with Steve months earlier, she was telling him about some bad dreams she was having about him hunting and how she wished he wouldn't go.

She also talked with Steve about not being able to sleep through the night, because of some uneasy feeling that something bad was going to happen to both him and her.

Steve tried telling Wendi that she was worrying too much, and that people always worry when they think that something bad is going to happen, but never reach that same level of emotion when they think something good is going to happen.

Steve also told Wendi that how can something bad happen to both of them when he was miles away hunting and she was in opposite direction.

Putting down his thermos Steve reached in his coat pocket for his flask and took a drink when Wendi said...

"*Don't give me that shit Steve...you heard what I said, I swear when a man has diarrhea of the mouth the first thing he says is...what did you say baby. So, what in the hell happened last night...and why didn't you call once you got to the cabin?*"

Steve asked Wendi if she was still going over to Deanne and Dave's place later, when Wendi asked Steve about the cabin they were staying in.

Wendi wasn't about to answer Steve until he told her about the cabin, and whether or not he'd be bringing ticks or chiggers or bed bugs home with him so Steve said...

"*The cabin's okay nothing special about it, it has four bunk beds, an old wooden table with four chairs an outhouse, plus the mattresses are covered in plastic.*"

Wendi told Steve...

"*Sounds like all the comforts of home but why didn't you call me like you said you were, and what's up with these kids?*"

Steve told Wendi how after they settled in and scouted where they were going to be hunting, that they heard children's voices, kind of a demonic singing and laughing, and they went to investigate it, and he just forget to call.

Wendi continued...

"*So who was it...boy scouts, girl scouts.... what?*"

Steve told Wendi...

"No...*these voices were loud, and demonic and chilling.*"

Wendi sighed and asked...

"*Well, what were they saying and why is your dumb ass still out there?*"

Steve said...

"*The best I can recall is, they were singing...*"

"*La-la-la-la-la-la-, la-la-la-la-la-la,*

Teddy Bear's a hunter, loading up his gun,

Click bang, what a hang, now it's time to run

"*La-la-la-la-la-la-, la-la-la-la-la-la.*"

Screaming at Steve Wendi said...

"*Wait a minute...you heard some weird shit like that and your still there?*"

Steve checked to see if his gun was still on safety and said...

"*Yeah we decided to stay and I also left out the part about me, Mike and Jeff drinking a whole quart of 'White Liquor' an hour earlier.*"

Wendi let out a big sigh and said...

"*Okay stupid ass...isn't that how the vice president shot his friend... drinking and hunting*"?

Steve told Wendi that they had a few drinks last night and won't be having anything else to drink until after they're through hunting for the day.

Steve spent another five minutes talking to Wendi and then ended their call. Steve climbed out of the tree stand and walked over to where Michael and Jeffery were perched and said...

"*Look, we're going to scrap today, let's get a real early start in the morning.*"

As the three men walked back to their cabin, Michael said...

"*Don't think I'm tripping or anything, but did you hear somebody singing a little while back?*"

Steve started to speak up and confirm what Michael said, when Jeffery sarcastically blurted...

"Yeah I heard it too, sounded like...'if you build it he will come."

Jeffery couldn't help but laugh, and Steve could have bailed Michael out but didn't...choosing to remain silent, even though he heard the singing too.

The three men were less than a mile from their cabin, when Michael said...

"Steve, is there any more of that juice left from last night?"

Steve reached into the inside of his pocket and handed Michael the flask, which refused and said...

"Oh no, I don't want any now I was just asking because before I hit the sack I was going to hit a shot or two to keep this cold from jumping my ass."

Steve passed the flask over to Jeffery who accepted it and drank two shots, before giving it back to Steve.

Steve also took a big swig and said, looking at Michael...

"Hair of the creature Mike...hair of the creature."

Michael asked Steve...

"So you have a cousin down in North Carolina who makes this, thought this was illegal?"

Steve took another swig and said...

"Yep sure do...shit, there are a lot of people back up in the mountains who make it. During homecoming we drive down for the church services, and there's my cousin out in the parking lot taking orders."

Steve told Michael and Jeffery on their way back to the cabin that it was a wrap and that some hot food and a warm bed was the only thing that was on his mind.

The trip back to the cabin should've only taken twenty minutes, but with each step the three hunters took, the longer it was taking them when Jeffery said...

"Hey Steve; don't tell me that I'm seeing things, but didn't we pass this section of woods?"

The sun was quickly setting but there was still enough light to see as Steve looked around the entire area and then and pulled down on the sling of his rifle said...

"You know what Jeffery...I think you're right."

Michael who was standing behind Steve walked over to the brush to relieve himself telling Steve and Jeffery...

"Well, while you two decide which is the way to the Land of Oz...I'm take a leak over here."

While Michael was busy taking care of business, Jeffery and Steve stood in the open pointing off towards the north, as Steve said...

"I swear; this is all jacked up. We left the cabin and walked along the creek for thirty but so far we've followed the creek for over an hour."

Michael walked over and joined Jeffery and Steve saying...

"Okay, so which way is the cabin?"

Jeffery and Steve looked over at Michael and Steve said...

"I'm not sure Mike...I'm not sure."

Michael was the least experienced of the three and looked over at Jeffery saying...

"Mike, I'm afraid he's not joking...think back to when we left the cabin, what was the first landmark we saw, and what did we follow?"

Looking all around Michael said...

"We followed this creek from the cabin...why?"

Steve was standing near the creek and pointed to a red ribbon tied to a tree and looked up at Michael and Jeffery and said...

"When we left the cabin we walked thirty feet down a hill and this creek was at the base of the cabin. We followed this creek for thirty minutes, and I tied this ribbon around this tree."

Michael stood looking puzzled saying...

"So all we got to do is follow the creek for thirty minutes...right?"

Jeffery leaned into Michael saying...

"I don't think you get it...our tree stands are right over there about thirty to thirty-five feet."

Steve interrupted saying...

"Mike, from right here to our cabin is only a thirty-minute hike, but we've been walking for an hour, and look where we are...right back where started from."

Jeffery, Michael and Steve decided after getting their bearings that they were going in the right direction, so they set out for their cabin, starting at the tree with the ribbon tied to it, and timed themselves for thirty minutes.

Michael yelled out...

"Seven thirty-six."

All three men looked up and they saw the trail that led to their cabin when Jeffery said...

"Okay, anybody want to tell me what just happened?"

Michael began climbing the hill and turned saying...

"Well, it appears as though we were walking in the wrong direction the first time."

Steve repositioned his gun across his back and said...

"Mike, if we walked in the wrong direction, how in the hell did we end up back where we started from, it stands to reason that we'd be further away in the opposite direction."

Wet, cold and hungry Michael, Steve and Jeffery climbed the hill until they reached their cabin to get some hot food, sleep and a fresh start early in the morning.

As Michael was reaching suddenly he broke wind when Steve and Jeffery said...

"Thanks for the warning?"

The three men laughed and joke and then entered the cabin for good night's sleep.

Chapter 3

Eternal Friends

Gahanna, Ohio

Wendi put her bag in the car and opened the garage door. Wendi was backing out of the garage when the garage door closed and landed a few feet from her rear bumper.

Hitting the brakes hard Wendi again pressed the garage door opener, but it did not engage to open.

Wendi pulled the car back completely in the garage, placed the car in park and used the key pad by the house door to lift the garage.

When she pressed the keyless pad the garage door opened fully and stopped at the correct position.

Wendi thought that perhaps she unknowingly hit the switch twice instead of once, but what Wendi didn't know was, something was warning her, telling her maybe she ought not to go anywhere today.

Wendi stood inside the garage looking at the clouds and the storm which was approaching Columbus and thought that perhaps the distant thunder interfered with the garage door opener.

After waiting a few minutes Wendi called Deanne and told her that she was getting ready to leave and should be there between thirty and forty-five minutes depending on the traffic on interstate seventy-one.

Wendi ended her call with Deanne and without thinking anymore about the garage door opener started backing out.

All was going well when just as Wendi's car cleared the garage the door, it came crashing down barely missing the hood of her car, as Wendi yelled...

"What the hell...a few more inches and the hood of the car would've been messed up."

Wendi slammed on brakes just outside of the garage looking at the garage door button on the sun visor, and thought...

"How in the world did that happen...I never even had a chance to hit the button...and if its messed up, Steve is going to blame it on me and say...I did something to it."

The night's storm that hit central Ohio, which included Gahanna was intense, and the day's forecast was for more of the same only the storm was forecasted to move through Columbus pretty fast.

Wendi put on her windshield wipers and slowly backed out of the drive waving to her neighbor Tonya Hill as she headed out of the subdivision.

Wendi's trip to Deanne and David's would take her down interstate seventy-one and around Alum Creek State Park and through a wooded area to a newly developed Condominium section.

Wendi turned to get her bag which she had packed in case she would have to stay the night at Deanne's, and put it in the front passenger seat.

Wendi placed her cell phone in the console and turned the heat up in the car and made her way towards interstate seventy-one, not knowing that there was a dark figure, hunched down in the back seat.

Coming from Wisconsin Wendi was no stranger to bad weather, but nonetheless she preferred not to drive in it.

She hoped that the worst of the weather would hold off until she arrived at Deanne and David's condo, and if need be she was prepared to spend the night.

The day's weather was nothing like the torrential down pours which all of central Ohio experienced the previous night.

The traffic was moderate and for a change every one on the highway seemed to be observing the posted speed limit that was all except one driver.

Wendi could see the dark eerie looking clouds a mile ahead of her which were becoming more and more threatening.

The drive around Alum Creek State Park in the day time is a little challenging but at night and in a storm, a person going too fast or not paying attention could end up running off the side of the road.

Wendi normally speeds wherever she goes, but her last few tickets came with a price, so Wendi slowed down and obeyed the posted speed limit.

Wendi was well into ten minutes on interstate seventy-one when she saw lightening flashing in the distance ahead of her and instead of hearing thunder, she heard voices.

Voices of children singing and laughing, their voices over lapping one another

"La-la-la-la-la-la-la-, la-la-la-la-la-la-la,

Teddy Bear Soda Crackers, Teddy Bear smart

Got a taste for Wendi's flesh, but first I'll eat her heart

La-la-la-la-la-la-la-, la-la-la-la-la-la-la."

Not knowing what to think about what she just heard Wendi reached for her cell phone to call Deanne, just to hear her voice.

Wendi pressed speed dial five which was Deanne's assigned number. Putting her cell on speaker phone, Wendi was about to lay the phone back in the console when she received an automated message saying...

"No Service Area".

Suddenly blinding headlights appeared in Wendi's mirror as she noticed headlights bobbing up and down and extremely close to her bumper.

Wendi noticed that there was a nineteen seventies late model ford pickup following her, which looked as if it was a poster vehicle for 'Junky-Truck Inc....", let alone out on a major highway.

Wendi wasn't real comfortable with driving Steve's Escalade but had no choice, since her Honda Accord was in the shop on a recall and Steve was hunting for the week.

All the other traffic behind Wendi sped up a little to pass her, but the old truck kept pace with Wendi. It seemed that with every bump in the road something was going to fall off of the truck.

The truck reminded Wendi of a cross between the Beverly Hillbillies & Sanford & Son's trucks.

Wendi kept a close eye on the truck because of the headlights on the truck, which were so loose, that with each bump in the road, the lights '*bobbed*' up and down.

Just then the hairs on the back of Wendi's neck began standing up as the truck was obviously keeping pace with her, slowing down as she slowed down, and speeding up when she did, and changing lanes when she did.

Wendi decided that she would get off before her exit, to see if the truck following her would do the same.

Wendi noticed that the exit she coming up on was a full service plaza and thought to herself...

"If I exit and then get back on the interstate, and this damn truck behind me does the same, then screw a ticket, I'll just have to out run it."

Wendi put on her turn signal and got onto the off ramp, and as she looked behind her, the truck continued on the freeway, showing no signs of following her.

Wendi exited and breathed a sigh of relief and noticed a Starbucks shop, up ahead and pulled into the drive thru to get a Cappuccino.

Wendi looked all around as she sat waiting on her Cappuccino and saw no signs of the truck, and thought...

"Well it's been ten minutes and it just might have been some old man, who drives slow...anyway once I get back on interstate I'll drive a little slower, that way I'll know the truck is far ahead of me."

After sitting for a few minutes and sipping some of her Cappuccino and looking at her cell phone for messages, Wendi decided to try Deanne once more before getting back onto the interstate.

Wendi dialed Deanne's number and after five rings was about to hang up when Deanne answered and said...

"Hello Wendi... please tell me that you are you on your way?"

Wendi took another sip of her Cappuccino and said...

"Dee, I was about to hang up. I tried calling you twenty minutes ago but I didn't have any service...I'll be there in a bit, I'm about fifteen minutes from you...had to stop to get me a Cappuccino."

Deanne said...

"With this crazy weather I thought for a moment that you weren't going to make it."

Buckling her seat belt and placing her coffee in the cup holder Wendi said...

"Well girl it's starting to get nasty out here, the wind and rain is picking up and it's almost pitched black out here and by the way.... how are we going to talk with David being there?"

Deanne replied...

"Just be careful, you can stay the night can't you... that'll give us plenty of time to talk. Don't worry about Blue, he'll be up in the bedroom and we can sit out on the patio and light the Fire Pit."

Wendi pulled up to the light to make a left turn to get back on the interstate, saying to Deanne before ending her call...

"The fire pit would be nice; you know I don't like cold but since you have a screened in Patio....it shouldn't be too bad."

Wendi entered the traffic and checked ahead of her to see if she saw the old truck, but all she could make out were newer model cars, as she said to herself...

"Oh well, I guess grandpas was ahead of me."

Wendi checked the Escalades GPS system for Deanne and David's address on Pecan Drive, to make sure she wouldn't miss her turn in the dark.

Alum Creek drive narrowed to a two lane winding road, with woods on one side and new homes and condominiums on the other side.

Wendi exited the interstate at state route seven ten, heading for Africa Road which winds around one side of Alum Creek.

That stretch of road is a dark and less traveled road, except for the residents living in the area.

Wendi turned onto Africa and reached to grab her cell phone to call Deanne to let her know she was about five minutes away...when out of nowhere... something rammed her from behind, causing her to drop her cell phone!

"Shit...you want to back up off my ass, mister!"

Wendi yelled as she looked in her rear view mirror to see the same headlights which bobbed up and down, as Wendi said...

"Oh shit...he's back...that damn funky ass old truck, he was waiting for me all this time...but how'd he know I was coming this way?"

Without warning the old truck which followed Wendi on the highway was now behind her on a ten mile, dimly lit stretch of road.

Wendi was so preoccupied that she had forgotten her cell phone was lying on the passenger floor board, which she dropped when the truck rammed her from behind.

Wendi frantically began searching on the passenger seat and the console area for her cell phone which had started ringing, and it was then that Wendi noticed it on the passenger floor board.

Again without any warning the truck behind her rammed into her again, which almost causing Wendi to run into the guard rail which separates Alum Creek drive from the reservoir.

Wendi screamed, and called out Steve's name...

"Steve"!

Wendi knew her turn off was ahead about three more miles and sped up to reach her turn before the truck behind her could catch her.

Wendi pressed the accelerator ...thirty, forty-five, fifty-five miles an hour when all of a suddenly the old truck which looked like it would fall apart, passed Wendi doing at least eighty miles an hour.

Puzzled and frightened Wendi's only thoughts were about getting to her turn off up ahead, and if she missed her turn off she'd have to go to the end of the road to a dead end and turn around.

All of a sudden Wendi's eyes got big as the old Truck was headed directly for her, when Wendi screamed...

"OH MY GODD......!"

The old truck grazed Wendi and knocked off her driver's side mirror, causing Wendi to swerve to the left and to the right... missing her turn off.

The only thing which lay ahead was a private road, and an old marine supply and parts building.

Wendi struggled to keep the escalade from flipping when she saw ahead, old boats, and a half torn down building.

Wendi hit the brakes and crashed into the front of one of the boats sitting in the yard. Shaken and in shock, Wendi opened the door to the escalade and slowly limped out.

Unaware of where she was at the moment and what had just happened. Wendi leaned against the hood of the Escalade when she noticed headlights coming up behind her.

The trucks tires slid and came to a stop in the gravel a few feet behind Wendi, as she searched her pockets for her cell phone.

Realizing where her cell phone was, Wendi limped around to the passenger side, when the truck began revving its engine with each step Wendi took.

With each step the truck inched forward when Wendi screamed...

"WHO THE FUCK ARE YOU, AND WHAT THE HELL DO YOU WANT?"

The reality of what was happening occurred to Wendi, and what was probably going to happen was sinking in as she limped as fast as she could to the door.

Opening the door Wendi bent down searching for her phone, which was partially under the seat.

Wendi started crying and talking to herself while her hands frantically searched for her phone until her finger tips felt it.

Grabbing the phone Wendi looked up in the direction of the truck which to her surprise was no longer there.

Wendi looked around for a minute but all she saw was fog, and then her phone started ringing.

Thinking that whoever was in the truck was scared off and left, Wendi put the phone to her ear and heard Deanne's voice...

"Hello, Wendi?"

Just as Wendi opened her mouth to answer, a large hand came up from behind her and covered her mouth and with the other hand, grabbed the cell phone from Wendi, closed it and tossed it into the woods.

Wendi began frantically reaching up towards his face, clawing, and kicking but the man was very strong and large. Wendi was lifted off of the ground as though she were a rag doll.

Finally, Wendi's hands reached his face but her nails slid off of his face because he was wearing a ...clown's face mask.

With one hand over Wendi's mouth and the other hand grabbing her hair, Wendi knew she was powerless to do anything, but kick her legs as hard as she could.

The man carried Wendi around to the back of the building and using Wendi's head as a battering ram... opened the large metal door and threw her to the floor.

As Wendi lay on the floor all she could see were candles lit and a very strong foul odor of something dead and rotting.

Wendi noticed chains suspended from a metal frame, attached to the ceiling swinging.

Closing the door behind him, the man dragged Wendi closer towards an old large work table which had vice gripes mounted at each corner of the table, which smelled of oil and diesel fuel.

Wendi's heart began racing as she imagined what this man intended to do to her and that's when she saw the man.

He was seven feet tall and about three hundred pounds, but the strangest thing was...he was wearing a ballerina's tutu, with stockings and a pair of old black converse sneakers.

Wendi struggled to get free and tried as hard as she could to scream until the man pulled a very large knife from his side and began cutting the buttons from Wendi's sweater.

One by one the buttons fell to floor revealing Wendi's shirt. Wendi began kicking and squirming knowing what the man's intentions were...she was going to be raped.

The man took the knife and began cutting away the buttons from her shirt and tracing the outline of her chest, from her neck, down to her left breast, and then to her right.

Wendi moaned each time the knife touched her skin, and there was one sign of hope in Wendi's mind...she did not think that the man in the ballerina's tutu was taking pleasure in seeing her nude breast.

Over and over the knife traced and each time he repeated this Wendi's breathed faster as the knife dug deeper and deeper into her skin until blood began seeping from the small cuts.

Wendi's muffled cries of...

"No.... No.... No."

Under the man's hand could barely be heard. Being raped is too horrific for Wendi or anyone for the matter to comprehend, but Wendi remembered a conversation she had several years earlier with Deanne, Mary and Kristin, when she said...

"I don't know how you guys feel but, if I'm attacked and there is a chance I can fight him off...I'm fighting, but if he has a gun or knife...well, being raped is totally fucked up but I'll be looking and waiting for a chance to get away...at least, I'll live."

The man kept walking away from Wendi and coming back, each time twirling the knife in the air and pointing at Wendi.

Then the big man in the ballerina's tutu walked over to Wendi and violently turned her head to the side as he took a few steps back and got in the stance of 'First Position' and began dancing like a clumsy ballerina.

Wendi thought to scream as loud as she could but another thought entered her mind...

"Even though I said I wouldn't resist...there is no way I'm just going to lay here and let this sick fuck rape me...if he kills me, then he kills me, but I'm not going to lay here and take it!"

The knife continued to cut away Wendi's shirt and her bra, as Wendi tried grabbing her shirt and pulling it back over her chest.

Wendi could feel the knife slicing her hands and arms and then all of a sudden, the man opened his right hand and let the knife fall to the floor.

When that happened Wendi thought to herself...

"Oh my god...this is it!"

As the knife hit the floor, the man reached over with his right hand and grabbed Wendi's throat.

Holding Wendi in the air, Wendi saw the clown face mask covering his face, and tried to scream but his grip was strong, so strong that it was almost impossible to breath, let alone make a sound.

Images of Steve, and her mother and sister flashed in her head as she felt it more and more difficult to breathe.

Wendi's bloody hands and arms began reaching and clawing at the man's arm and his face until she was able to grab a hold of the mask and pull it off, seeing the man's true distorted face.

Wendi's arms dropped and her hands fell and rested on the man's right arm, as she saw his face completely, and saw that the man had no nose or mouth.

Wendi felt herself about to lose consciousness when the man lifted her higher, and with his left arm under Wendi's back, slammed her down upon the table as a wrestler does, doing a body slam.

When Wendi awakened to her surprise, she had not been raped. Her jeans were still on, and while her shirt and sweater were cut open her clothes had not been removed.

Wendi sat up and tried to focus as her head throbbed in pain from being slammed down upon the table and as Wendi tried to move, she looked around to see where the man in the ballerina's tutu and white clown's face was, but the pain was too much for her.

Just then, the man appeared behind her and pulled her by the hair back upon the table.

He tied both of her wrists and ankles with ropes, and tied it to all four of the chains which hung from the ceiling.

At some point, Wendi had passed out from being repeatedly slammed onto the table. The man instead of sexually assaulting her had done other things, horrible things which Wendi hadn't noticed, but would soon discover.

The man in the ballerina's tutu retrieved Wendi's cell phone from the woods and went into her contacts to Deanne's number and texted her with a message that read...

"La-la-la-la-la-la-, la-la-la-la-la-la,

Teddy Bear Soda Crackers, picking at his teeth,

Got a taste for Wendi's flesh,

You're next just wait and see

La-la-la-la-la-la-, la-la-la-la-la-la."

The man in the ballerina's tutu went back over to the table were Wendi lay and placed the phone close to Wendi and placed her head in one of the vice grips and began tightening the vice until Wendi began screaming...

"Aww......Help me, aww... Steve."

As the vice gripped tightened on Wendi's head he held Wendi's head down turning the vice grip handle until the bones in Wendi's cheeks began to crush, and then he stopped.

The man in the ballerina's tutu then went to the ropes and tied it around Wendi's ankles, and after removing her shoes and socks, took a battery cable and connected one end on her toes.

The man in the ballerina's tutu attached one end to the positive side of the battery and reached down to a bucket filled with water.

The man in the ballerina's tutu did not want Wendi to pass out but only for her to suffer for some unimaginable reason.

The man in the ballerina's tutu put a rag soaked in ammonia to Wendi's nose which awakened Wendi, who screamed in agony as he poured water on her feet and connected the other battery cable to her toes, one at a time.

Wendi's ankles and wrists were bound with rope and her head tightly in the mounted vice. The man in the ballerina's tutu poured diesel fuel all over Wendi's hair and then he did the imaginable.

He took the hot wire battery cable close to Wendi's face...opening and closing it, and striking it against the metal table causing sparks to fly.

Hoping to die instead of going through hours of torment Wendi stopped screaming and opened her mouth and managed to yell...

"Go ahead you sick bastard...kill me. You don't have a fucking nose or mouth, and maybe you don't have any fucking balls either!"

Whether it was Wendi's grit or the words she spoke but which ever it was the man in the ballerina's tutu clearly seemed pissed off.

He began squeezing Wendi's jaws until her jaw bones snapped, and then with Wendi unable to close her mouth he connected the battery cable to her tongue.

At first Wendi was slightly moving her body and then her body started violently jerking and then it stopped.

The man in the ballerina's tutu bent down and got close to Wendi's face looking and perhaps wondering if she was dead and then her whole body began twitching and jerking again.

Smoke began coming from her ears and then her hair caught fire. The man in the ballerina's tutu after seeing this began dancing around the table.

In the beginning Wendi's body was twitching and jerking and just as the fire which engulfed her hair died down from the rain which poured in through the holes in the metal roof, so did the jerking and twitching of her body die down.

Wendi's body lay motionless upon the table. Her hands which had clutched the edges of the table revealed broken bloody chunks of nails from her fingers.

A disgustingly stench filled the room, as Wendi's eyes sunk down in the sockets emitting a rotten odor and smoke from the sockets.

Wendi's tongue was completely black and her pearl white teeth had dropped from her gums into her mouth.

The man in the ballerina's tutu wheeled the wheel barrel over near the table where Wendi laid, and sat down on the floor looking all around the dimly lit room.

The man in a ballerina's tutu with the clown's face sat looking around the dim lit room and noticed a single light shining through the dirty oil stained window, and in the background, there was the flashing lights of a police car.

Slowly the old metal door opened, creaking as the door opened wider and wider.

Officer James Murphy pushed opened the door, shinning his flash light all around the room until his flash light caught light of the candle sitting on top of the steel drum.

As officer Murphy entered the building his flash light shone on the table where Wendi was laying.

He slowly entered and approached Wendi's body and seeing the condition of Wendi, and smelling stench of burnt flesh he felt for a pulse, and upon finding none and believing that she was clearly dead, he backed out of the building and returned to his squad car.

Keeping his flash light trained on the door, he radioed in to dispatch headquarters saying...

"This is CP-10 to dispatch, somebody pick up."

The voice of a female answered...

"CP-10, this is dispatch, over."

Officer Murphy nervously said...

"Dispatch, I'm at the old boat yard off of Africa, and I discovered a deceased body. I need a unit and emergency services."

Officer Murphy's flash light was trained on the door that he exited, when he heard a banging sound directly behind him and turned, when the dispatcher replied...

"*CP-10, be advised...units are en route...ETA forty-five minutes, what's your status?*"

Officer Murphy stood up out of his patrol car and swung his flash light around in all directions and said...

"*There is a deceased body in an old abandoned boat yard building, and I am unable to determine if the perpetrator(s) are still inside. Waiting on back up before proceeding...over.*"

Officer James Murphy was a one year rookie fresh out of the academy with a newlywed wife and six month old son.

The patrol area of officer Murphy on this night was supposed to be a relatively quiet and boring assignment, but proved to be otherwise.

Officer Murphy volunteered to take this patrol to gain some extra money as the officer normally assigned on this night had called in sick.

Officer Murphy left the comforts of his home, wife and new born son because, it was storming badly, and all he expected to encounter on his shift was perhaps a motorist who slid off the road, but never expected that he would encounter something like this.

Officer James Murphy took duty on this night because it was storming, it was a quiet area and he and his wife Brenda were fighting over money issues and he thought this would be the answer to their problems.

What should have been a routine quiet night soon would turn into tragedy on the grandest scale.

Officer Murphy maintained his distance from the building waiting for back up as was protocol until he noticed a flash of light coming from inside the building.

Officer Murphy picked up the radio and told dispatch that he saw a flash of light coming from inside the building and that he was going to investigate.

As he laid the radio down on the seat of the squad car and walked towards the building, he did not hear the message from dispatch saying...

"CP-10, back up was rerouted to an accident on interstate seventy-seven...new ETA on assistance....one hour, set up perimeter and maintain surveillance...do not approach."

Officer Murphy approached the door and trained his flash light all around the inside of the room and spotted a large figure moving and coming towards him.

Officer Murphy shouted...
"Police...stop where you are and put your hands up!"

The figure continued to approach Officer James Murphy as he yelled and fired six shots...
"I said this is the police, stop and put your hands where I can see them!"

Officer Murphy backed against the door as the figured dropped to the floor inches in front of him.

Shinning his flash light on the figure laying in front of him, officer Murphy noticed it was a man. A very large man in a ballerina's tutu, and as the man lay in a prone position he could see that the man was wearing some sort of mask.

Officer Murphy quickly shone his flash light around the room looking for any other persons in the building, but because of the makeup of the building and the discarded old boat parts it was hard to tell who if any, were in the building.

Officer Murphy kept an eye on the man in the ballerina's tutu which lay before him on the floor as he walked back over to the body on the table.

Looking at the body he could tell that it was a woman, badly burned and bloody. Feeling for a pulse, but she was dead.

Officer Murphy shinned the flash light back on the floor where the man lay when he heard in the distance the sounds of faint sirens.

Knowing that assistance was near he began walking towards the door when he was grabbed from behind.

Then man in the ballerina's tutu had Officer Murphy in a bear hug. The grip was so tight that it was difficult for him to breathe.

Officer Murphy tried to free himself but the man in the ballerina's tutu was so strong, that he grabbed Officer Murphy's neck and snapped it, with one easy motion.

As the police were pulling up to the old Boat and Tackle shack, the body of Officer Murphy was being drug out the back door and into the woods.

With sirens blaring and guns drawn, one of the Sherriff's Deputies kicked the door to the old building open while police and sheriff deputies stormed the building.

As they entered the building they discovered the body of Wendi dead on the table, yet there was no sign of officer Murphy or the man in the ballerina's tutu.

Pecan Drive
10:30p.m.

Ever since Deanne got back home from my appointment at the VA, she was acting as if something was wrong, but didn't say anything.

I noticed Deanne was unusually quiet and so I wrote a note asking her...

"What's was wrong"?

Deanne just gave me a half smile and said...

"Oh, nothing's wrong Blue...just had a lot on my mind lately."

I've known Deanne for about as long as anyone could know someone so it was easy for me to tell when something was bothering her and when something was out of place.

Dinner was in the oven cooking, turkey and dressing with potatoes and Asparagus... all of my favorites.

Deanne was trying with all she knew to help me snap back to my normal self, because she needed me to be alright before telling me that she was leaving me.

Sitting on the sofa, Deanne was pretending to read a magazine... 'Vet Buddies...one of my magazines.

I thought to myself...

"I know something's wrong... she never reads that."

I noticed that maybe Deanne was expecting company because I caught Deanne's eyes going back and forth from the clock to the magazine.

I grabbed a piece of paper and wrote...

"I know something is wrong...won't you talk to me?"

Deanne folded over a page in the magazine and said...

"Blue, I'm just worried about Wendi, she told me she would be here by the time we got back from your appointment and that was hours ago."

I replied to Deanne saying...

"Maybe Wendi's taking her time or at the store or something... give her a little bit...if she said she's coming over then she'll be here."

Deanne laid the magazine down and said...

"Blue, I can't get her on her cell and the weather is getting nasty plus you know she hates driving in crappie weather not to mention driving at night."

I sat next to Deanne and began rubbing and kissing Deanne's feet hoping a good foot massage would ease her mind, when the doorbell rang.

Deanne jumped up and bolted to the door saying...

"There she is, it's Wendi!"

I started to head into the kitchen to pour a glass of wine and as I turned my head expecting to see Wendi coming through the door, Deanne was standing at the door all alone.

Deanne shut the door and told me...

"It is really nasty out there... maybe the storm caused our door bell to ring...Blue I'm getting way past worried about Wendi, it's been like four hours, and nothing."

I came back into the living room and offered a sip of wine to Deanne, who refused saying...

"Blue, do you think I should call the police about Wendi?"

As I turned around and placed my wine glass on the coffee table I wrote...

"If you're that worried call the Highway Patrol and give them a description of Wendi's SUV and ask if any accidents reporting her vehicle have been called in."

Deanne sat down on the sofa and attempted to call Wendi, and after not being able to reach her she called Mary whose number was busy.

Deanne sat down and said...

"I'll feel like a stupid ass if I call the highway patrol and then Wendi shows up.... I'll give her another thirty minutes and then if she's not here... I'll call."

Out of the twenty residents living in the condo development area, me and Deanne were one of the five who had a fenced in lot.

I leashed up Shone and headed out the back door.

I didn't realize how nasty the weather was until me and Shone stepped outside. I unleashed Shone who bolted all over the yard, circling to find her favorite spot.

After realizing Shone may have me outside for little bit I smacked my coat pockets for my cigarettes and discovered that I had left them inside, so I made a retreat to get them.

When I walked in I noticed Deanne was on the phone talking to someone so, I assumed it was Mary or Kristin...and I quietly went back outside.

The weather was getting worse hour by hour. The rain which was a mere sprinkle earlier, was now coming down hard.

The coldness in the air and the fog which was settling in was just a little eerie for central Ohio, especially given how cold it was.

Shone like most dogs was a particularly smart dog, and after I lit my cigarette I stood there watching her trying to catch the leaves that the wind was tossing to the ground and thought to myself...

"This poor dog is going to need some therapy."

I blew a puff of smoke from my cigarette when a face appeared in the cigarette smoke.

It wasn't a vapor image the kind that gets distorted as the wind grabbed hold of it and fashioned it, but a clear image of a face.

It was the face of the little girl which I'd seen at the farm, and at the farmer's market parking lot.

As the image of the girl's face swirled around me, I chucked my cigarette towards the image and the girl opened her mouth and screamed in a loud voice...

"BOO....and by the way...I don't smoke!"

I jumped back and bumped into Deanne who had just come out to check on me, saying...

"Hey you, whatcha doing?"

I showed a little irritation when Deanne put her arms around my waist and kissed me on my neck, saying...

"Still no word on Wendi so I called the highway patrol like you said, and they have no accident reports of anybody in an escalade."

Deanne and I quickly walked inside the patio as the rain began picking up and blowing sideways.

Once back inside their, Deanne said...

"Blue, I think I'm going to try calling Mary again maybe she's heard from Wendi."

Deanne sat down on the sofa and dialed Mary's number which went straight to her voice mail, indicating that Mary was either talking to somebody or had her phone off.

I walked into the living room when Deanne laid her phone down and said...

"Blue, you are going to dry Shone off aren't you?"

I nodded and held up the old yellow towel that we used whenever Shone gets a bath, or like today when she's been out in the weather.

Deanne tried calling Mary again and after not being able to reach her, dialed Kristin who answered.

Kristin and Deanne talked for about thirty minutes when our doorbell rang again.

Deanne hung up the phone thinking it was Wendi at the door but when she got to the door and looked out the peep hole she saw our neighbor Tonya Scott, standing there with her umbrella.

Deanne opened the door, and invited Tonya in who immediately said...

"Deanne I need you to save me."

Looking puzzled, Deanne asked Tonya to take a seat and then said...

"Save you, what are talking about?"

Tonya said...

"Oh Girl, we have some friends coming over in a few minutes, and I'm making Spaghetti and forgot to get the wine... Do you know Russ was planning on having beer with it?"

I pretended not to be interested in what they were talking about when I noticed Deanne lightly tapped Tonya on the leg as she was getting up, and said...

"C'mon girl we can't have your guest getting all Italiano without any 'vino'. You may want to pick two bottles of red or two bottles of white, to be on the safe side."

Deanne grabbed a wine bag hanging up by the kitchen closet and held it open as Tonya loaded the wine in the bag and said as she headed out the door, kissing Deanne on the cheek...

"Dee, you are a life saver and you know...tomorrow, you'll get four bottles back."

As Tonya was about to pick up her umbrella she turned to Deanne and said...

"This is some kind of weather we're having isn't it?"

Agreeing with her Deanne nodded and said...

"It sure is...good luck with your party, and tell me all about it tomorrow will ya?"

I watched as Deanne closed the door, when my mind drifted to thinking...when the farm was being renovated several years ago, Steve and I were supposed to move the wine racks to the farm, but we never got around to it.

Deanne watched as Tonya hurried next door, her mind raced back to Wendi and the feeling she had that something was wrong.

Deanne continued looking out the window, as the lightening flashed in the distance followed by thunder, which continued to get louder and closer.

Deanne sat down on the sofa and tried texting Wendi and Mary, hoping that one of them would call her back.

Kristin had told Deanne that she would let her know if she had heard from either of them, but there was no word from Kristin either.

Madison Wisconsin
Saturday, 8:30 p.m.

It was an unusual night as Mary sat in the kitchen talking to her mother on the phone and looking out the window at the ominous clouds gathering.

Winter weather in Wisconsin can be unforgiving, but something was unusual about this particular night.

Mary could feel that there was something ugly in the air and in a strange way felt that something bad was going to happen.

The grass on the hills and plains around town in Madison were dead and brown. The normal kind of bleakness that any rural place in the north has before winter.

A small and rapidly dwindling part of Mary started to panic, as the crisp air echoed that something bad was coming and Mary's own inner voice, sixth sense...or whatever you call it was slowly growing louder and louder.

Mary had taken lots of pictures of the early snowfall last week, but the following day when Mary had her film developed she noticed there was an extra picture that she didn't take.

It was a picture of her standing beside Tim, tied to a post and a large figure directly behind Mary.

"Who the hell took this picture and what's up with this?"

Mary thought as her mind was filled with thoughts all day long especially of her friends, Deanne, Kristin, and her cousin Wendi.

Alarming thoughts flooded Mary's mind until one single thought floated to the forefront of Mary's mind.

A thought so loud so demonic, that it made Mary check to see if she was alone in the room... thoughts which screamed in Mary's mind...

"You're going to die-you're going to die."

Mary's first thought was that it was just her imagination running away with her, but the thoughts and the voice in her head...were so real.

The voice Mary heard was like a whisper of a man's voice, not a voice she recognized and the more Mary thought of this, the more she found herself totally freaking out.

Mary got up and went over to the living room window to see if Tim's SUV was in the driveway but it was not.

One can call it three dimensional thinking, ESP, a woman's intuition, voodoo…whatever, but Mary looked at the picture again… wondering…

Mary grabbed her cell phone and tried to call Deanne, and then Kristin, and finally Wendi, but no one answered her calls.

Mary laid her cell phone on the end table and turned back to the window watching the darkness and looking into the night, unable to shake the feeling that something … wasn't right and said to herself…

'Damn, that was a fucked up thought…" I was going to die… what the hell did that mean and why would I think of something as fucked up as that"?

Not being able to reach Deanne, Kristin, or Wendi Mary tried calling Tim. She had to get in touch with somebody to shake her feelings, to calm her fears.

Suddenly her cell phone began vibrating just as she was about to lay her phone down.

Scrolling over to the voice mail icon Mary pressed, play and heard…

"La-la-la-la-la-la-, la-la-la-la-la-la,

Teddy Bear, Soda Crackers,

Teddy Bear laughs,

Are you flipping out and seeing things?

Horrible way you'll die,

La-la-la-la-la-la-, la-la-la-la-la-la."

Mary was so scared until she dropped the phone, and as she reached to pick it up, something touched her on the shoulder and she jumped backwards and screamed.

It was Tim, standing there laughing and singing that Teddy Bear tune.

Mary and Tim looked at each other for a brief moment and as Mary stood up she punched Tim in the chest and pushed him into the wall, saying...

"Tim, you fucking asshole...you scared the holy crap out of me!"

Tim stood there for a minute staring at Mary and said...

"Mar, what hell are you talking about...I came in and called your name... I didn't mean to scare you."

Mary told Tim that he called her phone and left that creepy ass song, and just a moment ago was standing there singing.

Mary always teased Tim about smoking too much Marijuana when Tim said...

"Mar, I think you've been in my stash yourself...I wasn't singing anything."

Mary told Tim that she heard what she heard and that it just makes it worse when he tries to lie about it.

Tim and Mary have both gone through a lot of bad things that year, Mary had confessed an affair to Tim, who at first took it hard... but later forgave Mary and gotten over it.

It was during the Easter weekend when Mary was hospitalized with a P.E. and the doctors were afraid Mary was not going to make it.

Mary was eventually released and thinking of how close she came to death, decided to Tim that she had an affair with a woman she met in a book store last year.

Mary told Tim that she was at the bookstore in the mall sitting in the reading section, when a woman came up to her and introduced herself as Kate.

Mary told Tim...

"All I did was respond but then the woman walked in front of me and then half way down the aisle stopped and brought back a book, sat down next to me, and began reading it."

Mary went on to say how she simply looked over at this woman and then found herself staring at her legs, and then her face.

Mary said she had the prettiest eyes and the cutest small black framed glasses, gently hugging her small pointed nose.

Then to Mary's surprise, this woman looked over and caught her staring at her legs.

Kate was five feet four inches, and one hundred and thirty pounds, black high heels, and a low cut button-down top with a mop of blonde curly hair.

Mary told Tim…

"I couldn't stop staring it was like I was glued to her. All I saw was two of the prettiest legs in a black skirt and grey button-down shirt, and the sexiest pair of heels."

Mary went on to say…

"I don't why, but I've never been attracted to women before but my eyes were fixed on her heels and her sexy legs."

Tim rubbed his head and responded to Mary…

"So, now you're into women?"

Mary nervously said…

"No…I don't know…it's just …. oh hell Tim, I'm sorry let me finish."

Tim sat back and said…

"Okay I'm just trying to understand why are you telling me now…what's up?"

Mary sighed and said…

"Anyway, Kate leaned over and just kissed me, not a long kiss but a quick, soft kiss and then she got up and walked out of the bookstore."

I ended up following her not knowing whether she wanted me to or not. I haven't seen Kate in over three weeks, but baby… I'm committed to you--to us, it's just…oh hell I don't know what to say."

Mary told Tim, she saw Kate again three days ago in a coffee shop. She had on jeans a tee shirt, and sandals, she'd recognize Kate anywhere, even from that brief encounter at the book store.

Mary explained how she couldn't go inside, because she didn't know what she was going to say and how she just stood there, looking through the glass.

Mary said, as she turned to leave, Kate touched her on the shoulder and after a moment of awkwardness and looking into each other's eyes, they went to her apartment and there they made love.

Tim had a hard time accepting Mary's honesty and went upstairs.

Mary after a few minutes followed Tim to apologize to him, but by the time she got to the bedroom Tim was sitting on the bed rolling up a joint.

Mary told Tim, she only told him all of this because of her near death experience and that she didn't want any more secrets between them.

Tim ignored Mary and continued rolling his joint, when Mary rubbed his shoulder and repeated herself...

"Tim, I know you're pissed, but at least act like you're listening...I mean we promised each other that we wouldn't act like assholes!"

Mary explained to Tim that it had nothing to do with his love making. In fact, Mary went out of her way to assure Tim that he was completely satisfying her.

Mary tried to get Tim to see that her being with another woman was something extra she wanted, and that her feelings, emotions and desire for Tim would never change or take a back seat.

Mary even tried to compare her desire for another woman with Tim's pot smoking. She tried everything she could to reassure Tim.

She told Tim, he has always smoked marijuana since college, morning noon and night. She reminded Tim that he once told her...

"My smoking pot is the one thing outside our relationship that I have to have."

Tim nodded and hugged Mary telling her he understood but something in their relationship changed at that moment... something was a little different.

Tim at times was a little cold towards Mary and at times would come home late on purpose...he would simply ride around for hours.

If Tim noticed that Mary's car was in the driveway, Tim would go to the store just to have something in his hands, so that he could avoid his usual routine of hugging her when he first walked in.

If Tim got home before Mary, then he would either make sure he was taking a bath or tinkering with something in the garage once Mary got home.

Tim and Mary have gone through professional counseling and their marriage was on the mend, but soon their love would soon be tested in ways that neither would be able to imagine or comprehend.

Deep down inside Tim loved Mary with a real love but because of her infidelity, Tim wanted Mary to know how much he was hurt; Tim reassured Mary that he would never walk away from her.

Chapter 4

The Drawing

Madison Wisconsin
Saturday, 1:30 p.m.

Mary sat in the kitchen looking out the window of the ominous clouds gathering.

Winter weather in Wisconsin can be unforgiving but something was unusual about it. Mary could feel that there was something ugly in the air and it felt, in a strange way, for what I don't know...that it was trying to warn her.

Mary had her camera and took lots of pictures, of the weather and the scenery, the first snowfall...heck, she just really felt that something was going to happen, and if she had her camera out she would catch it on film.

A small and rapidly dwindling part of me started to panic, as the crisp air echoed that something bad was coming, and my own inner voice, sixth sense...whatever you call it, was slowly getting quieter and quieter.

On the following day, Mary had her film developed, and noticed there was an extra picture that she didn't take.

"But, who the hell took the picture?"

Mary's mind was filled with thoughts all day long, especially of her friends, Deanne, Kristin, and her cousin Wendi.

Alarming thoughts flooded Mary's mind until one single thought floated to the forefront of Mary's mind.

A thought so loud, so demonic, that it made Mary check to see if she was alone in the room; a thought which seemed to scream at Mary...

"You are going to die- you are going to die."

At first, Mary thought it was totally unreasonable; but the thoughts were so real, the voice (it was like a whisper of a man's voice, not my own voice in my head) and the more reality set in, the more she found herself totally freaking out.

Mary didn't know why but she got up and went over to the living room window to see if Tim's SUV was in the driveway.

Call it three dimensional thinking, ESP, a woman's intuition, voodoo...whatever, but Mary immediately got the distinct impression that whatever this was in the picture; was in her house, watching Mary sleep... for god knows how long, and how many times before.

Mary grabbed her cell phone and tried calling Deanne, and then Kristin, and finally Wendi. Not one of them answered her call.

Mary thought...

"What was the possibility that all three of them were on their phones at the same time...was it merely a coincidence that all of them were unavailable at the same time?"

Mary laid her cell phone on the end table and turned back to the window; watching the darkness, looking into the night, unable to shake the feeling that, something ...' wasn't right'...

'I was going to die?"

Unable to reach Deanne, Kristin, or Wendi; Mary tried calling Tim she had to get in touch with at least one of them, or somebody, to shake this feeling, to shake her fears.

Suddenly Mary's cell phone began vibrating, just as she was about to lay her phone down.

Scrolling over to the voice mail icon, she pressed play, and heard...

"La-la-la-la-la-la-, la-la-la-la-la-la,

Teddy Bear, Soda Crackers,

Teddy Bear laughs;

Mary's flipping out, seeing things, horrible way you'll die...

"La-la-la-la-la-la-, la-la-la-la-la-la."

Mary was so scared that she dropped her phone, watching the flip top close. Mary waited a few seconds and then she reached down to pick it up, when something touched her on the shoulder, making Mary jump backwards and scream.

It was Tim, standing there, laughing with a joint in his mouth.

Tim and Mary both looked at each other for a brief moment, and then with both hands, Mary smashed Tim in his chest, pushing him into the wall, and saying...

"Tim, you fucking asshole...you almost gave me a damn heart attack!"

Tim stood there for a minute, as Mary stomped off into the kitchen. Tim knew Mary was pissed at him, and rather than fight, he went upstairs to take a bath.

Tim and Mary went through a lot of bad shit that year, Mary had even confessed to an affair she had.

During the Easter weekend, while Mary was pregnant, she was hospitalized because of a P.E., and while the doctors were afraid Mary was not going to make it, they were even more fearful of Mary's chances of carrying her baby full term.

Blood clots threatened Mary's life, and caused her to be placed on a BIPAP because of her low oxygen level.

It was during that time the doctors told her, that they no longer detected the baby's heartbeat.

For the first time since college, Tim stopped drinking and smoking Marijuana, he spent every hour with Mary even accepting to do telework.

Mary spent the next six months in a deep depressive state, continuing to withdraw from Tim. Mary confided in Deanne, that she always found herself daily, visiting the local book store.

Mary said, she would go out walking to think, or just be alone, because Tim was beginning to smother her and always, she ended up at the book store.

Mary eventually told Deanne, that she was having an affair with a woman, and she just couldn't stop.

She said, she wasn't looking for anything to happen, but was simply sitting and reading a book, when this woman named Kate came up to her and said...

'Hi; my name is Kate, is that book really as good as I heard it is?'

Mary said...all she did was respond, but then the woman walked in front of her and then half way down the aisle, picking up the same book Mary was reading and sat down next to Mary, and began reading.

Mary went on to say how the woman's perfume caught her attention and for a moment she looked over at Kate, and found herself staring at her legs, and then her face.

Mary went on to say, she had the prettiest eyes, and her cute small black framed glasses, gently hugging her small, pointed nose.

Mary told Deanne that had never thought about being attracted to another woman...but she found herself unable to keep her eyes off of this woman, and her mind from wondering.

Mary then said, as she was tracing the outline of Kate's legs from her ankles upward, Kate looked over and caught her staring.

Kate was, five-feet seven inches, one hundred and thirty lbs., black high heels, and a low cut button-down top, with a mop of blonde curly hair.

Mary told Deanne...

"Dee... I don't know what's wrong with me; I couldn't stop staring at her it was like I was glued or something.

All I saw was two of the prettiest legs in a black skirt and grey button-down shirt, and the sexiest pair of heels, and even though she was looking dead into my eyes, I could not stop staring at her."

Deanne took a deep breath and said...

"Hey Mary, there's nothing wrong with you, it's probably a phase you're going through...I mean Mary, this is the 21st century people are attracted to whomever, hey I'm not judging you girl."

Mary nervously said to Deanne that Kate closed her book and walked over to her, and gently grabbing Mary's face and kissed her.

Not a long kiss, but a soft kiss slightly parting Mary's lips and then Kate walked out of the bookstore.

Mary said her eyes followed Kate intensely, not knowing whether Kate wanted her to come after her or what, or if she was supposed to sit there.

Mary said she waited a few minutes, and then walked outside; looking for Kate, but Kate was gone.

Mary told Deanne, every day she went to the bookstore purposely looking for Kate, but has not seen her again until three weeks ago in a coffee shop.

Mary said, on her way to book store she passed the 'Coco Coffee Shop, and there she was, at the counter buying coffee.

Kate had on jeans a tee shirt and sandals, Mary she'd recognize her anywhere, even from that brief encounter at the book store.

Mary explained how she couldn't go inside because she didn't know what to say to Kate, so she just stood there looking through the glass.

Mary said that as she turned to leave, Kate came out and touched her on the shoulder, fondling her hair and the two of them went to her apartment and since then Mary has been a daily fixture with Kate.

Deanne told Mary that she was probably suffering from 'separation anxiety' over losing the baby and that perhaps, latching onto Kate was something that would eventually blow over...but 'not to tell Tim'!

Mary told Deanne the cat was out of the bag and that Tim knew.

Mary said Tim has devoted all of his time and attention to her during those difficult months and that Tim took the news of her affair better than she thought he would.

Mary told Deanne that she realized that something in her had changed.

Not because of her affair with Kate but Mary said she noticed she used to have a razor sharp, sarcastic tone in her voice, but that too changed to a milder cautious, mellow tone.

Deanne tried to comfort Mary by saying...

"It's called maturity Mary."

Deanne and Mary talked for another hour or so. Mary told Deanne how she missed it when all of them would get together for parties like they used to.

She told Deanne she felt all of them, Tim, Steve, Kristin and Wendi; never see her and Dave ever since he was released from the hospital.

Deanne told Mary that in a few months she would bring that up with David to see if they could plan something, since no one had small kids to deal with.

Deanne was a no nonsense type of person. When she is treating patients in the ICU, her patients and their family members get the same straight forwardness from her.

Deanne told Mary as people, we go through things from time to time. She did not believe that it was fate, or written in the stars, or it was some big morale experiment sent from God.

Deanne simply believe that we go through things and handling things isn't what defines us, because we continue to change, to evolve, to manifest from this to that.

Mary told Deanne...

"Wow Dee, we got shit twisted badly. I'm the Psychologist, and you're the Registered Nurse...but listening to our conversation...who would've ever known."

Deanne told Mary...

"There you go again with that mess...who was it that struggled in college....me, right, and who was it that partied from sun up to sundown and made 'Egregia Cum Laude'...you...hell, none of us knew that honor even existed until you won it.

Deanne told Mary to call her later, she had some things to do, and that if she ran into Kristin give her a hug from me and pinch her ass really good.

Mary agreed but said she wasn't into ass pinching.

Mary laughed as she got off the phone talking with Deanne.

Pecan Drive

Deanne grabbed her cell phone and dialed Mary's number all the while saying to herself...

"Pick up Mary, pick up!"

Deanne was relieved at the sound of Mary's voice as she answered the phone...

"Hello Dee, hey girl, what cha up to...we just talked a little while ago...what's up?"

Deanne tried to hide the nervousness in her tone...

"Nothing much Mary, how are you doing, I was worried about Wendi?"

Mary let out of breath of air and said...

"How's Dave, and why are you worried about Wen?"

Deanne sat down on the sofa and picked up an ink pen and began clicking the pen and said...

"Blue is good, he's still unable to talk, but his doctor says, it's normal and he'll be fine...so, when's the last time you saw Kate, or have you two slowed that part of things down?"

Mary scratched her head and said...

"Well, as a matter of fact, I spent the morning with her shopping...I just can't stop Dee; you know, I just have to be with her...but you're avoiding my question."

Deanne tapped her pin on the writing pad next to the sofa and said...

"Sounds like someone has a decision to make...but look Mary, I haven't heard from either Kristin or Wendi.

I've been trying to call them and besides that, Wendi said she was dropping by here last night and I haven't seen hide nor hair of here."

Mary said that since they talked earlier that she did run into Kristin at the mall, but she hadn't spoken to Wendi, since their family reunion last month.

At the same time Mary heard knocking at her door as she got up to go to the door she lost signal. Mary attempted to call Deanne back, but keep getting a busy signal.

Then all of a sudden there was banging on all of the doors and the windows in Mary's house, relentless and terrifying the banging

94

was that it seemed as if the wood frames encasing the door would splinter and crack.

On the third attempt Mary was able to get a signal and got Deanne on the phone. Deanne said she was going to drive over to Wendi's house as soon as David got ready, because she didn't sleep well, thinking about her.

Deanne was about to ask about Kristin and before she could, there was a loud insistent banging on the front door. Mary screamed and then the phone went dead.

Deanne jumped up from the sofa...

"Mary! Mary, what's wrong...Mary!"

Mary was backing out of the living room, when she was suddenly blinded by car lights coming through her front window....

"Oh yes baby, it's you.........TIM...TIM!"

Tim entered into the front door and was met by Mary, who hugged him and was crying hysterically in his arms.

Tim's arms were full of bags, which he softly let drop to the floor. Tim embraced Mary and said...

"Sugar...what's the matter, yogi-bear is here?"

Mary proceeded to tell Tim about her conversation with Deanne, and that in the middle of their conversation, someone was banging against the house and then on the door.

Mary helped Tim collect the bags that he dropped on the floor and as they walked into the kitchen, Tim said...

"Well who was banging on the door?"

Mary explained to Tim just how loud the banging was and that she was afraid to even go near the door, and just as she was about to go to the door, he pulled up in the drive way.

Tim pulled a joint from his pocket and lit it up and after several puffs laid his joint down, and looked up at Mary with the purpose of holding Mary, when there was a loud banging on the front door.

Tim got up off the sofa and peeked out the picture window, very stealthily. Upon not seeing anyone he turned to Mary and before he had a chance to say anything...

Every door in their house was being banged on relentlessly. Rhythmic and terrifying as if all the doors were about to splinter and crack.

The banging was so hard and loud that the chandelier shook at each knock, and the floor reverberated under their feet.

Tim grabbed Mary and ushering her into the living room and yelling towards the door...

"I don't know who you are or what the hell is going on, but whoever the hell this is, you're about to get your ass shot?"

Then the banging stopped! Tim and Mary slowly walked to the front door and Tim peeked out the picture window and said...

"There's no one that I can see in the yard, but who the hell was doing all the banging?"

As Tim looked out and to the right towards the driveway he noticed a truck. A large Dodge truck, sitting in their driveway.

Tim decided to walk over to the truck with his nine millimeter in his hand. Tim approached the truck and looked at the rear of the truck, and then he glanced in the cab window and stopped.

Mary was standing on the front porch looking intensely, and was not able to see how pale Tim's face had turned.

Tim pointed the pistol at the driver's side window and then he ran towards to the house, towards Mary and said...

"Baby, when I pulled up I didn't see anybody except for Carl and Jennifer and the kids in the yard, but where in the hell did that truck come from?"

I'm going to call the neighbors to see if they have a guest who unknowingly has parked in our front drive way.

Mary walked over to the kitchen sink and looked out the window and said...

"Tim I'm telling you, I was talking to Dee and then all this banging started and then the phone went dead."

Just then Mary jumped and said...

"What was that?"

Tim pointed to some bags on the table where Mary had laid her cell phone...

"Baby it's nothing just your cell ringing and vibrating underneath one of the bags on the table, gosh I've never seen you so rattled."

Tim called his neighbor and asked him, if he had company over who was parked in their front driveway when his neighbor replied...

"We don't have any company, besides whoever was in his driveway had left."

Tim went to the window and looked out. He did not see the large truck in his driveway and more importantly, he did not hear a door shut or the truck start up, not to mention seeing it leaving.

Tim went in the kitchen where Mary was and told her about the truck not being there.

Mary stated...

"Maybe some guy just pulled in to check his directions or maybe he was dropping off someone or something."

Tim replied to Mary that when he went to the truck, there was no one in the truck.

Mary told him what matters is the person is out of their driveway.

Lifting up the bag and locating her cell, Mary saw that it was Deanne calling...

"Hello, Dee?"

Deanne anxiously told Mary...

"Mary what happened, one minute were talking, and the next minute nothing?"

Mary went into the living room and left Tim putting away the groceries, to talk to Deanne...

"Dee, I know it sounds a little Cray-Cray, but when we were talking all of sudden, something started banging on the house. Tim says it was next door but I swear it was here."

"Mary, I'm starting to get worried about Kristin and Wendi, Kristin's not answering her phone and like I said earlier, Wendi was supposed to be on her way over here last night, and never showed up."

Shone was pressing her nose against Deanne's leg, signaling she wanted to go outside. David came into the living room holding the leash and took Shone out while Deanne continued her conversation...

"It's okay Mary Blue just took Shone out...well like I was saying, the Franklin County Sheriff's department said there was a grisly murder not too far from here last night.

They say a girl's body was found and they said she was so badly mutilated, that it would be sometime today, before they could positively ID her."

Mary walked over to her computer and logged in hoping to catch the news story from Columbus, Ohio and said to Deanne...

"*I'm a little worried too Dee, when none of you answered I was freaking out a little bit, so what does this dead girl's body have to do with Wendi, didn't you say her body was found not far from where you live?*"

"*Yes, that's exactly what I said...but you...*"

Deanne said before Mary interrupted her...

"*Dee, I don't mean to cut you off but you and Dave live far north east Columbus, and Wendi and Steve lives almost an hour away... right?*"

Deanne was still clicking her pen and doodling on the note pad...

"*More like forty-five minutes Mary, but like I was trying to tell you before you cut me off, Wendi told me that she would be here by the time I got Blue back from his doctor's appointment, yesterday around four.*"

Mary located the story about the dead girl's body and said...

"*Okay Dee I'm looking at the story on the internet, and it says.... they discovered the identity of the body and are waiting to notify the next of kin.*

Dee, have you tried calling Steve I'm sure the police would've called him if it was Wendi ...right?"

Deanne told Mary...

"*That's just it Mary, Steve is hunting this weekend and he wouldn't have his cell phone on. You're her cousin, has anybody heard anything?*"

Mary turned away from her computer and said...

"*No, her Mom would've called me...do you and Dave mind driving over to their house, maybe Wendi is sleeping in or something, and call me as soon as you find out something?*"

David and Shone just entered the house and Deanne walked towards them, still talking with Mary, saying...

"*Okay Mary, I'm going to see if Blue and Shone want to go for a little drive, do me a favor will you, try getting in touch with Kristin and see if she's okay...and tell her ass to call me?*"

Deanne began to tell David about her conversation with Mary and about the story on the internet news.

David and Deanne put Shone in the car and headed across town to check on Wendi. Deanne handed her cell phone to David and said...

"Blue can you send a text to Steve, and ask him to call us as soon as he gets this message. Tell him it's an emergency?"

David placed Deanne's cell phone in the console and used his own cell phone to text Steve, thinking he'd get a quicker response.

"Stevie, this is Dave...call me as soon as you get this...important."

David wrote Deanne a note and said...

"If Steve is hunting and doesn't have his cell phone on, the police have no way of knowing he is hunting...somebody might have to give the police that information."

Chapter 5

Circling Clouds

1640 Windsor Drive
Madison, Wisconsin

Northern winters range between the months of late November until late March, with a scenery of bare trees, bare landscapes and a glimpse of the coming snows.

Mary stood at the kitchen window looking out her back yard while she tried calling Kristin.

Mary became frustrated because each time she called Kristin the calls went directly to her voice mail.

Becoming frustrated, Mary said...

"Damn bitch answer your phone!"

Tim removed a cold beer from the fridge and shook his head at Mary and said...

"Baby, I don't know why you and Deanne are getting so jack up about this...how many times has Kristin said she'll call or come by and then she doesn't call or come by, knowing her she's probably out trying to find her next sugar daddy, now if you're that worried let's just drive over to her house?"

Mary walked over to Tim and hugged him saying...

"Babe Kristin might have worn the title of Miss Fake Ass, for the last twenty years without any competition but she's still our friend and yes, she's thrown me under the bus more than anyone, but I got bad vibes about this."

Tim was guzzling his beer, and after a disgusting belch said...

"*Bad vibes... baby you were tripping because you couldn't get either one of them, and didn't Deanne finally return your call...I'm telling you, you're getting all jacked up over nothing?*"

Mary opened up the curtains and pointing and turning to Tim, said...

"*What do you call that...every tree has leaves on them...but look at ours, and look at those clouds...all dark and spooky just circling, like we're going to have a tornado or something.*"

Tim looked out the window and then closed the curtain and said...

"*Okay so our trees are a little dead looking but that doesn't mean anything. Madison Wisconsin is too cold this time of year for tornados and what does the weather have to do with not reaching Kristin or Wendi?*"

Tim saw that there was no way in trying to get Mary to change her mind. Tim grabbed his coat and car keys and as he headed for the door, turned to Mary and said...

"*Well, you coming or not?*"

Tim backed out of the driveway, and as he was going down the street he reached up and flipped down the driver's side compact and pulled out a joint and lit it up.

Mary sat there texting Kristin and shook her head at Tim, saying...

"*Damn babe, you want to roll your window down a little I don't want to get high, just because you do.*"

Tim rolled his window down a little and began coughing and gagging as he took a big drag from his joint.

Tim and Mary pulled into Kristin's driveway and parked behind Kristin's car, and noticing her front door open, Mary immediately said to Tim...

"*She's home... but why is her front door open, maybe she's doing house work?*"

Tim threw the car in park and looked at Mary and said...

"*In all the times we've known her when was the last time she cleaned anything, but her nails?*"

Mary was opening her car door and as she was about to get out of the car, she turned back to Tim saying...

"Okay look we're not staying, we're just going to be here long enough to make sure she's okay and then we're out of here, okay"?

Tim nodded his head yes, as he put out his joint and put the butt in his pocket.

Tim and Mary walked up to Kristin's door. Once they got to the door they could hear the music blasting, coming from the living room.

Tim banged harder and harder and Mary tried to open the storm door, but it was locked. Mary took out her cell phone to call Kristin, but again the call went directly to her voice mail.

Tim walked around to the back door and found that it was unlocked and went inside. Once inside Tim looked around and began calling for Kristin, as he reached the living room Tim turned the music off.

Tim could hear Mary knocking at the front door, and headed for the door, continuing calling for Kristin as he unlocked the door, letting Mary in.

As they entered the living room Mary saw the vacuum cleaner sitting in the middle of the room plugged in and a clothes basket full of clothes by the basement door.

Mary took ahold of Tim's arm and pointed at the coffee table and said...

"Look babe, its Kristin's cell phone and purse...something's not right here those are the two things a woman always has with her."

Tim and Mary made their way through the downstairs of the house, looking and calling for Kristin.

Next they headed upstairs hoping that Kristin was putting away laundry, cleaning or something, but deep down they both Tim and Mary were sensing something was wrong, something was very wrong.

Mary stood at the top of the steps while she had Tim check Kristin's bedroom, and then the bathroom. Tim entered and exited each room, saying the same thing to Mary...

"Not in here!"

The only place left to check was the basement.

Tim found the basement light switch and turned it on as he and Mary started down the steps, unaware that a dark figure stood at the top of the stairs behind them.

Halfway down the steps the basement lights went out and Mary screamed...

"*Damn Tim, this is the wrong time to start fucking playing games... turn the lights back on!*"

Tim squeezed Mary's arm and said...

"*Mar, I'm right here and I didn't mess with the lights.*"

Mary stopped dead in her tracks and said...

'*Tim, let's just turn around and head back up the steps and call the police...Tim do you hear me...Tim...where the hell are you?*"

Mary began feeling around in the dark air for Tim calling him...

'*Tim...Tim...stop fucking around this shit isn't funny...Tim!*

Mary was frozen on the last two steps from the basement floor.

Mary started smelling a nasty, rotting, foul odor, something like flesh burning coming from the other side of the basement, which was becoming more and more overpowering.

Suddenly the lights flickered and flickered again, and then they came on illuminating the entire basement.

Mary stepped down into the basement and looked to her right and that's when she saw something which caused her to scream!

Mary stood looking in horror with her hands covering her mouth.

There was Kristin lying flat on her back on top of the laundry table, with a large bloody gash on her forehead.

Two drops of blood fell from the laundry table with a drip-drip noise that sounded like a leaky faucet...

"*Drip-Drip-Drip.*"

Scream after scream poured from Mary's mouth. Suddenly the lights began flickering and the basement door began opening and slamming shut... again and again.

Mary turned towards the basement door and screamed out for Tim, but Tim was nowhere to be found.

Just then Mary saw standing at the top of the stairs, the silhouette of a dark figure against the backdrop of the kitchen light.

Unknowingly Mary begin backing up towards Kristin's body when she heard footsteps coming down the steps, and slipped in a pool of blood, falling backwards.

The figure at the top of the stairs had not moved, but the sound of the footsteps caused Mary to scream hysterically as she hit the concert basement floor.

Mary's screams quickly stopped when her hands which were behind her back, felt the wet, sticky, warm coagulated pool of blood.

Whimpering and hyperventilating, Mary put her hands in front of her face and scream...

"OMG!!!"

Mary's hands were covered in Kristin's blood, and looking closer Mary noticed mixed with the blood were whole fingernails.

Whoever tortured Kristin had put a knife underneath the tip of her fingernails and toe nails, slicing not only the nails away from her body, but chunks of skin as well.

All at once the basement door slammed shut and started shaking violently, as if someone were pushing against it.

Mary began whimpering, she wanted to scream but when she opened her mouth nothing came out.

Just then the lights came back on, and standing in front of Mary was a very large man in a ballerina's tutu wearing a *clown's face.*

Mary was in shock and so scared that she didn't realize that she was urinating on herself. Then there appeared voices of children coming from all over the basement.

Mary turned in every direction and as she did she saw the faces of little children. Children who looked old and ghastly, who appeared from out of nowhere.

Mary began backing up on the floor looking left and right as she did, unfortunate for Mary she completely forgot about the man in the ballerina's tutu.

Mary backed into him and as she did he placed his big hand over Mary's mouth, and lifted her off of the floor and into the air.

He carried Mary over to where Kristin was, as the little children followed. The children move around the basement, without their feet touching the ground.

The man in the ballerina's tutu sat Mary in a chair directly in front of Kristin.

Once Mary was in the chair, four of the children approached Mary and one of them stood in front of her and began making swirling motions with his hands, as ropes mysteriously appeared and tied themselves around Mary's ankles and hands.

Mary began crying for Tim and pleading...

"TIM...TIM.... Please, no...no, let me go, please!"

The man in the ballerina's tutu backed away from Mary and sat on the basement floor in front of Mary and began pounding his fist on the floor.

Mary then heard the voices of the children singing in low demonic voices, over lapping, as two of them approached Mary.

The two creepy looking kids began circling Mary and as they did they held out their hands revealing a large needle and a roll of black twine.

Mary's eyes were fixed upon them and began screaming from the top of her lungs when one of the creepy kids motioned with his finger for Mary to be quiet.

Just then the chair that Mary was sitting in began twirling around and bouncing up and down as they two creepy kids began singing...

"La-la-la-la-la-la-, la-la-la-la-la-la,

Teddy Bear Soda Crackers,

Teddy Says don't scream,

If you do, your lips we'll glue,

And stitch them up with thread

La-la-la-la-la-la-, la-la-la-la-la-la."

With three of his disgusting large dirty fingers, he pressed Mary's lips together as one of the two creepy kids began threading a large needle with the black twine and sewing her lips shut.

As Mary moaned and cried the other creepy kid took a brush, and spread glue all over Mary's lips, and began singing...

"La-la-la-la-la-la-, la-la-la-la-la-la,

We told you once to shut your mouth,

Your screaming is in vain
Glue her lips, sew them shut,
He-he-he-he!"
La-la-la-la-la-la-, la-la-la-la-la-la."

Mary tried to scream out for help but all she could do was moan as tears ran from her eyes. Just then another child stood in front of Mary and pointed in Kristin's direction.

Mary didn't know what they planned to do but she knew she could not watch, so Mary closed her eyes moaning and whimpering in pain.

Just then the man in the ballerina's tutu grabbed Mary's head and tilted it back, and with a construction stapler began stapling Mary's eyelids to her forehead.

If Mary could scream, she would have screamed but the pain was so enormous until she passed out.

Mary awakened to water being poured over her head washing the blood away from her eyes. Mary's thoughts drifted to Tim and where he could be.

With Mary's head was tilted back and her eyelids stapled open, she saw that Kristin was suspended from the basement rafters by piano wire with six very large fish hooks, embedded into her back and her chest.

A piece of metal as long as a barbeque fork with two bi-pronged forks, resembling a double pitched fork was attached to a leather strap.

The metal prongs were barbed and serrated, and once they penetrated the skin the only way to get them out was to cut them out.

One end of the metal bi-pronged fork was pushed under Kristin's chin and the other to her sternum. A piece of nylon cord was wrapped around her neck which held the metal piece in place.

The pain of the fish hooks embedded in her back caused Kristin to straighten stretch her body and lower her head.

As Kristin lowered her head, the pronged fork was being driven into her chin, causing her to raise her head and fight against the pain of the fish hooks embedded into her chest.

If Kristin moved her head in the slightest from left to right the metal prongs would rip and tear at her throat and chest.

Mary's eyes were pinned to the torment which Kristin was subjected to, until her eyes began following the nylon cord up past the window and that's when she noticed Tim outside.

Tim tried to sneak back into the house, but was unaware that the man in the ballerina's tutu was sneaking up behind him.

Mary squirmed, and as she tried with all of her strength to make a sound, she could feel the skin on her lips beginning to rip and tear.

Mary moaned as blood and tears from her eyelids being stapled to her forehead trickled into her eyes.

Through her blood soaked eyes Mary saw Tim lifted off the ground by the man in the ballerina's tutu.

All Mary could see through the small window was the bottom of Tim's shoes being lifted several inches off the ground.

Tim was not a small man, standing over six two, and weighing close to two hundred and twelve pounds.

Mary knew that it must be the man in ballerina's tutu, but as her eyes scanned the basement she saw the man standing by the door... who had Tim...she thought?

Through her pain and before passing out, Mary thought...

"Omg...how many are they?"

Tim's legs quit kicking after a few minutes, and the man in the ballerina's tutu let Tim's limp body drop to the ground.

Mary could see the lower portion of a wheel barrel on the other side of Tim's body, as Tim was lifted off the ground.

The outside basement door suddenly opened and the man in the ballerina's tutu pushed the wheel barrel with Tim's body in it to the basement door.

The downstairs basement door flung open as Tim's body roll down the steps to the basement floor.

Mary knew that Tim was still alive, because of the moans she heard coming from him.

The man in the ballerina's tutu pushed the wheel barrel in the middle of the basement and after locking the door returned with two large clear gallon jugs.

The man in the ballerina's tutu attached the car battery jumper cable to one end of the barrel, and the other to an over-sized truck battery.

Next he poured something from two-five gallon clear containers inside the barrel and picked Tim off of the floor and lowered him in the barrel.

Mary struggled to see the label on the jugs from the dried blood which had gathered in her eyes, but was able to make out a few letters...

"S-u-l-f-u - H-y-d-r-o-f-l"

Mary could not make out the rest of the letters and when she was in college she wasn't the brightest crayon in the box, but she was one of the few students who paid attention to her professor in chemistry.

Mary remembered from her chemistry class, the two acid compounds...

"Hydrofluoric acid and Sulfuric acid."

Hydrofluoric acid and Sulfuric acid, were two of the deadliest acid compounds, and mixed together yielded deadly results, not just for direct contact, but the fumes can cause the lungs to fail.

When the mixture of the two came in direct contact with human skin, it caused excruciating pain, as it ate through skin, organs and tissue, causing massive bleeding, literally liquefying the body.

The man in the ballerina's tutu grabbed a sledge hammer and standing over Tim placed the sledge hammer on Tim's chest and proceeded to hold him down.

Tim was jerking and his legs kicking against the sides of the barrel as the acids began to burn holes in his clothes and saturate his skin.

The odor and the fumes of the acids dissolving Tim's clothes and burning his flesh, filled the entire basement.

The effects of the fumes also were taking their toll on Mary as well. Her upper and lower eyelids had begun to shrink, while her eyes were bulging out of its sockets, due to the fumes.

The man in the ballerina's tutu with the clown's face apparently had other plans for Mary, as he immediately picked her up slinging her over his shoulders leaving Tim and heading up the basement steps.

As the man in the ballerina's tutu carried Mary up the steps, Tim's lifeless body began jerking and thrashing which caused the wheel barrel to overturn and Tim rolled onto the floor.

Broad & High Street
J.C. Woolwood Building (Lobby)

Reggie stood at his post awaiting the arrival of his partner Amy and the executives who generally arrived thirty minutes before the employees.

Reggie paced the lobby checking his watch and wondered...

"Damn where is that girl, she's twenty minutes late... she better not be calling in sick today."

Reggie was unaware that there were over twenty murders in the city over the past several nights and that Amy, Jerry and Mr. Hargrove were a few of them.

Reggie tried calling Amy's cell phone several times, with no answer and said to himself...

"Now, I've got to call central dispatch and get someone here and in the meantime, I'm going to have to shut down one side, which means I'll have a line a mile long outside the door not to mention a lot of pissed off people complaining about how late I'm making them."

The executives began to filter in and as they did they gathered in the lobby near the Exec elevators.

Reggie wasn't aware of what was going on only that he heard some commotion coming from around the corner.

Thinking that maybe the elevator was not working.

Reggie locked the front door and walked around the corner, and it became clear as he heard Mr. Robert Owens, Operations executive of A.P.S. saying...

"Yeah it's sad...I got a call from a friend at the police station at three in the morning telling me that they found the bodies of James and Beverly dead in their homes. I tell you if the police can't protect us from these Jamaican killers then we all need to buy guns and protect ourselves."

Reggie interrupted Mr. Owens...

"Hold on did I hear you say that Mr. Hargrove and his wife were murdered by Jamaicans?"

Robert Owens tucked his newspaper under his arm, sipped his coffee and said...

"Yeah, my friend at police headquarters said they found bones and notes or something with the words...'Twisted & Dread'. It screams out Jamaican to me...and coach since you're the police, you know that already, or was that classified information...huh?"

Reggie stood looking shocked and puzzled and said...

"I knew something wasn't right...my partner said that Mr. Hargrove was acting strange on Friday."

Mr. Mark Hankins, Vice President of Ohio Atlantic said...

"What do you mean acting strange... acting strange in what way? Was he acting like he was in trouble or something...when he left on Friday, it didn't look like anything was wrong."

Reggie's attention shifted to the crowd massing outside the front door, and said...

"Mr. Owens, I'll let you know what I find out...I got a crowd of employees outside waiting to get in."

Robert Owens waved his hand at Reggie as he headed towards the front door to deal with the mass of employees anxiously waiting to get inside, as Reggie said...

"Okay people one at a time...we had a little emergency this morning, so I need everyone to come through on the Executive side."

Reggie laid a stack of newspapers on the desk, and began checking the employees I.D.'s.

Reggie decided that he would call central dispatch as soon as the first wave of employees passed through.

Once everything had settled down a bit, Reggie decided now was a good time to call central dispatch and ask for an extra body...

"Hello central, this is Reggie down at building one...my partner never showed today, so I am going to need someone down here fast."

Sgt. Margaret Holmes from central responded with a soft tone...

"I hear you Coach, someone is already on their way, and should be there within minutes."

Reggie looked shocked and said...

"Minutes... did my partner call in sick or what?"

Sgt. Holmes tried to respond, but her supervisor took the phone from her and said...

"Reggie, this is Lt. Meeks, I don't know how to tell you this but Amy, I mean Officer Smiles won't be there."

Reggie walked over towards the counter and sitting down said...

"Okay what do you mean you don't know how to tell me...I think somebody better be telling me something?"

Lt. Meeks replied...

"The State Troopers called in and said the bodies of Officer Smiles and her husband were found late Saturday evening, in an old abandoned building."

Reggie went to unlock the other door and noticed Amy's relief coming in. Reggie pointed to the desk that his partner Amy sat at, and walked back to his station and said to Lt. Meeks...

"Hold on Lt...you said ...'bodies were discovered'? What the fuck does that that mean, you say shit like that when somebody commits suicide or is murdered...how do they know they could be mistaken?"

Reggie and Amy had worked together for over eight years, and Lt. Meeks knew he had to control the situation and to handle the conversation as gently as possible when he said...

"Look Coach Amy's badge, weapon, identification...the whole smash was found at the scene. It appears they were murdered sometime late Friday night. Do you need me to send someone there to relieve you?"

Reggie slumped down in his chair, pounding his hand against his head...

"Okay, yea send someone, I'm coming down there and somebody better tell me what the fuck is going on...I was just with Amy and her husband Friday night.... aww no!"

Employees and venders began their daily entrance into the building unaware of what had transpired, only noticing that Amy was not at here station.

Reggie tried to keep his emotions in check, but did get a little overly aggressive and hostile with a few visitors, but nothing too serious.

Reggie packed up his things and prepared to give report, as his relief came into the building.

Chapter 6

Dying Notions

Southside Columbus Precinct

Reggie and Amy were police officers on detail to the Ohio Atlantic Power. In an attempt to lessen Post Traumatic Stress Disorder within law enforcement, officers are routinely detailed to various light duty assignments with local businesses after continued exposure to traumatic episodes.

Reggie and Amy worked closely with the Local F.B.I. office on a case involving a serial killer responsible for two dozen murders and missing bodies.

Reggie and Amy had been partners for eight years plus and had developed a very close bond.

The entire station knew that Reggie would take the news of Amy's death hard and were all prepared as Reggie walked into the squad room locker area and stood in front of Amy's locker.

The Southside police precinct was a relatively new addition to the police department and the many boxes of files lining the walls was an indication that the precinct was still in a transition phase.

Lt. Meeks and several plain clothes officers walked past the morning shift of twenty officers to the main interrogation room.

Lt. Meeks walked over to the locker room where Reggie was standing and said...

"Coach, you want to step in here for a sec?"

Reggie's large six ft. five frame towered over Lt. Meeks who was a mere five ft. six, as Reggie said...

"Did I understand that Amy was killed night before last? I was just with her and her husband eating dinner, I don't understand...we saw them get on the interstate...so what happened, where were they were found?"

Lt. Meeks interrupted him, saying...

"Coach Listen, they never made it home... their car was found in a ditch ten miles from their home. From the evidence, it looks like they slid off the road."

Reggie sat down on the desk and said...

"So did they have an accident or what...you told me over the phone that their bodies were discovered in an abandoned building... so, how in the hell did they end up there?"

Lt. Meeks walked over to Reggie and handed him Amy's badge and said...

"Detective Horton's at the scene and all we know based on the condition of the car was, there was some kind of struggle and Amy was taken to this building, and her husband's body was discovered outside about a mile away."

Reggie stood up and took a few steps towards the door when Lt. Meeks snapped...

"Don't even think about it coach, it's a crime scene and a muddy crime scene at that. It's going to be hard enough looking for clues as to who did this, you of all people know better!"

Reggie turned and said to Lt. Meeks...

"I'm going down there Lt., look if Mark tells me to leave I'll leave... hell, Lt. that was my partner!"

Reggie stormed out of the room and out of the precinct stopping outside the door momentarily chunking back tears as fellow officers passed him.

Reggie arrived at the crime scene just an hour after leaving the station.

When Reggie arrived at the scene Detective Mark Horton, a six-year homicide veteran was talking with several uniformed officers.

Det. Horton had received a call from Lt. Meeks informing him that Reggie was on his way there. Detective Horton met Reggie up on the road at the spot where Amy's car had slid off the highway and said...

"*Hey Coach sorry 'bout all this, I know she was your partner and all but...*"

Reggie cut Det. Horton off before he finished his statement and said...

"*Look I won't touch anything or contaminate the scene.... I just have to know. I don't want to find out second hand what happened.*"

Det. Horton reached in his coat pocket and handed Reggie a pair of rubber gloves and motioned for Reggie to follow him down a muddy slope, which had ropes anchored to the guard rails to two trees below.

There was little to no access for the first responders to drive their vehicles down let alone to bring up the bodies.

Using the ropes as guides Det. Horton stopped beside a tree where Jerry and Amy's car was, saying...

"*Skid marks show that the car left the road and slid down this embankment here and somehow ended up here. From the look of things her husband, Jerry was pulled out of the driver's side window, because of the driver's side glass was busted from the outside, and there is no evidence of the car flipping.*"

Reggie examined the shattered driver's side window and then looked down on the ground and said...

"*What makes you so sure that he was pulled through the window... maybe he was trying to get out of the car?*"

Det. Horton showed Reggie the evidence bag and said...

"*From what we can see here...the inside of the car is full of glass, and if you're trying to get out of a car window, you kick it or bust it, and all of the glass will be on the outside.*"

Reggie examined the evidence bag handed it back to Det. Horton and said...

"*Okay Mark this is not adding up...so you're saying that someone smashed the window and managed to drag Jerry, who weighed over two ninety through this little as window to that tree?*"

Det. Horton walked back and bent down to the front bumper pointing and saying...

"No only that, but it looks like someone rammed Jerry with the front of the car...we collected hair and bone fragments, and looking at Jerry's forehead his wounds are consistent with what the evidence is showing us.

Reggie walked around to the passenger side, looking at the contents of Amy's purse sprawled on the floor and said...

"Amy's weapon...where's her service revolver?"

Det. Horton tapped Reggie on the shoulder motioning for him to step out of the way, as he opened the glove compartment, revealing Amy's service revolver a nine millimeter P227 Nitron, and said...

"This is another reason why I feel this case has to go by the book...right here coach, but I'm not sure why she didn't draw her piece, in situations like this we're all trained to draw our weapon first.

Also, there are no visible signs of blood on the passenger side. If her husband is being attacked, and she is not wounded...why didn't she fire her piece?"

In an instant Reggie grabbed ahold of Det. Horton's collar and said...

'She was a damn good police officer! She knew how to handle situations...she was just in an accident and probably all shaken up... maybe that's why she never grabbed her piece!"

Det. Horton placed both hands on top of Reggie's, and said as they both slid a little in the mud...

"Okay coach...C'mon let me go, I'm not trying to question her ability as a cop, I'm just trying to do my job, just trying to ask all the right questions...C'mon coach, you know how this works.

Det. Horton reached in his coat pocket and removed a plastic bag containing a cell phone and said...

"Also when we located Amy's cell phone over there in the bushes, with a partial text message to you, which was never sent, which read..."

'big perp...killed jerry, trying to get out.'

Det. Horton smoothed out his collar and said to Reggie...

"No harm coach, I'd react the same way...anyway, her cell phone was crushed all to shit, it looks like whoever did this crushed the phone with his bare hands."

Det. Horton went on to say...

"*Another thing that bothers me is... no foot prints in the area, so I think Amy was trying to call for help, and the perpetrator came out of nowhere, up from behind and took her phone and threw it over there.*"

Det. Horton and Reggie walked away from the car, down the same path that Amy was taken by the man in the ballerina's tutu, which led to the abandoned house.

Det. Horton stopped and pointed at the ground directly in front of a row of trees, and said to Reggie...

"*Do you see these two indentations on the ground and the foot prints and the tire track, what do you make of it?*"

Reggie set his size twelve and a half foot carefully alongside of the foot print, and commented...

"*A single pair of foot prints...damn, this man is huge...I'm size twelve and a half and this looks to be about a size fourteen.*"

Det. Horton pulled the note book from his pocket and said...

"*Size sixteen all six feet nine inches of a very tall man, and judging from the deep impressions he must have weighed a ton.*"

Reggie stood up and asked...

"*What makes you say that he weighed that much?*"

Det. Horton placed his note pad back in his pocket and lighting up a cigarette said...

"*Well, my sister's son wears a size fifteen shoe, and weighs over two hundred and twenty pounds.....and once while we were putting up plywood over a busted window, in a storm, I noticed the depression he made the next morning which was an inch and a half thick.*

The cast impressions we made of these imprints were almost three inches deep, from heel to toe."

Reggie returned his attention back to the other tracks and said as he knelt down...

"*Let's see...the size of the tire track is about six to eight inches and the other two marks here are about three inches wide and thirty-six to forty-eight inches apart, I don't know...*"

Det. Horton tossed his cigarette off in the distance and said...

"*A wheel barrel...one single tire impression and two three inch flat marks...it's a wheel barrel, that's why we found no tracks of Officer Smiles on the ground!*"

Reggie stood looking and re-examining the tracks and said...

"*A wheel barrel... are you saying some wackadoo put Jerry and Amy in a wheel barrel?*"

Det. Horton turned around and pointed to the tree right in front of Amy's car, saying...

"*No... no way, we found Jerry's remains hanging from several branches of that tree, and with no tracks of any kind except these...I say, he wheeled Amy in a wheel barrel from the car to that house.*"

Reggie stood looking around and scratching his head, said...

"*Wait a minute. You said both of their bodies were found in the house and now you say Jerry was hanging from a tree, Jerry was a big man himself.*"

Det. Horton started walking towards the house and said...

"*I said we found his dismembered remains hanging from several branches of that tree over there, we also found some hair from Jerry on the door knob and inside on the table.*"

Reggie ducked and brushed limbs away from his face saying...

"*So it is possible that the perp wheeled Jerry to the house as well... and what about the perps tracks...where'd they lead to?*"

Just then a uniformed police officer approached Det. Horton and told him that they were unable to locate any tracks leading out of the area.

Reggie grabbed Det. Horton's arm and said...

"*Are you going to stand here and tell me this psychotic fuck vanished in thin air?*"

Det. Horton stopped in front of the door of the house and said...

"*All I'm saying Reggie is, the tracks and the wheel barrel go from the car to the house and back to the car, and then they stop here. There's no tracks of him or anything else outside of the ones here.... not around the house...not anywhere.*"

Reggie stopped to look around. The landscape and scenery mirrored something out of the television series... Twilight Zone.

A black and white, cold, picturesque scene, void of anything inviting except for the occasional dropping of the buildup of rain, making its way down the trees and the distant cawing of blackbirds.

As both men reached the side of the house aside from the wind blowing through the broken window panes, the stench of burned flesh could be smelled.

Det. Horton and Reggie ducked under the yellow police tape to enter the door.

Directly inside the front door were the remains of a rotted roof which had caved in overtime and the basement was visible through the missing floor boards.

Det. Horton snickered a little and said...

"Through here there's steps right off the kitchen leading to the basement but I got to warn you, the steps are a death trap, so watch your feet. I don't know how anyone let alone a three-hundred-pound man with a body..."

Reggie interrupted Det. Horton by saying...

"Amy...her name was Amy now you show her some goddamn respect!"

Det. Horton lowered his head and as he lifted it turned to Reggie and said...

"Amy. I don't know how the perp could carry Amy down these steps without them giving way."

Upon reaching the basement Reggie saw crime scene evidence markers which were centralized in one main area and walked towards them.

Det. Horton placed his hand on Reggie's shoulder and said...

"Okay buddy I got to stop you right here. We haven't finished processing this area completely. Crime scene folks had to put everything on hold because the roof began to cave in and one of the beams fell and damaged their equipment."

Reggie turned and grabbed ahold of Det. Horton's hand and swiped it, looking around the basement to a roped off covered table and said...

"Damn Mark...if the crime scenes not worked...that tells me that Amy's still laying in this shit hole?"

Det. Horton jumped in Reggie's face and said...

"Look, the captain has allowed you here at my discretion! The only reason I don't bust your ass out of here is because she was your partner, so if you want to stay here, let us do our fucking job!

Reggie bent over putting both hands on his knees and after a few minutes stood up saying...

"Okay, sorry Mark it's your show...its...it's just that, she wasn't just my partner, but she was also my sister."

Det. Horton lowered his head and then looked back at Reggie and said...

"Amy was your Sister!"

Reggie wiped a single tear from his eye and said...

"Yea, she was my sister...she never knew we had the same Dad. I was going to tell her when we were at dinner night before last, but she was so happy, and I didn't want to fuck up her night, by laying all of this on her."

Det. Horton placed his hand on Reggie's back and said...

"Oh man I'm double sorry, maybe you should..."

Det. Horton was about to suggest to Reggie that his being at this particular scene was the wrong place to be, when Reggie said...

"I know what you're thinking and I can handle it. I need to know Mark...I need to know."

Det. Horton walked closer to the table and then stopped, turning to Reggie and said...

"Are you sure coach?"

Reggie put both hands in his pockets and said...

"Yea Mark I'm a professional, I can deal with it...go ahead..."

Det. Horton took a deep breath and said...

"Okay, well the best I can imagine is, the perp had Amy handcuffed and based on the marks on her wrists, it appears Amy suffered horribly. He used a ripping chisel to..."

Det. Horton stopped and asked Reggie...

"You sure you want to hear all the details?"

Reggie covered his mouth, and after taking away his hand said...

"Go on Mark, I said I need to know so get on with it!"

Det. Horton pointed to a chisel laying on the floor next to a crime scene marker...

"He used a ripping chisel to dismember her body..."

Against one leg of the table lay a long-handled iron mallet covered with blood.

"I assume he used this because we found human hair and dried blood on it. On the other side of the mallet forensics found several teeth fragments, on the outer edges."

Det. Horton went on to say...

"There doesn't appear to be a motive. Nothing appeared to have been taken, Amy and Jerry both had money on them and none of their money, rings and watches were taken.

There is the possibility that we have a sick, psycho who enjoys killing...when you want to kill someone you do it, but this person appeared to take his time not to mention that he seemed to enjoy it.

Look Reggie, some time back you and Amy were working on the task force chasing a serial killer...does any of this look familiar?"

Reggie shook his head no...at Det. Horton and then walked a few feet away and bent over.

Det. Horton stopped briefly as he noticed that Reggie, was on the verge of vomiting and then he continued...

"We located the wheel barrel over there in the corner full of body parts. Each of Amy's severed hands covered her eyes, the sick fuck screwed both of her hands to her forehead."

Upon hearing the gory details of Jerry and Amy's murders and the emergence of the crime scene crew returning to photograph and collect Amy's remains...Reggie bolted from the basement, crawling up the stairs and out of the house.

Det. Horton came up after Reggie and as the two of them stood talking a uniformed officer handed Det. Horton a plastic bag containing a small green book and said...

"Detective...we found this underneath the passenger seat. It appears to be officer Smiles."

Det. Horton opened it and then flipped to the last three pages of the book trying to get a sense of Amy's last thoughts.

The final page read...

"Dinner with Coach, rib shack. Next week check on connection at Port Clinton farm...Twisted & Dread?"

Det. Horton turned to Reggie and handed him the green book and said...

"Do you recognize this Reggie, and what do you make of the last entry... Port Clinton Farm & Twisted and Dread...you said this didn't

look familiar so I'm asking again…does this have anything to do with the case involving the serial killer you guys were chasing."

Reggie looked at the last entry and the flipped several pages back and said…

"No Mark, it's nothing like that. That case…each of the murders, the killer always left a skeleton key with a red ribbon tied to it, you haven't found anything like that have you?"

Det. Horton turned around as members of the 'Crime Scene Unit' exited the house with bags, containing evidence and the remains of Amy.

Upon learning that Reggie and Amy were more than just partners, Det. Horton said…

"Reggie why don't you go on home and let us sort through all of this?"

Reggie stood motionless and in shock as the Crime Scene Unit passed them heading towards the van. Reggie softly whispered as they walked by him…

"Bye Sis…. I wished I'd told you."

Reggie sat in his car watching the van heading for the station with Det. Horton, following.

Reaching in his coat pocket for his keys, Reggie discovered that he'd forgotten to give Det. Horton Amy's green address book.

Reggie honked his horn several times but Det. Horton continued following the Crime Scene Van.

Thumbing through Amy's book, Reggie turned to the last page Amy had written, and looking at the entry…

'Dinner with coach, check on connection at Port Clinton… Twisted & Dread'.

With the crime scene roped off Reggie sat and watched as the last patrol car pulled off before leaving.

Reggie made a u turn and went passed the old house just out of curiosity, not knowing that he wasn't the last person at the scene.

Someone was watching Reggie as he drove past, from the woods behind the house.

The man in the ballerina's tutu, wearing the clown's face grunted as Reggie's car slowly went past the house.

Reggie drove about a mile down the road looking in all directions for anything which could explain where the killer disappeared to.

In the direction which Reggie was driving, there was no other houses or buildings, all that Reggie could see was miles of empty landscape, and so Reggie turned back around and headed towards Columbus.

Reggie slowed his car down to the spot where Jerry and Amy ran off the road and sat for a minute and then drove off, not paying any attention that the man in the ballerina's tutu had climbed the muddy hill and was watching him from the road.

Chapter 7

Peek A Boo

Pecan Drive
Columbus, Ohio

No matter what Deanne said, I sensed that she was upset over something because she sat looking at her watch and her cell phone. Each time I would write and ask her what was wrong, all Deanne would say was...

"Nothing Blue, it's nothing for you to worry about."

Tired of writing down messages, I got in front of Deanne and looked her in the eye, and mouthed the words...

"Nothing?"

Deanne and I were no different from other couples, we had problems like every other couple in communicating, but when you can't speak, and all you can do is write notes...that makes it even more difficult.

Suddenly the channel six news reporter caught our attention...

"This is Hiram Corcoran, at the channel six news room. We have a breaking story, and our very own Lisa Quam is live on the scene...

Good evening, I'm live here on the North East side of the city, where the body of a woman was found mutilated in the wee hours of the morning.

The body of a 48-year-old woman was found mutilated near the Alum Creek reservoir, in an old abandoned boat storage building. The police have identified the victim, but will not release the name of the victim until her next of kin are notified.

According to police the 48-year-old woman, was found mutilated, in what Police Chief, William Owens, called one of the most violent crimes in his twenty years in law enforcement.

When I talked with Chief Owens, he told this reporter, he would have more details later on. Again the body of a woman was discovered near the Alum Creek reservoir mutilated. We will get back with you, when we have more details."

I grabbed my cell phone and checked to see if Steve had left a message, or texted him...but there was nothing.

It was the second day of the last week of hunting season so the chances of Steve checking his phone, or listening to a radio was slim.

Deanne began crying and screaming at me, saying....

"It's Wendi I know it is...Blue...Wendi's dead!"

Next to Kristin, Wendi has been Deanne's closest and most trusted friend for the past twelve years.

I grabbed Deanne and hugged her trying to comfort her, but Deanne ran up to her bedroom and closed the door crying.

For the first time I didn't know what if anything to do. The news report didn't say who it was they had discovered dead.

For all we knew it could be anyone, but there were a few things which made me think.

For starters, Deanne told me that Wendi was heading to over here last night and she never showed, and the old boat marina is less than a mile from here.

Secondly Wendi is not answering her phone, and when Deanne did get a hold of Wendi last night all they heard was somebody breathing on the other end.

After feeding Shone and walking her outside David thought about going up and seeing if Deanne could eat something, even though he knew the answer would be no.

I made my way up to the bedroom when there was a knock at the door and then the doorbell rang.

I turned and went back downstairs and opened the door to find an undercover officer standing with his badge out, and behind him a female uniformed police officer.

I motioned for them to come in and have a seat, and made them aware that I could not talk, by using hand signals.

I turned to go upstairs and get Deanne but she was standing at the top of the stairs and asked me...

"Blue, who's at the door?"

For a moment I stood there feeling stupid at my feeble attempts to make hand signals for 'policemen', left Deanne frustrated.

Deanne came down the steps as I grabbed Shone and placed her in her kennel, and then joined Deanne on the sofa. As soon as I sat down next to Deanne, the plain clothes Detective said....

"I'm so sorry to disturb you people tonight, I'm homicide Detective Det. Fannichuci; and this if Officer Withers. We're here investigating the murder of a woman who was found less than a mile from here, and we'd like to ask you a few questions if we can."

I nodded to them and grabbed Deanne's hand gently to give her support as Deanne begin to cry saying...

"It's Wendi isn't it?"

The plain clothes detective took out a writing pad and positioned himself as though he was going to write something when the female police officer said...

"We didn't mention a name, what makes you say that the victim's name is Wendi"?

Detective Fannichuci looked at Deanne and said...

"We're here investigating a murder and before we even mentioned the victim's name, you know who it is...why do you suppose that is?"

Deanne scooted herself closer to the edge of the sofa and replied...

"Of course I know who it is....my best friend was just murdered, and you guys are here playing fucking games."

Detective Fannichuci replied...

"Look I can imagine you're' upset...we've been here a few minutes and we're not playing games, and the name of the victim has not been released yet you know who it is...now how is that it?"

Deanne, *let loose of my hand and said...*

"OMG!!! I can't believe this is happening."

Police Officer Withers interrupted and said to Deanne...

"Ma'am you say you know it's the body of your friend...can you describe her?"

Deanne grabbed her cell phone and said...

"*I can do better than that.... I have a picture of her that I took last week.*"

Locating the picture and enlarging it Deanne handed it to Officer Withers and said...

"*Here this is Wendi and her husband Steve.*"

As Officer Withers looked at the photo and then handed the cell phone to Det. Fannichuci, who nodded and said...

"*There is some resemblance, but I can't be sure.*"

Deanne threw her head into my chest crying...

"*Oh no.... Wendi, oh my God not Wendi!*"

Officer Withers whispered something in Detective Fannichuci's ear, and Det. Fannichuci, said...

"*As I stated, it resembles the body we discovered but...*"

Deanne stood up cutting Det. Fannichuci off, saying...

"*Yes you can, just tell us why you're here...do you know what happened to her, and you know her name...has anybody contacted her husband?*"

Still visibly upset and crying Deanne stood up and walked over to the mantel piece near the fire place and said....

"*If you weren't a hundred percent sure then how did you know to come to our house and question us?*"

Officer Withers looked down at Det. Fannichuci's pad and said...

"*For starters, your name and number were in the address book that we found on the victim, and it appears that you were the last person who spoke with her, according to a note we found written on a piece of paper. Can you tell me who would want to harm her, and what you two talked about?*"

Deanne walked behind the sofa and placed her hands on my shoulder and said...

"*First of all Wendi didn't have any enemies, and as for our conversation...Wendi was bothered about something and told me yesterday that she wanted to come over and talk.*"

Det. Fannichuci could tell that Deanne had just answered untruthfully.

He took the note recovered from Wendi's pants pocket and said to Deanne...

"So you say she was bothered about something. Did she tell you, what she was bothered about?"

Deanne came back over and sat beside me and said...

"No, she didn't say why she was bothered, but it's...well, you know what I mean, when you can sense something's wrong with somebody that's what I mean."

Officer Withers continued taking notes and said...

"We're not trying to turn this into anything major and I feel for the loss of your friend...but we found a note in a journal which your friend had written which says...she was coming to see you because you were the one bothered about something, not her."

Officer Withers handed her note pad to Det. Fannichuci briefly, pointing to something, saying...

"We also know from the weather report that it was raining and also the road from the interstate to where her car was found well, what I'm getting at is, did she ever make it here yesterday?"

I shook my head no, while Deanne said...

"Look, if she had made it here then she wouldn't be dead, would she?"

"That's what we're trying to find out also, her car was found five miles past your home on a dead end stretch of the road...did she ever have problems getting here?"

Det. Fannichuci said, as he sat back down.

Deanne grabbed a pad and ink pen from the table and began drawing the route Wendi takes and said...

"The news said her car was found at the old fishing storage building, that doesn't make sense because Wendi never goes in the direction.

In the whole six years we've lived here Wendi drives one way... she never goes across the reservoir...ever."

Officer Withers looked at Deanne's sketch and said...

"Perhaps there was traffic build up, or an accident or someone chased her...the point is she did go in that direction."

I tapped Deanne on the arm and pointed at her cell phone when Deanne said...

"Okay Blue, I'll tell 'em."

Officer Withers stopped taking notes and looked at Deanne intensely and said...

"Tell us what?"

Deanne grabbed her cell phone and said...

When we first moved here, for months I used to go across the reservoir to get home. David and Steve...' Wendi's husband' made us a bet that coming into the rear of the development was quicker than going across the reservoir, so we videoed it on our cell phones."

Det. Fannichuci said...

"Who won the bet?"

Deanne drew a deep breath and sighed and answered, but not before her voice began breaking....

"They did...Steve and Wendi came into our unit by the back of the development...they beat us here by ten minutes, and ever since then Wendi's been taking that route ever since."

Det. Fannichuci and Officer Withers stood up, to signal that they were through and said...

"Just a couple more things before we go...you stated that her husband Steve was hunting, can you tell us what area he hunts in, and a number we can reach him on?"

I took the pad and pen from Deanne and wrote...

"Woodgrain area, it's about an hour and a half from here. He normally drives his Escalade, but a friend of his drove, so I don't know what kind of truck they're in. He won't be using his cell phone, but his number is 614-235-0005."

Det. Fannichuci said as he handed the information to Officer Withers...

"I hate to ask but its routine...can you tell me where the two of you were at about eleven o'clock last night?"

I made hand signals pointing upstairs...when Deanne said...

"We we're asleep...we were waiting on Wendi to come by...do you honestly believe we had something to do with this?"

Deanne opened the door saying...

"Get out...just get the hell out of here...thinking we hurt Wendi.... GET OUT!"

Det. Fannichuci nodded his head and handed David his card and said...

"Again, thank you for your time and we're really sorry about your friend. If you think of anything or have any questions...please call me."

Deanne slammed the door and sat down on the sofa crying.

Deanne looked at me and said...

"Blue I know they won't let me near the boat area where they found Wendi, but they can't stop me from going to her house...I'm going over there."

I jumped in front of Deanne and opened my mouth to say no, and grabbed a piece of paper and wrote...

"Baby that was probably the first place they went to and are probably still there, besides they are not going to let you, me, or anyone near their house. I doubt if they'll let Steve in until they're through investigating."

Deanne took off her coat and grabbed and hugged me crying...

"Oh Blue...I can't believe this...Oh my God.....Wendi...."

I poured Deanne a shot of Vodka and after Deanne drank it she sat on the sofa beside me and fell asleep in my arms.

I laid Deanne's cell phone in the glass whale bone bowl which sat on the coffee table, and when it began vibrating, it made a high-pitched ring which caused me to jump, waking up Deanne.

Deanne sat up and picked up her cell phone and the expression I saw on Deanne's face was if she had seen a ghost.

In shock Deanne slowly lowered the cell phone from her ear as I plainly heard the voices of children singing...

"La-la-la-la-la-la-, la-la-la-la-la-la,

Teddy Bear Soda Crackers,

Twisted and Dread,

All at the farm will soon be,

Dead, Dead, DEAD....

La-la-la-la-la-la-, la-la-la-la-la-la."

I looked at Deanne and for a moment was glad that someone else was hearing what I'd been hearing and experiencing for the past six months, I couldn't help feeling that the timing was bad, in my mind I thought...

"*Now Deanne's got to believe everything I told her about Kristin, Steve, Mary, Tim and Wendi and all of the weird shit that happened was real... but*"

Before I finished my thought, Deanne let out a cry...

"*Mary!*"

"*Oh Blue...I'm losing it. I had a bad dream just now...before my phone woke me up, I dreamt that Mary was at the farm and some sicko was chasing her and now this crazy ass phone message!*"

I remembered how I felt the first time I saw a Doppelganger, and the little girl at the farm, so I wrote to Deanne...

"Baby I know! This is what I've been trying to tell you six months ago at the farm but you wouldn't believe me. All of that stuff at the farm I was seeing...it's the same thing and it's starting all over again."

Deanne turned and looked at me and said...

"*Blue I'm not talking about fucking hallucinations. I'm not talking about people appearing and disappearing.*"

I started writing something to Deanne when she snatched the pad and yelled...

"*Blue...I thought your doctor got through to you about this shit...talk to me! We get one weird message and I tell you about a dream and you start with this bullshit.*"

My mind drifted to what had happened in the shopping center parking lot when the girl came up to his car, when I wrote...

"*Deanne, that's how all of this crap begins, it starts with the creepy little kids singing, and then Doppelgangers start appearing and stuff.*"

Deanne had thrown her hands up in disgust when suddenly there was a screeching noise on the kitchen window, and when Deanne and I walked over to the window, we saw words forming on the window which read...

"The farm...the farm...Mary-Mary's at...THE FARM!"

I looked over at Deanne, and shook my head making the gesture...
no, no no! Then I snatched the pad off the table and wrote...

"There is no way in hell, I'm going to go back there!"

Deanne grabbed me by the arm and said...

"Blue I don't know what the hell is going on, Wendi was just murdered and if Mary's in trouble we need to go to the farm and find out what the hell is going on."

I flipped to a clean page on the note pad and wrote...

"No damn way. Call what's his name...farmer Brown!"

Deanne got up and stormed off to the bedroom and as I chased'
after her, Deanne turned and said...

"You mean Mr. Beck...what's he supposed to do?"

I pointed to Deanne's cell phone. Deanne walked over and picked
up her bottle of water and said...

*I don't get you Blue...you of all people should care about Mary...
oh yeah...I know about you and Mary's affair.*

*I've known for years how you lied to me about working and the
whole time you were in Mary's panties...C'mon Blue you're going to
have to get over what whatever trip you've been on and help me!"*

I handed Deanne her cell phone, and then wrote...

*"Call the police! Let them do a wellness check or whatever it is
they do, when somebody's missing or in trouble...and what do you
mean about me and Mary...what's up with that?"*

Even though I knew exactly what Deanne talking about, I tried to
play ignorant when she said...

"Blue you don't want to go there with me on that right now."

I tried to defuse the conversation by writing...

"Look you're upset, saying all kinds of stuff that you don't mean."

Deanne grabbed a jacket and her purse and started to walk out of
the bedroom when I grabbed her arm, shaking my head...No!

Deanne jerked away from me and said...

*"Look, I asked you to help me see if one of our best friends, the
one you fucked behind my back is in trouble, and you can't even do
that."*

I followed Deanne out of the bedroom and wrote...

"*Call that detective and ask them to check on Mary, then if there's something's wrong we'll drive to the farm.*"

I went into the living room and poured myself a glass of wine while I heard Deanne on the phone and wrote...

"*What did he say...did you call that detective?*"

Deanne had taken out her cell and tried calling Mary and Tim's number again and said...

"*Nothing it's useless... they are not going to do a damn thing! The detective said, getting a weird phone call, and the fact that she lives in Wisconsin and hasn't been reported missing...there was little they could do.*

Deanne tried calling Steve, Mary and Kristin and then came back into the living room and sat beside me and said...

"*Det. Fannichuci said the wildlife officials in Woodgrain told him they would leave a note on the cabin door for Steve to call the police, and for us not to expect a call until later tomorrow at the latest.*"

I placed my hand on Deanne's back and began massaging her, when Deanne's cell phone began vibrating. Deanne looked down at her phone hoping it would be a call from Kristin, Mary or Steve.

When Deanne picked up the phone it stopped ringing and vibrating. Deanne clicked on the '*missed calls*" icon and immediately recognized the number said...

"*Blue, look...567-234-2266. Blue that's our house phone at the farm, but that can't be... I had the power disconnected and the phone turned off over six and a half months ago!*"

Woodgrain Wildlife Hunting Area
Coshocton, Ohio
8 hours earlier

Steve climbed down from his tree stand and met up with his hunting friends, Michael Ward and Jeffery Fleming, who had just emerged from the wood line on the left and right of Steve.

Michael Ward and Steve have worked together for the past six years as letter carriers with the Post Office.

Jeffery Fleming, was a supervisor with the Supreme Tool & Die, and a good friend of Steve's.

The three men were on the first day of a three-day hunting weekend with no success. After three years of inviting Michael hunting, he finally agreed to go hunting admitting to Steve that he knew a lot about guns but nothing at all about hunting.

Jeffery on the other hand was the most experienced of the three having hunted in all of the four choice hunting areas in Ohio.

When Jeffery and Steve arrived at the Woodgrain Hunting office midafternoon on Friday they both laughed and commented on Michael's appearance as he pulled up in his jeep and parked beside Jeffery's Ford F150 pickup.

Michael, who had never been hunting, stepped out of his jeep resembling a 'poster-boy' for hunting and fishing.

Michael was dressed in brand new camouflage pants and jacket. A bright orange hat with fur earmuffs with the price tag still attached and brand new boots.

Michael walked around to the back of his jeep and pulled out a bag containing his sleeping bag and all the necessary things for the week of hunting...socks, long johns, shirts, two rifle bags, and a thermos full of coffee.

Steve and Jeffery had already paid for the cabin they were going to stay in for the week, so most of their gear was already inside.

Jeffery motioned for Michael to load his gear in the back of Jeffery's pick up, for the twenty-mile cross country trek to the cabin leaving Michael's jeep in the parking lot.

As Jeffery and Steve went to help Michael unload his things into the back of Jeffery's truck they noticed the smell of something like moth balls when Steve commented...

"It's about time you got here Michael, we were beginning to think you weren't going to make it."

Michael nodded his head and said...

"Yeah, had to make a couple of stops, before I got here."

Jeffery closed the tail gate of his truck and as all of them climbed inside, Jeffery looked over at Michael who climbed in the passenger side and said...

"Okay, Steve when we get to the cabin you and I are going to scout out the best places to put the tree stands, and look at the area

while there's still day light, because when we head out in the morning it's going to be cold, wet and dark."

Steve nodded and said to Michael...

"Mike the cabin has one of those old wood burning stoves so while we're out you need to crank up the stove and get rid of that odor."

Michael looked around puzzled at Steve's comment and said...

"Odor...what odor?"

Jeffery jumped in and grabbed Michael's hat from his head and sniffed his jacket and said...

"This is brand new... 'deer are not coming close to us with you wearing this moth ball funk' all over your clothes."

Michael put his sleeve up to his nose, smelling his sleeve jacket and said...

"I don't smell moth balls, besides this is all new I just bought them this morning."

Steve grabbed Michael's hat from Jeffery and tossed it at Michael saying...

"Mike a deer can smell this scent, and won't come within a hundred miles of us."

Twenty miles out Jeffery stopped the pickup and turned to Steve who was in the back seat, saying...

"Alright Steve we'll get out here. Michael, the cabin is straight ahead and off to the right. It's got a green flat-roof with wood stacked on the porch and deer antlers hanging over the door...you can't miss it."

Michael climbed out of the pickup and got into the driver's side and said to Jeffery...

"So you want me to unpack the truck and start up a fire...I can manage that?"

Jeffery walked back up to the truck before Michael drove off and said...

"Don't forget to wash the clothes you're wearing. There's a utility sink around back. Use water and baking soda, there's some in the cabin...

Steve hollered interrupting Jeffery...

"A lot of baking soda!"

Jeffery continued…

"*Like I was saying use baking soda and water to wash your clothes. That will neutralize the odor so the deer can't pick it up the scent….and hang them outside to dry. You can bring them in to finish drying before we hit the sack tonight.*"

Michael started the pickup and after closing the door said…

"*I've never heard of that…but hey, you're the subject matter expert here.*"

Michael drove off heading to the cabin as Steve and Jeffery disappeared in the woods. Michael pulled up to the cabin and began unloading all of the bags which were in the truck.

Michael grabbed the bags containing the rifles, making two trips to carry in all six.

Not sure who owned which rifles, Michael stacked them in the corner, and began bringing in a few wood logs from the porch for the stove.

Michael looked around the cabin for any signs of old newspaper to get the fire started when he remembered that he had seen a stack of newspapers in the bed of Jeffery's truck.

Michael gathered twigs which he saw lying around the side of the cabin along with some small kindling, and began rolling them in newspaper.

He lined the stove with the rolled up newspaper containing the twigs, and after they were burning good and producing red hot wood embers, he placed two small logs on top which immediately began burning.

Rubbing his hands over the stove and feeling the heat, Michael looked around the inside of the cabin to see what the comforts were.

From what Michael saw, outside of the cabin was a far cry from the inside.

The inside walls of the cabin were constructed of 'knotty pine', less than ten years old, but clean.

Two double stack bunk beds which looked like something '*Grizzly Adams*' made, sat on each side of the cabin.

A medium sized version of a picnic table, with two benches sat in the middle of the cabin. A roughhewn fire place with a mantle lined one side of the wall with an ash tray and an old smoking pipe resting in it.

Michael removed the clothes he was wearing and put on jeans and an old sweater. It never occurred to him, but he was the only one dressed in his hunting gear.

Michael grabbed his 30-30 lever action rifle, and before loading it swung it around the room several times in different directions, pretending to be shooting something.

Once Michael was through playing with his rifle he spotted the box of baking soda, and walked around to the back of the cabin to where the wash sink was.

Michael placed his jacket and pants in the cold water in the sink to soak, not realizing that something was watching him from inside the cabin.

Walking back to the front of the cabin Michael thought he heard the voices of Steve and Jeffery coming up the path.

Michael stood motionless and silent in front of the cabin until he noticed that the sounds he heard were coming from children...Children singing... "La-la-la-la-la-la-, la-la-la-la-la-la,

Teddy Bear Soda Crackers

Hunter in the woods

Think you're hunting something

But somethings hunting you.

La-la-la-la-la-la-, la-la-la-la-la-la."

Michael looked first to the left and then to the right and as the singing grew louder and louder Michael ran back inside the cabin and loaded his rifle, and walked back out on the front porch.

Just then, Michael jumped as he felt something from behind touch him, yelling ...

"WHOA!"

Michael turned to noticed Steve and Jeffery were standing there puzzled that he was startled and said...

"*Whoa there Elmer Fudd, you're way too jumpy...how are you going to hunt deer all jacked up like that.*"

It was a good thing for Steve and Jeffery that Michael was inexperienced because he still had the safety on. Michael lowered his rifle down and said...

"*You will not believe this but I-I just heard voices of children singing or something.*"

Jeffery looking in disbelief asked Michael...

"*You heard what!*"

Michael pointed to the direction which he heard the singing, saying...

"*It was like some creepy ass kids singing about we're being hunted, or something.*"

Steve removed a flask from his jacket and after taking a drink handed it to Michael, who was showing signs of still being rattled, saying...

"*A few hits of this, and you be won't be hearing anything.*"

Jeffery reached for the flask and after a few drinks said as he pointed to the east of the cabin...

"*We came up from behind that wooded area. We saw a lot of clumpy droppings so the deer are here and from the size of all the big clumps I'd say there are some pretty big Does and Bucks that are nested nearby.*"

Steve headed for the door and stopped and turned to Michael and said...

"*You better wring your clothes out so that they can start air drying before you bring them inside...it's going to get cold tonight.*"

Steve located the cooler which Michael sat in the corner. Jeffery was digging around on the small shelf next to the window and pulled down an old black frying pan and a medium size pot.

There are a dozen rental cabins located in all of the wildlife area, and each one is outfitted with the basic requirements of hunters.

Of course many hunters leave used items such as coffee pots, pots, pans, utensils for the next hunters to use.

Steve and Jeffery have hunted in this area and used the cabins before, so they had an ideal of what to bring, and what should be in the cabins.

Michael threw another log into the wood burning furnace and went outside for his clothes which had been hanging over the wash sink for an hour.

Jeffery lit the two lanterns and placed one on the table and the other over the fire place.

Steve wiped out the frying pan and put six large pieces of sliced ham which Wendi cut for their trip into the pan and placed it on top of the stove.

Jeffery had just taken another sip of liquor and after cleaning the pot dumped a large Tupperware bowl of Navy beans into the pot, along with a wooden spoon and began slowly stirring them.

Steve hollered for Michael to get the cake of corn bread which was wrapped in aluminum foil, which Wendi made for them and then he placed on the old stove to warm up.

Michael walked over to Steve commenting on how good everything smelled.

There were four wooden bowls sitting on the shelf above the window. Jeffery grabbed the bowls down and wiped them out and sat them on the picnic table.

Jeffery called to Michael and Steve, saying...

"Get it while it's hot...is the ham done?"

Steve nodded yes, and they all began filling their bowls with navy beans, a large slice of ham and corn bread.

The three men sat up until ten o'clock eating drinking beer and corn liquor which Steve bought with him from a trip to North Carolina.

Michael was not a heavy drinker and neither was Jeffery but after the first few drinks Jeffery came to life, laughing and joking.

Michael got up to go outside to relieve himself and have a cigarette... and Jeffery and Steve thought it was a good ideal if they all went out not to mention Jeffery had staggered to the door, and they didn't want him staggering around out in the dark drunk.

Steve bought one of the lanterns with him as a fog started to settle in, reducing visibility to just a few inches in front of your face.

When Steve stepped off the porch he could hear Jeffery and Michael off to his right, so he headed in that direction.

Michael and Jeffery were just finishing up as Steve approached the trees and said…

"Hey would one of you hold the lantern?"

Jeffery reached out for the lantern, and noticed he was in no shape to hold anything, seeing as how the tree had held him up while he was urinating.

Michael grabbed the lantern and held it is Steve finished his business.

The three men walked back to the cabin helping Jeffery up the steps as he missed the first step, nearly busting his ass.

Jeffery grabbed another piece of ham and headed towards the bottom bunk for the night.

Michael was checking on his clothes to see if they were almost dry and to his surprise the heat inside the small cabin worked well, if not better than a clothes dryer.

Steve meanwhile was setting the alarm on his cell phone knowing the amount of beer and liquor they drank and getting up at the crack of dawn may have proven to be a challenge.

The three men were finally asleep and from the sounds of all the snoring in the cabin, it's a wonder that all of the animals didn't pack up and leave the Wood Grain Wild Life area.

Somewhere in the dead of night the weather started turning from a dense fog to a slow steady rain, and then a down pour. The sound of the rain beating on the old tin roof provided the perfect sleeping weather.

The rain provided such a good sound cover that Steve, Michael nor Jeffery noticed that a dark figure was inside the cabin with them, standing near the stove, watching the three men as they slept.

This mysterious figure walked from the stove and all about the cabin, and as he pointed to the lanterns they both extinguished.

Chapter 8

Cooing birds

Pecan Drive

Deanne spent the rest of the day getting in touch with as many people as she could who knew Wendi, to tell them what had happened before laying down to take a nap.

I sat down next to Deanne who had fallen asleep and after yawing several times fell asleep next to her.

No sooner had drifted off to sleep that we were awakened by someone pounding on the front door.

I didn't pay it much attention at the time because Shone always barks her head off when someone gets close to the door, but she sat quietly in the corner her eyes glued to the door.

I sat up for a moment and thought not knowing if I was dreaming or if someone really was knocking at the door, until Deanne lifted her head from the pillow and said...

"Blue...someone's at the door."

I got up slowly, stretching and yawing and walked to the door. I looked over at Shone who was still lying in the corner, as I looked out of the peep hole but there was no one at the door.

I turned to Deanne and shook my head when suddenly there was a loud bang at the front door.

The banging on the door was so loud that it startled me and made me jump.

When I turned to the door, and after looking out of the peep hole and not seeing anyone, I slowly opened the door.

Deanne had joined me at the door as we both looked out onto an empty porch and driveway. Deanne tapped me on the shoulder and turned to go back inside and saying...

"That was weird...if Tim didn't live in Wisconsin, I'd swear it was him messing. around like he does."

I closed the door and turned curious as to why Deanne stopped in the middle of her sentence, and that's when I saw Deanne with her right hand over her mouth... staring at a dozen little children who were cooing like pigeons.

They were all over the living room. One in each corner of the house, several around the sofa, and a few by the entrance into the kitchen...they were everywhere.

The children were dressed in old dirty raggedy clothing with no shoes. Their feet were misshapen, and their eyes...their eyes were huge.

I looked over in Shone's direction to see one of the creepy kids patting her, as she lay silent wagging her tail.

Suddenly and without warning all of the children except for the one with Shone stopped cooing, raised their hands at me and Deanne and pointed their fingers and singing...

"La-la-la-la-la-la-, la-la-la-la-la-la,

Teddy Bear Soda Crackers,

Heating things up;

Farm's afire and you're invited,

See you when you come.

La-la-la-la-la-la-, la-la-la-la-la-la!"

Just then the house started shaking and all of the pictures hanging on the walls fell to the floor.

The cabinet glass in the entertainment system suddenly burst, and the figurines which were inside began shaking.

The children began disappearing one by one, until they were all gone.

Deanne screamed as I grabbed Deanne to the floor keeping her from getting hit by the broken glass, and the ceramic figurines which were flying out of the cabinet.

The figurines and glass nick knacks were spinning around in air and then violently flying in all directions smashing into the walls, and embedding themselves deep into our furniture.

Deanne had begun crying and screaming in my ear as each figurine hit the wall...

"*What is going on...Blue...what's happening?*"

I held onto Deanne as Shone began barking at the sound of glass breaking, as figurine after figurine crashed and exploding after hitting the walls.

Suddenly all the lights in the house went out and there was total silence.

I stood up and as I did I knocked over a glass from the coffee table which shattered on the floor.

Then suddenly something grabbed me on the shoulder...

"*Blue, are you alright! Blue you must have had a bad dream or something, what are you doing down here?*"

When I looked up the lights were on and Deanne was kneeling beside me cleaning up the spilled water from the glass and said...

"*I came down stairs because I heard glass braking...what's going on!*"

In shock, I looked all around the room but everything was normal. Deanne was looking at me as if I was losing it again. She had to have seen and heard all of this...but she said she was upstairs.

No pictures or figurines were disturbed or broken, the cabinet glass was intact, and Shone was quietly lying in her dog bed.

Deanne picked up the glass that I had knocked over and walked into the kitchen. I walked over to the cabinet and after inspecting the glass, reached into the drawer and pulled a cigarette out of the pack.

I called for Shone and walked outside on the patio...shaking my head in disbelief, as Deanne said...

"*Gosh Blue.... how much wine did you drink?*"

One of the features of our condo was that it had an enclosed patio, which was a good smoking place when the weather was bad.

I opened the patio screen door as Shone raced out in the yard, looking for her favorite spot to fertilize the yard.

I started thinking to myself, as my mind began racing...

"It's happening again... first at the Famers market in Polaris and now this. There's no way in hell that what I saw in there was a damn dream or hallucination...I don't how much of this Deanne is going to put up with."

For six months I pretended to be one bean shy of a bean pie which kept the Doppelgangers away from me, but now they're on to me, and I got a feeling this time, things are going to get worst.

I stood noticing Shone getting in the hunch-dog position, as a few drops of rain began falling and noticed something on the top fence behind Shone.

I wanted to call Shone but not being able to speak left it me with snapping my fingers and slapping my legs to get Shone's attention.

Shone looked over at me and then continued sniffing the ground where she had just made her deposit when all of a sudden it became clear something was climbing over the fence.

As the lightening flashed I got a glimpse of who and what it was.

It was that creepy girl...the same creepy girl that kept scaring me at the farm. Our back yard fence was over six feet tall, and she would have to jump to the ground but she didn't.

She began slithering head first from the top of the fence and by the time she made it to the ground Shone started racing towards me.

This creep girl didn't walk like you'd expect someone to, she took five very fast steps and then stopped, and then five more fast steps.

This creepy girl she was moving in a zigzag pattern, and coming straight towards me.

My mind told me to move and I wanted to move, but my legs wouldn't move... something was holding me to that spot.

It's said that animals can sense spirits and the supernatural... but whatever extra sensory perception animals have it was apparent that Shone did not possess it, because she was unaware of the girl's presence.

She was about four feet tall but the closer she got to me the taller she appeared, until she stood face to face with me at six feet tall.

The creepy girl didn't say anything to me and she didn't make a sound. She simply stood there staring at me and sniffing...and staring at me with her huge black lifeless eyes...and then she flashed a crooked wide grin.

The rain was picking up and my shirt was completely soaking wet and not from the rain, but from fear.

There was something terrifying about this creepy girl, so much till I felt a tightness in my chest.

My heart started beating extremely fast, and I began hyperventilating with beads of sweat running down my face, as if I were actually standing out in the rain.

This creepy girl's grin widened more and more until she exposed a mouth full of the ugliest teeth ever imagined.

The creepy girl stood right in front of me with her mouth opened wide and I saw tiny white maggots crawling in between her crooked grayish jagged teeth.

Then my heart pounded even faster when I saw what she was going to do as her face drew closer to mine as she puckered her lips, for a kiss.

I felt as if my heart was going to burst out of my chest as her lips touched mine.

Suddenly the outside patio light came on and I felt a hand on my shoulder. I was already frightened to death, and when I felt something touching me on my shoulder...I fell backwards into the patio furniture.

I immediately looked to my left and then my right and turning back around, I no longer saw the creepy girl but Deanne standing there, saying...

"Whatcha doing...I been standing her for a few seconds calling your name, what's going on?"

I'm sure Deanne saw how terrified I was as I turned around looking at her wide-eyed.

Out of breath and shaking I hugged Deanne tight kissing her neck and looking off into the night when Deanne said...

"Aww Blue...I know; I know...It's hard imagining that Wendi is gone I can't imagine how Steve is going to handle this when he finds out."

Wendi was one of our best friends, but I wasn't shaking over the loss of a friend, but terrified over what I had just seen.

As Deanne and I were going back into the house I stopped to lock the screen door and patio door, when I looked out into the yard and there she was again sitting on top of the fence in the rain, blowing kisses at me.

I spinning Deanne around so that she could see the creepy girl, and said...

"Baby, do you see that?"

Deanne shouted anxiously...

"OMG Blue, that's creepy looking...isn't it?"

I let out a sigh of relief and said to Deanne...

"Baby, I'm glad you finally can see that creepy little girl...I thought for a minute that you were going to suggest that I check myself back into the hospital."

Deanne closed the drapes and turned off the lights saying...

"Girl, what girl...what in the hell are you talking about Blue, I was looking at those creepy looking clouds. Why the hell would a girl be outside in our back yard in the rain?"

Deanne and I walked into the living room and sat down looking at television, Deanne was shaking her head at me and I could see that Deanne had a few tears in her eyes, as she softly called out Wendi's name.

A commercial came on and then the local news anchor came on with a short announcement about the upcoming news stories.

Deanne grabbed the remote and was about to turn the channel when the anchor said...

"...coming up at eleven channel six, we'll be standing by police headquarters, as Police Chief William Owens is expected to hold a briefing and answering this reporters' questions surrounding the brutal murder of the forty-eight woman found brutally murdered late yesterday."

I looked over at Deanne and reached for her as the tears began flowing.

Everything was coming at me real fast...I wondered if maybe I left the hospital too soon. The Doppelgangers are coming at me again, Wendi was murdered, some crazy stuff about Mary, Deanne mentioned knowing about me and Mary's affair, and to top everything off...that damn creepy little girl has returned.

Since losing her parents while she was in college, Kristin and Wendi are the closest people to family that Deanne has.

Me and Deanne made it through the news briefing from the chief of police, and the 0nly new information regarding Wendi's murder without going into the gory details was that, she was ran off the road, and the person or persons responsible, dismembered her body in an unimaginable way.

Ohio Wildlife Hunting Lodge

Steve and Michael climbed out of their bunk beds at three forty-five a.m., when Michael turned and pointed at the door saying...

"Damn...who left the door open?"

Jeffery hopped out of his bunk and tossed a log in the stove to get coffee going and looked around the room answering...

"Whoever was the last one out last night didn't make sure the door was locked."

Michael got up and after putting on his pants and a sweater closed the door and said...

"Don't look at me...someone else was up, and probably took a leak and forgot to lock the door."

Pouring hot water into a mug and spooning in instant coffee, Jeffery said...

"Correct me if I'm wrong, but you were the last one in last night not to mention the fact that you were still messing around with your clothes...did they get dry?"

Michael draped his jacket over the back of the chair and said, as he reached for a cup...

"That's what I'm talking about...last night I had my jacket and pants draped over the back of the chair, but when I got up they were on the top bunk over there."

Steve put on his boots and headed for the door and said...

"What are you two ladies arguing about this morning... the only thing you two should be arguing about is, me collecting two Benjamins for bagging the first deer."

Steve explained how after hitting the flask three times last night, and not eating enough food to absorb the liquor he fell right to sleep, but did admit to seeing someone moving around in the cabin last night.

The three left the cabin after several cups of coffee, bacon and eggs, and headed for the spot which Steve and Jeffery scouted the day before.

It was four-thirty in the morning; the temperature was close to forty degrees, with a light wind and mist falling.

A few stars were visible in the sky as they headed down the path and into the woods.

As planned they had a thirty-minute walk down the trail until they came to the creek, and then thirty to forty steps to the area where they were going to place their tree stands.

The three walked through the creek and came up on the spot where they picked out earlier not seeing that a fourth figure, a dark figure trailed them in the woods at a distance.

One by one they began climbing their ladder tree stands. Jeffery, Michael and Steve had anxiously waited on the first deer of the season, betting one hundred dollars to the one to shoot the first deer.

Everything was perfect, a light mist and a chill filled the air. They were perched in the same area where Jeffery saw fresh clumps of droppings the day before.

The one thing however which was far from perfect was the fourth figure, the dark figure that was perched in a tree behind and above the three men.

Steve sat motionless, still and quiet, and aimed his rifle to the left of the clearing, as he heard the sound of leaves rustling.

Steve was the most patience of them all having acquired this skill from the countless nights of laying and waiting to ambush Vietnamese soldiers while he served in Nam.

Soon Steve shifted his rifle aim from left of the clearing to resting on his lap, when he suddenly got the feeling that someone was watching him.

Steve has hunted and stalked in the darkest, deepest, jungles of Vietnam where the enemy was always watching his every movement, but this feeling was the most intense feeling he had experienced.

Without moving his head, Steve's eyes scanned left and then right with the slightest movements of Jeffery and Michael repositioning themselves in their tree stands.

Steve's eyes saw the movement of the leaves ahead of him, and knew it was the movement made by the antlers of a large buck in the brush.

Steve scanned the area looking for the place the buck was most likely to emerge into the clearing when he saw something out of the corner of his eye.

It was a faint shape of a dark figure which appeared directly above Jeffery slithering down the tree.

Steve's eyes went back to the place where the buck was rustling when he noticed Jeffery slowly raising his gun.

Steve's first thought was that because of Jeffery's location being closest to the deer, Jeffery would get the first deer and two hundred bucks.

Suddenly the biggest buck that any of them had ever seen emerged into the clearing, in Jeffery's kill zone area.

This massive buck emerged slowly and cautiously from the wood line directly below Jeffery.

Steve and Michael watched the deer slowly and followed the deer with their rifles ready to shoot if Jeffery missed.

Standing straight up the massive twelve-point buck surveyed the area as his keen sense of smell canvassed the entire area.

Suddenly and out of character for a deer, the deer began scraping his huge antlers against the tree when a single shot rang out.

Jeffery ejected and reloaded another cartridge and took aim right below the buck's ear...'the perfect kill shot'.

Michael and Steve waited for the second shot before climbing down from their tree stands, when another shot rang out.

Steve looked at the deer that had fallen against the tree and somehow managed to get one side of his antlers entangled into the tree limbs, when he heard a loud thud!

Steve looked over in Jeffery's direction wondering if Jeffery had fallen out of the tree when the second shot rang out.

Jeffery was still perched in his tree stand, only...his gun was not pointed at the deer, but on the ground below.

Resting his gun on his lap Steve scanned the ground, and that's when he saw Michael lying at the base of the tree.

Steve wondered if Michael had fallen out of his tree stand, when another shot rang out, whizzing past Steve's left ear.

"Mother... fuck... Jeffery; what in the hell are you doing, put your..."

Before Steve could finish his sentence, Jeffery fired another shot, missing Steve but ripping off a large chunk of the tree.

Scrambling to reposition himself but not wanting to shoot his friend... Steve took aim at Jeffery and fired.

Jeffery fell to the ground and landed face first, when Steve heard the strangest thing...the sound of pigeons cooing.

Steve started to scan the tops of the trees, when coming out of the woods into the clearing were a group of creepy looking kids.

These kids were inappropriately dressed for the weather wearing no shoes, and torn and raggedy pants and dresses.

Pointing and aiming his rifle at the children, Steve sat frozen and in shock over what just happened.

The children pointed to Jeffery and then over to Michael and then up at Steve cooing like pigeons.

Steve sat up in the tree looking at the kids, for the first time in his life he didn't know what to do.

Steve thought about shooting in the air to scare the kids off, when they stopped cooing and began singing in over lapping demonic voices.

Steve had been in many ugly situations, but never anything like this, as he yelled to the children below...

"I don't know where you all came from...but you need to get out of here, so you won't get in to trouble."

Steve sat looking at the children below as they joined hands and continued singing...

"La-la-la-la-la-la-, la-la-la-la-la-la,
Teddy Bear Soda Crackers,

Stuck up in a tree,
Teddy Bear getting mad,
Hunters, dead makes three
La-la-la-la-la-la-, la-la-la-la-la-la."

In an instant all of the feelings of being in the jungle in Viet Nam came rushing inside of Steve as he fired a single shot in the middle of the circle of children, who began disappearing one by one.

Steve still had that feeling that someone was watching him. Something from over in the trees in the direction where Jeffery had been sitting.

Steve lowered his head and to focus when a large dark figured came flying out of the trees straight towards Steve.

At first Steve thought it was an owl or some other type of bird until it got closer.

It had the outline of a person, but the figure was distorted. The dark figure flew closer to Steve as he fired a shot off balance and fell from his tree stand to the ground.

Dazed and shaken Steve scramble to his knees, his right shoulder and hip were in pain from the fall.

Wiping the dirt from his head and brushing the leaves off his clothes, Steve picked up his cap, and put it on his head.

Steve looked at Michael and Jeffery who were lying motionless on the ground, trying to figure out how a simple hunting trip ended up like this.

Looking up at the tree which he had just fallen from, Steve looked all around for what it was which flew at him, but saw nothing as the daylight revealed a fog which was setting in.

Steve got off his knees and attempted to stand not realizing that not only was his shoulder and hip sore from the fall, but his left leg was either badly sprained or broken.

Wiping the mud and leaves from his face and picking up his rifle, Steve limped slowly towards Jeffery who was clearly dead, with a large gaping hole in his forehead and a larger exit wound to the back of his head.

Steve shook his head thinking about all the news reports about how innocent outings suddenly turn tragic...and what possessed Jeffery to kill Michael and try to kill him.

Steve had known Jeffery for a long time, and there were never any harsh words between the two. Steve thought about the fact that he was godfather to Jeffery's and his wife Lynn's two children.

As Steve knelt beside Jeffery he heard Michael moaning. Using his rifle to help support his leg as he stood up, Steve made his way to where Michael was lying; unaware that the mud and leaves were clogging up the first three inches of his muzzle and barrel.

Steve approached Michael and the noise of the deer whose antlers were caught in the tree limbs, rested against the tree exhausted from trying to free itself.

Steve checked to see where Michael had been shot, and as Steve rolled Michael onto his back and opening his coat and shirt he saw a gunshot the size of a golf ball in his chest.

Looking at the condition Michael was in, Steve wondered how Michael could still be alive let alone semi-conscious.

Michael's eyes were open and Steve heard Michael making gurgling sounds knowing that Michael's lungs were filling up with blood.

Steve knew there was little that he could do for Michael except try to keep him comfortable, so Steve crawled over to Jeffery and after removing Jeffery's coat draped it over Michael, when another noise caught his attention.

Turning and looking in all directions Steve heard the singing and laughter of children, which were growing louder and louder and coming from all directions...

"La-la-la-la-la-la-, la-la-la-la-la-la,

Teddy Bear Soda Crackers,

Teddy has a gun,

Friends all dead... You're all that's left,

Teddy Bear aunt had enough?

La-la-la-la-la-la-, la-la-la-la-la-la!"

Steve raised his rifle and swinging it in all directions saw the collection of mud and leaves, lodged in the barrel of his rifle as he yelled...

"WHAT THE HELL DO YOU WANT!"

Steve knew he'd have to clean the mud and leaves out before he could even think about shooting.

The singing and laughing which was loud in the beginning suddenly grew faint until there was an eerie silence.

Michael had a single gunshot in the right side of his chest, a perfect kill shot and yet he was still breathing.

Blood was pouring from the gaping hole in Michael's chest and with each breath Michael took, blood was bubbling from his wound which was told Steve it was only a matter of time before one or both of his lungs would collapse.

Steve knew Michael's chances were fading with each breath he took, and with all of his military training there was little he could for his friend.

Steve's experience in combat with chest wounds told him, there was possibly damage to the lungs, liver and possibly the heart, not to mention the condition of the exit wound.

Not having any way to help Michael, Steve pulled the bright orange knit skull cap from under his camouflage hood and placed it over the wound and begin applying pressure.

Steve saw the look in Michael's eyes, a look Steve had seen many times in Viet Nam, as many members of his unit lay dying in the jungle.

A fixed stare which Steve knew all too well which said Michael had possibly seconds left to live.

Michael looked up at Steve and clutched Steve's coat when he took his last breath. Steve removed Michael's hand from his coat and with his other hand, placed it over Michael's face and closed his eyes.

Steve pulled Jeffery's coat over Michaels face and then sat down next to Michael trying to make some sense out of what happened when he heard the sound of branches snapping!

Grabbing his rifle, he started removing the mud and leaves from the barrel which were packed pretty deep.

Suddenly from the right wood line close to where Jeffery lay emerged a man. Taking aim, and knowing his gun would not fire, but hoping the sight of the rifle would be a deterrent, Steve hollered...

"Hey mister, I need some help over here!"

The man was massive in size about seven feet tall, three or four hundred pounds. As the man completely cleared the brush, Steve saw that not only was he enormously huge, but judging by the way he was dressed, Steve knew it was going to come down to shooting this man.

He didn't appear to be a hunter nor was he dressed for being outside. He wore a dirty white ballerina's tutu, tights, high top black all-star sneakers and wearing a clown's mask.

Not knowing who this was and what his intentions were, and judging by the outfit the man was wearing made Steve believe that the killing wasn't over.

As suddenly as the man appeared from the woods, he turned and walked back into the woods away from Steve.

Steve stood there for a few minutes trying to process all of the events which just occurred when the man appeared from the woods again, only this time he was pushing a wheel barrel.

The large man looked at Steve and stomped his left foot and then his right foot and go down in a low squatting position staring at Steve.

He then turned his head left and then right and then dropped down to both knees. Steve stood up to show this man that he was prepared to kill him if he didn't stop.

Steve pointed his rifle at the man who showed no signs of fear or intentions of retreating and chambered a round and yelled to the man to stop!

The cross hairs on the sight of Steve's rifle were dead center on the clown's mask.

Again he stomped his left foot and his right foot and clapped his hands once, and then he got into a stance something that a football tackler would be in.

As Steve aim at the man's face all thoughts of the barrel being jammed left him.

Steve pulled the trigger...

"Click"!

Steve tried ejecting another round into the chamber, but his rifle was not functioning, likely from the fall.

The man in the ballerina's tutu slowly began approaching Steve pushing the wheel barrel.

Steve quickly canvassed the ground looking for Michael's rifle, which was still hanging up in the tree.

Steve remembered that Jeffery's rifle was lying beside him when he fell out of the tree, but Jeffery's rifle was a closer to the man in the ballerina's tutu than it was to Steve.

Steve's only hope was to put enough distance between himself and the man in the ballerina's tutu, until he had time to clear the mud and debris from his rifle.

As Steve tried to run the pain in his ankle told him that trying to walk on it, let alone running, was going to be painful.

The sun was trying to peak out through the clouds as an eerie fog settled in, making it more and more difficult for Steve to see more than a few feet in front of him.

Over the past several years Steve had hunted in that area and pretty much knew several routes back to the cabin, but because of the denseness of the fog, he wasn't exactly sure he was going the right way.

Steve decided to put as much distance between himself and the man in a ballerina's tutu as he could and started hobbling through the brush.

Steve was no stranger to hand to hand combat having served two tours in Viet Nam, in sixty-eight and seventy-three but the average Vietnamese soldier was five-feet-four to five-feet-five.

The man chasing Steve was not a five-foot-five solider in the jungle, but a seven-foot-tall three hundred pound 'Twinkie' with a twisted attitude.

According to the way Steve's ankle felt, running was out of the question but Steve had created a little distance between himself and the man in a ballerina's tutu.

Getting away and making it out of the woods was Steve's only concern, once he was able to reach the wildlife area he would informed them of Michael and Jeffery.

Steve knew that he was in a tight spot with having to explain why both of his friends were killed.

Steve thought about what he was going to do once he made it back to the cabin, when his thoughts went to Jeffery's truck.

Having been hunting with Jeffery numerous times Steve knew where Jeffery kept the spare ignition key to the truck.

Steve kept the small creek to his right remembering that when they walked away from the cabin the creek was to their left.

Steve heard the panicking scatter of frightening birds leaving the trees as he made his way through the brush.

Occasionally Steve would look behind him for the man in a ballerina's tutu, and since the fog was so dense it was hard to tell exactly where we was, but he knew the man in a ballerina's tutu was close and that he could not stop.

As Steve rested against a tree, thoughts of his friends, Jeffery and Michael went through his mind.

He could not understand what made Jeffery snap like that... he'd known Jeffery for years, and while Jeffery could be obnoxious at times he wasn't a violate person.

Steve bent over to rest and massage his ankle which he knew for certain had swollen two maybe three times its normal size.

Resting against a large oak tree Steve saw coming through the fog, the man in the ballerina's tutu.

The truck was only a couple hundred yards, if only Steve's ankle would hold out.

Steve reached up and grabbed his KA BAR from its sleeve wondering how the man in a ballerina's tutu could have caught up with him so quickly.

Steve knew he had to get moving but the pain in his ankle was becoming more and more unbearable, not to mention that the rain had started picking up along with the fog which resembled pea soup.

Steve stopped in his tracks looking left and then to his right as he heard the laughter and singing of those creepy kids again, who were singing...

La-la-la-la-la-la-, la-la-la-la-la-la,

Teddy Bear Soda Crackers

Hunter on the run

Think you you're going to make it out

Teddy says think again...

"La-la-la-la-la-la-, la-la-la-la-la-la."

So many different things were going through Steve's head, especially hoping that the spare key was where it's supposed to be.

Steve also wondered how far he'd have to drive to get a signal on his cell phone to get the police or sheriff up here.

Steve noticed that the man in the ballerina's tutu was no longer behind him, and rested a few more minutes.

With the cabin and Jeffery's truck in eyesight, Steve felt satisfied that he would make it, and no longer being chased by the man in a ballerina's tutu, Steve made a sad miscalculation.

Could the man in a ballerina's tutu have ran ahead of Steve, so he slowed his pace down and began carefully looking all around him and as he did, he turned just in time to see another huge male deer confidently walking through the woods.

Steve's eye was not only trained on the deer but the background shapes for any possible movements.

Steve turned and as he did felt the pain from his ankle rushing up into his head, saying...

"Just another couple hundred feet and I'm there."

Steve raised his right leg to take a step and when he lifted his leg in the air, he heard movements coming from his right.

Steve looked to his right and saw the creepy kids coming through the woods, singing and laughing.

They were spread out a few feet apart against the back drop of the fog, appearing almost ghostly, and as they moved their feet were not touching the ground, Steve notice something even more unusual.

The children were…passing right through the trees! They didn't go around or duck down but they passed right through the trees coming straight towards Steve.

Just when Steve thought he had gotten away from the man in a ballerina's tutu, he's got to deal with a bunch of creepy kids.

Steve started to feel a sense of relief because now he could report the accident, and get some help for his ankle, help from the man in a ballerina's tutu who was chasing him but that warm sense of relief suddenly turned cold as ice.

Though the cabin and the truck were a short distance ahead… Steve had to climb up hill in the rain which was turning the solid ground to a mountain of muddy mush.

Though giving up was not in Steve's nature the pain in his ankle was challenging Steve close to reexamine that.

Steve realized that he had a real dilemma which demanded fast decisions. With his back against the tree, Steve really wanted to take off his boot to inspect his ankle because the pain had intensified.

Steve knew he was not going to have but one shot at climbing up the hill. He hesitated at first, and then when he thought about the man in the ballerina's tutu and wanting to see Wendi's face, gave him some added incentive to climb the hill.

A mile behind Steve laid the bodies of his two friends and somewhere nearby was the man in the ballerina's tutu and those creepy spooky kids.

The hunting site rental office was another ten miles but on level ground. As the rain intensified Steve knew that there was no way in hell that he could go another mile yet ten miles on foot.

Judging from the amount of pain Steve was in as he tried to raise his foot off of the ground that the thought of hoofing it a mile uphill in the rain to the truck was asking a lot, but Steve had no other choice.

Steve needed some relief for his ankle which was now throbbing uncontrollably. Slowly Steve tried to lower his foot to the ground and gently apply pressure, but the pain raced up to his head.

Steve knew that his ankle was in bad shape and the more he ran and hobbled on it, the more damage he was doing to it and without proper medical attention, the threat of infection and possibly losing his foot was becoming more likely.

Steve looked around the woods for a fallen branch which he could use as a cane, but everywhere he looked the branches were either too small or too large.

At any rate Steve was running out of time because he could hear the grunting sounds of the man in a ballerina's tutu behind him.

Steve scanned the area and after spotting the section of hill which was not the steepest, slowly started the one mile hike up hill towards the cabin, thinking...

"C'mon Steve climb this fucking hill and you're out of this nightmare!"

Steve had taken a deep breath and was about to move when he heard a snap.

Not the kind of snap when someone steps on a twig and breaks it, but a loud snap as though someone had just snapped a branch or piece of wood over their knee.

Steve continued at a steady pace but being very cautious, being very careful because one slip and it's all down a muddy embankment.

Steve thought about a time in Vietnam when he was out on patrol and they had to secure a hill top in the Shau Valley.

It had been raining for over 2 days and every time the unit tried climbing the hill, they would slide back down after only gaining a few feet.

A friend of Steve's named Private George Drisco, a farm boy came up with an ingenious plan to get up the hill.

From cutting and sharpening two branches he was able to stick them into the mud, and pull himself up.

Steve remembered that little trick and was making headway up the hill, thinking...

"Only a few more feet and I'd be at the top of the hill."

Just a couple more feet and Steve would be at the gravel road which led to the truck and the cabin.

Steve saw a tree up above him that had a long branch extending downward and reached for it.

Steve reached out to grab hold of branch and as he pulled himself up he saw the man in a ballerina's tutu above him.

Steve hollered as the branch slipped out from his grasp and he began rolling and tumbling down into the ravine.

Coming to rest at the bottom of the ravine, Steve screamed in agony as he could feel a bone protruding through his ankle inside of his boot.

Steve grabbed his leg and a look of horror came on his face as he noticed his left foot was twisted and pointing completely backwards.

Steve lay at the bottom of the ravine in agony and then lost consciousness.

When Steve came to he had no idea how long he been out, nor did he care where the man in a ballerina's tutu was.

Seeing the condition that his left ankle was in Steve laid back and put his arm up to his mouth and screamed, thinking that he wasn't spared the horror of Vietnam to die back home in the woods in a muddy ravine.

Steve knew he had to be about living and not dying. He knew that he was going to have to try climbing the hill again, and he'd have to make it...man in a sissy ballerina's tutu or not.

Steve knew that he was going to have to climb that hill with two hands and one leg. He knew that he was not going to be able to use his left leg or stop once he started.

Steve looked up the hill, but the man in the ballerina's tutu was nowhere in sight, nor where the creepy kids.

Steve said to himself...

"Okay, on the count of ten, I'm going to start crawling, and I'm not going to stop until I make it to the truck."

Chapter 9
The Search

19378 Austin Drive
Lancaster, Ohio

Reggie knew better than to interfere with an ongoing investigation but this was his sister and his partner, and Reggie had questions he needed answers to.

While Reggie was at the crime scene he discovered a small blue address book belonging to Amy, when he looked inside of the car, pocketing it without informing Det. Horton.

The drive from Columbus to Amy's house in Lancaster would have been a far more pleasant drive, had it not been for the rain which had started coming down again.

Being a seasoned cop normally Reggie would have shared the information he discovered had it not been for one thing.

In the little blue address book, there was an entry dated three days ago, saying...

"Thanks for the phone coach...I'm using it every day."

The problem with that entry was, Reggie bought the phone for Amy ten years earlier when they were first partnered up.

Detectives and police officers generally keep a secret hiding place, which only their partners know about.

The trouble with the entry for Reggie was, when he bought Amy the wall phone, it was a faux. It was an old nineteen sixties wall kitchen phone, which Reggie installed himself.

The phone was only a shell of a phone with a secret panel underneath.

Most law enforcement members have similar methods for information that they want shielded, which is only known to their partner.

Reggie picked up on the clue Amy left him in her address book by mentioning the phone.

Reggie knew that Amy was trying to tell him that I left you some information behind the phone.

Reggie's mind raced as to what could be hidden there, because he and Amy had no unsolved cases the whole time they were partners, except for the serial killer case, which was still ongoing.

Reggie and Amy were merely rookies fresh out of the academy and their only involvement in that case was when a new District Attorney developed a cold case division, and Reggie and Amy were assigned to that unit.

The case was known as the Red Ribbon murders. In nineteen nifty-four, police began finding bodies of mutilated men and woman all over central Ohio, and the links to these cases were a red ribbon was attached to the victim's apartment or house door, and all of the victims were mutilated.

Reggie's mind raced as to what Amy could have left him. As he drew closer and closer to Lancaster his only concern was hoping that he would be able to come and go undetected.

Reggie approached the street Amy lived on, and in noticing no patrol cars, marked or unmarked, Reggie decided to park along the street several houses down from Amy's.

Reggie sat in his car going through Amy's blue book and monitoring the traffic in the area before leaving his car.

Gaining access to Amy's house was not going to be a problem since Amy and Reggie exchanged spare keys to their houses when they were partnered up.

The rain was coming down harder which gave Reggie the perfect time to slip into her house.

Removing Amy's key from a chain around his neck, Reggie proceeded down the side walk and up the steps leading to her house.

While Reggie walked along the side of the house, he heard voices like singing and laughing as he walked pass the side window.

Reggie went to the back door, and slowly unlocked the door and entered.

The singing and laughing that Reggie heard when he was outside, was in fact coming from the living room of Amy's house.

Reggie drew his gun and cautiously crept down the hallway towards the living room. As soon as Reggie approached the living room he felt alongside of the wall for the light switch with his gun in his right hand.

The laughter and singing which Reggie heard was now silent.

The first thing Reggie noticed was several days of unopened mailed gathered under the mail door slot, and Reggie knew there was little time before members of his department would be on its way.

Walking through the living room to the kitchen Reggie saw the black and gold wall phone, and proceeded to remove it from the wall.

To the unsuspecting eye it looked like an old rotary dial wall phone against old paisley wall paper, but to the trained eye, it revealed so much more.

There was no electrical connection wiring, and the wall paper around the base of the phone was taped with double sided scotch tape.

Before Reggie could take another step he heard the sound of one of the doors creaking and he stopped, turned and cut the light out.

Standing in the darkness Reggie's first thought was that members of the department had arrived until something caught Reggie's attention.

Footsteps! Multiple small footsteps could be heard coming from upstairs, and then the sounds of children laughing and singing started.

"*La-la-la-la-la-la-, la-la-la-la-la-la,*

They were the sounds of children as Reggie stood thinking who all of these children in the house were?

The voices of the children grew louder and louder and more demonic sounding...

"La-la-la-la-la-la-, la-la-la-la-la-la."

Teddy Bear Soda Crackers,

Big man by the phone;

Teddy Bear, cut up Amy;
Port Clinton, you should go...
"La-la-la-la-la-la-, la-la-la-la-la-la"!

Suddenly the voices and the sounds of the footsteps stopped.

Reggie was about to take a step when suddenly lights from a car shone through the front room window.

Reggie quietly and quickly walked towards the back door thinking it was someone from his department pulling up when the lights disappeared.

With his hand on the back door knob Reggie slowly started turning the knob, when the front door bang rang twice.

Reggie knew it would only be a matter seconds before they came around to the back door, Reggie stood with his back against the kitchen wall and waited, but no one came to the back door.

Reggie watched as the car lights shone through the window again, and as the car backed out of the driveway.

Reggie's main focus was on getting to the phone and finding whatever it was Amy had left for him.

Not wanting to risk anyone else seeing lights on and coming to the house, Reggie kept the lights out and used the wall to guide him to where he had seen the phone.

Reggie carefully removed the tape revealing an access panel behind the phone, when Amy's house phone rang.

Stopping and stepping into the living room, Reggie stood near the phone which sat on a small desk and listened to a message being recorded.

Reggie stood there in disbelief as he listened to the message. It sounded at first like a woman's voice talking very low and then it grew louder into an almost mechanical and demonic tone...

"La-la-la-la-la-la-, la-la-la-la-la-la
Teddy Bear Soda Crackers,
Poor Reggie is on edge

Port Clinton, Take a trip

Count the body's dead.

La-la-la-la-la-la-, la-la-la-la-la-la."

One thing was clear whoever was calling Amy's phone was leaving the message for him...

"What the hell!"

Reggie said to himself.

Reggie walked back into the kitchen and removed the phone from the wall and retrieved a small box which Amy had placed in the wall behind the phone.

Not wanting to spend any more time at Amy's than he had to Reggie turned to leave out through the back door when something cold grabbed his ankle causing him to jump.

Reggie bolted to the door and as he opened it fled out and down the street to his car.

Reggie sat in his car trying to open the box which he discovered was locked. Reggie decided to head home and examine the contents of the box in private and away from Amy's.

Reggie started his car and started to drive off when the sounds of sirens came up behind him fast. Reggie ducked down a little over towards the passenger side as the emergency ambulance raced past him.

Reggie pulled into his carport and cut the engine off and began trying to open the box with his knife, when the door to his house opened and his wife Perry came out with a bag of trash.

Reggie laid the box on top of the car as he went to greet Perry.

Perry threw her arms around Reggie and kissed and hugged him, saying...

"Oh Reg...I'm so sorry Det. Horton's wife Shirley, called a little while ago and told me about Amy."

Reggie embraced Perry for a moment and pulled away from her and said...

"Honey I just don't get it...I mean I'm trying to wrap my head around this thing but nothing's adding up."

Perry gently grabbed Reggie's hand and said as she began walking towards the house....

"*Reg, you've told me a million times, nothing in this crazy world adds up anymore...I've got dinner ready, and I'll get you a nice cold one.*"

Reggie stopped Perry, patting her on the behind and said...

"*I'll be in about ten minutes...I got something I need to do.*"

Perry went into the house as Reggie took the box from the top of his car and walked over towards his work and sat the box on the table and sat down in his chair.

Reggie fished around in the drawer until he came across his pocket knife. Pulling out the finger nail file from the knife he inserted it into the lock until the latch flipped open.

Before opening the box, Reggie got up from the bench and went inside as Perry handed him a cold beer.

Drawing a deep breath Reggie raised the lid of the box as his eyes fixed on three items in the box.

A Dairy, which he had seen Amy writing in numerous times, an old skeleton key shinning as if it were just made with a red ribbon tied to it, and a map of Ohio with the route traced from Columbus to Port Clinton.

When Reggie opened Amy's diary he noticed Amy had made numerous entries about receiving strange calls in the middle of the night and finding messages about children being murder, on a farm in Port Clinton.

Amy's latest entry Amy wrote....

"*Going to dinner with Jerry, coach and Perry. Tell coach about the evidence.*"

Next Reggie looked at the shiny skeleton key with the red ribbon tied to it with gold etched lettering which read...

"15368 SR one sixty-three PC."

Reggie picked up the map and re-read the etching again...

"*One-five-three-six-eight, State Route one-sixty-three, Port Clinton.*"

Reggie knew that the skeleton key with the red ribbon was tied to the serial killer case that he and Amy worked on with the state police a year earlier.

He knew that somehow the killer or killers had drawn Amy back into the case or was leaving her a clue.

Reggie placed the box underneath the driver's seat and told Perry about his plans to go up to Port Clinton. Perry had a fondness for Amy and understood Reggie's reasoning for wanting to go, but was worried about Reggie's decision to go to Port Clinton.

Reggie told Perry he wanted to go within the hour but Perry convinced Reggie to wait until the morning and get some sleep and to get a fresh start in the morning and that she'd go with him.

Port Clinton is at the most northern tip of Ohio bordering Lake Erie, and ninety-seven miles northward and you cross over into Canada.

So while it is wet and cold in Columbus, the weather in Port Clinton was considerably worse.

Reggie shook off his wet cold clothes and proceeded to the bedroom with his beer, as Perry followed behind him saying...

"Sweetheart, I'm not trying to stop you because I know you got to do this but...it's cold, wet, and you won't reach Port Clinton until the wee hours in the morning, and then what?"

Sipping the last few swigs of his beer, Reggie said...

"Honey, I get what you're saying...I do, I just want to get up there and find out what Amy uncovered because it could tell me who and why Amy and Jerry were murdered."

Perry returned back to the bedroom as Reggie was going through his drawers and packing a large duffle bag, when Perry entered and Reggie said...

"Thanks Perry did you do laundry or something...I'm looking for my brown sweater and corduroy pants...."

Perry pointed over to the corner of the bedroom and said...

"Honey they're right over there... look let me pack you and me a bag, why don't you go on back downstairs, or better yet take a hot shower and close your eyes for a bit."

Reggie turned and saw the large bag against the nightstand and said...

"Hell no... no way you're going..."

With that said the doorbell rang. Reggie peeked out of the upstairs window, but didn't see any recognizable cars parked along the street or in their drive way.

Perry went downstairs to the door and peeked out the peep hole and after seeing nobody, begin unlocking the door.

Perry turned around sharply as she heard the sound of Reggie behind her inserting a magazine into his pistol.

Perry stopped and stood to the side, because Reggie's movements meant there might be trouble. Reggie motioned to Perry to stay back as he opened the door.

Reggie opened the door with his pistol drawn and seeing no one, looked both ways and shut the door not knowing that a skeleton key with a red ribbon around it, was left on the outside handle of the door.

Reggie came back into the living room where Perry was standing and said...

"Must've been the wind and storm triggering the doorbell."

Reggie sat down to fried chicken, green beans and mashed potatoes and corn muffins, as Perry bought him another beer and kissed on the neck, saying...

"It'll be okay just, eat and we'll get some sleep, and in the morning everything will look a little better."

Reggie knew that Perry was trying as hard as she knew to console him but there would be no consoling him not after just losing a partner and sister of ten plus years.

Reggie and Perry turned in for the night. The cold rain and expected dropping temperatures was ideal sleeping weather but Reggie found himself unable to fall asleep.

Perry turned away from Reggie dragging most of the covers with her, so Reggie decided to get up and make coffee and think about his plans once he arrived in Port Clinton the following morning.

Reggie stood in the living room drinking his coffee and watching the remains of the rain and high winds which was ripping through Columbus, and all the while his thoughts were on Amy.

All night the winds had been howling with gust up to forty miles an hour, blowing broken branches from the trees all over Reggie's front porch and yard.

Normally on a night like this, Reggie would have been planning Saturday's yard work but Reggie's mind was preoccupied with Amy, as he thought...

"I'll deal with the yard when I get back from Port Clinton or I'll get one of the yard service companies to deal with it, but I got to find out what Amy was working on."

Standing at the window with the drapes slightly open, Reggie watched as the wind tossed a branch at the window where Reggie was standing causing him to jump back, from fear of it shattering the glass.

Reggie gathered himself and then he saw the reflection in the glass of a little girl standing behind him.

Not thinking or knowing what his next move was going to be Reggie slowly turned, and as he did, saw the little girl standing behind him.

There was a little girl in a ragged torn white dress about three, maybe four feet tall. Messy strawberry hair with a usually large head with big bulging dark eyes staring at him giggling.

Reggie took a step backwards and before he could do or say anything he heard the sound of children's voices laughing and singing in a low pitched tone, saying...

"La–la–la–la–la–la–, la–la–la–la–la–la

Teddy Bear Soda Crackers,

Teddy will not stop,

Port Clinton you will find me

It's you I'm going to stalk...

"La–la–la–la–la–la–, la–la–la–la–la–la."

The girl in the white torn dress pointed her finger and then smiled at Reggie and then headed to go upstairs.

Reggie sat his coffee down and followed after the little girl stopping at the sofa, to retrieve his gun from under the cushion.

While Reggie was checking his gun he heard the sound of little feet chugging up the steps, and the voices of children giggling together.

Reggie made it to the stairs in time to see the children going into his bedroom, and the little girl in the white dress heading back down the steps towards Reggie.

Reggie pointed his gun at the little girl's head, when she said...

"Reggie, Reggie, Reggie, go ahead and shoot we're waiting on you and Perry ...go ahead shoot, but the gun won't work!"

Just then the little girl disappeared from the bottom of the steps and then reappeared at the top of the steps pointing at the bedroom door and waving for Reggie to come up.

Reggie raised his gun at the little girl and before firing six times, said...

"If you don't stop I'll put some holes in that ugly-ass head of yours."

Reggie pulled the trigger and fired six times as he watched as the shells ejecting from the gun, landing at his feet.

Reggie picked up two of the bullets and noticed that the firing pin had made connection with the bullets, but had failed to fire.

Reggie screamed for Perry as he bolted up the steps...

"Perry...Perry!"

Reaching the bedroom door which was fully open, Reggie saw the little girl climbing on the bed and straddling over top of Perry, who was still sound asleep and snoring, unaware of what was going on.

Reggie tried to enter the room but found himself being forced on both knees on the floor, writhing in pain, as one of the children had found Reggie's Taser, and shot Reggie in the back.

Reggie's six foot five, two hundred and ninety-pound frame was no match for the electrical shock and pain that the Taser delivered.

Reggie tried struggling against the pain but it was no use. Grabbing his head and dropping to the floor, Reggie saw the girl straddling Perry, and a thick dark vapor entering her nose.

Just as the shock from the Taser had worn off...The alarm clock rang out.

Perry turned over and shook Reggie who was fast asleep and snoring said...

"*Hey Hun...time to get up, we're still going to Port Clinton this morning...right?*"

Reggie opened his eyes, and propped himself up on his elbows, looking all around the bedroom.

Reggie sat up on the edge of the bed rubbing his back, not believing what had just happened, saying to Perry...

"*What the hell....*"

Perry was getting socks and her long johns from the top drawer, when Reggie ran past her going down stairs.

Reggie turned the light on at the bottom of the steps, and got down on his knees picking up six bullets and his gun which lay on the floor.

Perry was heading towards the bathroom when she saw Reggie at the bottom of the steps on his knees and said...

"*Gosh Reg...did you have a rough night? You were tossing and turning and talking in your sleep...shoot, you almost hit me in the face with your elbow.*"

Reggie looked down at himself and noticed that he was in his pajama bottoms and a tee shirt and said to Perry...

"*Perry, how'd I get in my PJ's and tee shirt, the last thing I remember, I was downstairs dealing with this...oh never mind, will you come down here for a minute?*"

Perry walked down the steps and kissed Reggie as he stood up showing Perry his gun and the six bullets and said...

"*Rough one my ass. What do you think about this?*"

Perry said sarcastically...

"*Okay... let me guess is it a gun and six bullets?*"

Reggie asked Perry to sit down and said...

"*Look I'm about to tell you something that is going make you think I'm drunk, or I'm losing my mind, or a little of both...but what I need you to do is, listen.*"

Reggie sat down and explained to Perry about the little girl, about how he shot at her but the bullets didn't fire and what had happened in the bedroom.

Perry turned her head sideways looking at Reggie and said...

"Really Reg, are you serious? You don't remember coming out the shower and then going downstairs for another beer...gosh...how much did you have to drink after I fell asleep?"

Reggie again tried explaining to Perry that he only drank several beers, and that there is no way in hell that everything that happened with the little girl, was some damn nightmare.

Perry told Reggie she was going into the kitchen to start coffee and then she was going up to take her shower and suggested to Reggie that he take it easy and try not to get all stressed out, that they had a long drive ahead of them.

Reggie finished his coffee and packed his service revolver and his back up, nine millimeter, and a pair of bolt cutters, and the strange key he found at Amy's.

The weather was cold and damp and according to the forecast for Port Clinton, it was supposed to be cold and windy with a high of thirty-eight degrees.

Perry had just walked downstairs from showering, dressed in jeans, boots, and a brown pull over sweater and carrying her blue jean coat.

Reggie stood up and walked over to her, hugging and kissing her saying...

"Mmm... you are one sexy woman...you know that?"

Perry kissed Reggie back and said...

"Reg, after all these years of being married you still know how to say all the right things...by the way are you feeling better?"

Reggie nodded yes, as he continued hugging and kissing Perry, gently pinning Perry against the wall.

Perry and Reggie lost all thoughts about where they were heading, as Perry dropped her coat and Reggie began unloosening Perry's jeans.

Perry removed her sweater and said to Reggie softly...

"Damn baby you're going to mess up my hair and everything."

Reggie passionately kissed Perry's neck and said as they both dropped to the floor...

"Your hair's not the only thing I intend to mess up."

Ten minutes of serious love making ended as they heard loud banging on the front door.

Reggie struggled to get up putting on his pants and saying...

"*Damn...this had better be someone real important, damn!*"

Perry emerged from behind the sofa running into the downstairs bathroom while Reggie answer the door.

Reggie opened the door only to see no one there. As he looked out the door he noticed that a large matted bird's nest had been flung against the door by the wind.

Reggie closed the door and went to the closet for the outside broom and a garbage bag to collect the large clump of nest when he noticed an old skeleton key with a red ribbon hanging on the outside door knob.

Tying up the garbage bag Reggie removed the skeleton key from the door, and closed the door.

Fifteen minutes later Perry came out from the bathroom and saw Reggie sitting on the sofa with a puzzled look on his face and said...

"*Who was it?*"

Reggie held the skeleton key up to Perry and said...

"*Not who, but what. The wind tossed a bird's nest out of the tree against the door, but I found this hanging on the door knob.*"

Perry took the key from Reggie's hand and said...

"*I don't get it...an old skeleton key with a red ribbon...who would leave a key at our door...I don't get it!*"

Reggie explained to Perry that he had found a similar key in a box that Amy had left for him with the same etchings and explained to Perry that the case he and Amy worked on a year earlier involved a key with a red ribbon.

Reggie got up from the sofa and went out to the car port and retrieved the box from his car.

Reggie and Perry sat down examining the key from the box with the key left on their door knob when Reggie looked over at Perry and said...

"*Well one thing is clear...we'll find the answer to all of this in Port Clinton.*"

Reggie and Perry grabbed all of the things needed for their trip and headed out to the car.

As Reggie backed out of the carport, Perry unfolded the map and on a separate piece of paper wrote the directions to Port Clinton, and the address that Reggie had written down.

Chapter 10

In The Woods

The cold rain began pouring on Steve's face, wakening him as he sat moaning and in pain and surveying the damage to his left ankle.

Steve knew that the ankle bone was clearly separated from his foot, and knew the damage he sustained in the fall from the top of the hill was extremely serious.

He could feel the swelling of his left ankle against his boot, and judging from the beating of the pulse in his ankle, which was gradually building...he didn't have a lot of time before the pain would cause him to pass out again.

With both hands Steve pushed against the ground, and sat himself up against the tree, all the while scanning the area for the man in the ballerina's tutu who was at the top of the hill.

It was a mile or less to the cabin to Jeffery's truck, which was all up the hill. A climb that Steve knew he could not make in his condition.

The hunting area registration office on the other hand was over ten miles, on level ground.

Steve contemplated as to which path he could make...ten miles on level ground, or a mile up a muddy hill.

He wasn't sure he could make the ten miles, and he also knew he couldn't go one mile up hill, he didn't think his strength would hold out.

Steve looked all around for something he could use to make a splint. Whether it was going to be one, or ten miles...he knew he had to splint his ankle, to stabilize it if he was going to go anywhere.

Steve felt around with his hands through the wet leaves until he came across a two inch tree limb, which had at some point been cut down or knocked down.

It measured about thirty-six inches long. Steve reached up and pulled out his KABAR, and went to work cutting it in half.

Steve removed his coat and then his sweater. He cut both sleeves off of his sweater and positioned them under the bottom of his ankle, and the other sleeve, just below his knee.

Placing the handle of the KABAR in his mouth, Steve leaned forward and positioned his hands on both sides of his foot.

Biting down as hard as he could Steve grabbed his foot and quickly turned his foot until it was pointing in the right direction, and then he passed out.

When Steve awoke he could feel the pulsating of his separated ankle and as the pain shot up his leg he sunk his teeth into his coat and screamed.

Steve knew he had to get moving, but it became much more apparent when he noticed off to his left and in a distance, the man in the ballerina's tutu returned and was slowly advancing towards him, pushing a wheel barrel.

Using his KABAR, Steve slammed the knife's blade deep into the tree he was resting against and used it for leverage to pull himself up.

Steve stood up hugging the tree, and wiggling his KABAR up and down until he was able to pull it from the tree when something caught his eye.

The man in the ballerina's tutu with the wheel barrel who was behind and to the right of Steve, was no longer there.

Stopping and trying to figure out what to do and which way to run Steve noticed something even more twisted and strange....

There wasn't just one man in a ballerina's tutu pushing a wheel barrel, but four of them blocking any direction that Steve might take.

Immediately in front of Steve the four men in the ballerina's tutu, with wheel barrels, all dressed the same with a stupid looking clown's face began moving closer to Steve, and then stopped.

The men in the ballerina's tutus were no longer moving but they had formed a line, blocking every direction in which Steve might take, except for behind him.

Steve knew there was nothing behind him, nothing behind him except....

The bodies of his dead friends.

Steve thought to himself before he let out a yell which echoed through the woods....

"*Who are you...what the hell do you want*"!

Steve turned around and began hobbling back to the hunting area where Jeffery and Michael's body lay.

Several times Steve almost lost his balance and fell, but for some unknown reason his ankle, which should be shooting pain up his leg, was no longer hurting.

Stopping and turning to see if the men in the ballerina's tutus were still on his trail, Steve began moving faster and faster, thinking to himself...

"*If I can make it to one of the guns these sons of bitches are going to regret the day you fucked with me.*"

Steve arrived at the spot where they had been hunting...but something wasn't right! Where were the bodies, and where was the deer which had his rack stuck in the tree?

The deer tree stands were gone and all three guns were gone. Did the game warden, or some other hunters come along and get Jeffery and Michael, and if so, why aren't there any tire tracks or anything?"

Though the fog had set in, Steve knew he was in the right spot, because he noticed Jeffery's coat which he had covered Michael with.

Hearing the sounds of stomping and seeing the men in the ballerina's tutus approaching him, Steve pushed on past the clearing into the woods...when Steve made a startling discovery....

"*The scenery was different.*"

When Steve left the clearing into the woods, he immediately left a temperature of fifty degrees and fog, into low thirty-degree temperature, with a light mist.

Looking, Steve could see a few farms in the distance and a familiar sight which shouldn't be there...the farm.....David and Deanne's farm.

Steve was no longer at Woodgrain Hunting & Wild Life area, in Columbus...but Port Clinton, Ohio, when he shouted out...

"*How in the world could this be?*"

Steve took a few steps forward and then backwards, realizing he was near some kind of dimensional doorway.

When he stepped backwards he was at the Woodgrain Hunting area, and the man in the ballerina's tutus were gaining on him, but when Steve stepped forward he was looking at David and Deanne's farm, almost two hundred miles away.

Steve stood for a moment thinking...

"How in the world can this be...this kind of stuff only happens in the movies."

Two things were certain...number one, directly ahead was David and Deanne's farm in Port Clinton, and behind Steve was the hunting area, with trouble on his heels, but in any case Steve was going to have to choose which reality he wanted to be in.

One other thing which was out of place was Steve's left ankle was no longer hurting him.

When Steve took a step forward his ankle was fine and there was not a splint on his leg.

Steve stepped forward and reached down and felt his ankle and foot which were perfectly fine.

Steve looked up towards David and Deanne's farm and after seeing several cars parked in the driveway, began running to the farm, all the while knowing...

"Everything about this day wasn't right...wasn't right at all"!

In the distance Steve could see the kitchen light on in the main house, and silhouettes of two people gathered in the kitchen.

The closer Steve got to the house, the more things began to change.

Instead of seeing several cars in the driveway, one by one they disappeared and so it was the same with the silhouettes in the kitchen they too disappeared, one by one until no one was there.

Steve stopped just short of the house looking around in all directions. The first thought which came to Steve's mind was...

"How was he going to explain to Deanne and David why and how he came all the way from Columbus without his car, and secondly why he was dressed the way he was.?"

Steve rested up against the barn next to the house trying to sort out the events of what transpired over the last few minutes, when a small pile of leaves caught by a gust of wind began swirling in front of him.

The leaves swirled around then up in the air and then Steve heard laughter and singing...the same voices he had heard earlier at the hunting area, singing....

"La-la-la-la-la-la-, la-la-la-la-la-la,

Teddy Bear Soda Crackers,

No time to think

Dark, ugly things

On their way...tick...tick...tick.

La-la-la-la-la-la-, la-la-la-la-la-la?"

Steve started running towards the house and had a thought... if his ankle is okay, then maybe his cell phone was still in inside his pocket.

Patting his pockets in search of his phone while his mind began racing and praying that his hands would feel his cell phone.

He began searching all of his pockets, when he felt a vibration in his inside right coat pocket.

Pulling out his cell phone and letting out a sigh of relief, Steve looked down and saw a message from David...

"Hey man, you coming in or are you going to stay outside playing with yourself?"

Steve looked up at the house, and standing at the window beside the front door was David, peeking out the curtains at Steve.

Unable to believe what was going on Steve placed his cell back in his coat pocket and stopped and took a deep breath.

The closer Steve got to the house, the more red flags begin going off in Steve's head.

The same type of feelings that he used to get when he was on recon patrols in Vietnam, when the Viet Cong would hide in the tunnels waiting for G.I. patrols to pass them.

Steve developed a weird but useful sense about that kind of thing in the Nam. A sense which helped not only keep Steve alive but his entire squad.

Once Steve explained it to Wendi after coming back from Nam. He told her he would get this warm feeling and then everything around him would become still, as if it were frozen in time.

The nighttime noises of the jungle would suddenly become so quiet and so still that he could hear the slightest sounds and then all hell would break loose.

Steve lifted his right foot to take the first step up to the porch, when he felt the air move behind him.

Turning, Steve saw a flash out of his left eye and realized it was the man in the ballerina's tutu reaching out for him.

Steve grabbed onto the railings and kicked the man in the ballerina's tutu in the mid-section, and when he tried to kick him again, the man in the ballerina's tutu grabbed Steve's foot and flung him in the air.

Steve landed fifteen feet from the porch near the basement storm door.

Stunned but alert Steve saw an axe handle near him and picked it up and began swinging it at the man in the ballerina's tutu with all his might.

Steve took aim for the man's face, and as the man in the ballerina's tutu inched closer Steve connected with the man's head.

The force of the blow was so hard that it turned the man in the ballerina's tutu head to one side, shattering the clown's mask.

The man in the ballerina's tutu with his half cracked clown's mask, turned as if the blow from the axe didn't hurt him.

Then Steve did it right, he planted his feet as if he were a major league baseball player in the world series, in the ninth ending with the perfect pitch, and swung the axe handle with all his might and caught the man in the ballerina's tutu on the chin.

The man in the ballerina's tutu shook his head, as if to shake it off and Steve hit the man again and again. The man in the ballerina's tutu, fell to the ground, and as he did the, clown's mask flew off, exposing a hideous face.

Out of breath and holding the cracked blood stained axe handle, Steve poked the man in the ballerina's tutu several times to make sure that he was not going to be getting up.

Steve looked up at the house wondering if he should go in, and thinking why hadn't David or someone came out to help, surely they must have seen what was going on.

Steve walked slowly towards the steps, not noticing that a dark figure had engulfed the man in the ballerina's tutu, who had slowly raised to a sitting position.

Suddenly and with cat like reflexes the man in the ballerina's tutu yanked the axe away from Steve, causing Steve to fall, hitting his head on the steps.

Steve knew that with the man in the ballerina's tutu so close to him that he'd never make it up the steps.

So Steve took off running towards the back of the house shouting David's name as he ran. Steve began pounding on the back door and calling David and Deanne's name.

Steve tried turning the door knob when he saw the man in the ballerina's tutu turning the corner of the house and coming at him.

Just then the door opened and someone yanked Steve inside.

Standing inside, the kitchen Steve expected to see David or Deanne, but what he saw he was not prepared for.

A group of children aging ten years old to early teens, with misshapen heads, and eyes which sunk deep in their sockets, stood starring at Steve and pointing at Steve.

Steve immediately recognized that they were the same creepy kids that were in the woods.

Their appearances were ghastly and their faces had a grey ashen look to it and their eyes were too large for their eyes sockets.

The clothes they wore were torn and old, as if they were made in another century.

Pointing at Steve the creepy looking kids began laughing and singing...

"La-la-la-la-la-la-, la-la-la-la-la-la,

Teddy Bear, Soda Crackers,

Sitting on the bed,

First you run, then you hide,

Teddy make you dead...

La-la-la-la-la-la-, la-la-la-la-la-la."

Without his gun, or KABAR and not even the axe handle to use as a weapon, Steve screamed at the creepy kids as he ran towards the living room, when he heard the voices of David and Deanne.

As Steve entered the living room, he noticed the door to the basement was slowly shutting and the sound of footsteps descending down into the basement.

Knowing that the psycho version of 'grandpa Jones' was outside and the creepy looking kids in the other room, Steve slowly approached the basement door and stopped, calling for David and Deanne.

Pushing the basement door completely open Steve heard voices of people in the basement, when one of the voices called out his name...

"Steve"!

Steve immediately recognized the voice...it was David's, but then suddenly the voice switched to a demonic tone, and Steve started to back up the steps.

Not sure of what to do, Steve heard another voice...it was Mary's voice...

"Run Steve...get out of here!"

Mary's voice confirmed what Steve was already thinking, and that was... something was really wrong here.

Just as Steve made up his mind to turn and run he caught a foul odor coming from behind him.

Steve heard Mary scream and as he turned to run the man in the ballerina's tutu was standing in the door way of the living room and the kitchen, blocking his exit.

Steve began patting his pockets searching for something, anything to help him fight off this psycho but found nothing.

Suddenly Mary screamed louder and Steve turned his head in the direction of the basement.

Steve had only turned his head for a micro second, when out of the corner of his eye he saw the man in the ballerina's tutu take a step towards him, cutting off the only way of escape, which was through the back door.

Steve glanced to his left and then to his right, until his eyes met the Christmas gift that he and Wendi gave David and Deanne...a four piece *Santoku* knife set.

Steve grabbed the seven inch Santoku knife and turned to the man in the ballerina's tutu...which mysteriously vanished from the room.

Knowing that the man in the ballerina's tutu was somewhere in the house, along with those creepy looking kids, Steve wanted to get out of the house...but he couldn't just leave Mary.

Steve's decision to help Mary or leave the house was settled when he heard the voices of the creep kids coming from all over the house...

"La-la-la-la-la-la-, la-la-la-la-la-la,

Teddy Bear, Soda Crackers,

Time to have some fun,

Locked inside, can't get out, which way you will run

La-la-la-la-la-la-, la-la-la-la-la-la."

Steve jumped when someone started banging on the doors and the walls of the house.

Steve turned around and looked in every direction and as he did, all of the windows in the house one by began raising and slamming shut over and over.

Steve ran to the front door and as he reached for the door knob and started to open it, there was the man in the ballerina's tutu trying to get inside.

Steve slammed the door shut and bolted for the back door. Steve was running out of options. Blocking his way to the door were the creepy kids, who were still singing.

"Teddy's going to get you

Teddy's going to get you,
Got you at the farm,
BOO!"

Holding the knife out in front of him and swinging, Steve lunged at one of the kids who was the closest to him, a boy who appeared to be sixteen and five feet tall.

The boy stopped singing and stared at Steve and then held his hands out to Steve, revealing his wrists which showed signs that he had slit his wrist, saying...

"Aim here...
Cut it real deep...
Just like I once did."

Steve hollered at the boy to get out of his way and then took aim at his oversized head and swung the knife cutting him and ripping open a large gash in his forehead which did not bleed.

The boy reached up to his head with his elongated skinny fingers, and pried open the wound as a thick black greenish looking glob began oozing from the wound.

The boy opened his mouth and as he did his mouth continued to stretch three times its normal size, revealing a set of grey crooked jagged teeth.

Steve drew the knife back ready to swing again when suddenly, the boy let out an ear piercing high pitched screech.

The sound of the screech was so intense that it caused Steve to bend over, dropping the knife as he covered his ears.

With his hands covering his ears Steve ran out the door and down the steps towards the side of the house when he heard the front door open, and heavy footsteps on the front porch.

Steve quietly sneaked around the side of the house, and saw the man in the ballerina's tutu with the clown's face coming out onto the front porch, looking and searching in all directions.

Steve noticed that the high pitched screeching had stopped. Just then to his left he heard the creaking sound of a door opening.

Steve could not believe what was happening. He couldn't believe that after all that he's had to deal with in his life, that it was coming down to some weird ass shit like this.

Not far from him the outside basement door had opened and he could hear moans coming from that direction.

The rain was picking up and a creepy fog started rolling in as Steve thought to himself...

"Alright...a sick ass nut has Mary in the house, it's raining like cats and dogs, I don't know what's going on here...now what do I do?"

Steve made a decision to go towards the basement because if he started running towards what looked like the direction to the main road...for all he knew he might run into a dimensional doorway and end up right back here, or somewhere worst.

Steve had to have a plan. He had to think of some way to get out of this mess, some way to get help.

Steve decided to go to the basement...he thought he'd at least be dry and out of the weather while he tried to make some kind of sense out of all of it.

As Steve drew closer to the basement door which was slightly opened, he saw a dim light and heard voices coming from inside.

Not the voices of the creepy kids he'd heard earlier, but voices of people talking, when all of a sudden the man in the ballerina's tutu with the creepy clown's face came up from behind him, grabbed his neck and threw Steve into the basement and slammed the door shut.

Steve hit the basement wall head first and as he struggled to get on his feet he lost his balance and fell.

Steve felt his head with his fingers and came across a large gash on his scalp.

Sitting there trying to clear the cobwebs from his head, the voices he'd heard a moment ago started up again.

Steve could barely see anything in the basement let alone tell who was in the basement with him, all he knew was that the crazy man in the ballerina's tutu would be showing up soon, and he needed to get out of there.

Steve quietly and cautiously made his way towards the voices when the main door to the basement opened and the man in the ballerina's tutu slowly started coming down the steps dragging something behind him.

Steve backed up against the wall and into the darkness hoping the man in the ballerina's tutu had forgotten that he was in the basement.

Pecan Drive
Columbus, Ohio

It was around eleven-thirty pm and me and Deanne were in the bed room watching television. Our plans were to get an early start out to the farm.

I was against the ideal but Deanne insisted I either go with her or she was going alone.

Deanne felt that, since the police weren't going to do anything that the least we could do was go up to the farm...and have a look around.

Deanne sat on the edge of the bed painting her toenails while I was lying across the bed flipping through the channels with man's second best friend...the remote control, hoping she'd change her mind.

I was about to reach over and rub Deanne's back when we heard a knock at the front door followed by the constant ringing of our door bell.

I got up to go look out the window, but did not see anyone standing on the porch, nor a car in their driveway.

Not knowing if it was caused by the wind, or something hitting against the house, I headed down stairs to check.

I went to the door and then stepped out on the porch, still no one was there so he locked the door and went back to the bed room.

Deanne asked me who was at the door and he motioned that there was no one there.

It was maybe an hour later after I had cut the lights out and had fallen back asleep, when there came another loud knock on the bedroom door.

Deanne jumped up and shook me as I lay dead asleep and snoring.

Just as David awakened the knocking on the door stopped, and then the knocking started again.

David and Deanne sat in bed for a second looking at each other, quiet and listening.

There was no one in the house but the two of them, so who could it be.

After a second or two, they heard a loud crashing noise coming from the living room, like the sound of glass breaking.

The crashing noise caused Deanne to scream, who was pretty rattled at that point, and she gasped before getting up to go with David to see what was going on.

David reached the bedroom door first and opened the door only to discover no one was there.

Deanne and David went downstairs and stood in the living room and that's when they saw, there on the floor by the sofa was the vase and the flowers, along with Shone who was lapping up the water.

Both David and Deanne felt a sigh of relief knowing that perhaps it was Shone who knocked over the vase and who probably was outside their bedroom door as well.

The vase was shattered and the water and flowers were spilled all over the floor, and after shooing Shone away, knowing that there were glass shards in the water...Deanne made a startling discovery.

The table that the vase sat on, was twenty feet away from the sofa, up against the wall by the window.

There was no way Shone could have accidentally bumped into the table, and even if she had been up in the window it doesn't explain how the vase ended up twenty feet away.

The vase sat on a small table in front of the living room picture window, and twenty feet away sat the dining room table with six chairs.

Besides all of that...there was no water or glass anywhere except in front of the sofa.

Deanne let out a scream as she heard footsteps and scratching noises behind her leading up the steps.

Deanne and I both turned and followed the noises with our eyes looking up the steps, but there was no one or nothing that they could see, so Deanne grabbed me and said...

"Blue.... *something just brushed my hair and touched the back of my neck!*"

I reached into the closet for the bat, unaware that behind Deanne was a dark lone figure, which pushed Deanne onto me, causing me to fall into the closet banging my nose and forehead.

I began swinging my arms, and pushing Deanne off of me. Deanne fell backwards as I emerged from the closet with a bloody nose.

Looking at Deanne and wiping the blood from my nose onto my tee shirt, Deanne cried out as she looked behind her rubbing her ass...

"*Blue...I'm so sorry, but something pushed me...oh my God... hold on Blue, let me get you some Kleenex's...your nose is bleeding!*"

Deanne grabbed a handful of Kleenex's from the table and handed them to me, as I was sitting in a chair holding my head back.

Deanne attempted to help me by wiping away the blood from my cheek as I pushed her hand away when Deanne said...

"*Blue...I told you I was sorry, but something pushed me hard into you. You know I wouldn't do something like that on purpose?*"

I threw up my hands in the air signaling, that there isn't anyone in the house and after the bleeding had stopped...walked back over to the closet.

Right before I reached into the closet I turned around and motioned with my hand for Deanne to stay right where she was.

I grabbed the baseball bat and walked over towards the steps, with Deanne directly behind me.

Deanne and I slowly made our way upstairs, as I tapped the baseball bat on each step, as we headed upstairs.

Deanne and I went back into our bedroom and after I checked the other rooms upstairs and every conceivable place that someone could have hid in, came to the conclusion...it was probably noises that a house makes when the heat is on...or was it?

Resting with the thoughts that perhaps Shone... did somehow knock over the vase, and that the knocking noises were the house making noises because of the heat being on, they settled back into the bedroom.

Before settling into bed Deanne walked over and stood looking out of the window, while I surfed the television channels.

Deanne propped up the head of the bed up with pillows to watch television and mid-way into the program, the television picture started showing only static.

Every few seconds into the movie, the picture would turn to static for a few seconds and the go back to normal.

Deanne noticed that I had dosed off and it would only be a matter of time before she was well asleep as well, so she cut the television off.

Looking at the clock Deanne saw that it was five minutes to midnight, and I must have already been calling hogs.

Deanne thought about going down stairs and getting a snack, but from all the noise that she had heard earlier...crawled up under the blankets and snuggled up close to me.

It wasn't long before Deanne fell asleep and joined me in a duel of snoring. Deanne was suddenly awakened by the blaring volume on the television, and looked over at me as she said...

"Blue...Blue what's going on. I'm trying to sleep; can't you turn the television down a little?"

I was lifting the blankets and sheets searching for the remote, until Deanne reached on her side of the nightstand and handed him the remote control.

Picking up the remote control and turning the volume down, Deanne said...

"Blue...I turned the television off, because you were asleep, why'd you turn the television on again?"

I was looking for the pad and paper to tell Deanne, that I didn't touch the television, it was on and woke me up too, when the television picture again became static, and the volume increased until it became unbearable.

Deanne tried turning the volume down, and when that didn't work she tried pushing the power button to cut the television off, but it would not go off.

I reached over and grabbed the remote from Deanne's hand and smacked it against my leg several times thinking the batteries were loose or jarred, and tried cutting the television off, but instead of the television turning off, the channels began changing.

I looked over at Deanne who was covering her ears and walking over and unplugged the television, which went off immediately.

I sat on the bed, and then pulled the cover of the remote control off to inspect the batteries. Once I saw that the batteries were in properly, I laid the remote on the nightstand, and glanced at the clock which read...

"Two-Twenty."

Deanne asked me if the batteries were in the right way, because she replaced the batteries a day ago and I nodded yes that they were in correctly before turning out the light and getting in bed.

Deanne and I both lay back in the bed to get what little sleep we could before getting up to get to go to Port Clinton.

Deanne and I had both fallen into a deep sleep when the television came on again. The volume wasn't loud but the television set was on, even though I had unplugged it before falling to sleep.

Deanne turned from her side and onto her stomach mumbling to me to quit messing with the TV, when the volume grew loud.

The television changed from one channel to another until there was static. The static slowly disappeared and an old black and white movie was on.

Deanne threw the covers off her head and said...

"Look Blue if you're going to sit up all night playing with that, I'm going into the other bedroom..."

Before Deanne could finish, she looked at the television and said...

"Blue...Blue...correct me if I'm wrong, but doesn't that look familiar?"

Waking I shrugged my shoulders, and repositioned the pillows from behind my head to my lap when Deanne tapped me again, only a little harder...

"Blue look! What in the fuck......that's the house at the farm! Blue look at the picture on the mantle...it's the picture taken of us when we were in Jamaica...Blue I'm telling you, that's the farm!"

David got up out of bed and walked over to the television to get a closer look. Deanne was beginning to shout at David as he turned looking pale.

She noticed that someone was video tapping the inside of their farm house in Port Clinton.

The camera went from room to room and then to the basement door, and down the steps.

I had the unplugged television cord in my hand, not looking at the screen, when Deanne screamed!

Turning my attention to Deanne and then to the television, I noticed on the screen black and white grainy images.

Instead of seeing a movie or even a commercial, there was an image of a basement in black and white with distorted images in the background.

I sat on the bed beside Deanne looking at what appeared to be a home-movie with a girl tied up in a chair.

As Deanne and I sat glued to the images on the screen, the image of the girl grew closer and closer, until her face filled the entire screen.

Suddenly the picture was reduced to normal size, as Deanne and I plainly saw that the girl on the screen was Mary.

It appeared as if she had been crying by the smudges of make up around her eyes and down her cheeks. When the angle of the camera changed, Deanne cried...

"Oh my God!"

Mary was partially nude only wearing panties and a bra, scratches and bruises covered Mary's entire body.

Deanne and I could see light coming through the small basement window, as Mary's outstretched hands frantically searched in front of her.

Deanne looked over at me as she reached for her phone and said...

"Oh my God Blue, Mary is at the farm...she's at the farm Blue!"

Deanne looked in horror as she attempted to dial Det. Fannichuci's number and heard...

"The number you have reached is not working at this time, if you need assistance, please stay on the line...or come to the FARM!"

Deanne closed her phone and then tried calling Kristin, and then Tim's number but no one answered at either number.

Just then the television screen which at first showed a black and white picture...turned to static.

I was scrambling for a piece of paper to write a note for Deanne, when Deanne tapped me on the shoulder and pointed to the television screen again and said...

"Look Blue!"

The static on the television screen disappeared and standing by the steps in the basement was a man in the ballerina's tutu.

The light which shone through the basement only provided enough light to see a small section of the basement.

Deanne and David could only see a grainy outline of Mary along the basement wall, about twenty feet from the man in the ballerina's tutu who was slowly walking in her direction when Deanne cried out...

"Mary, stop...get out of there!"

Deanne turned to David and told him that they've got to get the police or somebody up there to help Mary, as David wrote to Deanne saying...

"We're not leaving this house... you can call the police and let them handle this. You see what's going on, what are we supposed to do...go up there and do what?"

David and Deanne got off of the bed and stood right in front of the television set, as the image of Mary covered the entire screen when a voice in a distorted mechanical voice...

"Deanne...Deanne, help me!"

David and Deanne looked at each other, and then David walked over to the night stand and picked up Deanne's cell phone.

Dialing Mary's number again, David handed the phone to Deanne. Deanne reminded David that she already tried calling Mary's number, when David wrote down on paper...

"Mary's playing a sick joke...for over twenty years, Mary has always called you Dee, not Deanne?"

Deanne pointed to the television screen as David turned around.

In shock, David and Deanne watched as the man in the ballerina's tutu wearing the clown's face appeared next to Mary with a cell phone in his hand.

Suddenly Deanne's phone began vibrating...both David and Deanne starred at the phone for a moment before Deanne opened the phone to answer it, and heard...

"So you think this is a sick joke...is what happened to Wendi a sick joke too...your mute boyfriend doesn't really think it's a joke... he's just too scared to come up here."

Deanne looked over at David and said...

"Now what the hell did that mean...damn Blue, he's the one that probably murdered Wendi...we got to do something?"

The man in the ballerina's tutu grabbed Mary violently by the hair and put the cell phone to Mary's lips, as she began screaming and crying.

Deanne heard Mary's screams over the phone as they stood and watched in horror.

Next the man in the ballerina's tutu without hanging up the phone laid it on the table next to Mary...it was plain that the man in the ballerina's tutu wanted David and Deanne to hear what he was about to do.

Deanne screamed for David to look at the screen. The man in the ballerina's tutu was standing in front of Mary, with a large needle threading it with black twine.

Mary was crying and pleading with the man in the ballerina's tutu to let her go, but the man in the ballerina's tutu seemed more intent on Deanne and David's reaction than on Mary's pleas.

Just then David grabbed the television remote control and pressed the record button...but nothing happened.

Suddenly Deanne let out a loud cry and covered her mouth!

The man in the ballerina's tutu had pinched and held Mary's lips together and inserted the large needle through her lips sewing her mouth shut.

Mary started pounding and kicking at the man in the ballerina's tutu as he continued inserting the large needle through the top lip and then through the bottom lip, as blood began trickling down her chin and onto the man's hand.

David and Deanne could see how hard Mary was struggling to get away from the man in the ballerina's tutu and how this was not somebody's idea of a sick joke.

Once the man in the ballerina's tutu had sewn Mary's entire mouth closed, he grabbed a small can with a small brush and began sealing up her mouth with glue.

For what seemed like an eternity only lasted a minute...a minute of sheer horror.

The man in the ballerina's tutu with the clown's face, covered the entire television screen.

David and Deanne heard him say in the voice of porky the pig... *"Th-th-th-th-th...that's all, folks!"*

As soon as those words were uttered, David and Deanne could hear the theme to the looney tunes as the television went blank.

Deanne started shaking and crying and said...

"What the hell, what the hell...why did he say, to ask you, what's going on Blue?"

David took a note tablet from the night stand and wrote...

"Do what? I tried telling you, it's the Doppelgangers, but you wouldn't believe me...now do you?

Deanne looked over and cut David off and in a loud voice said...

"Blue don't start that evil Doppelgangers bullshit. This crap is crazy....this is about a sick psycho torturing people, not spirits and things like that. Blue you knew something was going on...Damn you Blue!"

David walked out of the bedroom on his way to the bathroom shaking his head. Deanne picked up a pillow and flung it at David, which hit the door as he left.

Regardless of what was going on and how messed up things were looking, David was not interested in going anywhere near the farm, but he knew that Deanne was going to do something that would drag him into it.

David stood in the bathroom brushing his teeth and then lowered his head over the sink...as so many thoughts ran through his mind.

David though about what happened six months ago at the farm, and how he went through a living nightmare once.

A nightmare so real much like a bad dream which he continues reliving day after day...but now Deanne is seeing and hearing what he hoped was gone forever...only this was different.

David stood at the mirror thinking...

"Okay, me and Deanne gets to the farm and by some odd chance Mary is there...she's not just going to be watching a movie and eating Bon Bon's! If the voices and the messages, and that twisted psycho is there...then what in the hell are we supposed to do?"

David lathered up his face to shave when something from inside the mirror reached out and grabbed David by the neck mashing his face smearing shaving cream up against the mirror.

Knowing that he couldn't cry out David started knocking off all of the things on the sink counter onto the floor...hoping Deanne would hear the noise and come in to investigate.

David's face was being mashed harder and harder into the mirror, when suddenly the mirror opened up and David's head was pulled inside the mirror.

First there was darkness, and then David saw a faint light emerging. Looking all around and then back to the dim light which was getting brighter and brighter, David heard voices, over lapping conversations.

Still engulfed in darkness David saw Mary standing in the living room at the farm calling out in Auntie Em's voice, from the Wizard of Oz...

"Where are you, I can't see you?"

The image of Mary and her voice quickly faded when David saw Deanne. Deanne was downstairs in the apartment, going out the door to the car and saying...

C'mon Blue. We're never going to make it to Port Clinton, if you keep jerking around."

As Deanne's image began to fade, grotesque images began to emerge. First the girl in the white dirty dress appeared, and then the man in the ballerina's tutu with the clown's face, and then those creepy kids with the large heads appeared.

Then they all began pointing at David and saying...

"You fooled us once, but not again

Come to the farm, or we're coming there!"

Just then David jumped as something grabbed his arm. David was no longer inside the mirror but in his bathroom, standing at the mirror with a face full of shaving cream.

Deanne stood behind me saying...

"Blue you've been standing there just looking in the mirror for almost five minutes... I thought you fell asleep?"

I quickly grabbed a towel and began wiping the shaving cream off my face, which already had begun to dry up.

Deanne turned around and began going out the door mumbling...

"I've already loaded up the car, C'mon Blue, we're never going to get to Port Clinton if you keep jerking around...we're going, and that's all there is to it."

At the sound of those words I dropped the razor and stood there looking at Deanne through the mirror as she left the bathroom.

I turned and placed the towel in the sink, and as I did that I saw the grotesque face of the girl in the dirty white dress emerge from the mirror and wink at me, and then disappear.

I jumped away from the sink and ran out of the bathroom and into the bedroom.

Chapter 11

Midnights Rain

Detective Mark Horton sat at his desk in deep thought over the day's events as well as Officer Amy Smile's murder.

No matter what side of the tracks you were born on, or whether or not your mother was a maid or the CEO of a large corporation... law enforcement remains "a *tight-knit family.*"

When any member of that family is harmed or in any kind of danger, members of law enforcement seem to turn one color...." *Tenacious.*"

Det. Horton jumped up from his chair and walked to the evidence room which was on the second floor room two thirty-four.

Det. Horton swiped his badge in the entry slot and the door clicked and unlocked, followed by a low pitched tone. Det. Horton stood looking around the evidence room thinking...

"No matter how many times I come into this room, it always smells like a leather and suede tanning shop."

Walking past cold corrugated metal shelves full of white boxes... marked 'evidence 'and a sea of vanilla envelopes containing the last names of the victims, Det. Mark Horton walked down the aisle labeled...S.

As a precaution Det. Horton grabbed a pair of disposable gloves from the box mounted on the wall.

When Det. Horton was trained in the academy he knew whatever evidence which was collected was always of use, and in this case there was mounds of it to sift through.

There were no foot print casts made of the crime scene because they were all washed away by the heavy rain the night prior except for the wheel barrel impressions.

All of the physical evidence was either soaked in rain, blood, grease or diesel fuel, not to mention some of the most telling pieces of evidence, were across town in the lab.

Det. Horton removed the five envelopes from the evidence box, and gently placed them side by side on the examining table.

The first envelope contained a set of car keys with a remote and a cell phone, presumably Jerry Smile's, because it was a 'flip' phone, and no woman would be caught so far behind in technology.

Det. Horton took out his pad and made notation for the folks in the Information & Technology department to retrieve the data from the phone.

Det. Horton set aside the phone and opened the next envelope containing Amy's green Clutch, a key ring with possibly the house and a car key on it, and as he began examining the photos and items he saw a piece of paper, rolled up around something.

Carefully unrolling the paper there was an old skeleton key with a red ribbon tied around it. Looking down at the paper were the numbers....

"15368 St. Rt. one sixty-three"

Det. Horton sealed the envelope up and searched through the remaining envelopes for any clues that could lead him to officer Smiles' murderer and after careful examination nothing jumped out at Det. Horton except the key and the note.

Det. Horton was just about to place the box of envelopes back on the shelf when he suddenly remembered something.

Reaching for the envelope which contained the crime scene photos, Det. Horton scanned through the photos until he came to the ones of Jerry and Amy's car.

Laying the five photos out the table side by side, Det. Horton looked closely at the photos, and at the box of evidence.

Everything in the photos were collected and accounted for except for one thing.... Amy's small blue address book!

Det. Horton placed all the photos back inside the envelope and on the outside of the envelope which contained the skeleton key, Det. Horton wrote 'skeleton key, note...Horton.

Det. Horton sat at his desk going through the department's emergency cascade roster, until he came to Reggie's number.

When Det. Horton dialed Reggie's number, it immediately went to his voice mail and Det. Horton said...

"Hey Reggie, this is Mark. I hope you're not going to screw this case up by trying to investigate it yourself. You're too close to this thing man, if you have information you need to share it with me and let me do my job....and by the way, I want officer Smiles' blue address book."

Det. Horton sat at his computer and pulled the skeleton key and the note from his pocket and typed...

"One-five-three-six-eight, state route one sixty-three"

Immediately the search box on the computer revealed a hit for Genoa and Oak Harbor Ohio. Det. Horton clicked on Genoa, Ohio which provided him with directions to Port Clinton.

Again Det. Horton typed in Oak Harbor which also showed directions to Port Clinton. Det. Horton printed the directions, and left the precinct.

Cinder Drive
Columbus, Ohio

Perry and Reggie backed out of the driveway, and Perry handed Reggie the directions so he could look over the route once he reached interstate seventy-seven.

Perry and Reggie were one of those rare couples who after twenty years of marriage, still found the preciousness of communication but today Reggie was obviously quiet, unusually quiet.

Perry tried to strike up a conversation but after all the years she spent with Reggie, knew not to push too hard.

Whenever Reggie was troubled by a case he was working on, he would sit up at night and listen to old Beatle's' records.

Reggie looked over at Perry and smiled as he started singing as the CD played...

"You say you want a revolution...well you,
know we all want to change the world."

Reggie reached over and gently held Perry's hand as Perry laid her head back into the seat and removed her shoes and put her feet up in the window.

She was extremely protective of Reggie even though Reggie was the perfect picture of a football linebacker...Perry stood a petite woman of five feet six inches.

Reggie set the cruise control on and settled in for a two-and-a-half-hour drive, not knowing what he was going to find or what good was going to come out of his logic to make the trip to Port Clinton.

All that Reggie knew was, Amy was investigating something, something that probably cost her, her life.

Reggie's thoughts went to why was so important for Amy to keep this from him...Amy was not the 'lone wolf' type.

She had planned on coming to Port Clinton to investigate something or someone... so perhaps Amy's murder and Port Clinton were connected some way.

Just as Reggie had cleared his mind of Port Clinton and relaxed to the CD that was playing...suddenly, there was silence.

At first Reggie and Perry thought that the CD was changing tracks, but more than a minute passed when both Reggie and Perry heard music playing on the CD, but it wasn't the Beatles...but the singing of children...

"La-la-la-la-la-la-, la-la-la-la-la-la

Teddy Bear Soda Crackers,

Sitting' in the back seat

Turn around, take a peek

A nightmare you will see...

La-la-la-la-la-la-, la-la-la-la-la-la."

Reggie immediately looked in the rear view mirror and Perry screamed as she turned around and looked in the back seat.

Reggie pulled over and came to an abrupt stop and looked in the back seat and at Perry saying...

"Perry baby, what are you screaming at.... I don't see a damn thing?"

Perry unlocked the truck and got out and stood on the shoulder of the road. Reggie turned on his four-way emergency flashers and walked around to Perry saying...

"Honey what's the matter, what were you screaming at?"

Perry stood and leaned against the front of the truck and pointed to the back seat saying...

"Reg, don't tell me you didn't see that...what the hell was that?"

Reggie looked in through the front windshield and then walked around and looked into the back seat and said...

"Baby, I don't see anything, what was that singing about...was that a CD?"

Perry grabbed hold of Reggie's arm and said...

"Reg, I got a bad feeling about this! I think we just need to turn around and head back to Columbus, and let the folks in your precinct handle this.

Baby I just saw children's faces in the back seat singing and pointing at me. This kind of shit is not supposed to be happening."

Reggie shook his head no, and then grabbed Perry and said...

"Look Perry, I don't know what the hell is happening. If you don't want to go, okay...I'll turn around and take you home but this is something I have to do. Amy was more than just my partner; she was also my sister."

Perry hugged and kissed Reggie and said as she turned to get back in the truck...

"I'm sorry for being jumpy and I know Amy that meant a lot to you...but I...I didn't know she was your sister, when did you find this out?'"

Reggie told Perry that he found out last year and got back on the interstate and started to turn around when Perry said...

"Reg, keep going...I just freaked when I heard those creepy kids singing...I'm sorry, just don't let me out of your sight."

Throughout the rest of the drive, Perry did not say another word to Reggie, she pulled the passenger side vanity mirror down every few minutes to check out the back seat.

Perry flipped the sun visor down and allowed the map to fall in her lap and reminded Reggie that he had a turn off coming in another forty-five miles.

Reggie and Perry looked all around at the scenery in Port Clinton, which wasn't what you'd call 'picturesque', it had rained some hours earlier, and everything had a gray desolate look to it.

Finally, after what seemed like hours of silence, Reggie said...

"Look honey, hearing that song with the creepy kids singing and all that... I really think it's nothing but a nut with a CB transmitter."

Perry tapped Reggie on the arm as she pointed to a sign off to the side of the highway, which read...

"Cabal Island – sixty-one miles, Milton's Ferry – fifty-six miles, and Drop in the Bucket Island – fifty-seven miles."

As they passed the sign Perry told Reggie...

"Like you told me, I checked up on Port Clinton and they have two really good restaurants, I want to try...um...McNeese' or Crossover Steak N Surf."

What Perry didn't know was, as they passed the sign, there was a little girl in a raggedy torn white dress standing behind the sign waving as they drove past.

Perry loved seafood, while Reggie's taste was a little more *'manly'* preferring meat and potatoes.

Reggie was keeping his eye on the road as the rain and fog began setting in. Reggie ignored Perry as he was trying to keep his eye on the road.

Reggie and Perry approached downtown Port Clinton, as Reggie looked for the police department.

He wanted to check in with them and to inform them that he was a police officer from Columbus who was checking up on his partner's case.

While they were sitting at a traffic light, Reggie notice a dark blue police cruiser to his left. Reggie turned and flagged the officer down, by flashing his badge.

Reggie and the police officer spoke for a few minutes before he returned to his truck and followed the police officer through town and out on a one lane paved road around Lake Erie.

After following the police car for ten minutes, the officer put on his lights and made a u turn in front of Reggie.

Reggie rolled his window down as the officer told Reggie he had a call to answer, but the address he was looking for was just a mile past Harmon's market and the first turn just as he passed Lake Shore drive.

The police officer waved and raced in the opposite direction as Reggie drove on. Reggie looked up ahead and saw the sign for Harmon's market, and began looking for his turn off, as the rain increased.

Reggie approached the first road to his left, but that appeared to go nowhere except into Lake Erie.

After driving another ten minutes, Reggie made a quick observance of his surroundings. One of the basics at the Police Academy is familiarizing yourself to the environment.

Reggie was concerned that he was in the right area, because the few farms he saw were empty shells of what used to be farms, and then off in the distance, Reggie got a glimpse of a farm house, way off the road, and thought...

"That has got to be what I'm looking for."

Reggie turned onto the gravel drive way, which turned into a partially paved driveway a hundred feet from the house. Reggie's instincts told him that something was wrong here.

Reggie lifted the console and removed a nine millimeter and placed it in his coat pocket and continued slowly up the drive way.

Perry on the other hand, had told Reggie that she didn't have a cell phone signal, when Reggie said...

"No cell towers out here...the last one I saw was about ten miles before we came into town."

Perry looked over at Reggie and asked him...

"What are you looking at"?

Reggie pointed in the direction of the house and the barn, and said...

"Look at that, something's not right... when we were in town the trees all had leaves on them, but look at the all the trees here... they're all barren."

Perry looked at the trees and said...

"You're right...there should be leaves on some of the trees, the whole area even the bushes are dead looking...as if..."

Before Perry could finish her statement, Reggie added...

"As if nothing here belongs!"

The first buildings they came to were old smoke houses which were converted into single room cabins.

Perry and Reggie's head both turned as they passed them. Next they saw an old barn, with a red metal roof, when Perry said...

"Reg, there are people walking in the field over there."

Reggie slowed down and looked in the direction that Perry was looking and said...

"Huh...I don't see anybody."

Perry looked in the direction where she had seen people walking and pointed...

"Right there Reggie...there they are!"

Reggie stopped the truck and to his surprise, there were a group of people, going towards the main farm house maybe three or four walking in the open field.

Reggie cut his lights off and slowly pulled up to a large barn.

Instead of seeing a huge double door structure as you'd expect with a barn, there was a large opening and a concrete slab, and a tractor in the background.

Reggie pulled onto the concrete slab and climbed out of the truck.

Reggie looked all around and could not see a soul, not even the people he'd seen a few seconds ago.

As a matter of fact, the only thing that they did see outside of themselves was a squirrel up in the tree near the tractor, which looked frozen.

Perry joined Reggie and both of them stood on the concrete slab looking up and all around.

They noticed at one time the old barn had stalls for horses or other animals, but by peeking in the window they saw that someone went through enormous efforts to convert it into a guest area, for company.

Reggie tapped Perry on the shoulder and pointed towards the steps inside the barn, which went up to the second floor. Obviously, two or three bedrooms were up there plus a bathroom.

Perry reminded Reggie that she would soon be in need of using a bathroom.

Reggie and Perry stood at the door and just as Reggie reached out to try the door knob, they heard a voice behind them which caused Reggie to jump, and Perry to cry out...

"Can I help you two...this here is private property you know?"

Reggie and Perry turned to witness an old man, perhaps in his early seventies, dragging a large bag of seed, or something behind him.

Reggie took his hand off of his pistol and out of his pocket as he reached for his badge, and said...

"Hi there, I'm Officer Reggie Parker from Columbus and this is my wife Perry. I was given this address from my partner and I wanted to talk to the people who live here?"

The old man stood for a moment, and the walked passed them towards the tractor, dragging the bag behind him.

Reggie walked up behind him as he saw the man wrestling with the bag, when the old man said...

"I don't need no help; I may be old but I can still handle a bag of seed. The people who own this place aren't here. They told me to watch the place, make sure the tractor doesn't get run down. Now who did you say you were looking for?"

Reggie stepped back a little and allowed the old man his space and said...

"My partner gave me this address of her friend who lives here, who might be able to help me with a case I'm working on."

The old man walked back over to where Perry was standing and said as he looked at Reggie...

"Ma'am, the names Thomas... your husband here is probably a fine officer of the law, but he sure is a lousy liar. If your husband really knows the people who live here, they would've least told him their names.

Perry extended her hand to shake the old man's hand and said...

"Oh no, his partner knows the folks who live here not us."

The old man told Perry after shaking her hand...

"I don't know how your husband's partner can be all that much of a friend to the folks who live here, when they didn't tell you folks their names."

Reggie stepped in front of Perry and said...

"Look Mr....huh Thomas, we're not here to cause problems, if you like you can check with Officer Terry Miller, of the POPD, I spoke with him not long ago and he led us out here."

Mr. Thomas scratched his head and said...

"Nope, I can't do that...don't own a phone...besides, the owners came up here six months ago, and one night the man got his eggs and chickens mixed up, and they put him in a nut ward somewhere in Columbus. The lady, Deanne...told me to watch the place."

Thomas pointed to a bucket beside the door and said the key was underneath there, and that they could look around, but that was it.

Perry and Reggie watched as Thomas emptied the bag of seed into a spreader attached to the rear of the tractor.

Perry and Reggie stood watching as Thomas climbed on the tractor, started the engine and slowly drove off, disappearing in the fog and rain at the edge of the property.

Reggie picked up the key from under the bucket and said to Perry as he opened the door to the barn...

"That old man's a weird ass fucker."

Perry followed Reggie inside closing the door behind her, saying...

"He sure pegged you as the weird one...by the way, who does this place belong to anyway?"

Reggie took Amy's green diary from his pocket, and finding the entry Amy made regarding the farm and showed it to Perry...

"April sixteenth investigate DB and DB at 15368 St. rt one sixty-three, call coach before going."

Reggie told Perry that the police found it in Amy's car, and that he had forgotten to give it back to Det. Horton.

While Reggie began looking around, his police instincts told him that a scuffle of some kind had taken place, because things were thrown around.

Perry watched Reggie as he looked in the closet which held the generator when Perry asked Reggie...

"So what exactly are we looking for anyway, and can we look for a bathroom...I got to pee?"

Closing the door to the closet Reggie noticed Perry picking up two unopened cans of green beans laying on its side, beside the sofa and said...

"We're looking for anything that looks suspicious, anything that looks out of place."

Walking over to Reggie and showing him two dinted cans of green beans which she picked up off the floor, Perry said...

"Does this qualify as suspicious?"

Reggie responded...

"Hardly, unless were looking for the jolly green giant."

Sitting the cans on the counter top in the kitchen, Perry walked around the kitchen looking in cabinets, as Perry mumbled under her breath...

"Smart ass!"

Reggie turned and looked at Perry and said...

"Keep it up babe, about right now you're starting to look kind of suspicious, yourself."

Reggie walked towards the door and in turning asked Perry...

"You don't have anything to say do you?"

Perry stood behind Reggie as he opened the door and began walking out, saying...

"I was just thinking ...suspicious sounds kind of kinky."

Reggie heard what Perry said, but wasn't about to let his mind go where it didn't need to at that moment.

On the other side of the concrete slab was another door which apparently was an inside walkway leading to the house.

Reggie walked in the direction of his truck when he noticed that the drizzle, was now a full fledge down pour.

Standing in the doorway and looking up towards the house, Reggie could plainly see that the end of the driveway leading to the house ended a good ninety feet from the porch, so they decided to use the walkway.

Reggie turned to Perry who was looking at the steps which led upstairs and said...

"Hey Honey, can you go to the truck and look under the driver's seat and get the black mag flash light?"

Perry at first was concerned with the rain, until she saw that her side of the truck was at the edge of the barn, out of the rain. Perry returned and handed Reggie the flashlight and said...

"Can we look upstairs...they got to have a bathroom upstairs and besides, I'm not nit-picking but wouldn't it be simpler to drive up to the house instead of walking through that tunnel thing...I mean it's dark, and we don't know what's in there?"

Turning the flashlight on, Reggie turned to Perry and said...

"I looked and it's got to be a good hundred feet from the end of the drive way to the front porch, unless you want to get soaked. We'll check upstairs then we'll head to the main house."

Perry followed Reggie up the steps to the first bedroom which was neat and tidy. Next to the bedroom was a bathroom and after Reggie checked it out, he stood outside the door as Perry went in to use it.

Perry came out of the bathroom and followed Reggie to the next bedroom.

The bedroom appeared to have been used, there were two pieces of luggage on one of the beds, and Reggie tried opening them, but was unable to because of the locks which were on them.

After checking the last bedroom Reggie and Perry headed down the steps unaware that a pair of eyes were watching them from one of the bedrooms.

Once downstairs Perry walked to the front door and looked out and after seeing how bad it was raining came back, saying...

"Okay Reg, it's cold and storming its ass off so I guess we are using this walkway... the last thing we need to do is to catch pneumonia and be laid up all next week."

Reggie and Perry stepped inside the walk way which led to the house, not noticing that the dark figure which followed them down the steps had also entered the walkway behind them.

The measurements of the walkway were just barely enough to accommodate Reggie's six-foot five frame. Reggie noticed from the first five feet that the height from the ceiling to the floor was uneven, as Reggie had to lower his head a couple of times.

Reggie and Perry also noted that the walkway, which was partially finished, had the smell of new construction.

Reggie shinned the flashlight on both walls and the ceiling, discovered that all of the windows had not been installed, so there were leaves and rain coming in, but for the most part they were dry.

Suddenly Perry screamed!

"What was that...something brushed the back of my hair?"

Reggie quickly drew his pistol from his coat pocket and shinned the flash light behind Perry and then all around her saying...

"Sweetheart, are you sure...I don't see anything, maybe it was..."

Perry cut Reggie off saying...

"Now Reg, don't say that I'm tripping because I'm not... I know the difference between the wind and something brushing my hair."

Reggie extended his arm out to Perry and said...

"Just hold onto papa bear."

Even though Reggie needed a flashlight, there was a little light in certain areas of the walkway, but still the flashlight made it much easier to see.

Reggie shinned the flashlight as far back behind Perry as he could and yet there was nothing to see...nothing except the dark figure which kept jumping in and out from the shadows whenever Reggie and Perry looked to see.

All the same, Reggie switched places with Perry by having her walk on the left side of him.

Reggie could see that they had perhaps another seventy to seventy-five feet to go before reaching the house.

Just then Perry and Reggie heard laughter coming from in front of them. First one voice and then another, and another until there were ten different voices laughing.

Perry was just about to tell Reggie that she had enough and wanted to leave when something came up behind them and shouted in a loud demonic voice...

"Boo!"

Reggie turned drawing his gun and shinning the flashlight behind him, when Perry started to run down the walkway towards the house until she realized that she couldn't see anything, and stopped...calling for Reggie.

The glare of the flashlight shone in Perry's face as she said...

"I'm sorry for freaking out but what the hell was that!"

Reggie grabbed Perry's arm and said...

"I don't know, maybe it was that old man fucking with us or something."

Reggie and Perry finally reached the end of the walkway, and found the door to the house open, thinking that the old man, Mr. Thomas wasn't as efficient as he thought.

Pushing the door open, Reggie and Perry noticed that they were standing in a small pantry, just off of the kitchen.

The pantry was neatly arranged and stocked with enough food as if, the owners were planning on a blizzard lasting for months, or some other natural catastrophe occurring.

There were four steps leading up and into the kitchen. Reggie motioned for Perry to get behind him, as he reached for his .35 caliber Marlin 336C and removed the safety.

There was a small amount of daylight coming in through the windows, as Reggie shined the flashlight on the walls looking for the light switch.

As Reggie shone the light on the wall opposite of the refrigerator, he located the light switch, and as he flicked the switch the light came on and flickered several times.

Reggie cut his flashlight off to conserve the batteries as they looked all around the kitchen, which appeared to be in good shape all except for a couple of cabinet drawers which were standing open.

Opening up the refrigerator both Perry and Reggie saw that it was completely full of food...some cooked, some in storage containers which had the appearance and the odor of mold and rotting.

In an attempt to judge when the last time the owners were in the house, Reggie grabbed the quart of milk which sat inside the refrigerator door and read the expiration date...

"Sept, twenty one-two thousand six."

Reggie held the milk cartoon up to Perry to show her the date and said...

"This is what I'm talking...this is six months old. Clue number one, no one's been here for over six months."

Placing the milk back into the refrigerator Reggie and Perry proceeded into the living room.

On a large table in the center of the living room sat playing cards with dealt hands in six place settings, and a bottle of vodka with six glasses, still bearing varying amounts of vodka inside of them.

Reggie picked up one of the glasses to smell its contents...it was weak, but it was vodka. Not certain what to make out of the things he had seen thus far, Reggie and Perry proceeded into the large front room.

Reggie tapped Perry on the shoulder and told her to stand where she was. Reggie had noticed a small gray box mounted beside the main circuit breaker on the pantry wall, and having worked as a guard inside a warehouse knew that it was a Manual Transfer Switch for a generator.

Upon opening the Transfer Switches panel door, Reggie's eyes saw on the left side of the box, a single relay switch with three sets of wires marked, On, Manual, and Automatic.

Reggie reached up and flicked the switch marked Manual, when Perry jumped as the generator came on illuminating the inside of the house.

The appliances lit up, and the television came on. Reggie rushed into the room upon hearing Perry scream, and yelled...

"PERRY...PERRY"!

There was no sign of Perry, as Reggie stood in the room saying to himself...

"*Now where in the hell did she go...I told her to keep her ass right here?*"

All of a sudden Reggie heard a small scratching noise and turned his eyes over to the dining room window where the hands of cards were.

Walking towards the window Reggie thought perhaps it was Mr. Thomas checking up on them, or maybe it was a branch being blown against the window by the wind and the rain.

Looking around the room again Reggie called for Perry but in a lower tone of voice...

"*Perry...Perry.*"

Reggie's attention was drawn to the window as he heard the scratching noise for the second time.

Reggie slowly grabbed the drapes and began sliding them open, and when he did he saw a large man in a ballerina's tutu with a clown's face mask just standing at the window looking into the house.

Reggie's heart was on the verge of exploding as he let go of the drapes. Reggie stepped to the side of the window and carefully peeped out, looking around for Perry.

The man outside on the porch was taller than Reggie, and looked as if he weighed a ton.

He made no movement to come inside the house nor did he act as if he saw Reggie, he just stood there his head turning slowly to the left, and then to the right.

Reggie was certain that the man hadn't seen him but had seen the lights come on in the house.

Just then the man in the ballerina's tutu started banging on the front door and then the side of the house near the window where Reggie was standing.

Reggie's only concern was where Perry was as he removed his .35 caliber Marlin 336C, and quietly chambered a round when behind him and to the right, the basement door started closing.

Thinking that Perry was frightened and went down into the basement, he firmly, but without yelling, Reggie said…

"Perry…Perry, is that you?"

Reggie saw that the man on the porch stopped banging on the house, and instead he was standing in one spot swaying back and forth as the wooden porch creaked under his weight.

Reggie was in a dilemma he needed to go after Perry, and from the fact of the basement door closing, perhaps Perry saw this sicko on the front porch and ran in the basement.

On the other hand, Reggie had to keep his attention on this reject, and running into a basement, with him outside was a sure recipe for boxing yourself in with nowhere to go.

It was a total feeling of dread and panic. Reggie was all too familiar with panic attacks, but this one took the cake.

Reggie decided he had no choice and he hoped that once down in the basement Perry would be hiding in a corner somewhere, and he could get her upstairs and out of that house.

Reggie's choice was made as he ran over to the basement door, keeping his eye on the front door.

As Reggie ran through the kitchen he saw a small steak knife and wedged it in between the basement door face plate and the door latch and then bent the knife until it broke off.

Reggie figured that if the lock doesn't work, then there'd be little chance of getting locked in the basement.

All of a sudden Reggie heard voices coming from down in the basement.

Reggie tried flicking the light switch at the top of the stairs, but either the bulb was burned out or the switch wasn't working, in any case Reggie shone his flashlight down the steps as he started his descent.

Before Reggie disappeared completely from the kitchen he took one last look at the front door where the man in the ballerina's tutu was standing making sure that he hadn't come in the house.

With each step Reggie called out for Perry, but there was no answer. Then suddenly he began hearing whimpering, as if someone was crying.

He saw several lights which were flickering, as if the light bulbs were not screwed in completely.

Reaching the first light bulb, Reggie reached up and screwed the bulb in, when he heard someone calling him...

"Coach...coach help me."

Reggie expected to hear the voice of Perry but this voice sounded more like Amy's voice. He knew that wasn't possible because Amy was dead, he had seen what was left of her. Again Reggie called out for Perry...

"Perry...Perry, is that you?"

Knowing the difference between Perry and Amy's voices, Reggie had the chills. It sounded a little like Perry, but the only one who ever called him coach was Amy.

Reggie heard a voice, very much like Amy's and a little like Perry say...

"Turn around!"

Reggie turned around, looking in all directions but the only thing he saw were boxes and some furniture. Again Reggie heard the voice say...

"I said Turn around!"

Reggie swung around to his right, and as he did he saw the ashen faces of a dozen little creepy kids laughing and singing...

213

"La-la-la-la-la-la-, la-la-la-la-la-la,

Teddy Bear Soda Crackers

Playing with a knife,

First goes Mary, next is Perry,

Teddy Bear, can't stop

La-la-la-la-la-la-, la-la-la-la-la-la."

As suddenly as the children appeared, the singing stopped and the children disappeared. Then Reggie heard is name being called again, as he looked over by the bottom of the steps.

The man in the ballerina's tutu was standing there holding Perry by the throat as Reggie cried out...

"Oh HELL No...just let her go, you don't want to go down this road, because I will blow your twisted head off...now LET HER GO!"

Reggie took aim at the man in the ballerina's tutu head and as he did, the man in a ballerina's tutu lifted Perry off of the ground until her face was directly in front of his, blocking any clean shot that Reggie might get off.

As the man in the ballerina's tutu lifted Perry in the air, she began kicking trying to get free, but the man in the ballerina's tutu grip around her neck was tight.

Reggie had stepped a little to his left hoping that he could get a clear shot, when from behind him he heard...

"Teddy Bear Soda Crackers

Teddy Bear says

Got your woman

by her neck

Whatcha going to do?"

Reggie turned his attention to the man in the ballerina's tutu and again shouted...

"I'm not going to tell you again...put the lady down or your sick ass can cancel Christmas!"

Just then the man in the ballerina's tutu sat Perry on the floor and as he did Perry ran over to Reggie crying and coughing saying...

"Let's just get out of here...Reg, I told you I had bad vibes about this place...let's go!"

All of a sudden the basement door slammed shut and the lights went out, and Perry screamed!

Just as suddenly as the lights went out, they came back on again and Reggie found himself face to face with the man in the ballerina's tutu and the clown's face.

The reason for Perry's scream was that the man in the ballerina's tutu grabbed her again.

Reggie took aim and fired three times at the man in the ballerina's tutu, being careful not to hit Perry.

Though Reggie didn't miss the three well placed shots did not phase the man in the ballerina's tutu.

The man in the ballerina's tutu let go of Perry and began walking towards Reggie who fired several more times at his head.

Reggie's shots found their mark, as from underneath the clown's mask, blood started to run down his face.

Normally six shots fired would have been more than enough for any man, but the man in the ballerina's tutu was different... demonically different.

Reggie ejected the empty clip from the nine millimeter and grabbed another clip from his pocket, loaded it and fired several more shots at the man in the ballerina's tutu' head.

The clown's face mask was being torn apart from the impact of the bullets, as the man in the ballerina's tutu dropped to one knee.

Believing that the man in the ballerina's tutu was dead, Reggie grabbed Perry's hand as they both headed to go up the steps to the kitchen, when from out of nowhere, and the man in the ballerina's tutu grabbed Reggie from behind and had him in a head lock and dragged him back off of the steps.

Reggie struggled to get free from the man in the ballerina's tutu, and as he was being dragged off the steps, he looked up and in the darkness saw a pair of red eyes coming down the steps towards him.

Perry began screaming as the red eyes got closer and closer. Reggie noticed that the red eyes were only two or three feet off of the steps, until a flash of lightening revealed for a second...a small brown stuffed teddy bear.

The teddy bear was the kind of stuffed toy a child would have in its bedroom. Reggie started to lose consciousness as the flash of lightening disappeared.

When Reggie regained consciousness, he found himself tied to a chair and noticed that Perry was also bound and gagged sitting across from him.

The man in the ballerina's tutu stood in front of Reggie as he struggled to prevent the man in the ballerina's tutu from stuffing an old dirty rag in his mouth.

The man in the ballerina's tutu then wrapped a cord over Reggie's mouth and tied it to a beam directly behind Reggie stretching his head back, making Reggie gag and choke.

Perry sat motionless with her head down until the man in the ballerina's tutu bent down and lifted a car battery from the floor and placed it in her lap.

He connected jumper cables from each of the battery post and walked over towards Reggie.

The man in the ballerina's tutu attached one of the cables to the table and the other to the metal chair which Reggie was tied to causing Reggie to moan and groan in agony as sparks flew off of the chair legs when the man in the ballerina's tutu clamped the cables onto it.

Reggie jerked and twisted in his chair until he suddenly collapsed as his head dropped.

Chapter 12

Dark Intentions

Central Precinct
Columbus, Ohio

Det. Fannichuci waved at his partner and headed for his car, he had been divorced from his wife Sandra for over two years, but still insisted on wearing his wedding ring.

Det. Fannichuci wasn't in that much of a hurry to get home but if he had any idea what was waiting on him in his house, he would never have gone home...ever!

Det. Fannichuci had a habit of being predictable all the way down to how he prepared himself for bed at night.

His nightly habit consisted of picking up takeout food from the same Italian diner, to eating in his bedroom and going outside on the patio for a smoke and then going to bed.

Since his divorce from Sandra several years earlier, Det. Fannichuci kept the bedrooms of his children, and the entire house just as Sandra had left it, believing that one day they would return, which of course was not in the cards.

Another thing which was not in the cards was what was going happen later that night.

Det. Fannichuci gathered his plate and the two empty beer bottles and headed downstairs to the kitchen.

After washing the single plate and placing it in the cabinet, Det. Fannichuci reached to turn out the light when he heard a noise over by the fireplace.

Turning on the living room lights Det. Fannichuci noticed that the family photo of himself, Sandra and his two children had slipped off the wall and lay on top of the fireplace mantle.

Det. Fannichuci stood looking at the picture and with his fingers, traced the outline of his wife's face.

Det. Fannichuci's mind began drifting back to a year ago, when his wife sat down to talk to him about the amount of time he was spending on the job verse the time he wasn't spending with his family.

If only he had heeded her words…her pleas to change, she'd never taken the children and left him.

A tear formed in his eye, and then in a fit of anger Det. Fannichuci flung the photo against the opposite wall, smashing the glass.

Standing there with his head down on the mantle, Det. Fannichuci hadn't noticed that the glass in the picture frame had slowly reassembled itself, as if it had never been smashed.

Det. Fannichuci walked over towards the steps leading upstairs and turned out the lights, and headed back upstairs not paying any attention to the mysterious dark figure which emerged from the kitchen and picked up the picture and hung it back on the wall.

One hour earlier….

Det. Fannichuci thought that this night would be like every other night, where he'd go in to the restaurant, order and flirt with the waitress Diane, but Det. Fannichuci's plans were about to be interrupted.

Instead of going in and flirting with Diane, there was another man standing at the counter talking with Diane so that Det. Fannichuci couldn't talk with her.

Det. Fannichuci shrugged off and sat at the area designed for takeout orders, when another waitress came to where he was sitting and took his order.

Det. Fannichuci explained that he was here for takeout, and he only sat down because he'd been on his feet all day.

Det. Fannichuci paid for his order, and then left the restaurant without doing what he came in for and that was to speak to Diane.

On his way home Det. Fannichuci questioned himself as to why he was able to interrogate and get just about any criminal to talk, but couldn't make himself talk to Diane.

Diane Pritchard was forty-nine years old, a red head, with an amazingly toned figure. Diane stood five feet seven and a hundred and forty pounds. She was divorced and Det. Fannichuci had first noticed her while he and his wife Sandra and the kids frequented the diner several years ago.

Det. Fannichuci pulled into the car port and collected the mail from his box and climbed the steps to his house.

Once inside Det. Fannichuci put his dinner for the evening on the counter, kicked off his shoes at the front door, and reached in the fridge for a cold beer.

Det. Fannichuci sat on the sofa and turned the television on to catch the nightly news and then after grabbing another beer and his dinner...retreated to the bed room for the night.

Det. Fannichuci grabbed a towel from the bathroom closet and spread it on the bed, to prevent food crumbs from getting all in the bed...something Sandra taught him to do.

After climbing into bed, he began eating and then fell asleep, unaware that he was not alone in the house.

One of the things about sleeping alone and being by yourself is, when you're asleep....and when you think you're alone...you never really know if there isn't someone or something watching you sleep.

On this night, there was something watching Det. Fannichuci as he lay asleep in his bed.

Something dark and cold. Something that looked like a man and had the shape of a man, but was something else.

Det. Fannichuci awakened just before midnight and sat up looking at the television which was still on.

Det. Fannichuci grabbed the remote and changed the channel to a movie, when something caught his attention. To the right of the television he noticed a small hole on the bed room wall.

Not sure of what he was seeing, Det. Fannichuci stared more intensely at the hole in the wall as it began growing larger.

Looking back in hindsight, Det. Fannichuci probably should've never noticed it, or for the matter...left the house all together.

The more Det. Fannichuci looked at the hole getting bigger and bigger he got this feeling that there was something or someone behind the wall watching him.

Discreetly Det. Fannichuci reached under the side of the mattress and found a gun he kept there, and slowly got to his feet and headed towards the wall.

As Det. Fannichuci got to the wall he was able to see that the hole was being pushed from inside the walk-in closet.

On the other side of the wall was the bedroom closet, so slowly and cautiously Det. Fannichuci opened the door.

Det. Fannichuci pulled the light string and once he was certain no one was in the closet, turned his attention to the inside of the closet where the hole should've been, but saw nothing.

Looking back to the bedroom wall, the hole was still there about the size of a golf ball.

Thinking that he had overlooked the hole from inside the closet, walked inside the closet to where the hole should have been, but again saw nothing.

Det. Fannichuci grabbed the flashlight which lay on the top shelf in the closet beside a shoe box to inspect the inside of the closet, only to see nothing...no shavings, no drywall peelings, no nothing.

Det. Fannichuci was about to walk out of the closet, when he placed the flash light back on the shelf and as he reached up to pull the light string something grabbed his wrist.

Everything happened so quickly that Det. Fannichuci didn't have time to react. The grip was very powerful until Det. Fannichuci found himself being forced to the floor.

Det. Fannichuci tried to reach for his gun which was in his bathrobe, when whatever or whoever had him, grabbed his other wrist pinning him to the floor.

Det. Fannichuci struggled in the darkness as the closet door closed and began shaking violently.

Det. Fannichuci wanted to yell or holler or even cry out, but it seemed as if the air had been sucked out of the closet, making it hard to breathe.

Det. Fannichuci head started swirling around and around and going down into a deep dark hole, when he suddenly passed out.

No more than a few seconds had passed when Det. Fannichuci awoke, gasping for air. Det. Fannichuci looked over at the place where the hole in the wall was, and saw nothing.

He knew that what had just happened was not a dream, because he hadn't gone to sleep.

Det. Fannichuci threw the blanket off of him and as he threw his legs over the side of the bed, he saw his plate of half eaten lasagna and a beer sitting on the night stand.

Det. Fannichuci wiped his eyes and his face and said to himself...

"I'll be damned...how'd I get in bed...I washed and put my plate up, besides that...I didn't have lasagna, I ordered Rigatoni, what the fuck!"

Det. Fannichuci knew that there was no way in hell that this was all a dream.

Det. Fannichuci walked over to the wall where he'd seen the hole, and after examining it and finding nothing, grabbed the plate and went downstairs.

Det. Fannichuci walked towards the kitchen, and then stopped in the living room and looked expecting to see the picture of himself, Sandra and kids which he had flung against the wall, smashed...but wasn't either.

Det. Fannichuci scratched his head and walked into the kitchen and slowly opened the kitchen cabinet expecting to see the plate which he had eaten off of earlier that evening, but the only plate missing was the one which he held in his hand.

Next Det. Fannichuci grabbed the plastic bag which he'd gotten from the diner and inspected the receipt. He expected the receipt to show that he ordered Rigatoni...and when he looked at it, the receipt showed an order for Rigatoni.

Det. Fannichuci, thought for a moment and then said to himself...

"The receipt shows I ordered Rigatoni, but on my plate is Lasagna...maybe the girl at the diner gave me the wrong order."

Det. Fannichuci wasn't a person driven by emotions, he was a man, an Italian who more than anything, loved his momma was stubborn and a real man's man...but what he saw next changed all that.

Looking down at the plate which he bought with him from the bedroom was Rigatoni and not Lasagna.

Det. Fannichuci grabbed a fresh cold beer from the fridge and sat on the sofa, looking at the plate of food and called his partner, Officer Kathy Withers.

Not knowing exactly what he was going to say to her, or even if she would believe him, Det. Fannichuci waited for her voice which finally said...

"Hello."

Getting up and walking over towards the living room window, Det. Fannichuci said...

"Hey, Kathy, it's me Tony...hope I'm not disturbing you?"

Even though Det. Fannichuci really was interrupting his partner she insisted...

"No, me and Robert were looking at a movie and about to go to bed...what's up?"

Det. Fannichuci knew that he had intruded in on Officer Withers when he said...

"Hey if you don't have any plans in the morning, how about stopping by in the morning, I need to run something across you?"

What Det. Fannichuci didn't say was how scared he was, and that he really needed company right then and there.

Another two beers later, Det. Fannichuci was sitting in the recliner watching television, he tried shaking sleep away from him, but ended up falling asleep.

At three o'clock in the morning, Det. Fannichuci woke up and looked around the living room. He checked to see if the doors were locked and then cut the television off before heading to the bedroom.

Det. Fannichuci glanced around and noticed four empty beer bottles on the coffee table next to an empty plate and said...

"This shit is getting too damn weird...I took my plate into the kitchen...and what's up with four empty beer bottles, I only drank two!"

Heading upstairs and making a stop to the bathroom, Det. Fannichuci stood over the commode and the thoughts of the plates and the hole in the bedroom wall and the beers.

He knew he wasn't dreaming… it's impossible, things like that don't just happen.

Det. Fannichuci took his cell phone from out of his pocket and looking at the activity on his phone, saw where he had called Officer Withers twice when he said…

"Wait a minute…I called Kathy once…what the hell."

Det. Fannichuci plugged in his cell phone and set up in bed with his gun sitting next to him, for the first time ever Det. Fannichuci drifted was experiencing fear and anxiety.

No more than an hour had passed when Det. Fannichuci was startled by a noise that sounded like someone with roller skates on a hard wood floor, going back and forth.

Looking at the clock radio next to the bed, it showed…'Four twenty-nine'

Det. Fannichuci sat on the edge of the bed thinking…

"Damn…now what!"

Det. Fannichuci got dressed and grabbed his and made his way into the hallway to investigate the sounds.

There were only the two bedrooms of his two daughters besides his bedroom. Det. Fannichuci entered the first bedroom which was empty, when he heard the sound of roller skates going down the hall.

Running out into the hall, Det. Fannichuci heard the sounds of children laughing and the sounds of roller skates…but there was no one else in the house.

Satisfied that no one else was in the house, Det. Fannichuci went downstairs and into the kitchen and loaded up the coffee pot, putting in two scoops more coffee than usual.

Det. Fannichuci, made himself some breakfast, two eggs, sausage links and toast. On his way into the living room he stopped at the cabinet and topped off his coffee with a generous amount of whiskey and cut the television on, when a story caught his attention…

"Here live on your six – to recap…two hunters were found dead from gunshot wounds and a third hunter is wanted for questioning during the last weekend of deer season in Woodgrain, Ohio.

The Ohio Department of Conservation on Monday said after an examining the area that, both hunters were shot by a third person or persons unknown, who was also perched in a tree stand according to the trajectory of their wounds and the discovery of three tree stands.

The identity of the dead hunters' and the third man sought in the killings are pending notification of their next of kin, and the conclusion of the investigation..."

Det. Fannichuci was finishing his spiked coffee as the doorbell rang. Det. Fannichuci looked out through the peep hole only to see standing on his porch... his partner Officer Kathy Withers.

Det. Fannichuci opened the door, as Officer Withers shook the rain from her umbrella and came inside saying to Det. Fannichuci said...

"Whew...it's going to be one of those days."

Officer Withers unbuttoned her coat and hung it over a chair which sat by the door, and after leaning her umbrella near it said...

"Now what was so hot that you had to call me when I was right in the middle of some action...huh, damn you just about ruined everything and why'd you have to call twice...do you know how long it's been for me?"

Det. Fannichuci poured Officer Withers a cup of coffee and said...

"Look Kathy, what I'm about to say might sound a little nutty I mean, hell when it happened I couldn't believe it either...but it's true."

Officer Withers walked over to Det. Fannichuci, sipping her coffee and said...

"Whoa, slow it down a little...what might sound nutty, what are talking about?"

Det. Fannichuci told Officer Withers everything that happened that night about the food, and the beers and the noises.

Officer Withers scanned the room and saw four empty beer bottles and a half empty bottle of Jack Daniels, pointed to the bottles as she said sarcastically...

"It looks like the thing or whatever it was that was messing with you, must've had one too many also?"

Det. Fannichuci sat down beside Officer Withers and said...

"Don't even go there...I just put a little in my coffee this morning, and it's like I said...last night I only drank two beers not four.

I'm trying to be serious here Kathy, I know it sounds insane, I experienced it and I still can't believe it...but it happened just the way I say."

Just then there was a knock on the door. Det. Fannichuci looked at his watch and then got up to answer the door.

Det. Fannichuci came back into the room and sat beside Officer Withers and said...

"That was strange..."

Officer Withers sat her coffee cup down and said...

"Who was it...oh let me guess...was it the thing coming back for another drink?"

Officer Withers started laughing and then handed Det. Fannichuci an opened envelope.

Taking the envelope, Det. Fannichuci asked...

"What's this?"

Officer Withers sat back in her chair and continued drinking her coffee and said...

"An old skeleton key...you left it on the seat yesterday when I dropped you off."

Det. Fannichuci looked puzzled as he opened the envelope and read the note attached to the key...

"15368 state route one sixty-three...what the hell does that mean?"

Officer Withers sat her coffee cup on the table and said...

"First you call me twice at midnight and now you're trying to tell me that this not your key...I mean, no one else was in the car except you and me, and I was driving remember?"

Det. Fannichuci read the note again and examined the key and said...

"I'm telling you Kathy, I've never seen this key before and where the hell is state route one sixty-three?"

Officer Withers stood up and asked det. Fannichuci...

"How am I supposed to know...pull it up on your computer?"

Det. Fannichuci motioned for Officer Withers to follow him into the kitchen where his computer sat on the countertop.

The computer showed that state route one sixty-three passed along the rural area of Port Clinton, Ohio.

They both looked at each other with a puzzled look in their eyes when suddenly, there was a loud knock on the front door.

"Now who in the hell can this be at this time in the morning?"

Det. Fannichuci said as he got up to see who was knocking on his door so early in the morning.

Det. Fannichuci walked back into the kitchen to tell Officer Withers that there was no one at the door, when he noticed Officer Withers bent over the computer with a look of shock on her face.

Tapping Officer Withers on her shoulder he said...

"Earth to Kathy...what's wrong kiddo?"

Officer Withers pointed at the computer screen as Det. Fannichuci read...

"Twisted and Dread
Teddy Bear Soda Crackers,
Killers on the run
Bloody scene, both hunter's dead
Teddy Bear says you're next!"

Det. Fannichuci firmly grabbed Officer Withers by the shoulders and said...

"Kathy are you out of your mind or something...you just wrote that, okay I had a few beers last night and I tell you some weird shit and now you're messing with me."

Officer Withers pointed at the screen as the two of them saw the curser on the screen moving and typing all by itself.

Officer Withers closed the computer and walked in the living room and cut the television on to the news.

Det. Fannichuci followed Officer Withers saying...

"This is getting a little weird Kathy... what in the hell is going on, and where are you going?"

Officer Withers began flipping through the news channels until she came to channel six news...

"...At six thirty yesterday evening, the bodies of two hunters were found dead at the Woodgrain Wildlife reserve.

The Ohio Department of Conservation discovered the bodies of Michael Ward and Jeffery Fleming, both of Columbus with single gunshots.

Since the bodies were discovered on Federal property, the FBI and Federal Marshalls have been called in to head up the investigation. A news conference is scheduled today at 11:30 and channel six news will be there covering the story."

Officer Withers got up and walked over to Det. Fannichuci and said...

"Don't you find that a little odd that they found two hunters murdered yesterday, and your computer mysteriously has this message about them?"

Det. Fannichuci stood looking at his computer and then back over to the television, and said to Officer Withers...

"Kat, this is more than just a little weird, I don't claim to know everything about computers but I do know that they aren't supposed to type all by themselves."

Det. Fannichuci started rifling his hands in his hair and said...

"Okay, okay let's think about this for a minute...hackers. It's got to be hackers...right?"

Officer Withers replied...

"I don't know...if it were hackers how would they know to send that message to you? For my money I'd say that someone you sent to prison is screwing with you...that's what I think."

Det. Fannichuci nodded his head in agreement and said...

"Yeah, you could be right but I'll play the hacker thing out until something else prompts me to think otherwise."

While Det. Fannichuci and Officer Withers were re-reading the message on the computer, suddenly they heard large pounding on the front door.

Det. Fannichuci raised his voice and said...

"Who the fuck is playing around!"

Det. Fannichuci opened the front door but there was no one standing on the porch. Det. Fannichuci opened the screen door and stepped out and looked left and then right, but saw no one.

As Det. Fannichuci was about to head back inside, he noticed what seemed to be smeared blood on his front door.

Storming back inside Det. Fannichuci grabbed his phone and began dialing, when Officer Withers asked...

"What's wrong, what is it?"

While he was waiting for someone to answer, he yelled to Officer Withers...

"Look at the front door, someone smeared blood on my front door!"

While Det. Fannichuci called the precinct and asked to have a car sent to his house along with someone from the lab to collect samples of the blood smeared on his front door, he turned to Officer Withers and ask...

"Hey while you were waiting for me to answer the door, did you see that on the front door?"

Officer Withers shook her head and said...

"No...I mean you have a white door, I would've noticed red blood, besides... your screen door was locked, and it was raining...I could've missed it."

A squad car from the precinct arrived and two officers took both Officer Withers and Det. Fannichuci's statement, while the technician from the lab collected multiple swabs for testing.

Det. Fannichuci filled a bucket with water, dish detergent and bleach and begin removing the blood stain words from his front door.

After cleaning the door Det. Fannichuci walked into the kitchen and said to Officer Withers...

"That envelope...where did I put that envelope you just gave me?"

Spotting the envelope lying beside his computer on the counter top, Det. Fannichuci asked Officer Withers...

"Didn't you say that state route one sixty-three ran in the boonies somewhere in Port Clinton?"

Officer Withers replied as she put her jacket on, saying...

"I said rural area, and knowing you as well as I do, you're thinking about a road trip, and dragging me along...right?"

Det. Fannichuci grabbed his jacket and re loaded his pistol and walked towards the front door, as Officer Withers pointed to herself saying...

"Do you see what I'm wearing?"

Det. Fannichuci continued towards the door and said...

"Okay you got on boots, white jeans and a thick sweater and a jacket...we're not going to a fashion show, besides this won't take

long…just look around a little and ask a few questions and we're out of there."

Det. Fannichuci told Officer Withers that he was going to drive, and for her to call into the precinct and tell the desk sergeant they wouldn't be in until after lunch…that they had to check on something.

Before pulling off Officer Withers removed the map from the glove compartment and gave Det. Fannichuci directions…

"Okay it's pretty much a straight shot, fifty-three towards Upper Sandusky, and do we even have a plan or are we going to just wing it?"

Det. Fannichuci told Kathy all he had at the moment was to simply ask two or three questions, and if they knew anyone who hunted in or near Columbus, and what the skeleton key unlocks.

Det. Fannichuci taught new recruits coming into the academy and one of his pet pees is, the art of asking questions.

Det. Fannichuci believed that there are really only two or three questions which should be initially asked and the answers to those will tell you if you should or should not pursue anything further.

The one hundred twenty-five-mile stretch of highway from Columbus to Port Clinton offered nothing much in the way of scenery except farms, wooded areas and more farms.

Generally, it takes the average person a little over two hours to complete the trip, but for Det. Fannichuci and Officer Withers, this was going to take an eternity and would be the ride of their lives.

Route twenty-three takes you from Downtown Columbus north, before connecting to fifty-three. Other than trees, abandoned farms and a few bridges with an occasional house set back off of the road is all one could expect to see.

About thirty miles outside of Columbus the houses become scarcer and the woods begin to take over the landscape.

The weather was brisk and the trees bare of leaves, and the drive was lonely and tiring.

To take the sheer boredom out of the trip Officer Withers began reading and commenting on all of the signs that were posted on the side of the road and on the sides of the worn out barns and structures, except for one.

It was an old barn one with a red rusty metal roof and a sloppy hand-written sign in red paint which read…

"THE FARM AHEAD DEAD!"

As they passed the sign Officer Withers turned to Det. Fannichuci and said...

"Tell me, I did not see that...did you see that. There was a sign on the side of an old barn that read...THE FARM AHEAD DEAD!"

Det. Fannichuci looked over at Officer Withers with a not so concerned look on his face and continued driving.

Ahead was a sign that read...

"Harmon's Market five miles"

Officer Withers said to Det. Fannichuci...

"Good I hope they have a restroom, both cups of coffee are working on me."

Seizing the opportunity to liven up an already boring trip, Det. Fannichuci remarked...

"Hey if you got to go that bad, I can always pull off the side of the road, and you can go in the woods."

Officer Withers was an exceptionally attractive woman. Five feet seven, a hundred and forty pounds.

Det. Fannichuci would never admit it, but he secretly flirted with Kathy, who had tried on one occasion to seduce Tony at one of the precinct's cook outs.

Officer Withers cocked her head to the left with a...

'I can't believe you just said that' look on her face.'

Det. Fannichuci chuckled a little and then said...

"C'mon, I don't know why going in the woods is a big deal for women. I think if you have to go bad enough you'll do what you have to do wherever you have to."

Officer Withers explained to Det. Fannichuci that for starters, it was raining outside, and number two...there are things in the woods like bugs, and number three it was unsanitary.

Det. Fannichuci straightened up in his seat and said...

"Well you can relax, the sign I just passed says...Harmon's Market, next right and they'll probably have a bathroom there."

Det. Fannichuci pulled into the parking lot, and as he was putting the car in park, Officer Withers jumped out and ran inside the store.

With her legs semi folded and crouching down Officer Withers desperately said.

"*I need to go really bad, where's your restroom?*"

The old man in the store said...

"*It's out back but...?*"

Before the old man in the store finished his statement, Officer Withers was heading to the door, when he hollered at her...

"*You're going to need this key to get in... the doors locked!*"

Officer Withers turned round and snatched the key from the old man and ran out the door, nearly knocking down Det. Fannichuci.

Mr. Hennessey stood on the front steps next to Det. Fannichuci and said...

"*Boy I'm glad your lady came back and got the key...I'd hate to see what would've happened if she hadn't.*"

Putting a stick of chewing gum in his mouth, Det. Fannichuci said...

"*I'd hate to see it too, and she's not my lady...she's my partner.*"

Officer Withers turned on the lights in the restroom, and locked the door and after checking the commode and sat down.

No sooner had Officer Withers sat down when the lights went out, and she heard the bathroom open.

Officer Withers fished around by the commode for her purse to get her gun out and said...

"*Hello, who's in here?*"

In the dark Officer Withers started to stand up, wiggling and pulling her jeans up without wiping.

Officer Withers felt that if she had to run or fight, having her pants down around her ankles was not the place they needed to be.

When Officer Withers entered the restroom, it was empty no one was inside but her, but seconds after she closed the door, the door opened up, so she remained quiet listening for and waiting.

Suddenly the lights came on and when they did Officer Withers was not alone.

Standing in front of her was a woman about five feet, four inches tall. Heavy set, with short brown hair neatly arranged covering her ears.

David Ray

The woman looked as if she was in her mid-fifties, a hundred seventy-five lbs. Her eyes were solid black and lifeless like a dolls' eyes, and the size of golf balls.

Officer Withers held her gun down at her waist and said to the woman...

"Ma'am, I was just finishing up, the restroom is all yours, I-I was just leaving."

That's when the woman smiled and when she did, her mouth revealed the ugliest set of broken and jagged teeth, and her smile stretch across her entire face from ear to ear, and the woman said...

"Leaving, who said anything about you leaving? Tonight, we're going to have fun with you...he-he-he-he-he-he-he."

Officer Withers raised her gun and pointed it the woman and said...

"Hold it right there!"

The woman placed both hands on her hips and said...

"Are you planning on shooting me sweetie?"

Officer Withers cocked her gun and said...

"I don't want to have to shoot you but if you don't get the hell out of here I'll blow your bug-eyed face the fuck off."

The woman stuck her face out in front of Officer Withers, taunting her and said...

"And while you're blowing my bug-eyed face the fuck off, what am I supposed to be doing. Do you want me to lie down and die like your father did when your mother killed him?"

With an expression of anger on her face Officer Withers said...

"What did you just say bitch...what did you just say?"

The woman took two steps towards Officer Withers and she fired her gun twice.

Just then someone was pounding on the restroom door and Det. Fannichuci yelled...

"Kathy...Kathy, are you alright... open up the door."

The woman turned to the door and then back to Officer Withers and said...

"Well, it looks like I got to go sweetie...but I'll see you again, real soon."

232

Just then the door was kicked in as Det. Fannichuci and Mr. Hennessey came rushing in.

As they burst into the restroom, Officer Withers was standing there alone in the rest room as she swung her gun around pointing it at them, as Det. Fannichuci said...

"Whoa...Whoa... partner it's me, now lower your gun Kathy."

Officer Withers lowered her gun as Det. Fannichuci grabbed it from Officer Withers and said...

"What gives, we heard two shots...what the hell are you shooting at?"

Officer Withers looked around the restroom and upon seeing no one else there but the three of them, said as she broke down in tears...

"Tony...she was standing right there. There was a creepy ass old woman in here coming towards me."

Mr. Hennessey whispered to Det. Fannichuci and said...

"Look I don't know who you two are, but...I think you best be leaving, I can't have my damn restroom shot all to hell."

Det. Fannichuci walked Officer Withers out to the car as Mr. Hennessey followed close behind.

Det. Fannichuci turned to Mr. Hennessey as Officer Withers got in the car and said...

"Can you give me some directions... we're looking for this address on state route one sixty-three, are we pretty close to that?"

Mr. Hennessey looked at the paper Det. Fannichuci handed him and said...

"Umm, I know this place...well I don't really know it but I know the people that own it, a young couple from Columbus.

What you want to do is go out of here, make a right and at the second stop sign, turn right before the rail road tracks.

Follow that for about fifteen to twenty miles around a winding road and start looking for the first paved driveway on your right... but I wouldn't go there, if I was you."

Det. Fannichuci looked a little puzzled and showed him his badge saying...

"I'm Det. Fannichuci and my partner is Officer Withers. We're investigating a case, and all we have to go on is the owner's house... you say you know the people, mind telling me what their names are?"

Mr. Hennessey scratched his head and said...

"I'm not that sure about names, let me see...I know the lady kept calling him Blue, but for the life of me, I can't recall what her name was...Debbie, or Deanna, something like that."

Det. Fannichuci got inside the car when Mr. Hennessey came up to the window and said...

"The folks I told you about...something strange happened up there six months ago...I really wouldn't go up there if I was you."

Det. Fannichuci and Officer Withers drove off in search for the farm, but what neither of them knew, was they should've listened to the old man at the store.

When Det. Fannichuci left the store several miles back, the weather was chilly with a light drizzle, but that was suddenly going to change.

The rain changed from a drizzle to a steady down pour, and the chill in the air was replaced by an eerie warmth which bought with it a heavy milky white fog.

As Det. Fannichuci and Officer Withers continued on, neither one was prepared for what was about to happen next.

One minute there was a heavy rain with a light milky fog, and then the fog intensified and engulfed their car which was so thick that Det. Fannichuci had to reduce his speed to less than five miles per hour.

Suddenly and from out of nowhere something darted in front of Det. Fannichuci's car, causing him to hit the brakes.

Officer Withers, who was trying to recover from the events which happened in the bathroom screamed...

"What the hell was that?"

Det. Fannichuci stopped and rolled the window down to see if he had hit an animal and that's when he saw it.

It was a big man dressed in a ballerina's tutu wearing something some kind of mask.

Det. Fannichuci turned to Officer Withers and said...

"Where the fuck did he come from.... shit he came from out of nowhere?"

Officer Withers climbed in the back seat and rolled the rear window down looking with Det. Fannichuci at what he'd hit.

Det. Fannichuci and Officer Withers looked at each other debating on what they should do and then, the man which they hit started getting up and they saw his real size.

Det. Fannichuci and Officer Withers commented that he was massive. Det. Fannichuci checked his gun while the man in the ballerina's tutu continued approaching towards them.

As Officer Withers climbed back in the front seat, Det. Fannichuci tried driving off, but felt a loud thud on the car and turned around to see that the man in the ballerina's tutu was on the back of the trunk pounding on the back window.

Not wanting to shoot the man, Det. Fannichuci slammed on brakes but instead of the man in the ballerina's tutu falling off the car he was thrown and embedded into the car's back window.

Officer Withers hadn't completely recovered from her experience at the restroom, and was still a little rattled as she searched for her gun, when Det. Fannichuci gave her, his.

A few moments had passed and Det. Fannichuci heard the sound of the back window being smashed and yelled at Officer Withers...

"Shoot the damn gun...shoot it!"

Officer Withers aimed and fired six shots in succession, and the man in the ballerina's tutu, fell backwards and off of the car.

Det. Fannichuci stopped the car about thirty feet away and put the car in park. He turned to Officer Withers and said...

"Get a grip...even for a twisted fuck like this we can't just leave him on the side of the road without reporting it."

Det. Fannichuci told Officer Withers he was going to go check on the guy, and not to worry because he was dead anyway.

Det. Fannichuci took his gun from Officer Withers and headed to check on the man and as he stood a few feet from the man in the ballerina's tutu, there were bullet holes to his chest but no signs of blood.

Det. Fannichuci slowly bent down besides the man in the ballerina's tutu, and gently picked up his wrist to check for a pulse.

Det. Fannichuci turned to yell to Officer Withers that there was no pulse and that the man was dead when the rain intensified.

Det. Fannichuci stood up and slowly began walking back to the car. He noticed that Officer Withers was sticking her head out of the rear window where the man in the ballerina's tutu had crashed into, yelling something him.

Officer Withers was yelling at Det. Fannichuci but he could barely hear what she was screaming because of the rain.

As Det. Fannichuci got closer to the car he could hear Officer Withers yelling...

"Run you son of a bitch...run!"

Det. Fannichuci turned around just in time to see the man in the ballerina's tutu sitting up.

Seeing that the fog had reduced visibility and that Det. Fannichuci was close to the man in the ballerina's tutu, Officer Withers began yelling and screaming at Det. Fannichuci and fired one shot in the air, saying...

"WATCH OUT!"

Det. Fannichuci lowered his head a little trying to focus on Officer Withers through the rain and fog, when Officer Withers got out of the car and began waving her arms and pointing the gun at the man in the ballerina's tutu.

The man in the ballerina's tutu was within inches from grabbing Det. Fannichuci, when Det. Fannichuci turned and saw the man in the ballerina's tutu and started running for the car.

Det. Fannichuci yelled for Officer Withers to get behind the wheel and get ready to take off. Officer Withers jumped behind the wheel and stepped on the brake pedal placed the gear selector in drive, and waited for Det. Fannichuci to jump in.

Det. Fannichuci's hand reached the door handle and as he opened the door began yelling,

"GO...GO...GO"!

Officer Withers pressed the gas pedal as Det. Fannichuci hopped in the car, slamming the door.

Officer Withers was so fixated on Det. Fannichuci making it inside the car, that she did not see that the man in the ballerina's tutu had grabbed the rear bumper of the car.

The front of the car started sliding from side to side as the man in the ballerina's tutu begin lifting the rear of the car off the ground.

Det. Fannichuci looked out of the window and yelled at Officer Withers...

"Throw it in reverse!"

The man in the ballerina's tutu was incredibly strong he was holding the car in place, without slipping in the rain and mud as the front wheels just spun in place, when Officer Withers throw the gear selector in drive.

Officer Withers began screaming as the man in the ballerina's tutu let the car slam to the ground, causing the car to dart forward and veer off to the right into the bushes.

Crashing into the bushes and stuck in the mud, Officer Withers saw the man in the ballerina's tutu coming towards them and parting the bushes when she yelled...

"Tony...shoot this crazy fuck...shoot him!"

Looking over to the passenger side, Det. Fannichuci's head had smashed into the window and was bleeding.

Det. Fannichuci grabbed his head and began moaning and looking around as Officer Withers started screaming when she heard a *"POOF"* sound coming from the engine and then the car engulfed in flames.

Officer Withers completely forgot about the man in the ballerina's tutu as the flames began rising from under the hood to the front windshield.

Officer Withers tried several times over to open her side of the car, but it would not open.

Det. Fannichuci managed to get his door open with a push, and fell out onto the muddy ground.

Officer Withers started yelling for Det. Fannichuci to help her, as he reached in and began pulling her from the car.

Det. Fannichuci and Officer Withers lay on the ground in the mud beside the passenger side of the car, when two things caught their attention.

Number one they noticed that the heavy rain dissipated to a drizzle and they could see the man in the ballerina's tutus feet on the driver's side.

Officer Withers whispered as her voice trembled....

"Were going to die...we're going to die!"

Unfortunate for Officer Withers because the man in the ballerina's tutu heard Officer Withers, and started coming around to the other side of the car where they both were.

Officer Withers and Det. Fannichuci jumped up as Officer Withers cried in a loud voice....

"OH MY GOD...WHAT DO YOU WANT!!!"

Not knowing where or which way they were running, Det. Fannichuci and Officer Withers lowered their heads and ran out into the woods until they came to a clearing.

Hearing grunting sounds coming from the man in ballerina's tutu, they pushed on past the clearing until they came to another wooded area.

They stopped by a tree which provided some shelter from the rain to think about what they were going to do and where they were going to go.

Det. Fannichuci turned behind him to see if the man in the ballerina's tutu was still chasing them or if they could still hear the sound of his grunting.

Det. Fannichuci searched his coat to see how much more ammunition he had left, and as he began to turn around, Officer Withers grabbed his arm and tugged on it.

Standing in front of them was the outline of a man, tall but not as large as the man in the ballerina's tutu.

Det. Fannichuci pulled his gun from his pocket and pointed it in the direction of the man and said...

"Okay Mister that's close enough unless you want to get shot, you'd better stop right there."

The man in front of them shinned a flashlight in his face and stepped forward and said...

"Whoa pal...don't shoot, my name is Tim and you got to help me... there's some people up there in that house that has my wife tied up!"

Det. Fannichuci cocked his gun, not knowing who Tim was and said...

"Look man I don't know you, for all I know you could be with that big ass man in the ballerina's tutu who's chasing us!"

Tim shinned his flashlight back into his own his face revealing his cuts and bruises and said...

"Some big man creepy fuck wearing a ballerina's tutu wearing a clown's mask? He's the one. My best friend David Blue owns the farm where my wife Mary is tied up...you got to help me."

Det. Fannichuci kept his gun pointed at Tim and said...

"You say the man wearing the ballerina's tutu has your wife tied up...well, how come he's behind us, chasing us then...he can't be two places at one time?"

Tim handed Officer Withers the flashlight and said...

"I need help damnit... My wife Mary's in the basement all tied up, and there's some other people too."

Det. Fannichuci said as he lowered his gun...

"So we're supposed to just follow you, huh?"

Tim turned to run towards the small cabin and then turned back to Det. Fannichuci and said...

"If that big son of a bitch gets a hold of your ass, you'll wish you'd listened to me... now either trust me or shoot me!"

Det. Fannichuci pointed his gun at Tim's back and said...

"Well just don't go pulling no funny stuff, or I'll drop your ass."

Det. Fannichuci and Officer Withers began following Tim when he turned and said...

"You still haven't said who you were?"

Det. Fannichuci said...

"I'm Det. Fannichuci and this is my partner Officer Withers. We're from the Columbus PD up here investigating a case we're working on... that was until our car collided with that big country fuck. Who the hell is he anyway?"

Tim threw up both of his hands as his pushed brush away from in front of him and said...

"Hey not too much further, and as far as that twisted fuck with the ballerina's tutu ...I don't know who he is or what he is, but I can tell you this much...he won't die."

A little small shack dotted the landscape as Det. Fannichuci said...

"Well if we hadn't see him with our own eyes, we'd think you were on drugs or just plain crazy."

For the first time in over twenty minutes since running into Tim, Officer Withers spoke up...

"Tim, does this place have facilities and don't tell me I got to go outside... cause I'm really not feeling that."

Tim raised his right hand to signal everyone to stop, until he had a chance to check out the area before going into the clearance.

As the three of them quickly ran across the clearance and were on the side of the cabin, Det. Fannichuci said to Officer Withers...

"I thought you took care of business back there at that market?"

Officer Withers whispered in Det. Fannichuci's ear and said...

"I was about to when the crazy bitch came at me...hey where did that guy go?"

Det. Fannichuci and Officer Withers looked around but Tim had disappeared.

Suddenly the front door opened and Tim was standing there, saying...

"Hurry up, come on in."

As Det. Fannichuci and Officer Withers entered the small room, Tim closed the door behind them and took a log beam and placed it against the front door.

Officer Withers was looking around the cabin while Det. Fannichuci said to Tim ...

"Why didn't you tell somebody where you were, don't just go running off?"

Tim removed his coat and placed several of the lit candles on the floor of the cabin, and replied...

"When I got here, I noticed that the door needed a skeleton key to open it. Only trouble with this this old fashion lock is... that once the door closes, it locks automatically.

I found a ladder outside which I've been using to climb in and out through the upper window."

Det. Fannichuci walked over and looked at the small window and commented...

"So every time, you leave here in order to get back in you have to climb up through there?"

Before Tim could respond, Officer Withers said...

"I don't think so Tony, unless I'm dead wrong you have a key in your pocket that might just work...remember?"

Looking puzzled Tim looked over at Det. Fannichuci and said...

"A key...how do you have a key to this place...Dave and Deanne never mentioned anything to me about giving keys to anyone?"

Det. Fannichuci felt all of his pockets until he ran across the one which had the skeleton key, which Officer Withers gave to him the day prior.

Det. Fannichuci had forgotten all about putting the key in his pocket, once he had made up his made to drive to Port Clinton earlier this morning.

Pulling out the key along with the note attached to it, he said...

"Oh yeah I totally forgot about this...nobody gave me the key, it just sort of appeared in our squad car yesterday."

Tim also informed Det. Fannichuci and Officer Withers that he's keeping the candles on the floor, because the light doesn't reflect through the small window, and that they need to keep their voices down.

Det. Fannichuci handed Tim the key as Tim knelt down on the floor examining the key, and Det. Fannichuci said...

"Have your friends ever used a key up here, like this before?"

Tim crawled over to the door and inserted the key into the key hole slowly and turned it...

"Click."

Tim locked and unlocked the door several times, and then handed the key back to Det. Fannichuci and told him...

"This is the first that I've ever seen that key. Dave and I have been friends since college, but this is the first time I've been up here, because they just finished remodeling this place last year, besides that key didn't magically appear, someone wanted you here, just like they wanted all of us here."

Officer Withers said...

"I'm curious, what makes you say...'they' wanted us here...who are they?"

Tim leaned his back up against the wall and told them all about David's mental breakdown six months ago, and how his girlfriend Deanne told them that David claimed that there were evil Doppelgangers or spirits up here who were appearing and disappearing.

Tim went on to explain how he and Mary live eight and a half hours from Port Clinton, in Wisconsin and just a few hours ago they were at the home of a friend, and somehow mysteriously appeared here, in an instant.

Officer Withers and Det. Fannichuci looked at one another and immediately the looks on their faces revealed and confirmed that their hunch to investigate the farm at Port Clinton was a valid one.

Officer Withers responded…

"So wait a minute, you want us to believe that you and your wife mysteriously just ended up here all the way from Wisconsin in a matter of minutes?"

Tim shook his head and said…

"No not minutes….it was more like seconds.

You see, when Deanne told us what David had said…I was just like you…I didn't believe it either…but now I do, now I believe that and much more."

Det. Fannichuci said…

"Okay, Tim, we're just police officers not voodoo witchcraft experts…so your friend was in a nut ward, and he said all this crazy crap?"

Tim took another deep breath and said…

"Look, that big guy…he's been shot six times in the head and won't die, and then there are these creepy looking kids that keep singing…I'm telling you, this place is haunted or something."

Officer Withers said…

"Do you think you can be a little less vague than that…I mean we had weird things happening to us all day? Some sick psycho is chasing us…that's all. Just one man, and no creepy kids either."

"Tim looked over at Officer Withers and said…

"You happen to have a key that fits the doors here and there are people tied up and being tortured, all of this stuff's been planned… I'm trying to tell you."

Det. Fannichuci interrupted…

"That's what we're trying to uncover what all of us are doing here okay, Tim you and I are going to see what's what, Kathy you just hang tight until we get back."

Officer Withers walked over to the window and turned and said…

"Man, would you look at that rain coming down. It's like cats and dogs outside and I have a real need going on right now, if you know what I mean."

Tim walked up to Officer Withers and said...

"Well, it looks like you're going to get a little rain in your panties, huh?"

Officer Withers snapped back at Tim and said...

"You know, the worst thing a guy can do is to get a woman pissed off who has a gun and a badge."

Officer Withers stormed past Tim and slowly closed the door saying...

"Damn...Damn...Damn...Tony...you got my back right?"

Det. Fannichuci nodded as he was discussing with Tim what they were going to do when Det. Fannichuci hollered to Officer Withers, saying...

"Hurry it up partner, you okay?"

Officer Withers replied...

"Yeah...I'm good."

Tim sarcastically said as he smirked...

"Yeah, good and wet."

Det. Fannichuci asked Tim for the skeleton key and told Officer Withers not to leave the cabin under any circumstances.

Tim and Det. Fannichuci headed out the door into the rain, towards the house.

Det. Fannichuci spotted the walkway and suggested going through there to keep from walking in all the rain, but Tim refused saying...

"No way am I going through that again, there's something in there man, I don't know what, but I'll take my chances in the rain."

Det. Fannichuci couldn't understand Tim's refusal to go through the walkway, so the two men headed up to the house in the rain.

Tim showed Det. Fannichuci where the basement window was located as they approached the house.

Everything was as Tim told Det. Fannichuci it was... Det. Fannichuci saw Mary tied to a post and another woman strapped down on a table.

Sitting in two chairs was a man and a woman, bound and gagged. Upon closer inspection Det. Fannichuci recognized the man in the chair as Officer Reggie Parker.

Det. Fannichuci and Tim scanned the basement for the man wearing the ballerina's tutu, when they spotted him over by the steps heading up the steps into the house.

Det. Fannichuci tapped Tim on the shoulders and motioned for him to head back to the small cabin. Reluctantly, Tim followed all the while asking...

"Why didn't we do something...all we had to do was go in and grab Mary and get the hell out of dodge?"

Det. Fannichuci told Tim that without a plan, all they could hope to do was to give him another hostage or two, or even... worse get everybody killed.

Once they returned to the cabin, they found Officer Withers asleep on one of the bunk beds.

Officer Withers did not hear the men come in but later awoke as she heard them talking about rescuing the others.

Officer Withers said...

"Sorry I dozed off, what did you find out?"

Det. Fannichuci removed his rain soaked coat and said...

"Everything checks out, there are several people bound and gagged and unless I'm mistaken one of the people looked like Officer Parker...you remember coach don't you?"

Officer Withers responded as she wiped her eyes...

"Yeah I met him once when I was a recruit, but what's he doing here?"

Det. Fannichuci told Officer Withers the plan that he and Tim had put together.

Tim was going to create a diversion in the house to draw the big man upstairs, so that Det. Fannichuci could free the people in the basement.

Officer Withers asked what her part in the plan was going to be, when Det. Fannichuci said...

"Nothing...stay here and just be ready to shoot whatever comes up behind us."

Officer Withers shook her head and said...

"Shoot whatever comes up behind you... how am I supposed to be able to tell who's who, in all this rain and fog...that's pretty lame Tony?"

Det. Fannichuci checked the magazine clip in his gun and said...

"This cabin is our only option, the people in the house are probably hurt and will have to have somewhere safe to hold up in, until we can deal with the psycho in the ballerina's tutu.

We go busting in there and try to run out in all of this rain with injured people, we're just screwing our own chances, besides we got to see what we're dealing with first."

Det. Fannichuci told Officer Withers she might as well shut her eyes for a few minutes, because him and Tim we're going to wait twenty minutes before heading out.

The pouring rain provided some comfort that the man in the ballerina's tutu, or anyone else for that matter would be confined to staying inside.

Tim double checked the wooden beam which was braced against the front door. Little concern was given to the window on the side of the house as it was too small for an adult to fit through.

Somewhere in the twenty minutes Officer Withers, Det. Fannichuci and Tim found themselves fast asleep.

Had the snoring not awakened Officer Withers, the three would have slept until the morning.

"Three-Twenty-two."

Officer Withers was about to waken Det. Fannichuci and Tim, when all of a sudden she heard a noise outside.

It was a quiet tapping on the window behind her. There was no way she was going to pull the ragged curtain away from the window to peek out.

Officer Withers hoped it was nothing more than a small animal, like a squirrel or chipmunk, or bird or something.

The tapping was back...but only this time it was more like fingernails tapping against the window. Officer Withers started to get nervous. After each tapping, she could hear the sound of children giggling.

Officer Withers began whispering for her partner and Tim in the darkness of the room in a small quiet voice...

"Hey...Tony...wake up, hey you guys?"

Officer Withers tried calling them again a little louder, but all she heard was the snores of two very tired men.

Just then, Officer Withers felt something cold and wet on her lips.

Her first impression was that Tim was making a move on her, because she'd seen the way he eyed her ever since they arrived.

Officer Withers wasn't going to shoot Tim, she was only going to scare him a little by putting the gun in his face...but something was wrong, something was very wrong.

Officer Withers tried lifting her hands up, but she couldn't. She was literally being held down, but there was nothing that she could feel holding her.

She tried to scream but something held her to the bunk and was preventing her from screaming and getting free.

Every time she tried to make a sound, it was as if her breath was being sucked out of her.

Officer Withers could not understand why her partner or Tim wasn't able to hear her struggling.

Officer Withers could not tell who was wrestling with her or how many, the only thing she be could sure of was, there was something holding her.

Det. Fannichuci and Tim began stirring around in the small cabin. The rain was still as heavy as it was several hours earlier, as Det. Fannichuci shook Tim saying...

"Tim, damnit Tim wake up...we must have both dozed off."

While the cabin was dark, Det. Fannichuci immediately sensed that something wasn't right. Even through the cabin darkness enough light shone in through cabin window to see.

Det. Fannichuci stood up and said...

"Where in the hell is Kathy?"

He thought to himself...she probably had to go again.

Det. Fannichuci tapped Tim on the shoulder again, as Tim jumped up and lit the only candle which he found.

Tim awakened saying...

"How long have we been asleep?"

Det. Fannichuci grabbed Tim's arm, and shook it and said...

"Forget about how long we've been asleep...where's my partner?"

Tim was a little more puzzled as he crawled over to the door, saying...

"I was going to say, she had to pee again, but if she went outside she didn't use the front door...look the log is still against the front door!"

Det. Fannichuci was pretty good at his line of work, but this had him stumped. The only other way out was through the upper window, but something was not adding up.

Det. Fannichuci said to Tim...

"Officer Withers would never have gone out that way; she would have awakened us and used the front door."

Det. Fannichuci started to remove the beam from against the door, when Tim asked ...

"Hey, what color of fingernail polish was Officer Withers wearing?"

Det. Fannichuci left the beam and walked over to Tim and said...

"She didn't wear fingernail polish, why?"

Tim told Det. Fannichuci...that's what he thought as he handed Det. Fannichuci four whole fingernails which looked as if they had been ripped off.

Det. Fannichuci examined the fingernails and the small window when Tim said...

"Now do you believe what I've been saying, there's something spooky up here."

Turning his attention back to the beam, Det. Fannichuci said...

"One thing is for sure Officer Withers is not inside the cabin and God help that big cheese eating son of a bitch if he's done anything to Kathy."

Det. Fannichuci repeated himself saying...

"I just don't understand how she could have left the cabin without us knowing it, and without using the door...I just don't get that."

Tim interrupted Det. Fannichuci by saying...

"You might as well save your breath it's like I've been trying to tell you...there are spirits or some kind of evil supernatural shit happening up here."

Det. Fannichuci cut Tim off by saying...

"Put the brakes on that evil spirit shit."

Tim walked up to Det. Fannichuci and said...

"Okay well you tell me, how did your partner get out of the cabin, because she surely didn't use the door, and I doubt if she went out the window...the window is close to eighteen feet off the floor...she didn't fly did she?"

Det. Fannichuci backed Tim off of him a little and said...

"I don't know what the fuck is going on...but we're going to that house, and I'm going to get some answers...I'm tired of playing these sick ass games!"

Tim sarcastically sniped at Det. Fannichuci...

"I guess what we got to get our minds around right now is... whatever evil is up here, nothing is going to be like we think it is."

Det. Fannichuci told Tim that they were heading in the direction of the house, because that's where we'll find his partner.

Det. Fannichuci also told Tim that his first priority was to his partner, and everything else was a distant second.

Before reaching the house they stopped at the barn, but it was completely dark, and both doors were locked.

Det. Fannichuci whispered to Tim that the barn may be a better place to hold up in, as the two men searched for a way to get inside.

As Tim and Det. Fannichuci walked to the back door of the barn, Tim made a suggestion to Det. Fannichuci that they use the skeleton key since the locks looked as if they'll fit.

Upon entering the barn, Det. Fannichuci commented to Tim about the amount of money it must have cost to refurbish the barn.

Tim told Det. Fannichuci that his friends David and Deanne told him that they inherited a lot of money and used it fix up the farm.

Tim and Det. Fannichuci left the barn and headed up to the house. As they circled the entire house, Det. Fannichuci told Tim to keep an eye out for any signs of Officer Withers.

Det. Fannichuci told Tim he has three things to do, number one was to climb into the second story window and make as much noise as he could, anything that would make the man in the ballerina's tutu leave the basement and come upstairs.

Number two was once the man in the ballerina's tutu began chasing him to run in the opposite direction of the farm away from the cabin, because he didn't want the man in the ballerina's tutu to look there.

Number three was to stay away from the basement because he wasn't coming back to save Tim's ass after he gets everybody else out.

Det. Fannichuci and Tim picked up the ladder and extended it so it would reach the second floor window.

Tim began climbing up the ladder, as Det. Fannichuci peeked in through the basement window to wait for the man in the ballerina's tutu to head upstairs.

Just when it looked as if he would never come back to the basement, the man in the ballerina's tutu wearing the clown's mask returned.

Det. Fannichuci noticed the man in the ballerina's tutu was carrying something and walking towards the outside door, hoping that he did not lock the door.

Before giving Tim the signal and making sure the man in the ballerina's tutu was away from the door, Det. Fannichuci quietly turned the door knob and to his surprise, the door was not locked.

Just then something tapped Det. Fannichuci on the shoulder causing him to jump. It was Tim. He whispered into Det. Fannichuci's ear and said...

"We need to regroup and find another way in."

Knowing they could not stand there in the rain talking without being discovered, the two men made their way to the barn a couple hundred feet from the house.

Det. Fannichuci peeked in the window besides the barns backdoor, but it was completely dark inside.

Quietly he turned the door knob until the door opened with a slight squeak. As both men entered, Det. Fannichuci told Tim they were going to have to check from top to bottom, to make sure the place was empty.

Det. Fannichuci found a closet to the left as they entered the room, where there sat a generator, with several burnt candles.

Picking up the candles, Det. Fannichuci asked Tim...

"Do you have matches or a lighter?"

Tim reached into his inside coat pocket and pulled out his prized zippo lighter and an old cigarette case where he kept his marijuana.

Looking down at the case, Det. Fannichuci said...
"Wow, haven't seen one of them in a minute."

Det. Fannichuci lit one of the candles and handed the lighter to Tim, who lit his candle as well as a joint, which he pulled from his cigarette case, when Det. Fannichuci said...
"You've got to be kidding me...are you out of your fucking mind?"
Tim took a big drag, and cupped his candle to conceal the outline of his shadow and replied...
"It is, what it is...you got your gun, and I got my pot."
As they headed upstairs Det. Fannichuci mumbled....'fucking pothead'.
After searching every room upstairs, Det. Fannichuci and Tim came back to the downstairs living room area.
Tim said to Det. Fannichuci...
"We're going to have to come up with another plan to get into the house...the windows have bars on them."
Det. Fannichuci told Tim, he was going to have to break the downstairs window, and when the man in the ballerina's tutu comes to see what the noise is, try to draw him out of the house.
He told Tim to let the man in the ballerina's tutu chase after him, with a man that size, he would never catch Tim.
Tim reminded Det. Fannichuci...
"Dumb-dumb-dumb, look Dick, I'm high, and it's dark and raining its ass off and all I'm going to end doing is slipping in the mud or running right into him...no way, why don't you be the one he chases?"

Det. Fannichuci replied...
"For starters, I'm over weight, and plus I'd stand a better chance of getting everybody out alive...you said it yourself...you're stoned."
Tim reluctantly agreed to the plan that he would be the one who the man in the ballerina's tutu was going to chase.
The rain and fog which had set in was making it hard for Tim to see, not to mention getting a good grip on the bannister.
Det. Fannichuci watched as Tim started climbing up onto the porch and walked over to the basement window and got down on his knees to observe the man in the ballerina's tutu.

Just then Det. Fannichuci saw the man in the ballerina's tutu turn his head upward towards the door at the top of the steps as Tim smashed the living room window.

The man in the ballerina's tutu began walking up the steps as Det. Fannichuci got up off of his knees and headed towards the basement door.

Slowly Det. Fannichuci turned the old rusty door knob and slowly pushed the door open. He could see that there were six people bound and gagged in the basement.

Det. Fannichuci's plan was to untie Reggie first and then the two of them would free everyone else.

Removing his gun from his coat, Det. Fannichuci took two steps in the direction of Reggie and Perry, when he felt something sticky under his shoes.

Det. Fannichuci tried taking another step but couldn't. His shoes were stuck in some sort of epoxy.

Det. Fannichuci squatted down and attempted to wrestle his shoes from the epoxy when he realized that the epoxy was all over the floor on the inside of the door, and that his shoes were completely stuck to the floor.

Unable to move, Det. Fannichuci untied his shoes and looked for a place on the floor which did not have this glue on it.

The lightening flashed and Det. Fannichuci noticed a dry spot to his right, about five feet away.

Wiggling his feet out of his shoes, Det. Fannichuci carefully stood on them and tried to get himself ready to jump five feet, something which he doubted given his weight but he realized that he had no other choice.

The man in the ballerina's tutu was surely on his way back down in the basement, and Det. Fannichuci knew if he didn't make the jump, then everything else was pointless.

Det. Fannichuci heard footsteps and then the front door closing, and counted to himself before he jumped...

"One, two, three."

Det. Fannichuci jumped with all his might and made a landing onto his stomach just at the edge of the glued area.

Being careful to keep his legs in the air, Det. Fannichuci could
feel his socks barely touching the glue. As Det. Fannichuci when he
rolled himself over onto the dry basement floor, his socks remained
in the glue.

Det. Fannichuci took the gun from his pocket and quickly crept
over in Reggie's direction.

The sound of Det. Fannichuci hitting the basement floor caught
Reggie's attention, which began shaking his head...

"No-no-no!"

Det. Fannichuci didn't understand why Reggie was signaling for
him to not come in his direction until he took another step.

Directly in front of Reggie and Perry the entire floor area had large
nails protruding from the floor boards, as Det. Fannichuci stepped
onto barefoot.

Grinding his teeth into the sleeve of his coat, Det. Fannichuci
looked down at both feet which had nails protruding out them.

The boards with nails were screwed to the floor directly in front
of Reggie and Perry, as Det. Fannichuci took a deep breath and slowly
lifted both feet.

Three to four rusty nails penetrated both feet, that when Det.
Fannichuci lifted his feet, blood dripped from the holes in his feet.

Det. Fannichuci was careful about not losing his balance and
looked for a safe place in the darkness to place his feet when he lost
his balance and fell backwards onto the floor, his gun coming out of
his coat pocket and sliding into the darkness.

Det. Fannichuci decided to stay on his knees and feel his way
towards Reggie, when out of the darkness, a hideous face appeared
directly in front of him and in a loud voice cried...

"Boo!"

Startling Det. Fannichuci, he quickly scooted backwards on his
hands and feet, forgetting about the glue and landing in the glue, only
this time instead of his shoes sticking to the glue, now his hands, feet
and the bottom of his pants were now stuck.

Det. Fannichuci struggled and struggled trying to get free, but the more and more he struggled...the stronger the glue permanently bonded to his hands, feet and his pants bottoms, bonding him in a crab position to the basement floor.

The time for rescuing the people in the basement without being detected had long come and gone, as the basement door opened and the man in the ballerina's tutu stood at the top of the steps.

Of all the bad luck that a person could have in the world, Det. Fannichuci was having his share as he let out a loud cry...

"AWWWW!"

The man in the ballerina's tutu began descending down into the basement, dragging something behind him which hit each of the basement steps as he slowly walked down.

Suddenly the basement lights came on as Mr. Thomas appeared standing next to the man in the ballerina's tutu.

Det. Fannichuci cried out to the two men, not being able to see them from the position which he was stuck in, saying...

"Look, I don't know you or what you're doing, but I'm a Detective and one of the people you have down here is also a police officer... you can't hope to get away with this...there'll be more police here than you'll know what to do with, if you don't let us go."

Mr. Thomas positioned himself in front of Det. Fannichuci so that he could see him and said...

"You're a police officer and he's a police officer, huh...well what about this one here?"

At the sound of that the man in the ballerina's tutu drug Officer Withers over in front of Det. Fannichuci and dropped her limp body on the floor, saying...

"Get away with it...we don't want to get away with anything, and as for more police coming to look for you...No one else will come."

Det. Fannichuci looked at Officer Withers limp and lifeless body and said as she whimpered...

"Oh my God Kathy...what have they done to you...You sick son of a bitches...what have you done to her?"

Mr. Thomas reached down and grabbed the face of Det. Fannichuci and squeezed it and said...

"Not...what we've done...it's what we are going to do. In a little while you'll all experience life on a whole new level...our level. All over your world and in every city, there are gatherings just like this one. Some a little more inventive, but all fun I can assure you."

Det. Fannichuci struggled to speak when Mr. Thomas said...

"Oh...I beg your pardon...are you trying to say something?"

Det. Fannichuci cried out in pain as he tried to relax his arms which were locked behind him. Catching his breath Det. Fannichuci cried out...'

"Listen, I don't know what you're talking about...you're talking about something you're going to do..., maybe we can talk, try to get you some help."

Mr. Thomas walked into the glue and pulled Det. Fannichuci's head back, allowing his hair to become stuck in the glue and said...

"Does it look like I need help...and I know you're thinking I'm stuck in here with you, right! We'll this stuff here has no effect on me, as a matter of fact nothing in your reality has an effect on any of us."

Mr. Thomas walked out of the glue unaffected and stood before Det. Fannichuci as Det. Fannichuci said...

"Please, who are you...I can't stay like this, if you're going to kill me, well kill me."

Mr. Thomas stood up, and with one hand he scratched his head, and putting the other hand in his back pocket, said...

"You couldn't comprehend who I am...where I come, from should be the question to ask. Let me just say for now...we are from a dimension parallel to this one. Your existence was privileged and honored above us, but you don't deserve it!"

Det. Fannichuci cried out in pain as his feet and arms were in excruciating pain...

"Oh, Jesus...help me God!"

Mr. Thomas raised his foot and brought it down hard in Det. Fannichuci's stomach and cried...

"And don't use His name either...you don't deserve to say His name!"

Mr. Thomas walked back over to the man in the ballerina's tutu who was tying Officer Withers to one of the wooden posts.

Then after cutting off the lights in the basement they both started up the steps as Mr. Thomas began singing a song in the tune of the Muffin Man...

"Oh....do you know the game we'll play,
The game we'll play, the game we'll play,
Do you know game we'll play?
I...don't think so."

Mr. Thomas and the man in the ballerina's tutu disappeared up the stairs; a lone figure peeked through the small basement window at the captives below.

From the position which Det. Fannichuci was stuck in he could see the small window from his angle very well, but from upside down.

The lightening flashed and as it did, Det. Fannichuci could see that it was Tim. Somehow Tim escaped. A second later the lightening flashed again and Tim was gone.

Det. Fannichuci hoped that the image he saw was Tim and not a figment of his imagination and if it was Tim, he hoped that Tim had ran away to get help.

Chapter 13

Cold Chills

What started out as a simple hunting trip for Steve, had fast become a nightmare.

The cool temperature and over cast skies and light drizzle which seized the whole day, turned into a torrential down pour.

Steve couldn't find an explanation as to why he ended up almost two hundred and fifty miles from the wild life park in Columbus to the farm of his best friend in Port Clinton, some two hours away in a matter of minutes.

Thinking to himself, Steve said....

"How am I going to explain this to David and Deanne, just showing up and with no transportation or anything...that's if they're here?"

Steve's thoughts gave way to reality as the rain was now running down the back of his neck, and the fact he could see David and Deanne's farm in the distance.

Though the farmhouse was in sight the barn was closer, because it sat almost a hundred feet from the house, when something caught Steve's eye.

When he first looked and saw the farmhouse, it looked as though thick smoke was pouring from the chimney and rising up into the night sky, but as Steve got closer to the farmhouse, he noticed something strange.

It wasn't smoke from the chimney which he saw, but fog. The fog resembled a huge white funnel cloud which circled and settle all around the farmhouse.

Nowhere else was the fog moving in on but David and Deanne's farmhouse, and the fog seemed to be circling and engulfing just this one area.

Steve remembered how David talked about building a covered walkway leading from the barn which was converted into guest sleeping areas, to the main house.

Steve pulled his collar up around his neck, lowered his head and ran in the direction of the barn.

When Steve arrived at the barn he found the barn door partially open and what appeared to be wet and muddy tracks leading to the walkway.

Steve let out a sigh of relief as he realized his friend was there at the farm, as he ran upstairs to the bathroom.

Racing into the bathroom as fast as he could, and sitting down on the commode, Steve threw his head back and sighed as if it seemed as though he hadn't used a bathroom in days.

Steve scanned the toilet paper roll and sure enough... if you don't check for wiping paper before you sit down, the roll could be empty as Steve sat staring at an empty roll.

Steve's eyes searched the immediate area for something he could use to wipe his behind, when he spotted the paper towel rack on the wall between the door and the commode.

Steve jumped up and snatched down several sheets, cut on the water at the sink to wet the paper towels, when he jumped.

Instead of water coming out of the sink, there was a thick black goo, oozing out of the faucet.

Steve reached to cut the faucet off when the entire fixture began vibrating and then the thick black goo started thinning out as the water made its way through the faucet.

Within a few minutes the water was clear, as Steve wet both paper towels and wiped himself.

Steve was about to flush the toilet when suddenly there was a lot of stomping or someone walking very loudly in the hallway.

Steve was about two feet from the door and was about to open it and call for his friends when someone begin pounding on the walls and doors all over the barn...

"Bam...Bam...Bam!"

Thinking perhaps David had seen someone enter the barn, and was attempting to scare away an intruder, Steve said...

"*Hey Dave...Dave it's me, Steve.*"

The pounding on the door stopped as Steve opened the bathroom door expecting to see his friend David Blue.

Steve stepped out into an empty hallway, and upon not seeing his friend or anyone, called out...

"*Dave, hey man quit screwing around...it's Steve.*"

Steve didn't get a reply so he slowly walked out into the hallway when he heard the sound of a door creaking loudly.

When Steve turned, he noticed the door to one of the bedrooms was beginning to close.

Normally something like this would not have bothered Steve, but what Steve has just gone through in the past few hours, he wasn't about to walk blindly and follow something into a closed room.

Steve decided to get his behind downstairs and out of the barn to the farmhouse. Steve walked down the steps and into the living room area when he heard voices echoing in the walkway.

With the amount of rain and the thick fog which was setting in, Steve initially thought he'd take the walkway, but now he wasn't so sure.

Steve wasn't a coward or afraid of things, but prided himself on when he took chances.

Steve looked around for a flashlight, or candles to provide some light for the walkway.

The walkway bore little light, and while Steve had no problems with the dark, he needed a light of some kind, because he had never been in the walkway, or at the farm for that matter and didn't know what he was walking into.

At the entrance of the walkway was a small closet where the farmhouse generator was, and inside on top of a shelf was a box with two large candles and a box of strike anywhere matches.

Steve noticed as he started to make his way through the first few feet of the walkway that not all of the windows had not been installed, but a few windows were covered with plastic which was ripped in several places.

The rain and wind easily made its way through the ripped pieces of plastic, and just as Steve approached the first window, he noticed several hundred feet in the darkness, a light swaying back and forth.

Holding both candles to the opposite side of where the windows were, to prevent them from being blown out, he noticed something odd.

Looking out one of the windows through the fog and heavy rain he saw a light, a light which looked like the glare of a flashlight.

Steve hollered out hoping that it was David...

"DAVE!"

Steve's sense of calm suddenly turned to icy apprehension as the hairs on the back of his neck stood up, and he knew *"something wasn't right in Kansas."*

As Steve was backing away from the window, he didn't notice the dark figure behind him, and backed into something cold, wet and solid like flesh.

Steve jumped and turned so quickly that he forgot about the candles he was holding, as they both blew out as he dropped them on the ground.

Whoever or whatever was behind Steve, suddenly grabbed him and Steve struggled and began yelling...

"Get the fuck off of me! Get your damn hands off me...now get the fuck off!"

As quickly as Steve was grabbed by the dark figure behind him, he was released. Standing in darkness, Steve tried focusing on what was in front of him, trying to at least make out an outline...a shape anything.

Steve stood looking around and then he felt the wind behind him howling and the feeling that something was watching him.

Just then an eerie voice laughed and said...

"David Blue, David Blue, David Blue...

You think you know David Blue...well we know him too

He'll be here soon...and coming here is something all of you will

come to regret...

If you survive...Aha, ha, ha, ha, ha, ha, ha, ha, ha...

Twisted and Dread, Twisted and Dread"!

259

The wind stopped howling, and on the floor to Steve's right he saw both candles flickering and sitting upright… still lit.

Steve cringed as the coldness of the rain beat against his neck, and brought him back to reality…the reality of what in the hell was he going to do?

Steve's mind went over the course of events of the past several hours, and pondered in his mind, how in the hell a simple hunting trip could transpire into a full blown demonic nightmare.

Scared but knowing he had to make it to the house…Steve picked up the candles which barely gave off just enough light for him to see that there was nothing or no one in the walkway with him.

Steve turned back looking for the light which he had seen through the window, which was no longer there.

Steve continued through the walkway feeling a little better because now he could see that the house light was on lighting up the last few feet of the walkway.

Steve expected to be greeted by David or Deanne, however, what Steve didn't know, was…that beyond the door, he was about to experience evil, and a darkness which would forever permeate the recesses of his mind and shatter everything that he had ever believed in.

Steve was perhaps twenty feet from the house door entrance when he heard a voice behind him calling out through the darkness…

"Oh Steve… thank God it's you!"

Steve turned and standing in front of him was Wendi. Steve placed both candles on the window near him and reached out and grabbed Wendi saying…

"Honey, sweetie…damn baby…you don't know how good it is to see your face. Did you and Deanne just drive up?"

Steve barely finished his sentence when Wendi put two fingers up to his lips to silence him, and began kissing him and saying…

"Oh babe, it's okay, it's okay. Deanne called me, and we drove here."

Steve was unaware of Wendi's murder, in Columbus the day before, and that the person standing in front of him, kissing and holding him was not Wendi as he would soon find out.

Steve had just been through a nightmare and the sight of Wendi clouded all of the red flags that he should have seen.

Steve and Wendi stood hugging and kissing, and as Steve ran his hands through Wendi's hair and held her back to ask about David and Deanne...he saw something that made him sick to his stomach.

Steve was about to tell Wendi about all the weird things he'd seen and how they needed to get out of there as he looked down at his hands.

Steve noticed his hands were full of wet clumps of hair and leaves from Wendi's head. The person standing in front of Steve, whom moments ago, he had been passionately kissing, no longer looked like Wendi, but had a grayish demonic appearance, as if she'd been dead for some time.

The woman began to laugh as maggots wiggled and protruded through her crooked grayish jagged teeth.

Suddenly Steve felt the movement of something in his mouth, and after wiping the clumps of hair on his pants leg, he reached up and placed his finger in his mouth.

Steve began spitting and hollering with disgust as he noticed his hand were covered with maggots.

The person whom Steve thought was Wendi, was an old woman in the late stages of decomposition. All that was left of what should've been her eyes, were two wrinkled sunken hollow places.

Steve backed up and then took off running towards the house until he reached the pantry, just inside the back door.

Not certain of what to do next, Steve quickly felt for the light switch and turned on the lights.

Taking a deep breath, he ran into the open kitchen and turned on the faucet and rinse his mouth out.

A big part of Steve already knew he would not find a living person in the house, let alone
David or Deanne.

It was just an undeniable feeling which stayed with Steve for a while. Feelings never prove anything rational, but feelings were all that Steve had left.

Steve began thinking about his two dead friends, and the man in the clown's face when suddenly...

It felt like there was someone standing behind him. Steve could feel the breath of someone and when Steve turned to look, obviously there was no one there.

Steve walked over to close the back door when he heard a faint sound.

It sounded very much like laughter, which was coming from the woods.

Steve would've been the last person to run and hide, but he was freaked out. Steve locked the door and stood there for a moment, unaware that he was not alone in the house.

Steve opened the fridge out of instinct and discovered a six pack of beer and a half fifth of Vodka, saying...

"This is what I'm talking about...thank you Dave."

With the Vodka in his hand, Steve climbed the stairs, when he heard people talking and as he stopped to figure out where the voices were coming from.

There was A faint conversation with several people. Steve listened as hard as he could, hoping it was David and Deanne, but then there was dead silence.

Steve walked into the first room when he started calling David and Deanne's name as he pushed open the door saying...

"Hey Dave, Deanne, anybody here...there is some strange shit happening you guys."

As Steve pushed open the door he found the room empty, and a noise coming from the window got his attention, and he decided to go over and look out the window.

Steve crept slowly towards the window to peek out, when something tapped him on his shoulder.

As Steve turned around a loud voice screamed.......

"Boo!"

Steve hollered. The upstairs lights were on so Steve knew David or Deanne was somewhere nearby.

Outside of the window where Steve was standing there was a clanging sound, and against his better judgement, Steve looked out to see a man just standing in the rain.

It was Mr. Thomas, David and Deanne's neighbor...just standing by the fence, and then as if he heard Steve's thoughts, Mr. Thomas looked up in the window at Steve and pointed his finger saying...

"They're going to plant you like winter wheat...he-he-he-he-he!"

Steve was completely frozen by fear or shock but for some reason he couldn't tear himself away from the window.

Steve started thinking that everything was just a product of being too tired and delirious, but before those thoughts cemented themselves in Steve's mind, there was a loud pounding and stomping coming from the hallway on one of the doors.

The sound of the pounding on the walls seemed to be headed in Steve's direction, and just before the pounding got to the room Steve was in... the door slammed shut.

Hearing the pounding on the walls getting louder and louder and coming closer, Steve grabbed the bedroom vanity chair from the vanity and flung it violently against the window.

Steve's heart switched gears and went from survival mode to desperation, after seeing that the window was not smashed.

Steve was about to make another attempt to smash the window when he noticed Mr. Thomas pointing up at the window laughing, and dancing in a circle.

Steve looked around the small room for something, anything that he could use to defend himself with.

Steve didn't see anything that he could use, so decided to leave the room.

Steve opened the door and saw the man in a ballerina's tutu going into a room down the hall.

Steve crept over across the hall to another bedroom leaving the bedroom door open, waiting for the man in the ballerina's tutu.

Steve grabbed a small lamp from the nightstand and positioned himself by the door. Steve watched as the man in the ballerina's tutu went into the bedroom that was one room from where he was waiting.

Steve's plan was to throw the lamp into the opened bedroom, and when the man in the ballerina's tutu ran inside to check on the noise, Steve would shut and lock the bedroom door, giving him time to run out of the house.

Everything was going as planned. Steve threw the lamp into the opened bedroom and when the man in the ballerina's tutu rushed in to the room.

Steve crept out and closed the bedroom door, locking it with the skeleton key he'd found on the door knob of the basement door.

Steve ran down the stairs listening as the man in the ballerina's tutu violently shook and pounded on the bedroom door, as he ran out the front door towards the side of the house.

The rain continued pouring as Steve watched the man in the ballerina's tutu appear in the window of the bedroom.

Not a second had passed when Steve looked back at the front porch, and noticed the man in the ballerina's tutu was standing there.

Steve remembered when he was being chased in the woods, he'd seen four or five men in ballerina's tutus, so fear took hold of Steve as he stopped dead in his tracks and began scanning the area.

Just then he heard a noises coming from over by the basement.

Bending down to look into the basement window Steve saw people. The mud which the rain splashed against the window made it hard to see, but Steve counted four maybe five people.

Steve thought to himself that maybe David and Deanne are in trouble in the basement. He couldn't leave his best friend in trouble and not help.

Steve also realized that he was going to have to do something that he didn't want to do and that was going back inside the house.

Standing there Steve saw foot prints in the mud about size thirteen maybe larger, and knew the man in the ballerina's tutu was using the outside basement door to enter and exit.

Not knowing exactly what to do, Steve's attention was drawn once again to voices coming from the basement.

Steve knew that getting as far away from the farm was the most sensible option, but Steve was not a coward, he just couldn't leave the people in trouble.

Not knowing what or who he would find, he made the decision to go into the basement, Steve carefully opened the door.

Directly in front of Steve and in a crab position was a man, who motioned to Steve not to enter.

The man told Steve he was a Detective and that there was some kind of glue all around the inside of the basement door, and for Steve to go get help.

As Steve's eyes scanned the basement he could faintly see and hear voices, moans and crying coming from the far side of the basement.

A single light which hung from the ceiling was swaying back and forth, revealing the outline of four people.

A strong musky rotten odor, mixed with the scent of burning flesh filled the damp basement.

Bound, gagged, blindfolded and strapped to chairs were two people, a man and a woman.

David and Deanne's best friend, Mary who was tied to one of the support columns.

Steve had met Mary six years earlier when he moved to Columbus after marrying Wendi, but had no clue who the other two people were.

Steve stuck his head in the basement trying to make as little noise possible, knowing that the man in the ballerina's tutu may be on his way, and said to the man glued to the floor...

"Shh...my name is Steve...I'm going for help but I'll be back."

Steve crept away from the basement door and headed in the direction of the road.

Up ahead of Steve and going inside the barn, Steve saw the shadow of the man in the ballerina's tutu, and decided to turn around and go back into the basement from inside the front door of the house.

Steve tried the front door and when he found that it was locked, he went around to the back door, which was unlocked.

Steve could use all the help that he could get, so he scanned the basement from the top of the steps and decided he could untie everyone before the man in the ballerina's tutu returned.

The first person Steve saw was Mary. She had a fair amount of blood which had dried on the left side of her face.

Not thinking, Steve placed his hand under Mary's chin to lift her head up, when Mary opened her eyes.

Steve was at the point of motioning to Mary to be quiet, when Mary began moaning.

Steve immediately placed his hand over Mary's mouth when he noticed that her lips were sewn shut and sealed with glue.

Mary began whimpering as Steve told her to be quiet, and that he was going to get her out of this mess.

Steve stepped over to the man bound in the chair and reached to untie the nylon rope which held him, when Steve noticed something unusual....

The knot used to tie the couple up was something which Steve had heard about, but had never seen it with his eyes, until now.

Whoever was responsible for holding Mary and the others captive, had used a 'Gordian Knot'. A very old and almost impossible knot to untie...

The Gordian Knot was difficult to untie and had to be cut, because no matter which end or loop of the rope you tried to loosen, would only make the knot even tighter.

Steve looked over at the table where Mary was for something to use to cut the nylon cords, when Mary moaned again.

Steve turned in time to see the neighbor Mr. Thomas coming up behind him with an axe handle raised in the air.

Steve reached out and grabbed Mr. Thomas's hand as the two men wrestled and fell onto the table.

Steve thought as he wrestled with Mr. Thomas that it would be a no brainer over powering an old man in his seventies, but soon discovered for an old man, Mr. Thomas was incredibly strong.

In a surprising move Mr. Thomas released his hand from Steve and with the axe handle, smashed Steve on the right side of his face, knocking him to the floor.

Steve struggled to get to his feet when Mr. Thomas, again raised the axe handle and took a violent swing at Steve knocking him out.

Mr. Thomas hogtied Steve's wrists and ankles behind his back while he lay unconscious. The basement door opened and the man in the ballerina's tutu stood at the top of the steps grunting.

He had just come back from the barn, after checking on Officer Withers who was bound, gagged and locked in the upstairs closet.

The man in the ballerina's tutu grunted as he came down each step. Mr. Thomas looked at the man in the ballerina's tutu and then at Steve.

The man in the ballerina's tutu threw a rope through the top of the basement steps, and then looped the ropes around the steps which bound Steve and left him suspended in air under the basement steps.

The man in the ballerina's tutu slowly made his way up the steps, as the dark figure with red eyes trailed him and started to break up and disappear... like smoke when a fan hits it.

Reggie began squirming and trying to work his hands free when Perry screamed. Looking over at Perry, Reggie saw what frightened Perry.

A woman stripped naked with her hands tied behind her back and around her neck with a nylon cord. It was plain to see that she had large clumps of her hair pulled out.

The nylon cord was fastened to the ceiling rafter, with the woman's feet barely touching the floor.

Perry whispered to Reggie...

"OMG Reg, who is she...look at what they did to her lips...oh fuck...Reg do something."

The woman was suspended from the ceiling by ropes and dangling.

Her feet were grotesquely deformed and doubled in size. The man in the ballerina's tutu had suspended her over white hot coals, until her feet slowly, roasted and swelled, releasing large pockets of pus, which formed and then burst.

Reggie leaned over to Perry and as he was about to tell her to pretend to be unconscious, the basement door opened.

Mary's husband Tim came crashing down the steps onto the basement floor, with the man in the ballerina's tutu following close behind.

Reggie whispered to Perry to keep her head down and to be quiet no matter what happens and he would get her out of this mess.

The man in the ballerina's tutu stood over Tim's body and nudged him several times with his feet to see if he was conscious, and then picked him up and placed him in one of the chairs.

Reggie lifted his eyes slightly, watching the man in the ballerina's tutu while secretly trying to free his hands.

Reggie knew that he would only get one shot at rescuing Perry and the others in the basement, but everything hinged upon him getting free.

The man in the ballerina's tutu walked past Reggie and Perry and headed upstairs into the house. Meanwhile Reggie was trying to work his hands free, when he heard loud footsteps coming from upstairs as if a lot of people were running back and forth from room to room.

David Ray

Reggie looked over at Perry who was motioning for Reggie to look at the man who was lying on the floor. As Perry looked, he noticed Tim had gotten to his feet.

He had a large nasty wound to the right side of his head, and his left arm appeared to have been broken, due to the fact that he dangled it at his side.

Tim looked at Reggie and Perry and then his attention was drawn to Mary his wife. Tim slowly walked in her direction softly crying at first, and then crying louder...

"Mar, oh Mary...what has he done to you"?

Reggie tried telling Tim to lower his voice and help him get untied but Tim ignored him. In shock Tim raised his right hand up the Mary's face, his fingers lightly touching her lips which were sewn shut.

Tim's words went unnoticed by Mary who was unconscious. Reggie tried telling Tim to help him get free and that he was a police officer, and he could help.

Tim began crying and kissing Mary's face as his hand stroked Mary's face and arms, when the basement door open.

Tim backed away and hid in the corner out of the light as the man in the ballerina's tutu with the clown's face mask came down the steps.

He first walked over to Reggie and Perry, lifting up their heads to see if they were alert.

Dropping their heads, he moved over in Mary's direction and then slowly started looking for Tim's body.

Mary's head was already tilted back so the man in the ballerina's tutu grabbed Mary's cheeks and began to squeeze them and finger the stiches in her lips when out of the darkness Tim appeared with a hatchet in his hand.

The man in the ballerina's tutu after squeezing Mary's cheeks began gently slapping her in the face, trying to get her come to not realizing that Tim was coming up behind him.

Tim emerged from the darkness and with all his strength buried the rusty hatchet deep into the man's back.

The man in the ballerina's tutu frantically tried reaching back to pull out the hatchet, falling into the table, and then backing against the wall, trying to get the hatchet to dislodge itself but Tim did it right.

He buried the hatchet deep in the center of his back where neither of his massive hands could reach it.

Tim started backing away from the man in the ballerina's tutu, when he tripped and fell. Without the use of his left arm Tim struggled to his feet, and when he did the man in the ballerina's tutu caught hold of Tim by the throat.

As he lifted Tim in the air all Tim was able to do was to hit the man repeatedly on his arms, and when it looked as if Tim was running out of time the man in the ballerina's tutu dropped to his knees, releasing Tim.

Feeling light headed and dizzy from the choke hold, coughing and gagging, Tim got to his feet and walked back over to Mary when Reggie began whispering to Tim...

"While he's down head upstairs and get out of here...go get help... hurry."

Tim turned to look as the man in the ballerina's tutu slowly sank on the floor of the basement. Looking all around the basement, Tim ran over towards the outside basement door.

Tim climbed the steps all the while looking back at Mary, and he wanted to turn and go back to her, but noticed that the man in the ballerina's tutu was slowly getting up.

After putting the weight of his right shoulder into the door and turning the knob with his right hand, the door opened.

Tim started out the door and then stopped and took one step to come back down, when Reggie yelled...

"You can't do anything for her man get...the hell out of here!"

Tim turned, whispering...

"I love you Mary"

Then Tim ran into the kitchen and out the door into the rain and the darkness.

The man in the ballerina's tutu got to his feet and began thrashing and throwing his back against the basement walls, and moving from side to side again trying to dislodge the hatchet.

After several attempts the hatchet suddenly dislodged from his back and dropped to the floor.

The man in the ballerina's tutu reached down and picked up the hatchet and headed up the steps after Tim.

Once the man in the ballerina's tutu was plainly out of sight, Reggie began working his hands free and said to Perry…

"Perry, look it's now or never. Once we're free we are getting out of here. As soon as I get you lose…run, hang onto me and don't look back until we got to the SUV."

The ropes on Reggie's hands were starting to loosen and then gave way, when the outside basement door suddenly opened and then slammed shut.

Perry and Reggie looked up to see the man in the ballerina's tutu and Mr. Thomas, standing at the basement door and then coming towards Perry and Reggie, stepping on the body of Det. Fannichuci who yelled as the man in the ballerina's tutu stomped on him.

Perry's muffled cries bought the man in the ballerina's tutu directly in front of her as she began crying and shaking, not realizing that she just urinated on herself.

The man in the ballerina's tutu cocked his head to the left and then to the right, and began sniffing Perry as her urine ran down the chair and onto the floor.

Reggie's hands were now free, but his ankles were still tied to the chair when the man in the ballerina's tutu, grabbed Reggie by the throat and started to squeeze tight when Mr. Thomas tapped him on the arm.

Looking out of the small basement window, something or someone caught Mr. Thomas' eye.

Mr. Thomas and the man in the ballerina's tutu headed towards the steps to go upstairs and just before leaving the basement, Mr. Thomas and the man in the ballerina's tutu re-tied Reggie's hands and left.

Pecan Drive,
Columbus, Ohio

In addition to suffering from PTSD, one of the things I suffered from most was experiencing new degrees of all of the symptoms. I would get an almost paralyzing fear and feelings of being suffocated.

Feelings far worst and more reoccurring than the ones people experience, who suffer from panic attacks.

My last night before going back to the farm was the most restless night that I have ever had since I left the hospital.

While Deanne was asleep, I would often stay up in the middle of the night watching her sleep that was until I began having terrible migraines.

Migraines which would drive me from the comfort of my bed into the bathroom, hung over on the side of the bath tub for hours on end.

The thought of going back to the farm gave me the worst suffocating, panic attack… because I knew firsthand what was going to happen.

Only this time, instead of hanging over the side of the tub clutching the sides of my head, I started completely freaking out in the bath room, hearing and seeding things, jerking around and hyperventilating.

Then I heard the most terrifying sound of my life… it was a long screech like from a horror film.

Then the screech turned into laughter, a demonic laughter which grew louder and louder.

The lights flickered off and when they came back on there was a dark red glow like someone had put black paint in a red light bulb.

My migraine began to ease up, and when I got up off my knees I was literally shaking, and I tried with everything in me to get out of the bathroom but it was like I was frozen in that spot.

I started to feel as if I was really losing my mind and close to being a hop, skip and jump from being back at giggle central.

Not being able to speak, seeing things and people appearing and disappearing, was having their toll on me.

Suddenly there was a knock on the bathroom door, as Deanne said...

"Hey Blue, I'm going to take Shone over to Cathy's so that'll give you about thirty minutes to get ready...okay?"

My migraine subsided a little and the shaking in his hands and knees also lessoned.

The laughter and the red light, that I was hearing and seeing grew brighter and louder as I backed into the wall covering my eyes.

Looking into the mirror I saw the image of a man standing by an open door. It was the man I saw at the farm.

The big man in the ballerina's tutu wearing the clown's face.

I turned and as he did, all I saw was my bathroom door open. Not wanting to deal with seeing anything else...I quickly ran downstairs to catch Deanne but was too late.

Just as I opened the front door, Deanne was turning the corner.

I would've stayed outside on the porch but I closed the door as the cold rain reminded me that I was only wearing boxer briefs and a tee shirt.

I stood in the living room with my back against the door terrified and determined that I wasn't going to move one inch from that spot until Deanne returned.

One of the classic symptoms of PTSD is the need for isolation, not wanting to be around a lot of people, but being alone was the last thing I either needed or wanted.

I stood looking around the living room when all of a sudden I started itching all over. The television and the CD player suddenly came on, with both volumes blaring.

I took a few steps into the living room and grabbed the remote control and as I went back over to the door the power in the condo went out. Everything that I could see...lamps, clocks, everything was out but the volumes grew louder than they were originally designed to go.

Suddenly the cabinet drawers over the sink in the kitchen swung open and cups and glasses began shooting out, swirling in the air and then crashing all over the kitchen and living room.

I backed closer against the front door, when just then I heard loud demonic laughing coming from upstairs, with the sound of heavy footsteps coming from the bedroom towards the steps.

I turned and grabbed the front door knob, trying with all of my might to open the door, but wasn't able to turn the knob.

The heavy footsteps seemed to be getting closer as I turned back around but there was no one coming down the steps.

I was the most terrified that I have ever been in my life. Whatever it was that was after me, literally scared the piss out of me as I looked down and noticed a puddle in front of me by the front door.

There I was a grown man, who had been to war, and survived a variety of things that would make the strongest person crap all over themselves, standing there crying and shaking like a little girl.

I couldn't believe it, but there I was inside my own house and pounding on the door and shaking the door knob in fear...but these spirits or whatever they were brought with them a fear which I've never felt before.

Just then, demonic voices of those creepy kids started singing...

"La-la-la-la-la-la-, la-la-la-la-la-la,

Teddy Bear, Soda Crackers,

Swinging from a tree,

All your friends are at the farm

But it's you we want to see...

La-la-la-la-la-la-, la-la-la-la-la-la."

I wished I could have opened my mouth to scream to make some kind of noise, but I was helpless to do anything.

Panic and sheer terror set in as I continued to bang and kick on the door, trying to turn the door knob.

The thought of running upstairs entered my mind but each time I tried to make a run for the steps, a dish or glass flew at me, crashing into the walls.

Sliding down to the floor, about to give up, I gripped the door knob with both hands when at last...the door knob turned.

I stood up and opened the door and when the door was opened... Deanne was standing there with her door key in the lock, and her hand on the knob looking at me yelling...

"Damn Blue, you're still in your underwear...what's the matter with you?"

I grabbed Deanne's arm and pulled her into the living room and pointed towards the kitchen.

I knew that once Deanne saw the mess, she would know that there was something in our house which was evil.

Deanne walked into the kitchen while I stood in the living room by the door biting my finger nails, when Deanne yelled...

"OMG Blue, just look at this mess."

Certain that Deanne now was able to see that something had been after me, I walked over to the kitchen doorway, as Deanne pointed out...

"Look at this will you... you have a half-eaten plate of food in the sink and a cigarette butt in one of my coffee cups... Blue I told you, if you're going to smoke, smoke outside!"

I turned around and slowly walked into the kitchen, and looked around and everything was in place except for the plate of food in the sink and the coffee cup which Deanne was pouring in the disposal.

I walked over to the fridge to get a bottle of water and almost jumped out of my skin, when Deanne tapped me on my back and said...

"...Look I told you I was going to the farm, so if you want to play fucking games, then stay here by yourself!"

Being alone was the last thing on my mind. I ran after Deanne and motioned for her to wait. I pulled a pair of jeans and a sweat shirt from the dryer, and threw my coat on and ran out the door after Deanne.

Deanne got in on the driver's side, while I was locking the door to the condo, when Deanne rolled down the window and shouted...

"Don't forget the alarm...set the alarm, Blue."

As Deanne turned and backed out of the driveway, I noticed the living room curtains moved a little and the creepy little girl in the ragged white dress was peeking out the window and waving as we drove off.

As Deanne turned off of our street onto Nelson road, I was still looking back and wondering, when Deanne said...

"Blue, I need you to keep it together okay don't fall apart on me...I need you, why don't you get sleep and I'll wake you once we're at the farm."

Deanne jumped on the interstate while I sat hunched down looking out the window and every once in a while turning around looking at the back window.

Deanne put her hand on my leg rubbing it saying...

"I know your little episode six months ago at the farm has you all jacked up, but your doctor said...this is what you needed, to get you over the hump...to show you that it was all in your head."

I took a deep breath and nodded my head yes, and sat back in my seat. I knew what was waiting for us at the farm, and the only thing that was 'all in my head' was that I was scared shitless.

The drive down the two lane highway was especially bleak looking and void of any signs of life early in the fall season.

The trees were empty, with remnants of bird's nest wedged high in the branches. The cold rain which was sure to turn into a full blown downpour added to the already bleak scenery that went by me as a blur.

Six months earlier, me and Deanne were on our way to the farm, for what was supposed to be a week of celebration, when everything just went to hell in a hand basket.

The beginning of all of my troubles of seeing the Doppelgangers started at the farm and at a little mom n pop country store only twenty minutes from the farm.

The closer we got to Port Clinton, the more my stress level rising not to mention seeing the Harmon's market again.

Deanne had already mentioned to me that she wanted to stop at the store to call the sheriff and have him meet us at the farm, but just the very thought of thinking about to store had me perspiring and breathing heavy.

Deanne's expecting to see a normal store, with normal things and people, but I know what's there...and I know who's there too.

Out of the corner of my eye, I kept catching Deanne looking at me with this look on her face which read...

"I wonder if I'm going to need to take Blue back to giggle central... to be committed for good after we leave the farm."

The only two things I hated to do while I was in the unit were... medication time, and visitor's day.

Don't get me wrong, I know I'm not the brightest crayon in the box but I'm receiving treatment.

I don't know why my mind thought about visitor's day and the people who show up. Have you even been in a psychiatric hospital and looked on the faces of those who visiting someone there?

They have a look on their face as if they are embarrassed to be visiting someone in a psych ward.

How and why in the world could that be sane and healthy... thinking...feeling embarrassed and trying to hold it together, and when they leave they act as if they merely went to the grocery store or something.

I don't know why so many thoughts are running through my head...the main one is that Deanne would turn this car around and head back to Columbus...but that won't happen.

I guess I was trying to think about anything I could to keep from focusing on the store, the Doppelgangers and the farm... heck I even thought about my little chili stain along the drive.

I continued to read the road signs in my mind and amuse myself with looking at every single thing on the landscape.

Just then we approached a sign which displayed a car dealership and a little girl with her father.

Nothing was all that out of the ordinary about the sign except for two things. For starters the girl on the bill board waved at me, and secondly she looked just like the little girl in the Polaris parking lot.

That's when my mind went into over drive I remembered what the little girl said at Polaris...

"Ooh...ooh...I'm telling!

Wait till the Others find out that you've been pretending this whole time.

Ooh... this is going to be fun.

Twisted and Dread......

Twisted and Dread,

Fooled us once, now it's really on again

Twisted and Dread!"

I tried sitting back and closing my eyes, but the images in my head were much too strong.

I thought that there had to be a way out of this nightmare...there had to be a way to get back to feeling like a normal person.

I wondered for a moment if this wasn't one of the reasons people check out of this world. If this isn't the reason people do the things they do, knowing they'll be killed.

I thought that it wouldn't be totally unbearable if there was someone else who was witnessing what I was, seeing what I was seeing.

I know that Deanne heard and saw the messages of Mary on the television, but she was thinking that a living person was responsible and not the Doppelgangers.

I felt that surely I wasn't the only one who was going through this nightmare, there's got to be someone else, but how do you find them...this isn't the type of thing you put on social media or the kind of thing you place an ad in the newspaper for either.

Suddenly my heart began racing and my hands got very sweaty as we approached a sign which read...

"Harmon's Country Market...42 mi."

Deanne noticed that I had become a little anxious and nervous, so she grabbed my hand to reassure me that everything was okay... but I knew that it was not okay nor was it going to be okay...instead it was going to be a nightmare.

I let go of Deanne's hand and began wiping my hands vigorously on my pants and slowly, exhaling, as my palms were wet and clammy from my nerves.

Deanne looked over at me saying...

"Blue, are you going to be alright...Babe, once we get there we'll stop and get the police...and you don't have to even leave the car... okay?"

I looked over at Deanne and smiled and shook my head ok....and tried to show her that I getting it under was control.

I started taking deep breaths and slowly exhaling trying to show her that I was alright, when Deanne said...

"This morning I had planned on stopping and talking to the police, no matter what they say, they got to help us."

I nodded my head okay, as Deanne turned off onto highway fifty-three which led to the farm, when Deanne looked over and said...

"Okay, almost there Blue."

Deanne knew that she was less than ten minutes from downtown Port Clinton, and the Sheriff's Office. She looked over at me and said instead of going to Harmon's market she was going straight to the police.

I sat there visibly showing my nerves were getting worse when Deanne said...

"Another ten minutes and we'll have someone from the Sheriff's department follow us to the farm, so relax Blue...it'll be alright."

I heard Deanne but I still feared that it was not going to go as simple as that. Nothing in my life in the past six months has been simple; it seemed everything was complicated and disturbingly depressing.

Deanne approached the out skirts of Port Clinton a little after seven in the evening and began thinking out loud as she slowed down to look at street signs...

"Okay...if I remember, the Sheriff's Department is in the same area as the boat landing on a service road...right Blue?"

I nodded my head yes, and pointed to the street where Deanne would have to turn on, and a sign which read...

"Road Closed"
Detour Ahead."

Deanne slowed down to look at the sign and continued a few more blocks and followed the detour signs to the service road.

Deanne had to go down several back streets and through a section of Port Clinton which she was unfamiliar with, until she saw the service road and turned on to it, reading out loud the sign which read...

"Sheriff's Department"

Pulling into the small parking lot at the top of the hill which overlooked a section of Lake Erie, Deanne parked the car and turned to me and said...

"We made it Blue, you want to go in with me, or will you be alright here?"

I nodded my head yes that I preferred to go inside with Deanne. The thought of being alone especially there in Port Clinton was way too difficult for me to deal with...I mean the doctors gave me pills, but not to deal with this crap.

I looked around and thought... I was right back where all of this mess started and I know it would only be a matter of time before the Doppelgangers knew I was back.

The weather in Port Clinton, like any other port city in the north was ten to fifteen degrees cooler in the fall and winter, especially when there is rain in the making.

I opened the door of the Sheriff's department for Deanna as we both went into the lobby area.

Inside the lobby waiting area were three chairs, a door and a glass partition. Deanne pressed the 'help' buzzer and after five minutes or so, a young woman in her thirties exited out of the side door saying...

"How are you folks doing, my name is Tara Johns...I'm the dispatcher, what can we help you with?"

Deanne reached out to shake her hand and said...

"Hi Tara, my name is Deanne Byrd, and this is my boyfriend David Blue. We're from Columbus, but we have a farm up here and we need help with a friend of ours who is at our farm."

Tara closed the door behind her and as she buttoned up her coat saying...

"What kind of help are we talking about...you see, I'm off duty, and the only person who is on tonight is Deputy Andrews who is about to go on an accident call."

279

Deanne tried not to act too emotional, but felt she needed to express how serious it was, saying...

"Well, that's who we need Deputy Andrews.

We got a call from a friend of ours named Mary, she's house sitting for us, and she called and said that there's someone on the property trying to get in the house, and we need someone to ride out to the farm with us."

Tara Johns sat down with Deanne and removing a small pad began taking notes and said...

'So let's back up a little...you said that your friend called you and told you she was being bothered by someone trying to get into the house...how long ago did she call you?"

Not having enough experience with lying, Deanne hadn't thought out her story and the possible questions Tara might ask as she said...

"Mary called us yesterday around eleven in the morning."

Tara placed her pen on top of her pad and looked at Deanne and said...

"Look, uh...Deanne, has your friend contacted either one of you since then?"

Deanne looked over at me and answered...

"No, she called us last night and that was it."

Tara scribbled something onto the pad and then said...

"I'm not trying to make light of your situation but it doesn't seem much like an emergency to me, first you said she called yesterday morning, and now you say she called again last night...if you're friend called you yesterday, and you waited a whole day to report this, it doesn't seem like your friend is all that worried."

When Deanne first walked into the Sheriff's department, she felt that once she said a friend at their farm was in trouble would've been enough to get help, but didn't count on lying and being asked a lot of questions.

Deanne was visibly getting upset and irritable as she said...

"What the hell difference does it make if she called yesterday or last year, I'm telling you she's in trouble and she needs help...look, I'm done talking to you, let me speak to the Deputy...what's his name!"

Tara Johns stood up and looked at both me and Deanne and replied...

"Just calm down...there's no need to go down that road...Deputy Andrews is gone on an emergency accident call...as a matter of fact he was leaving just as you folks walked in. I'll call him and relay the message to him and he'll come out and give you whatever assistance you need as soon as he's through with his first call."

Tara handed Deanne the writing tablet and her pen as Deanne irritably said as she wrote down their address and her cell phone number...

"I can't believe this...what kind of place is this where there's only one Officer on duty!"

Deanne handed the tablet back to Tara and looked at me and said...

"C'mon, Blue I'm sorry but looks like we got to handle it ourselves."

I nodded at Tara, giving her a half smile as we left the Sheriff's Department.

When we left the Sheriff's station, I had a warm sickening feeling as Deanne and I got inside the car, when Deanne looked at me and said...

"Blue I tried; it looks like it's going to be up to you and me until 'barney fife' shows up."

After Deanne drove off, Tara closed the outside door to the station and went back inside.

Tara grabbed her keys from her purse and opened the inner office door and walked back to the dispatch room.

Sitting at the control desk she put on her head set and dialed a number, waiting for the caller and said...

"Are you out there Thomas?"

Ripping the page off of the tablet and placing it in front of her, the voice on the other end replied...

"Yep it's me Tara...so did my two neighbors stop in to ask for help?"

Tara read him the information and said...

"Yes they did Thomas; I did just as you told me. They were just in here talking about their friend was in some kind of trouble and they needed help."

Right before Tara ended the call she told Mr. Thomas...

"*They just left and are on their way to the farm and should be there in about ten to fifteen minutes.*"

Tara hung the phone up after talking with Mr. Thomas and reached in her desk and pulled out a handful of skeleton keys and tied red ribbons on them and placed them in her purse and left the station.

Chapter 14

Det. Horton

Det. Horton pulled a map from the glove compartment of his car, and rechecked the directions to Port Clinton.

He had made several calls to Reggie that went unanswered, so decided on a trip to Port Clinton to investigate what Amy Smiles was working on, and what Reggie was hiding from him.

Det. Horton had worked with Reggie when he was a rookie on the police force, and knew that if Reggie was taking chances by obstructing and interfering with an investigation, then, there was some meat to it, there was something solid going on.

Det. Horton thought...

"Other than driving in cold rainy weather there is two hundred miles of black and white barren landscapes, and a damn car radio which plays nothing but static."

Det. Horton noticed dead ahead a sign which read...

"Port Clinton...120 miles."

Det. Horton alternated between chewing gum and smoking cigarette during the entire trip to Port Clinton, and familiarizing himself with the surroundings.

Det. Horton thought about stopping at the rest area plaza just ahead, but decided as he saw the sign...

"Harmon's Country Market...10 miles..."

That he would stop there.

Det. Horton flicked the fire from his cigarette and tossed the butt out of his window as he pulled into the parking lot.

The entrance to the store had an old fashioned look to it. There were four old wooden steps leading to the front door, and an old wooden screen door, with a bell over the entrance of the door.

Det. Horton stood there reading a sign on the door, which read...
"Fried bologna sandwiches-$2.50
Ham & cheese sandwiches-$3.00
Fresh dough pizza slices-$4.00"
Det. Horton approached the counter, where an older gentleman stood reading a newspaper, and said...
"Excuse me sir, can I interrupt you a bit?"
The old man slowly lowered the newspaper and replied...
"Why ask if you can interrupt me when you already done did it."
Det. Horton apologized for interrupting the man and said...
"My name is Mark Horton, I'm a detective from Columbus... and I'm looking for directions to a farm up here."
The old man looked past Det. Horton and replied...
"The name's Hennessey and I bet you're up here looking for the young couple's farm, aren't you?"
Det. Horton reached in his pockets and grabbed his cigarette pack, and asked...
"Do you mind...if I um..."
Det. Horton was almost finished with his question when Mr. Hennessey butted in...
"Smoke...oh yeah go ahead, you might as well enjoy them whilst you still can."
Det. Horton turned and looked back at the door, thinking...
"What the hell is up with this smart ass man and this thing about...'enjoy them while you still can...what the hell is that supposed to mean?"

Trying to avoid any further unnecessary conversations Det. Horton turned back at Mr. Hennessey and said...
"How would you know what farm I'm looking for?"
Mr. Hennessey placed an ash tray in front of Det. Horton, saying...
"All kinds of folks been coming up here and heading to that place...I don't go anywhere near that place, if you were to ask me...I think the place is alive."

Det. Horton put out his cigarette and stated…

"What do you mean…the place is alive?"

Mr. Hennessey picked up his newspaper and said…

"Well, you'll find out soon enough."

Not certain what to make out of Mr. Hennessey or what he was hearing, Det. Horton said…

"By the way, how long would it take to get a slice of Fresh Dough Pizza?"

Mr. Hennessey walked over to the end of the counter and replied…

"Honestly, do I look like I know anything about making pizzas?"

Det. Horton told Mr. Hennessey that all he wanted was some directions and perhaps a pop, fried bologna sandwich and to use the restroom.

Mr. Hennessey went to the counter on the opposite side of the store and began to hand slice some fresh bologna, and turned to Det. Horton saying…

"Sorry the grill's not working, so you're going to have to make due with a cold sandwich, several people's complained about the restroom, so I closed it…do you want cheese on this?"

Det. Horton nodded his head, reached into the cooler for a red pop. Det. Horton took a drink of his pop and watched Mr. Hennessey as he sliced the bologna, thin at the top, and thick towards the end.

Watching Mr. Hennessey pull a long block of cheese from the cooler and unwrap it, Det. Horton thought about uneven the bologna was cut, and imagined a huge chunk of cheese n his sandwich, when he said…

"You don't have to worry about any cheese…I'll eat it plain."

Mr. Hennessey placed the cheese back in the cooler and said…

"You don't want any mustard on your sandwich…bologna isn't any good without mustard."

Det. Horton reached into his wallet for money to pay for the sandwich and pop, when he saw Mr. Hennessey put a large spoonful of mustard on his sandwich and spreading it and handed it to Det. Horton.

Mr. Hennessey said…

"That'll be eight dollars."

Det. Horton took a bit from his sandwich and said…

"Eight dollars?"

Mr. Hennessey walked over to the register to get Det. Horton's change, saying...

"Yeah, I gave you a double slice of meat, plus I used my own homemade mustard."

Mr. Hennessey walked over to the door and stood beside Det. Horton, looking at his service revolver in his holster saying...

"Turn right on the highway, and the place you're looking for is... about thirty-five or forty miles...depending if the weather isn't bad.

Det. Horton looked up in the sky while chewing his sandwich and said to himself while Mr. Hennessey chuckled...

"Weather...what the hell's he talking about. It's just partly cloudy."

Mr. Hennessey stepped outside and pointed to the road, saying...

"Any way, you're going to go past an old run down boat repair place on your left, then start looking to your right, and you'll see a paved driveway and then a gravel one... take the paved driveway... it'll lead you through the woods, and you'll see two farms, the farm to your left if you really want to go there."

Det. Horton started walking to his car when Mr. Hennessey called after him...

"Detective, I say detective...I almost forgot something."

Det. Horton turned after taking another bite of his sandwich and nodded his head to say yes, when Mr. Hennessey said...

"That gun of yours...isn't going to help you none."

Mr. Hennessey started laughing and then he walked out of the store and ahead of Det. Horton and began dancing 'round and round in circles and singing...

"Teddy Bear, Soda Crackers,

Heading to the farm,

'Thousand things, in your car

Horrible way to die..."

Det. Horton thought to himself as he headed for his car...

"That old man's Wheaties are soggy."

Continuing to eat his sandwich as he pulled out of the store's parking lot, Det. Horton noticed up in the sky and heading north, what looked like a very large swarm of some kind.

Not paying much attention to it and thinking its bees going south for the winter, finished eating his sandwich and drinking his red pop.

Det. Horton rolled his window down a little and lit up a cigarette and following Mr. Hennessey's directions, and turned right.

There were two things that Det. Horton was unaware of and that was, the swarm which he saw, would be circling over the farm, and that he was heading into a strange and unexpected storm.

According to Mr. Hennessey, Det. Horton had roughly twenty-five to thirty minutes before reaching his destination so; Det. Horton carefully began scanning the area for the boat repair shop and his turn off when from out of nowhere he ran into a storm.

The rain was coming down so hard it was as if he'd run into a wall of water. Suddenly and from out of nowhere Det. Horton was not only driving through a torrential down pour but he was engulfed by a thick fog.

Slowing his car down to twenty miles an hour, he caught a glimpse of something in front of him before hitting it and slamming on brakes.

Due to the rain and the thick fog, Det. Horton didn't realize that he had ran off the road and into a ditch.

Sitting in his car dazed, Det. Horton cut on his emergency flashers and rolled his window down as he lit a cigarette trying to get a glimpse of what he'd ran into.

Det. Horton knew that if it was a deer or some other large animal and it was lying directly in the road, he would have to drag it to the side of the road to prevent any other motorist from running over it.

Taking one last drag from his cigarette before getting out of his car, Det. Horton noticed as he blew the smoke out of the window, that as he blew the smoke from his cigarette out of the window, that it was lost in the fog.

Staggering out of the car, Det. Horton first inspected his car to see what, if any damage was done to it when he saw two things.

The entire front end of his car was smashed, and just about two feet in front of him was another car which looked as if it had smashed into a tree, and abandoned.

He walked back a few feet onto the road looking for the deer or animal that he believed he hit.

Det. Horton walked to where he believed he'd hit the animal when he saw that he'd been mistaken...he hadn't hit a deer or any other kind of animal...but a man.

A very large man in a ballerina's tutu wearing white tights and something on his face.

Det. Horton approached the man lying in the road and turned towards his car to make certain that he and any approaching cars could see his car lights...but all he saw was the faint red color of his tail lights.

The fog was so thick that, when det. Horton looked down at the man in the road, he could not clearly see the outline of the man's body.

Det. Horton bent down to check on the man's condition, not noticing there was a dark figure emerging from the trees on the other side of the road.

Det. Horton's only concern was seeing if the man was alright, and getting him off the road and rendering whatever assistance he could.

Det. Horton checked the man for injuries but neither saw nor felt anything signs of injuries. The man was breathing but Det. Horton felt no pulse.

Searching his pockets for his cell phone, and not feeling his cell phone Det. Horton believed that, when he ran off the road, his cell phone must have fallen in the car somewhere.

Det. Horton raced back to the car looking for his cell phone, which he was unable to locate. He felt all under the seats and in the glove compartment, but came up empty handed.

Det. Horton popped the trunk of his car, looking for his emergency gear. He lit another cigarette, and hoped to use the light from his cigarette lighter to help him see, when he spotted his flashlight.

Det. Horton located one flare, a folded up yellow tarp, spare tire, and jack, when he remembered that he kept a backup pistol stashed with the spare tire.

Det. Horton grabbed the flare and the tarp, and headed back to help the man that he'd hit.

Det. Horton lit the flare and laid the tarp out beside the man. Det. Horton was an average sized man about five feet nine, two hundred and twelve pounds, and found it extremely difficult as he rolled the man onto the tarp.

Det. Horton, after slipping in the mud several times was finally able to drag the man out of the highway and off the road underneath a tree, when he heard the sound of a tractor trailer's horn blasting in the distance.

Grabbing the flare and going back to his car, Det. Horton stood off to the side of the road and began waving the flare and the flash light hoping that the truck would be able to see him and stop.

The sound of the eighteen wheelers horn blasted again, only much closer this time. Det. Horton couldn't see anything through the rain and fog, but could tell from the sound of the ruck's horn, that it was getting close.

Again the horn of the semi-truck sounded and Det. Horton knew the truck was right upon him.

Through the rain Det. Horton heard the sound of the trucks engine, and then everything went quiet.

Believing that the truck stopped, Det. Horton walked in front of his car and behind his car and on both sides of the highway waving the flare, trying to locate where the truck had stopped, but saw nothing.

Det. Horton laid the flare back in the road and made his way back over to his car and again to look for his cell phone.

Shinning the flash light all around the front seat area he heard the ring tone of his cell phone which was lodged in between the driver's seat and the console area.

Det. Horton picked up his phone to check for a signal when the thought hit him...

"I didn't feel the truck pass, plus there were no sounds of braking... maybe, he turned off up the road a little way."

Det. Horton felt the vibration from his phone when he answered it, saying...

"Hello, hello!"

At first there was only silence, and then he heard the voices of children singing...

"La-la-la-la-la-la-, la-la-la-la-la-la,

Teddy Bear Soda Crackers,

Detective all alone

Big man's up

Having fun

Think you'd better run.

La-la-la-la-la-la-, la-la-la-la-la-la."

Det. Horton looked up in his rear view mirror in the direction of where he had laid the man, and then all around the car, and when he didn't see anything or anyone, he dialed nine one-one, but his cell phone displayed...

"No service area."

Det. Horton slowly got out of the car and walked back over to where the man was laying...but when he got there, all he saw was the tarp... the body was gone.

It was too foggy and dark to see any foot prints to determine which way the man in the ballerina's tutu went, so Det. Horton decided to go back to his car, get out of the weather, and think about his next move.

With the front end of his car badly damaged and the front right tire half on and half off the rim Det. Horton locked the car, and checked the clip in his gun to make sure it was fully loaded.

In between thinking about the strange phone call he just received and the disappearance of the man he hit with this car, Det. Horton knew that he could not sit in his car all night; he had to get out of there and find where he was going and anyone to help him.

Det. Horton looked at his cell phone, and saw that the time was eight twenty, and thought...

"What the hell...when I left the store it was just a little after five, but how in the world did I lose three hours?"

Det. Horton came to the conclusion that when he hit the man and slid off the road, he must have hit his head and knocked himself out.

Det. Horton's attention went back to the man which he'd hit with his car, and where he could've disappeared to.

With all the rain and the thickness of the fog, Det. Horton couldn't see or tell where the man was, whether he was directly in front of him, behind him or in what direction he walked.

Det. Horton didn't recall seeing any houses or business between where he was and the store behind him. From where Det. Horton stood, he was closer to the farm than he was to the store, and chances were Mr. Hennessey was probably already closed for the night.

Grabbing the flash light and looking around, before getting out of the car, Det. Horton went to the highway and started walking straight.

Det. Horton tried walking and keeping one foot on the highway and the other on the shoulder, so that he could tell where the gravel and paved driveways were.

The weather was uncomfortable and with the fog and not being able to see through it… made Det. Horton a little nervous and uneasy, so much until he had his right hand in his pocket holding his gun, and the left hand holding the flashlight.

Det. Horton continued walking down the road with one foot on the pavement and the other on the shoulder until he felt loose gravel underneath his right foot.

Shinning the flashlight down at his feet, and moving his feet left and right, Det. Horton's right foot was standing on the entrance of a gravel driveway.

Hoping that Mr. Hennessey didn't give him bad directions, Det. Horton said to himself…

"Not too much longer and I should be coming to a paved driveway."

Det. Horton zipped his coat up to his neck and turned the collar up, lowered his head and continued walking until felt the gravel give way to a paved driveway.

Not knowing who or what he'd find at the farm house, Det. Horton said to himself….

"Reggie, this had better be good…got my ass going through all of this… all I got to say is, you have a lot of explaining to do."

Det. Horton lifted his head up every few feet in the hopes of seeing a house, or a farm, anything other than fog and rain, just then... he noticed in the distance a small light, barely visible.

The closer Det. Horton got to the light, the smaller the light appeared to get. Then suddenly through the rain and the fog, Det. Horton heard what sounded like little kids laughing.

Shinning his flashlight in all directions and wiping the rain from his face, Det. Horton stopped dead in his tracks as the sound of laughter stopped.

Assuming it was nothing more than the howling of the wind, Det. Horton started walking again, until he came across a lot of thick brush.

Det. Horton had only taken about twenty steps when he heard the sound of little kids laughing singing again...

"La-la-la-la-la-la-, la-la-la-la-la-la,

Twisted and Dread...Twisted and Dread,

You weren't invited, if you continue

You'll be dead,

La-la-la-la-la-la-, la-la-la-la-la-la."

Det. Horton swung the flashlight over in the direction where he thought he heard the voices and said...

"All right whoever you are...I'm a Police Detective, why don't you show yourself."

Suddenly, Det. Horton was no longer in the fog...it was as if Det. Horton walked out of a wall of fog and into a clearing.

Standing there in the clearing, Det. Horton scanned the area and behind him was a wall of fog, while ahead he saw a small cabin in the distance, a barn beyond that, and an old farm house up ahead.

The rain was still coming down, but more disturbing was the fog which lay behind Det. Horton.

Det. Horton had taken at least twenty steps since coming into the clearing, and no matter how much distance he put between himself and the fog, the fog remained behind him touching his back.

Det. Horton saw in front of the barn and to his left, there was a SUV parked alongside of it, and the closer Det. Horton got to it, it looked like the same one Reggie was driving when he came to the crime scene.

There was a light in one of the upstairs windows of the barn, and Det. Horton decided that would be the first place to look for Reggie, because of the light and his vehicle being parked there.

As Det. Horton knocked on the barn door he noticed up at the house, an outline of someone on the porch, and then the porch light went out.

Det. Horton knocked again on the barn door, and as he did it opened. Slowly pushing the door completely open Det. Horton announced who he was, called for Reggie but got no answer.

Hoping whoever had cut the lights out at the house, was on their way to the barn, as Det. Horton backed out of the doorway and stood at the entrance.

The last thing Det. Horton needed was to trespassing on someone's property outside of his jurisdiction, not to mention letting someone have access to evidence in a murder case is always a good way to be suspended without pay by the department.

As Det. Horton stood waiting, he unzipped his coat and placed his badge which was on a strap around his neck on the outside of his coat.

Det. Horton turned and looked around in the direction which he had walked and noticed that fog, was still there, as if it were waiting for him to start walking again.

Det. Horton pulled his gun from his pocket and checked it again, and that's when he heard the voices of the little kids, the same voices he had heard thirty minutes ago, only this time, the voices were too distorted to make out what they were saying.

As Det. Horton stood at the barn, he saw that someone went through the incredible expense of keeping the barn looking like a barn on the outside, but inside it was a fairly modern living room.

There was a small open kitchen, a large living room area and from what he could see there were steps leading to a second level.

Det. Horton waited and waited, but no one came to where he was so, since he had come this far, he thought he might as well go all the way, and that's when he decided to walk up to the main farmhouse.

The whole time Det. Horton walked he kept glancing back as the fog was actually following him.

At one-point Det. Horton stopped, turned and tried sticking his hand into the fog, which when he did...the fog opened up and then closed around his hand again.

Det. Horton came to within a few feet from the house when he noticed a small window a few feet from the ground, revealing that a light was on, and someone was inside.

His curiosity got the best of him and he knelt down and peeked through the window and saw four people tied to chairs, and one woman nude, bound and gagged, and another suspended by fish hooks.

Det. Horton looked closely at one of the people bound in the chairs...and it was Reggie.

Det. Horton took an extra clip from his left pocket and placed it in his right pocket along with his gun.

Just when Det. Horton was about to move away from the window, he noticed a large man in the ballerina's tutu standing in front of one of the girls who was bound in the chair, pouring something on her.

This man looked like the same man in the ballerina's tutu that he had hit with his car an hour ago. He couldn't be certain, but he was sure it was the same man in the ballerina's tutu with the clown's face.

What Det. Horton didn't see was the dark figured behind him which slithered from the roof and onto to the ground behind him, and a pair of red eyes following him in the fog and the darkness.

Reggie looked up and saw Det. Horton's face outside the window peeking through and Det. Horton placed a finger up to his mouth, motioning for Reggie to be quiet.

The rain was still coming down, but also coming straight for Det. Horton was the wall of fog, which had engulfed the cabin, barn and everything behind him.

In many places in the world, it can be raining and foggy in one place and then a few feet away it can be dry, but what was so unusual about this was, that this fog seemed to have purpose...it seemed to have a plan.

When Det. Horton was driving from the store there was no weather and a mile or so everything was clear and then out of nowhere there is an eerie spooky fog.

Det. Horton stood up and brushed the dirt and leaves from his pants, and began thinking of a plan to help the people that were being held by this maniac.

Det. Horton thought about drawing the big man outside of the basement but thought if he did might put the people in the basement in more jeopardy, so decided he would just barge into the basement.

Det. Horton walked over to the outside basement door, and looked all around, and carefully turned the basement door knob to see if it was locked.

Det. Horton had only seen the big man in the ballerina's tutu, and didn't know who else was inside...but he had no other choice except to take a chance.

Det. Horton wasn't a trigger happy person, nor was he proud of the fact that he's killed people, but he took his oath to protect and to serve very seriously, and these people were in danger and there wasn't a lot of time waste.

Det. Horton thought that the man in the ballerina's tutu may have walked away from a car accident, but the game's a little different... like the saying goes...'bullets kill'.

When Det. Horton walked up to the house in the fog, he really couldn't remember seeing the walkway...all he was focused on was, Reggie's SUV and the man which he had hit.

Whatever Det. Horton was or was not going to do, had to be done quickly because the man in the ballerina's tutu returned to the basement, and not alone.

Det. Horton noticed the man in the ballerina's tutu was with the old man, Mr. Thomas, who handed the man in the ballerina's tutu a pair of old hog ring pliers and headed towards Reggie.

Det. Horton grabbed the door knob, turned it and burst through the basement door.

Mr. Thomas and the man in the ballerina's tutu wearing the clown's face turned around slowly, almost unconcerned that Det. Horton was there with his gun aimed at them.

The man in the ballerina's tutu dropped the hog ring pliers and took a step towards Det. Horton, as he took careful aim and said...

"Alright big man, if you want to be shot all to hell and back, take one more step."

The man in the ballerina's tutu cocked his head to the right and then raised his foot to take another step, when Mr. Thomas grabbed his arm, and the man in the ballerina's tutu stopped.

Det. Horton was about to enter the basement, when he noticed in front of him on the floor was Det. Fannichuci.

Reggie hollered for Det. Horton to watch his step and Det. Horton stepped to the side and approached the man in the ballerina's tutu and Mr. Thomas.

Without a word and without doing anything Mr. Thomas and the man in the ballerina's tutu walked up the stairs and then out into woods.

Det. Horton walked back out to ensure that they were leaving and came back into the house through the front door and down into the basement.

Det. Horton began untying Reggie as he said…

"Damn glad to see you Mark!"

Det. Horton went to untie Perry, as Reggie untied the cords from his ankles.

Reggie told Det. Horton about all the events which transpired, and how Tim was able to escape, and he's probably wondering around outside somewhere.

Det. Horton began untying Mary who was still unconscious and told Reggie…

"We got to go upstairs and out the back door and through the walkway to the SUV. Using the basement door isn't going to work, besides, the rain and fog and the mud's only going to slow us down."

Det. Horton turned to Reggie and said…

"These other girls…are they alright…what in the hell is going on up here Reggie?"

Reggie replied…

"These two were already here when we arrived…let's get to the SUV and once we're out of here, I'll explain everything."

Perry followed behind Reggie, who had grabbed Mary, while Det. Horton shouldered Kristin and made their way upstairs through the kitchen and to the back door which led to the walkway.

From the back door to the entrance of the walkway was twenty feet, and then onto safety.

Once inside the walkway Det. Horton stopped and knelt down to rest from carrying Kristin and said to Reggie…

I passed your SUV right at the end of this walkway, beside the barn…a hundred feet dead ahead, we're almost out of this mess…you got your keys coach?"

Reggie positioned Mary on his shoulders and said…

"No…but there's a spare key under the driver's side floor mat."

Det. Horton grabbed his flashlight and shinned it on the faces of Mary and Kristin and said…

"Coach thirty minutes away is Port Clinton, and we've got to get these girls to a hospital, just then Perry screamed!"

Reggie cried out…

"What the hell…Perry, Perry!"

Reggie and Det. Horton looked for Perry, who was just in front of them as Det. Horton shinned his flashlight in front of them and as far down the walkway as he could, but did not see Perry.

Reggie sat Mary's limp body on the ground and frantically going in circles, began calling for Perry…

"Perry, Perry…babe where are you?"

Det. Horton tapped Reggie on the shoulder and said…

"Hey Reggie, we got to get these girls to your SUV, something probably just scared Perry, we'll run into her up ahead.

Reggie had almost lost Perry once and said…

"What if she's behind us?"

Det. Horton told Reggie…

"Well stay here and wait if you like, but I got to get this girl to the SUV…*keep the flashlight on me and don't let that sick son of a bitch sneak up on me."*

Reggie grabbed the flashlight, when Det. Horton snapped…

"Reggie, get a grip think man we're out in the middle of nowhere… at least shine the light towards the SUV so I can get this girl to safety, I'll watch for Perry."

Reggie pointed the flashlight down the walkway as Det. Horton disappeared in the darkness. Mary moaned and Reggie told her not to worry, she was safe and that he was going to get her to a hospital.

Reggie picked up Mary and started to walk down the walkway to the barn slowly when he heard someone hollering.

It was a little hard, carrying Mary and juggling the flashlight in his hand, but Reggie picked up his pace when something from behind tapped him on the shoulder.

Thinking it was Mary whom he was carrying, Reggie ignored it, when he felt anther tap on his shoulder, but this time he realized that it could not be Mary as both of her arms were dangling over his shoulders in front of him.

Reggie sensed that there was something or someone else inside the walkway that kept coming up behind him and brushing up against him, but couldn't see a thing.

Just then a voice from in front of Reggie cried out, it was Det. Horton...

"What took you so long, and what was that I heard?"

Reggie explained to Det. Horton as he placed Mary in the SUV next to Kristin.

Locking the rear door, Reggie said...

"Perry...where's Perry?"

Det. Horton told Reggie that, since he did not run into Perry coming or going to the SUV, that she must've gotten turned around outside, and that they should start their search beginning on the other side of the barn.

Reggie headed back into the walkway, when Det. Horton said...

"Where the hell are you going?"

Reggie turned and said...

"I'm going back after Perry...where's the flashlight...it was right there on the ground."

Unable to see anything Reggie and Det. Horton had no clue where they were searching or in what direction they were going in, when Reggie said...

"How in the hell could she have gotten turned around in the weather...The SUV is right here...she had to run smack into it."

Det. Horton told Reggie...

"Look I got a bad feeling about this place, and I'll be a big happy ass once we're out of here."

Reggie looked at Det. Horton and said...

"Bad feeling. You haven't seen half the weird ass crap that I've seen."

Reggie and Det. Horton left the SUV running and searched around the barn for Perry. They both met back in front of the SUV, with no sign of Perry.

Surprisingly, Mary and Kristin were both still alive and in the back seat. Reggie slammed his fists down upon the hood of the SUV saying...

"Damn, damn, damn...where'd you go Perry?"

Det. Horton said...

"I know I can't tell you what to do or not do, but we are in way too deep, and one of us needs to go get some help."

Reggie nodded his head in agreement and reached into the glove compartment where his back up gun was and said...

"Okay, Mark you know I have to stay here, I got to find Perry, my gut is telling me somehow she ended up back in the basement...I'll be okay, just bring the Calvary back with you."

Det. Horton said...

"What I don't understand is, you say the old man and the big wackadoo, subdued six people and when I arrived...they just ran off into the woods without any kind of fight...it doesn't figure."

Reggie shut the SUV door and Det. Horton climbed into the driver's seat, and said as the engine died...

'It's like I said weird ass shit....and I don't think it's over, and I don't think they ran away because they were scared either."

Det. Horton tried to restart the SUV over and over, until Reggie tapped on the window and Det. Horton opened the door and said...

"Man, is anything going to go right in this nightmare."

Reggie motioned for Det. Horton to get out of the SUV. Both men stood against the barn, out of the rain when Reggie said...

"That's exactly what this is Mark...it's a nightmare, and I'm afraid we may not make it out either."

Det. Horton reached in his inside coat pocket and pulled out his cigarettes, offering Reggie one, who to Det. Horton's disbelief took one. Reggie hadn't smoked since high school, after his grandmother died of throat cancer.

Det. Horton gave Reggie a light and lit his cigarette as well and said...

"Hey coach, don't go getting all weirded out on me, talking about not making it and all. There's some weird shit happening I'll admit that, but just because the SUV quit running, don't get all 'Casper' on me."

Reggie took a long drag, and blowing out the smoke said...

"Look Mark, when I was walking away from the SUV, something caught my attention. I was smelling gas, and when I bent down for the flashlight I could see that someone intentionally punctured my gas tank from underneath."

Bending down Det. Horton saw the remaining gas dripping from the gas tank. We need to lock these girls in the SUV and then go find Perry as Reggie said...

"Okay, we're going to have to go back into that house, but I feel the basement is where we're going to end up. I figured we could enter in through the front door, and one by one search each room, and we use the buddy system."

Det. Horton took the flashlight from Reggie saying...

"Hey partner you have your piece, just want to check and see how many rounds I got left, by the way what bought you up here?"

Letting Det. Horton have the flashlight Reggie said...

"I was reading Amy's entry and she mentioned coming up here to check on some leads she had, so I wanted to see what was what."

Det. Horton patted Reggie on the back and said...

"Listen man, I know what it's like losing a partner, and to learn she was also your sister...I don't even know how're you handling it, but you should've kept me in the loop and maybe all of this shit could've been avoided."

Reggie didn't respond to Det. Horton's statement, because it is what it is, and there were more pressing issues to deal with at the moment, as Reggie stated...

"The way I see it, we leave the two girls here, and go back to the house, and everybody comes out alive or we don't."

Det. Horton turned on the flashlight and said...

"How about we just try to make it out alive, okay...I can't do the hero bit."

Before leaving Reggie looked back at Mary and Kristin in the back seat and then turned with Det. Horton to head through the walkway.

As they entered the back door into the kitchen, the first thing Reggie did was lock the basement door; they were going to save that for last when, all of a sudden the front door slammed shut!

Jumping, Det. Horton shinned the flashlight in direction of the front door, while Reggie had his gun trained on the least little movement.

Det. Horton walked over to the door and turned the door knob which opened without resistance and said as he locked the door...

"Must have just been the wind."

After closing the door Det. Horton pointed past Reggie and said....

"Look!"

Det. Horton shined the flashlight past Reggie to a figure who stood in the door way between the living room and the dining room.

Reggie wiped away the rain away from his face, and relief came over Reggie, recognizing the person standing in front of him was Perry.

Reggie ran over to Perry hugging her and kissing her said...

"Honey...oh my God...I thought I lost you...I was looking everywhere for you, where'd you go?"

Reggie turned to Det. Horton to tell him, let's go, let's get out of there, when he noticed standing behind Det. Horton on the front porch was the man in the ballerina's tutu.

Without any warning, the front door glass smashed, and the man in the ballerina's tutu grabbed Det. Horton and pulled him outside.

Reggie grabbed onto Perry's hand and pulled her with him as he made it over to the kitchen doorway. Reggie wasn't letting go of Perry's hand again.

Though the fog was still thick and the rain showed no sign of easing up, Reggie could see easily the man in the ballerina's tutu had Det. Horton in a head lock and was dragging him down the steps, when he heard several gun shots.

Reggie and Perry then ran to the front door as Reggie took careful aim, and fired six shots into the man in the ballerina's tutu back.

The man in the ballerina's tutu was unaffected by the bullets, as Reggie looked on in disbelief, saying to himself...

"There's no way in hell I could have missed something that damn big."

This time Reggie aimed at the man's head and fired three more shots. The man in the ballerina's tutu turned his head looking at Reggie, cocking his head to the left and to the right.

Reggie knew that he had to do something to help Det. Horton after all, if it hadn't been for Det. Horton, all of them would've still been in the basement tied up.

Reggie stepped back and told Perry, that once the man in the ballerina's tutu drops Det. Horton and comes after him, for Perry to start running through the walkway and to the SUV, and not to look back or stop.

In a low voice, Perry said...

"Oh no you don't...what the hell's the matter with you, have you lost what's left of your fucking mind? Look Reg, I'm not leaving you and you'd better not let me go either."

The man in the ballerina's tutu began to drag Det. Horton down the steps. Reggie turned to Perry and said...

"Help me out here babe, it's raining like hell, its foggier than shit, car won't start, and just a minute ago I shot that fucker eight times, and he's still standing....so am I missing something here?"

Reggie started yelling at the man in the ballerina's tutu, and taunting him to come back and fight like a man. In the beginning the man in the ballerina's tutu ignored Reggie, until he did something totally unexpected.

Reggie ran up to him and struck him several times in the back of his head with his gun and said...

"Yeah, that's right! I'm not afraid of you, you big pussy.... C'mon, you Jolly Green Giant bitch! You know I'll kick the shit out of you... you damn freak!"

The man in the ballerina's tutu stopped dead in his tracks, and Reggie motioned for Perry to go to the far side of the porch, and to be ready to climb over the railings and get Det. Horton.

The man in the ballerina's tutu dropped Det. Horton and slowly turned to face Reggie, and as he did, Perry was sitting on top of the railings and then jumped to the ground.

Reggie began backing up to the door, to lure the man in the ballerina's tutu towards him, so that Perry could get away.

With each step that the man in the ballerina's tutu took, Reggie continued taunting him...

"C'mon...bring your big happy ass over here...you think somebody's scared of you!"

Reggie had three bullets left and had to make each shot count. Reggie took aim at the man in the ballerina's tutu' face and fired a single shot from five feet away, hitting him in the right eye.

Reggie was shocked. He stood there for a second wondering how he could have missed from that distance until he saw blood pouring from beneath the clown's mask.

The man in the ballerina's tutu lowered his head and then reached up and removed the clown's mask from his face.

Reggie quickly scanned the area on the porch for a possibly escape route when the man in the ballerina's tutu began digging in his right eye, blood pouring profusely from the eye socket.

Reggie seized his opportunity and bolted to the right of the man in the ballerina's tutu until he was at the far end of the porch and near the railing.

Placing the gun in his pocket, Reggie threw one leg over the railing and then the other, when he heard Perry scream.

Even though there was a porch light on, Reggie was unable to see anything in the night because the rain continued coming down and the fog which was up to a moment ago several feet away, engulfed the entire porch.

Not knowing where the man in the ballerina's tutu was, or what was below him, Reggie slowly jumped from the porch onto the ground.

With absolutely no visibility and not knowing in what direction to go, Reggie recalled that the inside walkway which was connected to the house was only a hundred feet to his right.

Using the siding of the house as a guide Reggie slowly made his way towards the walkway hoping that Perry and Det. Horton went in the same direction.

Reggie finally made his way to the corner of the house, now the trick was to find the door into the walkway.

Reaching the entrance to the door, Reggie entered inside thinking and wondering if Det. Horton was there, when he heard a soft familiar voice call out to him...

"Reg, is that you babe?"

Recognizing that it was Perry's voice, Reggie whispered...

"Perry, it's me... Damn babe, I'm so glad I found you, but how did you find your way here?"

Perry stretched out her hands until they found Reggie's.

Perry helped Reggie into the doorway as she explained that once she had jumped over the railing, she was in a crouched position until she saw a light on the ground coming out of the fog and that's when she screamed.

As they walked cautiously through the walkway, Perry explained how Det. Horton had met up with her, and that his leg was busted and that he was headed down the walkway to the barn.

Perry went on to say that, Det. Horton begged her to go with him to the SUV, until she heard a gunshot and decided to stay by the doorway entrance hoping that Reggie would be there.

Reggie and Perry just about made it through the walkway to SUV when they saw a single beam from a flashlight pointed at them.

Thinking that it was Det. Horton they hurried their pace until they arrived at the barn. Standing in the door way was someone with a flashlight, but it wasn't Det. Horton.

Reggie and Perry stood for a moment in shock, because the man standing there wasn't Det. Horton, but someone else they didn't know.

Reggie stood looking at Steve who was dressed in hunters' camouflage clothes. Steve pushed open the barn door wider and said...

"Your Det. friend is inside on the sofa, I think his leg is busted... and if that gunshot I heard means you killed that psycho in the ballerina's tutu with the clown's mask, I suggest that everybody get back inside.

Steve introduced himself and explained how he got there, and where he had been hiding, and said...

I took Mary and Kristin inside, and I hope you know that your SUV won't start...it's out of gas...I think...anyway it's much safer inside the barn than it is locked in a car that won't go anywhere."

Just as Reggie, Perry and Steve entered the barn and closed the door, Perry yelled...

"Aww shit!"

Reggie turned and asked her what the problem was and Perry said...

"Damnit…I broke a nail."

Reggie stopped for a moment and then all three broke out in laughter. Det. Horton told Reggie…

"With all the weird ass shit going on, a twisted psycho chasing us and your woman is worried about her broken nail."

The laughter which was heard coming from the barn was interrupted by a loud bang and the door and scratching on the windows.

Steve and Det. Horton went to the windows and peeked outside to see the man in the ballerina's tutu wearing the clown's face and Mr. Thomas standing at the front door of the barn.

Realizing that their only way of escape was through the back door, Det. Horton told Steve…

"All we got to do is keep an eye on the back door, since they've nailed shut the front door."

Steve looked away from the window and over to Perry, who had grabbed a couple of wash cloths, trying to provide comfort and clean up Mary and Kristin's wounds.

Steve walked over and asked Perry…

"How are they doing?"

Perry was attempting to remove the staples from Mary's eye lids, which had swollen her eyes with fluid and blood, making it difficult to remove the staples when she replied…

"I hadn't started to work on the other girl, but this woman…"

Steve interrupted saying…

"That's Mary, and the other woman is Kristin."

Perry asked Reggie to look in one of drawers and get her a small knife and to soak it in salty water, along with these wash cloths, saying to Steve…

"You know these girls?"

Walking over to the sofa and checking on Kristin, Steve said…

"Yes, we're all friends. The owners of this place David and Deanne are friends of ours…damn Kristin, what in the hell did he do to you?"

Reggie bought Perry a pot of salty water, with two wash cloths and a small steak knife.

Perry soaked the wash cloths in water and laid them across Mary's eyes and turned her attention to Mary' feet which had been literally baked until they were double in size.

David Ray

Perry sat both of Mary's feet in the salty water, as Mary moaned.

Steve and Reggie thought that Mary was running a fever and was sweating profusely and asked Perry, who responded...

"No she's not running a fever. This is what happens when your body is severely burned. Our bodies hold blood and fluid, and because her feet are so badly burned...fluid is going to leak out anywhere and everywhere it can."

Reggie placed both hands on Perry's neck and massaged her saying...

"Well it's good that we have someone who's experienced with traumas up here."

Next Perry grabbed the small steak knife and asked for one of them to help hold Mary still while she removes the staples from Mary's forehead.

Perry explained that this was going to be a little tricky because she would have to make a small slit across the inside of the eyelids, and then she would work on getting the staples out of her forehead later.

As Perry and Steve worked to remove Mary's eyelids from the staples in her forehead there was a loud bang on all sides of the barn and then there was a sudden silence.

Looking out the window Det. Horton saw the man in the ballerina's tutu with the clown's face and Mr. Thomas getting on a tractor and driving off in the direction of the other farm.

Reggie looked at Det. Horton saying...

"Now what do you suppose they are up to?"

Det. Horton and Reggie watched as Mr. Thomas and the man in the ballerina's tutu rode around in circles, over and over going from Mr. Thomas' property to David and Deanne's farm.

Steve came up to the window to see the two men out in the rain riding around and around in circles saying...

"Hey you know...if they keep this up, this might give us the break we need to make a run for it."

Det. Horton walked away from the window saying...

"We're not going anywhere tonight...not in all of this rain and fog. Those nuts are playing some kind of game and we're not going to fall into their trap by going out in the middle of the night."

Perry and Steve were able to remove all of the staples from Mary's forehead, when Perry had noticed that some of the swelling had gone down a little.

Det. Horton asked Steve if he'd walk Perry upstairs to look for some clothes that they could dress Mary and Kristin in.

Steve walked away from looking out of the window saying...

"Did you all hear that...it sounds like somebody's dogs are chasing something out in the rain?"

Det. Horton and Reggie walked back over to Kristin, who still had a few fish hooks in her back and her breast saying...

"If I had a pair of wire cutters it would be easy, but he's got these hooks embedded really good...looks like I'm going to have to push them in deeper and wiggle them around until they come out but it's going to be painful as hell."

Reggie replied as he turned to see Perry coming down stairs with Steve carrying an armload of clothes saying...

'One of the good things is, Kristin is still unconscious."

Removing the fish hooks from Kristin's body proved to be a lot harder than Det. Horton had planned on.

The fish hooks were extremely large and because they held up the weight of Kristin's body for hours, a lot of damage was done to the surrounding tissues and muscles, causing massive swelling where each of the hooks were.

Det. Horton began the process of removing each hook as carefully as he could, and he noticed all around the area of each hook infection had set in.

With each pushing in of the hooks, Kristin gasped and moaned.

Around each hook the skin was swollen with large pus filled blisters which had begun to ooze with the slightest touch of Kristin's skin.

It was clear from Kristin's wounds that she was in need antibiotics, but the immediate need was to remove them.

Perry went searching the upstairs bathroom and the down stairs kitchen cabinets for hydrogen peroxide, bleach or anything to treat the infections.

Coming back in from the kitchen Perry placed in a bowl on the table, cayenne pepper, honey, baking soda and sesame seed oil.

Looking at all the ingredients Perry was mixing, Det. Horton asked...

"Okay, what is all of that?"

Perry mixed all of the ingredients together until it was thick and said...

"Just something I remembered from my grandmother...it won't cure the infection, but it will draw out and dry up the pus and the other fluids."

Each time Det. Horton removed a hook, Perry applied a thick batch of the mixture to Kristin's infections.

Reggie went back to the window and peeked out saying...

"Hey Mark, we still got a big problem?"

Det. Horton pretended to ignore Reggie as he was busy removing the hooks from Kristin's skin, when Reggie said...

"Hey Mark...."

Det. Horton looked up at Reggie with a bloody hook in his hand saying...

"I hear you coach, what's up?"

Reggie turned his back to the window and said...

"Det. Fannichuci. Det. Fannichuci is still stuck to the basement floor...what are we going to do about him?"

Det. Horton was about to answer when the window behind Reggie busted. Perry screamed as something started pulling Reggie through the window.

A bunch of hands small hands like children's hands were grabbing and clutching Reggie's shirt as he struggled to pull away.

Det. Horton jumped up and grabbed a large butcher knife from the counter top and began striking and slashing at the hands holding onto Reggie's clothes, until one by one they let go.

Reggie, who was half way out of his shirt said...

"WHOO! Thanks Mark, damn those little bastards were strong, where'd they come from?"

Det. Horton stood looking around the room saying...

"This is why we are not doing or going anywhere until morning, and in the meantime, we're going to have to barricade all the windows.

Reggie, while I finish removing these hooks and watch guard down here, see what you can find to barricade the windows...okay?"

Reggie nodded and went upstairs, Det. Horton and Perry were tending to Kristin's wounds when Mary began squirming around on the sofa, pointing to the window and moaning.

Reggie, Get your ass down here quick!"

Det. Horton yelled as he jumped up and ran to the living room window. Mary had seen that one of the creepy children was squeezing itself in through the window.

Det. Horton ran to the window and began beating the creepy kid, whose body was nearly through the window, when Reggie came running down the steps yelling...

"Oh shit, hang on Mark."

Reggie looked around the room and then ran over to the refrigerator and began pushing it up against the window and saying to Det. Horton...

"Here, this ought to take care of this window but there are other places where they might try to come in."

Reggie and Det. Horton stood watching as the hands of the creepy kids tried unsuccessfully to get past the fridge, but could not.

Det. Horton and Reggie stood talking as Reggie said...

"When I was upstairs there are three windows we need to board up and I saw in the back bedroom a lot of two by fours and a box of nails, but no hammer?"

Det. Horton went to search inside the storage closet by the back door as Reggie went back upstairs to grab as much wood and the box of nails which he saw.

Mary had regained full consciousness and tried to get up off of sofa, looking down to see that her feet were inside of a bucket of water.

Perry laid Kristin's body slowly on the floor and covered her and went over to Mary and said...

"Mary; your name's Mary right?"

"My name is Perry...honey you can't stand right now, your feet...."

Perry tried telling Mary that her feet were baked over a bed of white coals and there were third degree burns covering her entire feet.

Mary pulled her feet out of the bucket of water, and crossing her legs to bring her feet to where she could examine them...and began crying and moaning and crying...

"OMG…. TIM!"

Perry helped her place her foot back down into the water and said…

"Don't worry Mary we're going to get you out of this. My husband and another Det. are here. Just give me a few minutes to finish up with your friend and I'll see what I can do to help you."

Perry went back over to Kristin and as she uncovered her, Mary saw that it was Kristin and started shaking her head from side to side, moaning and crying.

Det. Horton returned from the storage closet just as Reggie was coming back downstairs with the wood and the box of nails, saying…

'Hey Coach…I couldn't find a hammer, but I found a Mechanical Jack… we can use this end to hammer the nails in."

Reggie looked at the two by fours and then over to the jack and said…

"Well anything is better than nothing, just hope that this jack will drive the nails through these boards."

Det. Horton placed the jack over near the window on a table saying…

"It'll do the trick the outside is steel and inside there is a three inch solid rod of steel…so, you and Steve will start, I'll come help you guys when I'm done here."

Reggie and Steve began placing the boards up to the window and began nailing them in place.

The Jack that Det. Horton found was getting the job done without any problems, but was also wearing Reggie's large arms out, from all the pounding.

Reggie and Steve nailed up the living room window which was the only window downstairs, before going up stairs to work on the three bedroom windows.

Steve took a two by four and braced it under the back door knob and the floor, and then went upstairs to help Reggie.

Perry and Det. Horton removed all of the fish hooks from Kristin's body as Perry applied the last amount of the concoction she made up to draw out the infection.

Perry stood up and started to go upstairs when he Det. Horton asked…

"Can I ask you where are you going?"

Perry turned at the bottom of the steps saying...

"I'm going to look in the bathroom for some fingernail polish remover, I- I thought I saw some up there earlier."

Not knowing why Perry wanted the nail polish remover, Det. Horton said...

"You're going to do your nails?"

Perry walked over to Det. Horton and said...

"No, nail polish remover and soap will loosen the super glue off of her lips...hopefully there's enough in the bottle I saw."

Heading upstairs, Perry turned and looked back at Kristin and Mary, and for brief moment a tear formed in Perry's eyes as she continued up the steps.

Reggie and Steve were nailing the bedroom windows shut when Perry stuck her head in the bedroom and said to Reggie...

"Hey hon, I'm just getting something to help with one of the ladies downstairs."

Reggie turned looking at Perry saying...

"Okay babe, we got those two rooms left so hurry up and get back down stairs with Mark."

Perry left the bedroom and went into the bathroom, and recalling that she'd seen the fingernail polish under the sink in the bathroom cabinet, grabbed the bottle and took off the lid and smelled it, saying to herself...

"Well, it doesn't smell old, and it looks like there is enough."

Walking out of the bathroom, Perry was met in the hallway by Reggie and Steve who were heading into another bedroom, saying...

"Okay Reg, I got what I need, see you down stairs in a bit."

Reggie hugged and kissed Perry saying...

"Thanks babe, you've been great through all of this...I promise, we'll hold up in here tonight and in the morning this nightmare will be over."

Steve and Reggie returned from boarding up all the windows in the three bedrooms upstairs and came down stairs to see Det. Horton double checking the board braced against the back door.

Outside of the condition of Mary's feet Perry managed to get her Lips unglued, but they were still swollen and Perry was working to

311

remove bits and pieces of the twine which were stuck inside of her lips.

Steve, Reggie and Det. Horton were standing over at the window discussing plans for getting out of the barn in the morning and watching Mr. Thomas and the man in the ballerina's tutu, who were still on the tractor.

Reggie looked over at Det. Horton saying...

"*Mark, I know we're talking about doing something in the morning, but I'm thinking maybe we shouldn't wait, you and I can take on the big man, and Steve here can handle an old man.*"

Det. Horton checked his coat pocket for a cigarette and said to Reggie...

"*Coach, I had the same thought too but, there are too many things riding against us if we try anything tonight.*"

Steve walked over towards the kitchen cabinet and grabbed a bottle of vodka down and some glasses saying...

"*Look...everything's been against us since day one, I'm not against trying something... what do we have to lose.*"

Steve offered everyone a glass as Reggie asked Perry to check the fridge and cabinets for food.

Perry walked over and handed Reggie a can of pineapple juice and a bottle of ruby red grape fruit juice, when Det. Horton walked over saying...

"*For starters, the rain and fog is against us hatching any kind of successful plan, and then there's the fact that none of us know the area up here.*

Lastly...we have three women, two of them are injured and I just think our first priority is to get them out of here safely, I just think if we try something and one or more of us are injured...the woman won't stand a chance."

Perry discovered a canned ham in the fridge along with a box of crackers and some canned foods in the cupboard and said...

"*This is all I can find, and I'm afraid we're going to have to eat it cold. I tried the gas range, and it's not working.*"

Sitting his drink down, Reggie went to help Perry by opening up the ham saying...

"*Cold ham, crackers and whatever is better than no ham and crackers.*"

Things appeared as if there was a little light at the end of the tunnel for the folks in the barn.

Det. Horton was sitting in a chair with a drink in one hand and his feet up on the arm of the sofa.

Mary who was sitting on the sofa, her feet still in the bucket of water and baking soda, was actually talking.

It was difficult hearing what she was saying all the time because she was trying to form words without her lips touching one another, which she found hard to do.

Steve was sitting next to Kristin, occasionally checking on her infections.

Perry got up from Reggie's lap to put the left over ham in the fridge saying...

"*Would there be a problem with the women sleeping in the beds upstairs...I mean all the windows are boarded up right, and both of these women need to lie down?*"

Reggie blurted out saying...

"*Yeah, I don't see anything wrong with that.*"

Det. Horton got up from the chair saying...

"*I see something wrong with it. We'll have two men downstairs keeping an eye out on both doors, and one man upstairs making certain no one gets in through the windows...I think we ought to stay together in one room.*"

Steve laid Kristin's head down on the sofa saying...

"*I agree with Reggie and his wife...the way I see it, if that big man someone how gets in here, then women are going to be in our way. As far as someone coming in through the windows...I doubt that, the windows are about thirty-five forty feet off the ground.*"

Det. Horton thought for a moment and then agreed that maybe that was not a bad ideal.

Reggie picked up Mary to carry her upstairs as Steve and Perry stood Kristin up to help her up the stairs when the lights went out and Perry let out a scream.

Det. Horton yelled...

"*Shh...don't anybody make a move!*"

313

Chapter 15

The Collection

20 Miles outside
Port Clinton, Ohio
9:30 p.m.

I was doing a piss poor job of pretending t0 be calm, but when they approached the road sign which read...Port Clinton, twenty miles, Deanne thought that I was going lose it.

I reached up and started turning the tuning knob on the radio looking for a clear station when Deanne said...

"Blue, I can't believe that the Sheriff's department said if something's wrong when we get to the farm, they'll try to send a car out. All I wanted them to do was send one deputy with us now... damn!"

I sat back in my seat and stared out of the window and then looked over at Deanne as she put the wipers on and began slowing down from seventy to twenty miles an hour...

"Gosh Blue where did all of this weather come from, we must've rode right into a storm."

I reached up and switched the control to defog the windshield for Deanne, because she showed no sign of removing her hand from the steering wheel.

The windshield became a milky screen, when Deanne suddenly slammed on brakes.

I looked up and saw the reason Deanne slammed on brakes so hard. The entire car was engulfed in fog, and not your typical light fog...but an eerie milky white fog with a strong vanilla scent.

Deanne tried switching from low beams to high beams, when I remembered there was a toggle switch so I flicked the toggle switch for the fog lights, which offered very little help...we still couldn't see anything in front of us.

Deanne looked over at me and said...

"Blue, I know what you're thinking and yes...this does not look good."

I motioned for Deanne to let me drive. Deanne placed the car in park and climbed over to the passenger seat, as I got out of the car and into the driver's seat.

After I shut the driver's side door, Deanne noticed some of the fog had drifted into the car.

Deanne tapped me on the arm and pointed to the fog which was hovering over the back seat.

When I turned the fog looked as if it were a misshapen balloon, not completely round...more oval with misty edges.

Deanne had turned back to the front and cut the wipers on full as the rain started pouring down on the windshield when I jumped almost out of the car.

Deanne turned back to look at me when the fog which was hovering over the back seat began taking the form of a person's head.

Deanne grabbed hold of my arm as the fog form a face, a little girl's face.

Suddenly, the image was clear....it was the face of the little girl which I had been seeing all along when I looked at Deanne, pointing to the face...when the little girl screamed...

"Boo!"

Deanne looked over at me and smiled, as I sat there shaking, when Deanne said...

"Blue...Blue, for once it's good to see a man scared to drive in bad weather...you men all act like women are the weak ones when it comes to driving in nasty weather."

I looked at Deanne and said...

"So that's it...you're smiling at me because you think I'm scared... what about the fog and the little girl's face?"

Deanne looked at me and said...

"Blue...it was just a little bit of fog that drifted in the car, and no I did not see a girl!"

I sat there for a moment shaking my head and in disbelief that Deanne still was not able to see and hear what I was.

I looked out through the rear view mirror, thinking about turning around, but with visibility of minus zero...turning or doing anything but going straight was impossible.

Slowly I inched the car forward watching for the broken yellow center line in the road, which was barely visible.

I inched the car up to five miles an hour until finally I was able to see the yellow center line a little clearer.

Suddenly there was a loud bang on the rear of the car as if something rammed into us from behind, while Deanne screamed as I hit the brakes.

Looking out the driver's side mirror and then the rear view mirror I didn't see any lights or anything else for the matter.

Deanne turned to me saying...

"Are you going to see what that was?"

I shook my head and said...

"HELL NO!"

I continued slowly inching forward until the fog looked as though it was clearing up a little at a time.

Deanne looked at me and said...

"Whew...it's about time...it can't be too bad up ahead, I can see Harmon's market sign pretty clear."

Hearing the name of Harmon's market brought a chill to me. It was at Harmon's market six months ago, that this damn nightmare began.

It was there at Harmon's market where he first saw the Doppelgangers and the little girl, and I knew it was only fifteen more minutes before they would be at the farm.

For the next ten miles as the rain increased and the fog briefly disappeared, when Deanne screamed at me...

"Look out Blue!"

From out of nowhere the man in the ballerina's tutu with the clown's face mask appeared in front of their car.

I swerved to the right and hit a parked car which was sitting on the side of the road.

As I looked over at Deanne and reached out to see if she was alright, when I noticed Deanne's knee hit the dash board.

Deanne let out a soft moan, as she grabbed her right knee and saying...

"Ooh...I'll be okay. Damn Blue, the man in the road...where did he go?"

I looked to his left but the man in the ballerina's tutu was nowhere in sight. David tried putting the car in reverse, but the front fender of my car was knocked loose on one side and was digging into the right front tire.

I slammed his hands on the steering wheel and put his head down, when Deanne said...

"It's not your fault Blue...we're just going to have to do some walking, we're not that far away."

I held the umbrella over us as she linked her left arm through mine.

The fog had dissipated a little, but the rain was still coming down hard, sometimes blowing sideways.

The walk to the farm was not the first time that Deanne and I had done this.

Several years ago, in summer when they decided to renovate his family's old farm, their car had broken down at Harmon's market, and Deanne and I walked the entire twenty mile trip.

The walk from Harmon's market several years ago, took Deanne and I forty-five minutes to do, and since we had driven at least ten miles past Harmon's, our trip was almost over.

A gust of wind caught the umbrella and made short work out of it, bending the ribs and destroying it, as I let loose of it.

Deanne and I continued down the highway with their heads bent when I lifted my head up and pointed to a mail box on the opposite side of the road...

"C. Thomas 15350"

When Deanne saw the mail box she looked up at me and smiled knowing that in less than five minutes we'd be at their neighbors' house, and then at their farm.

Deanne wiped the rain from her face and said to me...

"C'mon Blue let's go, we can cut through this field to Mr. Thomas's house first and get him to help us."

Mr. Thomas's house bordered our farm, and just like our property, it sat a half a mile off the road and would be another five to ten minute walk through the muddy field.

Deanne knew that Mr. Thomas always stayed up late tinkering with something, especially when it wasn't planting season, so a little late night unexpected visit wouldn't create too much of a disturbance.

Unlike our driveway which was paved, Mr. Thomas preferred to keep his graveled, so pulled Deanne arm so that they would walk more on the gravel than in the muddy field.

As we made our way Deanne couldn't help but notice that the trees looked as if there were 'things' up in them slithering down.

What Deanne didn't know was...there were 'things' up in the trees, slithering down, and soon she would see them.

Our fast pace walk soon became an all-out run, as we began hearing the sound of horses snorting and knew we were a few feet from Mr. Thomas's barn.

Directly ahead of us we noticed Mr. Thomas's porch light come on, and then the milky fog which they drove through was behind them setting in again.

Deanne and I slowed our pace down as the fog rolled in behind them and stopped right against their backs.

Both of us cried out for Mr. Thomas who upon hearing us, stepped out of the house and onto the front porch.

We ran up on Mr. Thomas's porch wet and out of breath, shaking the rain from our clothes as Mr. Thomas opened the screen door to let them in, saying...

"Whoa...folks, what are you two doing out in this weather, let me guess your boyfriend's cheap foreign car broke down...told ya, you should've bought American."

Mr. Thomas grabbed a couple towels from the closet and handed them to me and Deanne as Deanne replied...

"We didn't break down, but we hit some car that was parked up there on the turn off, and had to walk the entire way here."

Mr. Thomas motion for me and Deanne to follow him in the kitchen as he put a kettle pot of water on.

I dried the rain from his head and face, while Deanne dried her hair, when Mr. Thomas said...

"What are doing up here this late at night, you folks are going to have to pay attention to the weather report before setting out... besides, I thought your boyfriend here was getting his 'cheerios' checked out?"

Deanne handed Mr. Thomas the towel and said...

"No Mr. Thomas, David is fine...he just needed a little rest... they released him last week."

Mr. Thomas poured water into two cups and a teaspoon of instant coffee into each cup along with a shot of whiskey from his flask, and said...

"Well if you don't mind me saying...he can't be too fine, letting you get up here in all this weather at this time a night, and why don't he say something?"

Mr. Thomas was unaware of my condition, only that six months ago on their farm emergency had to take him to the Psychiatric hospital.

Deanne kissed on the cheek and rubbed his arm as she said to Mr. Thomas...

"The reason we're here is... has there been anybody up at our place lately?"

Mr. Thomas placed the flask back in the fridge and said...

"Come to think of it there was a couple up here real early this morning. I think the husband said he was a detective, but like I said that was early this morning, and they left."

Deanne sat down and drank her coffee and asked...

"Do you think you can drive us to our farm, and are you sure, nobody else has been up there, because a friend of ours called, saying she was at our farm?"

Mr. Thomas grabbed he keys from off the rack and said...

"Sure I'll give you a ride over and it's like I said... nobody comes around except my friends, and I only have two of them and they died years ago.

Deanne had reached in her coat pocket to locate her house key and said...

"Mr. Thomas we we're wondering if our friend Mary and her husband Tim were the ones who you saw earlier, because...

I interrupted Deanne by tugging on her coat, because I didn't want her saying the real reason they came to the farm.

After we finished their coffee we waited for Mr. Thomas to come out of the bathroom and then we headed out of the living room towards the front door.

Mr. Thomas walked out of the kitchen and turned around and said...

"If you want that ride, my trucks out back, easier to go through the kitchen though."

Mr. Thomas grabbed his keys off the kitchen table, saying...

"So, what was so all important that got you folks up here in the middle of the night and in all this...you could've called...are you two in trouble or something?

Deanne walked slowly through the kitchen and began telling Mr. Thomas how her friend Mary had a fight with her husband, and got in her car and drove out to the farm to have some time to think.

Mr. Thomas opened the back door and as we exited and reached the truck, Mr. Thomas started the truck and got out and said...

"I'll be right back... forgot something."

Deanne looked over at me and then sat down on the seat inside the truck. Mr. Thomas's truck had two bucket seats, so it was clear Deanne was going to have to sit on my lap.

Looking through the rear view mirror Deanne screamed...

"Oh My God... BLUE!!!!"

I was about to turn and look at what caused Deanne to scream when the truck began to shake and the man in the ballerina's tutu was standing in front of the truck.

The man in the ballerina's tutu turned his head sideways and began pounding on the front of the truck, and in between screaming, Deanne yelled...

"Blue... Mr. Thomas, who is this!"

I slid over into the driver's seat and put the gear selection into drive and, and as he did, the man in the ballerina's tutu wearing the clown's face, lifted the front end of the truck off the ground.

I pressed the accelerator pedal as far as it would go until the rear tires began spinning and kicking up the gravel and mud under the tires.

I put the gear in drive and then in reverse, again and again until the man in the ballerina's tutu began losing his grip on the bumper and began sliding in the mud.

The man in the ballerina's tutu tried to get from out of the front of the truck when he noticed that the fringe of his ballerina's tutu was caught in the grill of the truck.

I continued to accelerate the truck until the man in the ballerina's tutu fell onto the hood of the truck and then was being driven backwards, towards a tree.

I saw the large tree directly behind the man in the ballerina's tutu and I opened my mouth and hollered as I slammed the man in the ballerina's tutu into the tree.

My eyes were closed as the man in the ballerina's tutu was being crushed between the truck and the tree, until the man in the ballerina's tutu, slumped onto the truck.

I hadn't noticed at first and maybe it was because of the adrenaline, but when I opened my mouth to scream, I was surprised that sounds actually came out of my mouth...

"Augh!"

Deanne grabbed onto my arm and looking around said...

"Blue...oh my God Blue...you can talk...you can talk!"

Throwing the gear of the truck into reverse, the truck started backing up and the man in the ballerina's tutu dropped to the ground.

I tried putting the truck in drive, and as I did the truck started to slide and the rear tires started spinning.

I tried going from reverse to drive, but there was too much mud, and Deanne said...

"Blue...Look... Blue!"

When I glanced up, the man in the ballerina's tutu was no longer slumped on the ground, but was beginning to stand up.

looked over at Deanne and with a low raspy voice said...

"*Okay Deanne, we're going to have to make a run for it...let's go baby.*"

I watched as Deanne tried to open the passenger side of the truck, when I leaned in and said...

"*C'mon baby, forget it, C'mon this side.*"

Just then Deanne let out a scream...

"*Watch out Blue!*"

It was too late...Mr. Thomas was standing behind me and drove a hay pitchfork into my back.

I stood for a moment in shock, looking at Deanne and looking down at the prongs protruding out of my chest, and then I slowly slumped to the ground.

The last thing I saw was the man in the ballerina's tutu, grabbing Deanne by the hair.

The echoes of Deanne's cries for help faded away as thunder cracked and lit the sky up with a bright blue traces and streaks.

Mr. Thomas walked over to the man in the ballerina's tutu, who was nudging my limp body with his foot, seeing if I was alive.

Mr. Thomas's quiet demeanor changed to menacing as he instructed the man in the ballerina's tutu to forget about me, and to carry Deanne to the gathering place.

The man in the ballerina's tutu, who towered over six feet eight inches seemed to fear Mr. Thomas, or better yet...mindlessly obey Mr. Thomas.

As Mr. Thomas and the man in the ballerina's tutu approached the basement of Deanne and David's farm house, the man in the ballerina's tutu suddenly stopped and turned his head to the left in the direction of the small cabin, several hundred feet away.

Tim was crouched down beside the cabin, watching as Mr. Thomas had just stabbed someone with the pitched fork, not knowing that it was me.

Tim nervously turned from watching Mr. Thomas to check behind him every few seconds, because the fog and rain, limited his visibility to just a foot or two, hoping no one was sneaking up on him.

When Tim escaped from the man in the ballerina's tutu, he said that he was running to get help but not knowing which way to run and where to go, Tim hid out at the small cabin, hoping that someone else would come.

Tim reached in his pocket for a joint, believing that the rain and fog would the smell of marijuana, when he heard in the darkness a twig snap.

Tim ducked back on the side of the cabin putting his back against the cabin when he heard another twig snap.

Tim strained his eyes to both the left and the right, but wasn't able to see anything except fog, and when he poked his head out to see where Mr. Thomas and the man in the ballerina's tutu was, something grabbed Tim' shoulder.

Tim jumped and as he did, the marijuana cigarette which was dangling in his mouth fell to the ground.

Tim balled up his fist to defend himself, when he realized that the person who had grabbed him was none other than Officer Withers, who said...

"I never thought I'd say it...but it's good seeing you again, by the way...they'll be able to smell that pretty good if you lit it up."

Tim reached down to pick up his marijuana joint and said to Officer Withers...

"Damn...you made me drop my joint sneaking around on people. What happened to you, me and your Detective friend looked all over for you...what happened."

Officer Withers traded places with Tim as she poked her head around the corner to get a peek at what Tim was looking at, and said...

"My God, this is crazy...what's going on up here. One minute I was lying in the bunk listening to you and Det. Fannichuci snore, and the next thing I knew...I'm being dragged out in the woods."

Tim explained everything to Officer Withers regarding the last several hours saying...

"It's all a mess now. Me and your Detective friend went looking for you and that's when that big fucker grabbed me and your partner.

I got away...but he's got him inside the basement along with Mary, and some other people."

Officer Withers asked Tim who was he spying on, and if there was anybody else inside the house.

Tim continued explaining everything which had happened, since she disappeared when Officer Withers suggested...

"Look there's a barn right there, a little closer to the house, why not make it there?"

Tim explained that when he got away from the man in the ballerina's tutu, that he's been behind the cabin the whole time watching the house, and at one time the man in the ballerina's tutu carried something to the barn and left.

He explained that staying near the cabin was the safest place to be. Officer Withers disagreed with Tim and saying...

"Tim, regardless of what's going on up here we can't just stay here far away from house and just do nothing while people are in trouble."

Tim peeked around the cabin looking at Mr. Thomas and the man in the ballerina's tutu, and looked at Officer Withers as she checked her gun, saying...

"Oh yes we can, every time someone goes up to the house to help the others escape...something happens and they end up in the basement all tied up.

I'm telling you that big ass man in the ballerina's tutu, he's not human... he was shot four times by your partner and he's still up walking around....no, no, no, staying our asses right here is what we're going to do."

Officer Withers explained to Tim that, if they stay there at the cabin, her partner and everybody else in the basement is going to die, and then the man in the ballerina's tutu is going to come after them, and then what are they going to do?

The heavy rain and thick fog normally would have provided the perfect cover especially when you want to be undetected, but Tim and Officer Withers would soon discover that when you think nobody can see you...there is always someone watching you.

Tim leaned against Officer Withers and said...

"Look at them...it almost looks like that big son of a bitch can see us through all this fog, huh?"

Officer Withers in a whisper, said...

"Unless he's from the planet Krypton...there is no way in shit that he can see us, we're too damn far away, and look at this fog?"

The man in the ballerina's tutu wearing the clown's face stood quiet and began sniffing the air, looking in the direction of Tim and Officer Withers.

Mr. Thomas tapped the man in the ballerina's tutu on the arm and said...

"Yes.......I smell them too; their odor will lead us right to them."

Officer Withers and Tim secretly continued to watch the man in the ballerina's tutu, who had thrown Deanne over his shoulders when Mr. Thomas stopped at the front door of the house and turned in the direction of Tim and Officer Withers.

Officer Withers and Tim crouched down, wiping the rain from their faces, when they noticed Mr. Thomas opening the front door and heard him whistling as he went inside.

The heavy fog was hard seeing through, but Tim and Officer Withers could faintly pick out that something or someone had emerged from inside the house and onto the front porch.

Officer Withers looked over at Tim and said...

"What the hell do you think that is?"

Tim leaned against the side of the cabin and reached into his pocket, pulling out a joint and lighting it saying...

"Hell I ...don't know and I'm not so sure I want to find out either."

Tim tried opening the door of the cabin, and when he remembered that the door locks as soon as it's closed said...

"Fuck!"

Officer Withers walked up t0 Tim and said...

"What's wrong now...since the door is locked all you got to do is use the ladder and go through the window around back, right?"

Tim shook his head no, and said to Officer Withers...

"No can do...me and Det. Fannichuci took the ladder over to the house when we were trying to help the people inside, and we left it there."

Tim explained to Officer Withers that the only real option is to hide out in Mr. Thomas' house, that it was their best bet, since they probably would not look for them there.

Officer Withers shook her head and agreed with Tim and said as Tim took a deep long drag on the joint, and mumbled at Tim...

"With all the shit going on, now I got to deal with 'captain pothead...if that shit you're smoking marks us, I'm going to shoot your ass myself."

Tim blew the smoke from his mouth in the direction of the back of the cabin which was being engulfed in the fog, and tapped Officer Withers on her shoulder and pointed towards the front door of David and Deanne's house and said....

"C'mon, let's go."

Officer Withers and Tim slowly began making their way to Mr. Thomas's house, careful to use the tree line so that their movement would go undetected.

Officer Withers had grabbed a hold of the back of Tim's coat, so that she would not get lost in the fog and go in the wrong direction.

Tim looked back and said to Officer Withers...

"You okay back there, it's not too much longer, I think it's just on the other side of the ravine that we should be coming up on."

Officer Withers gave a sharp tug on Tim's coat saying...

"Should be! I thought you knew where you were going, I won't to be lost out here when we could easily have gone to the barn back there, where we'd at least be dry."

Tim suddenly stopped and turned to Officer Withers who had let go of his coat, saying...

"Shh...I heard something...did you hear that?"

Officer Withers turned with Tim and cupping her hands over her forehead to shield the rain from her face, looked in the direction of David and Deanne's farmhouse.

Tim and Officer Withers saw the outline of two very large Rottweiler's at the top of the ravine against the outline of the fog, racing towards them.

The Rottweiler's were a good distance away from Tim and Officer Withers, if they could only make it to the house before the dogs caught up with them, but this was the dog's territory and the dogs no doubt have been all over the area, when Tim hollered at officer Withers...

"Move girl...move, give me your hand, move your ass...and if you fall down, you're on your own!"

Officer Withers and Tim made it to the rear of Mr. Thomas' house, and discovered that the back door was locked.

Hearing that the dogs were closing in on them, they ran around to the front door which to their surprise was open.

Running inside and closing the door, they heard the snarling, barking and the clawing of the dogs against the back door, when Tim said...

"Whew...we made it."

Officer Withers and Tim went to the back door to make sure that there were no open windows or anything that would allow the dogs' easy entry as Officer Withers said to Tim...

"How'd I let you talk me into this...damn?"

Tim looked at Officer Withers said sarcastically...

"Now what are you bitching about...the cabin door was locked, going to David and Deanne's barn was the first place they'd look, not to mention we just had two dogs chasing us, being a cop doesn't automatically mean you're the only one with common sense."

Officer Withers got up in Tim's face saying...

"That's about all the shit I'm going to take from you 'captain pothead'. Shit happens, and the last fucking thing I want to do is to be stuck in this mess with someone whose idea of courage is puffing on a piece of white paper filled with wacky weed."

Tim threw his hands up and walked back to the front door and pushed the sofa against it, and placed a glass lamp on top of the back of the sofa to ensure that they could not be sneaked up on by Mr. Thomas.

When Tim returned to the back door, Officer Withers was standing and looking out of the kitchen window when Tim said...

"Look Off...hey can I just call you Kathy, all this officer shit is getting old. Your courage is in your holster, and mine in rolled up... and all this bickering is gonna do is get us both killed."

Officer Withers removed her gun from her holster, ejected the clip and turned and stared at Tim for a moment and then turned back to kitchen window.

Tim walked up to Officer Withers and said...

"Look, I apologize for all the drama...but we're in this together, and we need each other if we're going to do anyone or ourselves any good...let's say we call a truce?"

Officer Withers slowly turned her head to look at Tim, and then extended her hand, as she and Tim shook hands, saying...

"Okay, I get what you're saying okay, just call me Kathy...and yes I have a gun, a gun with only four bullets left."

Tim began pacing the room and talking to himself, while Officer Withers slowly opened the door to see where the dogs were.

Roaming through the kitchen, Tim found a half full bottle of red wine in one of the cupboards. Raising the bottle in the air motioning to Officer Withers who gladly said yes, to some wine.

Officer Withers walked over to the window and said to Tim...

"It looks like the rain is not going be letting up anytime soon... and you know I was thinking...back at the cabin when I said all that about just marching right in...that might not a bad idea after all."

Tim poured a drink and said...

"Well we got two meat eaters outside, just sitting at the door. It looks as if, they were sent here to keep us trapped, I mean after all... we're dry, and we could even eat, I mean if one of them comes after us, they're going to have come over the ridge and we'd see them before they got to us...right?"

Officer Withers said to Tim as she watched the dog's movements...

"If I could take out both dogs with just two shots, that'd leave me with two shots for the man in the ballerina's tutu."

Tim said to Officer Withers...

"Kathy, I don't mean to sink your boat but, I saw your partner shoot that twisted psycho not three, but four times in the head, and he's still not dead...I just think your two shots will only piss him off."

Officer Withers holstered her gun and said to Tim...

"Well it looks like we're going to need more fire power. Listen Tim, he's an old farmer, and farmers always have a shotgun or rifle, right?"

Tim nodded and said to Kathy...

"Right?"

Officer Withers said...

"Here's what I'm thinking about. I'll keep an eye out at the kitchen window while you search the house, and if I see any one of them headed this way, I'll let you know."

Tim nodded in agreement and disappeared in the living room, checking closets and underneath furniture, when he heard a door slam upstairs.

Thinking that was Officer Withers' signal that someone was coming, Tim walked over towards the second floor window which faced the direction of the ridge when he heard a voice behind him, saying...

"Tim...Tim, help me."

Tim turned from the window as he recognized the voice...it was Mary's. Tim turned to see Mary standing a few feet from the door.

Mary's hair was ringing wet, and she was clothed only in her panties and bra. Mary's legs and feet were covered in mud, and her eye shadow was smeared and running down her cheeks.

Tim moved away from the window, grabbing a quilt which was on the bed and wrapped the quilt around Mary's shoulders and body, saying...

"Oh Mary, baby... Mary you're okay...how'd you get away?"

Tim embraced Mary and held Mary in his arms calling for Officer Withers to come up stairs.

Tim's attention returned to Mary who was shivering.

Tim started to massage her shoulders with the quilt when Mary started singing with a soft tone...

"Teddy Bear soda crackers
Teddy says listen up,
Safe inside is what, you think,
You'd better think again."

With a look of shock on his face Tim's arms dropped to his side as Mary threw off the blanket and with her hands, reached up to Tim's face, as she began caressing him and then tilting his head to the side and then smiled at Tim and then began kissing Tim.

Tim ignored the red flags going off in his head telling him that this couldn't be Mary.

When Tim last saw Mary, her face was bloody her lips were sewn together and large clumps of her hair were yanked out, but due to the stress and the terror that Tim had experienced he ignored the obvious when Tim' face was slapped and he heard in a loud voice...

"Tim... what in the hell are you doing?"

Tim opened his eyes expecting to see Mary who was embracing him and kissing him...but it was Officer Withers, who Tim had by the arms as she said angrily...

"You son of a bitch...don't you ever touch me again. What do you mean grabbing me and kissing me...I should've never fallen for that...'let's call a truce shit'?"

Tim jumped back looking all around the room and then shouted...

"Aww...Fuck this shit, I'm getting the hell out of here!"

Officer Withers followed him to the door and said...

"Have you forgotten about the 'meat eating dogs out there... maybe you ought to go out there, so they can grab a chunk of your ass?"

Tim stopped dead in his tracks and took his hand off of the door knob when they both heard pounding on the front door.

Racing to the front window, and with her finger slid the curtain back a little and whispered...

"Hey, those crazy fucks are out there, locking us in!"

Tim ran over to the window saw the man in the ballerina's tutu nailing boards against the front windows and then the front door.

Officer Withers fired one shot through the door, when Tim grabbed her arm and said...

"What are you shooting at...you can't see a damn thing and you're shooting through the door?"

Walking away from the front door and pacing back and forth Tim mumbled...

"We're screwed, we're screwed. Damn twisted psycho locking us in, and I got to get stuck with Barney Fife' sister."

Officer Withers lowered her gun and turned to Tim and replied...

"Look asshole, if he nails us in here we're fucked, which means there'll only be one way in or out, which is the back door...now did I leave anything out?"

Tim searched his pockets for a marijuana joint and was about to light it when Officer Withers slapped the joint from Tim' mouth and snapped...

'Hey...melt what few fucking brain cells you have left after we get out of here but I am not about to be trapped inside this fucking house, with a pot head trapped in the sixties!"

When Officer Withers slapped the joint from Tim' mouth, the neatly rolled joint had come apart and marijuana was scattered on the floor.

Tim scrambled on the floor scooping up what marijuana he could and said...

"You stupid bitch...you stupid bitch, this was my last one!"

Tim managed to collect most of the marijuana and stood by the back door re-rolling his joint.

Tim was about to light his joint when he heard the sound of kids singing and laughing on the other side of the door...

"La-la-la-la-la-la-, la-la-la-la-la-la,

Teddy Bear Soda Crackers

Having all the fun,

Front door locked, back door blocked

Coming in upstairs?

La-la-la-la-la-la-, la-la-la-la-la-la."

Tim let his marijuana joint fall to the floor as he turned to Officer Withers and said...

"What the hell is that? This is the kind of stuff I'm talking about...I can't take any more of this shit...I can't stand it, I got to get out of here."

Officer Withers bowed her head and started giggling saying...

"Oh yeah, you're a big man as long as you got something to smoke on, but let things get real and you fall apart....so tell me, where you going to go?"

Tim had taken all that he could stand and was ready to leave the house and take his chances whatever they might have been, when Officer Withers called Tim over to the window and said...

"Come take a look at this...what do you make out of this?"

When Tim got to the window he saw the man in the ballerina's tutu in an old wagon being pulled by Mr. Thomas on a tractor and heading towards David and Deanne's house.

With puzzling looks on their faces, Officer Withers and Tim looked at one another. Whatever the man in the ballerina's tutu and Mr. Thomas' intentions were, Tim and Officer Withers knew it was going to be bad in every sense of the word.

Officer Withers continued to stare out the window watching the two dogs that hadn't left the back door, as well as Mr. Thomas and the man in the ballerina's tutu on the tractor going round and round all over the three acre farm.

Just what they were doing, and why they just left them alone, they didn't a clue but one thing was clear, they were going to be coming back for them.

Officer Withers called for Tim to come take a look out the window and just as Tim was able to see Mr. Thomas and the man in the ballerina's tutu going around and around in the tractor, there was a huge bang on the back door.

Officer Withers and Tim jumped away from the window and scramble around the living room.

Tim looked around the room and noticed Officer Withers' face was pale. He walked over to Officer Withers and whispered in her ear as she jumped again...

"Hey Kathy, you don't look so good...are you okay?"

Officer Withers shook her head and then told Tim, she didn't know where her head was at a few minutes ago...but that she was alright.

Tim grabbed one of the cups from the cupboard and poured Officer Withers a half of cup of the whiskey which he found in the fridge in a flask, and with one motion she drank it all.

While Officer Withers watched nervously out the window she said to Tim...

"Thanks a lot...even though I don't drink that often, I needed that."

Tim went to the back door and sure enough... Mr. Thomas and the man in the ballerina's tutu were still going around and around in the tractor.

Officer Withers turned to Tim and asked...

"Well, I feel like the color in my face has returned...what do you think?"

Tim told her that her color looked fine and it was alright to be a little scared. Tim went on to tell her that when the big man in the ballerina's tutu grabbed him in the basement, he literally crapped in his pants, so everyone gets a little scared.

Again checking her gun, Officer Withers said to Tim...

"T.M.I. Tim, since you mentioned the basement, how many were in the basement, and were they all alive?"

Tim explained that he noticed five at first, and now judging from the fact that her partner is also in the basement, it makes six.

Officer Withers asked Tim if he knew Mr. Thomas and the man in the ballerina's tutu, or the rest of the people in there, and what he was doing at the farm.

Tim recanted the entire story about him and Mary getting a call from the friend Deanne, who owns the farm with her boyfriend David and how they were in Wisconsin checking on a friend when all of this happened.

Tim went on to say that while he and Mary were in Madison, Wisconsin, checking on their friend Kristin when they stumbled across her bloody body.

He said that Kristin was alive but in bad shape, and as he picked up Kristin's body to carry her upstairs into the living room, the next thing he knew... they were standing in David and Deanne's living room at the farm, some six and a half hours away.

When Tim had said that, Officer Withers looked at him in shock and said...

"Are you trying to tell me that one minute you and your wife were in Wisconsin, over four hundred miles away and then the next second you ended up here...c'mon now... things just don't happen like that!"

Tim walked back over to the window and looking out said...

"Look, I'm telling you what happened... you wanted to know, besides, just look at where we are and what's happening to us can you explain any of this...you can't can you?"

Just then, while Tim was staring out the window a very ugly and hideous face appeared in the window causing Tim to jump back and holler.

It was the face of a young teenaged girl. Her face was ashen in color and were her eyes should have been, were dark black budging eyes.

Her hair was unkempt, uncombed and matted with leaves all through her hair.

As Tim stood there pointing at the window Officer Withers slowly walked to the window, and turned to Tim saying...

"There's nothing out there...what were you looking at?"

Just then they heard over lapping voices of kids singing and laughing coming from upstairs.

The sound of their voices began in a normal tone, but quickly changed and sounded like a radio, whose battery was dying.

Tim and Officer Withers stood there in shock listening to voices of laughter which turned to singing...

"La-la-la-la-la-la-, la-la-la-la-la-la,

Teddy Bear Soda Crackers

Wicked little Imps,

Trapped inside with no way out

Teddy Bear wins again.......

BOO!

La-la-la-la-la-la-, la-la-la-la-la-la."

Immediately as the singing died down, heavy footsteps could be heard coming from all over the upstairs.

Officer Withers ran back to the window to check on the whereabouts of Mr. Thomas and the man in the ballerina's tutu, who were still riding around and around on the tractor.

Tim went over to Officer Withers with a suggestion...

"A little while ago you said something about killing both dogs with two bullets, right?"

Officer Withers walked over to the windows to where both dogs sat motionless, only turning their heads as Mr. Thomas and the man in the ballerina's tutu rode by, as Tim said...

"What I got in mind is, when Mr. Thomas and the man in the ballerina's tutu makes another pass by here and are heading away from here, you shoot both dogs and then we make a run for it."

Officer Withers turned to the Dogs, and then back to Tim and said...

"Okay, I shoot both dogs and then we what!"

As soon as Officer Withers had made that statement, both dogs turned in their direction and slowly got up from where they were sitting and walked off towards the side of the house and sat down.

Watching both dogs walking off, Officer Withers looked at Tim saying...

"No don't tell me that you think they heard what we were saying... and they just walked off?"

Tim raced into the living room to see if he could see the dogs through the living room window and said to Officer Withers...

"As long as those dogs are guarding outside we won't stand a chance of getting out of here...but if we cross the dogs off, we might have a chance to make it out of here to get help.

Unless you're some kind of a super hero masquerading as a cop, three bullets is hardly enough to take care of that Psycho, Mr. Thomas and the two meat eating dogs...remember you shot one through the door."

Officer Withers stood in the window with Tim looking at the dogs who were on the side of the house and said...

"I don't know Tim...we can wait it out or something, but killing two dogs...I mean, for all they know, we are trespassers on their property you want me to kill two dogs and for us to run and go where?"

Tim stood next to Officer Withers pacing and saying...

"I don't believe this shit!

Kathy, I love dogs too...maybe a poodle or a hotdog dog, but these are meat eating dogs, on a mission to rip us a new ass hole as soon as we step one foot outside."

Tim explained to Officer Withers that regardless of what she felt and thought, time was not on their side and the only option left, was getting away from the farm and finding help somewhere.

Officer Withers still disagreed about killing both dogs, but was in complete agreement with Tim regarding their chances on staying alive.

Officer Withers told Tim about and idea she was thinking about of luring the dogs inside, and then locking them inside the house.

Tim replied to Officer Withers that, for starters the front door was boarded up, and in order to lure both of these dogs inside, somebody was going to have to be bait...and Tim stated that he wasn't up for that.

Officers Withers plan provided a greater margin of hope than did Tim's plan. By luring the dogs inside Officer Withers would not have to waste any of her remaining three bullets, which she could use on the man in the ballerina's tutu.

For their plan to work timing was critical. Everything had to go like clockwork. Officer Withers told Tim, that she would be the one to lure the dogs inside because of her small build.

Tim was almost six feet four, and he would have to run from the outside into the service porch which had a low opening and low ceiling, and it was more practical for Officer Withers to do it.

Officer Wither and Tim put their heads together in just a few short minutes and came up with a plan on luring the dogs in and getting away.

First of all, Tim was going to be waiting in the sitting room behind closed doors for Officer Withers.

Across from the sitting room lay a small bedroom, with the door open and a roped tied to the door knob, with the other end in Tim's hand.

The plan was to have Officer Withers waving her sweater out the window at the dogs, teasing them and giving them a good whiff of her scent.

Next Officer Withers would step outside the back door through the service porch and taunt the dogs until they started chasing her inside.

Officer Withers would then run inside and toss her sweater into the open bedroom and then run into the sitting room where Tim was waiting to pull the rope locking the dogs inside the bedroom.

To seal the deal and offer a little insurance, Tim found their dog food bag and dumped a large amount of dog food on the bedroom floor on the far side of the bedroom.

The trap was set and all Officer Withers had to do was to haul ass into the sitting room after tossing her sweater into the sitting room.

While Tim was keeping an eye on Mr. Thomas and the man in the ballerina's tutu, Officer Withers raised the window in the sitting room and began taunting the dogs.

At one point the dogs didn't seem too interested in Officer Withers, and then they became agitated as the sweater kept hitting the dogs in the face.

Officer Withers kept lowering her sweater and pulling it back up teasing them, until one of the dogs grabbed hold of the sweater and tore one of the sleeves off.

Each dog had an end of the sweater, and after getting a good whiff of Officer Withers' scent, began a violent came of tug of war with the sleeve, ripping it to shreds.

Officer Withers turned to Tim and said...

"Okay partner, how do things look...from where you're at...I'm almost ready, got the dogs pissed off and ready to chew me a new butt hole?"

Tim gave Officer Withers the *'thumbs up'* sign saying...

"Be ready to go in about five minutes, I want to wait for Mr. Thomas and the man in the ballerina's tutu to pass this side of the house...they're just on the other side heading this way."

Officer Withers had been on many stake outs and patrols, but waiting to have two large angry dogs chasing her was throwing her nerves in overdrive.

Tim tied one end of a nylon cord around the bedroom door and pushed the door open, signaling to Officer Withers that it was time.

Officer Withers went to the back door and opened it slowly as Tim yelled...

"Good... one of the dogs just heard you open the door...okay now, there both coming."

Officer Withers' heart was racing as she got closer to the edge of the house.

The rain was still pouring and the only thing on her mind was not to slip in the mud or on the steps while she was running.

Just then she heard one of the dogs growling as she stuck her head around the corner and hollered at the dogs...

"COME AND GET MEEE!"

Officer Withers turned and began running as fast as should could, being extra careful not to slip as she ran up the rain soaked wooden steps.

With her sweater in her hand, Officer Withers dropped it just inside the bedroom as she bolted inside the sitting room where Tim was waiting.

Standing behind Tim who was crotched down on his knees, Tim started shaking his head as both dogs entered the house.

The dogs stopped right at the bedroom door, and while one of the dogs was sniffing Officer Withers' sweater, the other dog did something very strange...

The larger of the two dogs, lowered his head and with his eyes followed the nylon cord which was lying on the floor all the way to the cracked door of the sitting room.

Tim whispered to Officer Withers...

"Recliner"

Bending down to hear what Tim was saying, Tim hollered...

"PUSH THE FUCKING RECLINER OVER HERE, NOW!"

And with that, Tim slammed the door shut and held onto the knob as he struggled to turn the small lock.

Officer Withers, yelled for Tim as she had the recliner near the door, and Tim reached over and pulled the recliner in front of the door.

Officer Withers began yelling at Tim...

"What the fuck...what the fuck...happened?"

Suddenly one of the glass window panes shattered as one of the dog's head came crashing into to it.

While the dogs were growling and snarling, Tim could feel the weight of the dog pushing the recliner as it continued to crash into the door.

Tim hollered at Officer Withers as he laid his weight against the recliner...

"Get to the window...."

Officer Withers began crying and saying as she opened the window...

"What do we do...what do we do."

Tim hollered back at Officer Withers...

338

"This chair is only going to hold for a little while longer, I need you to go out the window, and close the back door...now!"

Officer Withers climbed out of the window as Tim continued to struggle holding the recliner against the door, as both dogs were pushing the door open with their body weight.

Tim felt that his chance of getting out, before the dogs could come through the door, would be when Officer Withers shuts the back door, hoping it would distract them log enough.

Just as Tim figured, he heard the back door slam shut and with that, the dogs raced to the back door giving Tim the time he needed to go out through the window, shutting it behind him.

Tim was unaware, that had he and Officer Wither's went inside the bedroom and turned the light on, he would have seen his friend David, bleeding and lying in the bed.

Tim ran to the rear of the house where Officer Withers was waiting, watching Mr. Thomas and the man in the ballerina's tutu, who was making a turn at David and Deanne's fence line and heading their way.

Officer Withers was being pulled by Tim who said...

"We got to go. We got to run as fast and as far as we can...c'mon."

Officer Withers and Tim took off running in the rain and fog, heading away from Mr. Thomas and David and Deanne's farm.

Neither Tim nor Officers Withers had any ideal where they were running to or if they were running in a circle.

Just then Tim and Officer Withers, stopped and rested against a tree, as Tim said...

"I think we're going to make it. We just got to keep running until we get somewhere, and find someone."

Just then Officer Withers whispered to Tim...

"Do you hear what I hear...oh my God, it can't be!"

Officer Withers and Tim heard the sound of the two dogs coming after them, apparently, Mr. Thomas either released them from the house, or they jumped out of the sitting room window.

Tim yelled to Officer Withers, to run as fast as she knew how, and don't stop for anything. Officer Withers and Tim reached a ravine and could see in the clearance the highway.

Looking behind them, they noticed that the entire area from where they had run from was engulfed in fog.

Where Officer Withers and Tim were standing was an early morning fog, and a light drizzle, but not the downpour or the thick fog that they had just been in.

They started down the ravine sideways, as the bare field had turned to a muddy mess during the rain, which seemed to be letting up.

Tim had cautioned Officer Withers about not falling, but it was Tim who first slipped and fell in the mud, rolling into Officer Withers.

Officer Withers and Tim came to rest at the bottom of the ravine, twenty feet from the highway.

Officer Withers had a slight limp from rolling down the ravine, and they could still hear the dogs, only their barks and growling seemed further and further away.

Officer Withers and Tim got to their feet and continued running, but not as fast, not as deliberate as before, and then finally they saw something up ahead, coming down the road.

Officer Withers shouted to Tim excitably…

"It's a car…Look Tim, it's a car we made it!"

Officer Withers began hugging Tim and saying how glad she was that they made it, as Tim said…

"Let's just hope that we can get the car to stop for us."

As the car got closer, Officer Withers drew her gun from her coat and as Tim was attempting flag the car down, she fired a single shot in the air.

Just then a welcomed site appeared…the emergency lights of a police car appeared and slowly approached them.

The police car stopped twenty feet in front of Tim and Officer Withers, and immediately, the spot light was shining on them lighting up them as well as the night.

So happy and elated Tim turned and hugged Officer Withers and then Officer Withers laid her gun down and they both held their hands in the air, as the doors to the police car opened.

Two men exited the police car and the officer on the passenger side hollered…

"*This is Sheriff William Odem and Deputy Andrews from the Port Clinton Sheriff's Department, now slowly get down on your knees.*"

Both Officer Withers and Tim immediately dropped to their knees as both the Sheriff and his deputy approached them. Officer Withers shouted...

"*Sheriff, we're glad to see you...I'm a police officer... I laid mu gun down over there, and my badge is inside my coat pocket.*"

Sheriff Odem still training his gun on them glanced over at Deputy Andrews and said...

"*Okay Deputy search the young lady first she says she's a police officer.*"

Deputy Andrews gently tapped Tim with his foot and said...

"*Now, don't move a muscle.*"

Dropping down to one knee, Deputy Andrews searched Officer Withers pockets until he found Officer Withers badge.

Deputy Andrews retrieved Officer Withers' gun and walked towards Sheriff Odem saying...

"*Yep, that's a big ten-four...it says here...Columbus Police Officer, Kathy Withers...she's good alright Sheriff.*"

Sheriff Odem pointed at Tim and asked him...

"*What about your young man, you a police officer too?*"

With his arms still spread out Tim replied in a calm voice...

"*No, I'm not a cop...my-my wife is being held hostage a few miles back at a farm...you got to help me.*"

Sheriff Odem told Tim and Officer Withers to get on their feet and slowly and place their hands behind their backs.

While both Tim and Officer Withers complied with Sheriff Odem, Tim glanced over his shoulder and said while Deputy Andrews handcuffed him and searched him...

"*Wait a minute...she's a police Officer, you saw her badge, why are you handcuffing her?*"

Sheriff Odem held the rear doors of the squad car open, saying to Officer Withers...

"*Do want to explain it to him, Police Officer?*"

Officer Withers told Tim as they were being placed in the back seat that, anytime law enforcement happens upon a suspicious person(s), until they are identified...they must treat them as a possible threat until their identity is first confirmed.

Sheriff Odem and Deputy Andrews both got back into the squad car, and turned on the inside lights, and then began questioning Tim and Officer Withers.

Tim and Officer Withers were told that they were going back to the station, until their identities were confirmed and their stories checked out.

Tim became agitated and said...

"But you don't understand Sheriff, my wife is in danger back at there and they're going to kill her if we don't do something."

Sheriff Odem turned to Tim and said...

"What you can do is to close your mouth until we get to the station."

Officer Withers cautioned Tim to just shut up and not make things harder until everything is checked out.

She told Tim the sooner he settles down and cooperates, the sooner they'll get back out there and help Mary and everybody else.

As Deputy Andrews drove back to the station, Sheriff Odem watched Tim the whole time through the rear view mirror.

Chapter 16

Doubt Thomas

Sheriff Odem order Deputy Andrews to lock Officer Withers and Tim separate cells, while he brewed a pot of coffee.

Deputy Andrews was a young deputy of only two years on the force, born and raised in Pittsburgh, fresh out of the academy and single.

He had asked the Sheriff which one of the two he was going to be able to question when Sheriff Odem stated...

"Boy, you're not questioning neither! I'll do the asking, you just watch and learn."

Sheriff Odem asked Tim and Officer Withers if they wanted some coffee, and both replied...yes.

Sheriff Odem had deputy Andrews to hand them each a cup of coffee, as Officer Withers was first pulled out of her cell to be questioned.

The Port Clinton Sheriff's Station was a one floor building, with one small room used for questioning and three cells and one restroom.

Sheriff Odem escorted Officer Withers in the interrogation room and began questioning her.

"Now you're a police Officer from Columbus, so what brings you all the way up here in the middle of the night, and why didn't you check in with me first?"

Officer Withers held onto her coffee as the cup was warming her hands and said...

"I came up here with my partner yesterday, because he was investigating a murder which happened in Columbus, and we had

343

only anticipated being here no more than an hour…but Sheriff, there are some strange things happening at one of the farms up here, there are people…."

Sheriff Odem stopped Officer Withers before she had a chance to finish her statement saying…

"Okay, Let's get on the same bus for a minute…you know if you're investigating anything out of your district, you first make contact with the governing authority…which is me…now you know that?

Officer Withers realizing that the Sheriff was right lowered her head and said…

"Yeah understand all that, but we were not even sure that there was anything to what we were looking into, it was a hunch is all… but still we should've paid you a visit first."

Sheriff Odem sat back in his chair and asked Officer Withers, if she wanted another cup of coffee, and she replied…

"No I'm fine, but you got to get some people up at that farm…I'm telling you there are people being tortured and held in a basement… you got to do something."

Sheriff Odem leaned back in his chair and looking at Officer Withers said…

"Now let's see… we took off of you a Glock 40.cal which still had one in the chamber and two in the clip…did identify yourself as a police officer and try do anything …huh?"

Officer Withers stood up and told Sheriff Odem…

"Listen, what I'm about to say you might not believe me, but it's true. There is a very large man up there who was shot four times in the head, and he's still walking around."

Sheriff Odem said as he sipped his coffee…

"Oh, I was waiting for this to come out…and I guess this big man is from outer space right?"

Officer Withers said as she sat back down in her chair…

"Look Sheriff I don't know the people who own the farm, I only know the neighbor is a crazy man with two vicious Rottweilers named Thomas."

Sheriff Odem sat in chair laughing saying…

"*You mean old Creton Thomas…why hell, now I know your mush isn't fried…for starters he doesn't like people, especially strangers, can hardly get around without his cane and he hates dogs even more.*"

Officer Withers placed both hands on the table and leaned into Sheriff Odem saying…

"*I'm telling you Sheriff, this old man didn't walk with a fucking cane, and he has two mean Rottweilers, and he's with a man in a ballerina's tutu, wearing a clown's face, they're killing people up there.*"

Sheriff Odem slammed his fist down on the desk and said as he stood up…

"*Do you know how old he is…he's eighty damn years old and can barely get around…I was just about to believe you…until this crap came out of your mouth.*"

Officer Withers described the man she encountered at the farm, and Sheriff Odem agreed with her description as being that of Mr. Thomas.

Officer Withers asked Sheriff Odem what he planned to do about going up to farm and checking out their story, when Sheriff Odem said…

"*As soon as we run a make on your boyfriend back there…we'll all take a drive out there, and if things aren't the way you say, then we'll have us another little talk.*"

Officer Withers was locked in her cell while Deputy Andrews bought Tim out for questioning.

Tim's story was just a little more disturbing and in more depth than Officer Withers' story.

Sheriff Odem placed both Officer Withers and Tim in the back in their cells and told them…

"*We're all going to go up to the farm you're talking about, but not until the morning, so you can all make yourselves a little comfortable back there.*"

Tim began shouting to Sheriff Odem…

"*We can't wait until morning, my wife and a bunch of other folks are in danger up there… Sheriff if we wait until the damn morning, they're all going to be dead…don't you understand that!*"

Sheriff Odem stormed over to Tim's cell and removed his night stick and called for Deputy Andrews to open the cell saying...

"This smart ass here is about one minute from needing medical attention...now open this damn cell!"

Deputy Andrews walked slowly towards the cell that Tim was sitting in saying...

"Sheriff this man's obviously got some mental issues, and you go smacking him upside his head...it's only going to make matters worse, don't forget the election is next month and this is the kind of stuff McCombs will use against you."

With the cell opened, Sheriff Odem stepped in Tim's cell and poked him in the chest with his night stick saying...

"You're lucky Mr. Noodles, thanks to my deputy he saved you from a bad beating, now my advice for you is to shut up, and don't let me hear a peep out of you until morning."

Sheriff Odem and Deputy left the cell area and walked back into the control room as Sheriff Odem said to Deputy Andrews...

"Do you mind taking the squad car over to the seven and eleven and filling up the tank, and after breakfast...we'll take a trip out there?"

Deputy Andrews grabbed the keys from off his desk and turned to Sheriff Odem and said...

"Hey Sheriff, if they have those loaded burritos you want me to pick one up for you?"

Sheriff Odem began searching his pockets for some money to give deputy Andrews when Deputy Andrews stopped him saying...

"I'll get this you can pay for lunch later on."

Deputy Andrews drove off to the seven and eleven as Sheriff Odem started making a fresh pot of coffee.

Tim and Officer Withers cells were side by side, while they could speak to one another, they couldn't see each other.

Tim got up off of the cot and said...

"Hey Kathy...Kathy you awake over there?"

Yawning and stretching, Officer Withers walked up to the bars and replied...

"Yep, I'm awake was just sitting here thinking, is all. What's on your mind?"

Trying not to sound too paranoid Tim said...

"Don't you smell something fishy about this hick Sheriff's department, because things don't happen this way, it's almost like they were reading a script or something."

Officer Withers sat back down on her bunk saying...

"Tim I was following you in the beginning, but you kind of lost me at the end...what are you even talking about?"

Trying to keep his voice down, Tim said...

"We told him that people were in danger up at the farm, and they act like they don't even care, and secondly, they know that you're a police officer, and have you in a cell too...I mean it's not adding up."

Officer Withers told Tim...

"That's not what I'm getting out of this, I mean the business about waiting until the morning bothered me at first, but there's not a whole lot we're going to be able to do about it...right, the more we keep complaining the more they're not going to believe us at all?"

Officer Withers could hear Tim pacing in his cell and saying...

"Damn, I need a joint bad."

Giggling and laughing to herself, Officer Withers told Tim that he didn't need a joint but what he needed was to learn to deal with things like normal people do.

Tim continued pacing in his cell, while Officer Withers laid down in her bunk and pulled the blanket up around neck and fell asleep.

Deputy Andrews came into the cell area and woke up Tim and Officer Withers saying...

"Hey folks it's six thirty in the morning, time to rise and shine... we got coffee, eggs, bacon and toast."

Officer Withers jumped up out of her bunk and said...

"That sounds good to me, but I need to use the facilities first."

Deputy Andrews opened Officer Withers cell door saying...

"Okay, it's out the door and to your right, but I have to unlock the main door, just waiting on your friend here."

Tim got up and stood at the cell door waiting for Deputy Andrews to unlock it, saying...

"Say, you guys got more than one restroom in this place...right?"

Deputy Andrews walked over and stood at the door motioning for them to follow him, saying...

"*Yep, we're real modernized here, we have two restrooms, one for inmates and one for staff, and no you cannot use the staff restroom so you'll just have to hold it.*"

Tim followed behind Officer Withers who turned and said to Tim...

"*Don't worry I'll only be a minute or two.*"

While Officer Withers was using the restroom Deputy Andrews asked Tim...

"*Say, all that stuff you told the Sheriff earlier about things and people appearing and disappearing, and the man in the ballerina's tutu taking four bullets to the head and all.... You were just making all that shit up, right?*"

Tim stood wiping the crusties from his eyes, looked around and said...

"*No I wasn't making anything up...once we get there, if we ever get there...you'll see for yourself...speaking of, where is Marshall Dillon?*"

Deputy Andrews shook his head in distaste saying...

"*I can see what kind of morning we're going to have already. You need to lay off of all this, Sheriff Odem is good man, and a good Sheriff.*

When we ran into you and your friend, I was driving him home after he pulled a twelve hour shift...so excuse him if he was a little grumpy."

While Officer Withers was in the restroom, Deputy Andrews handed Tim a cup of coffee, and after taking a few sips Tim said...

"*Look, all I'm concerned about is my wife, who's up there at the farm, I don't care about anything else...so what time are we going out there?*"

Before Deputy Andrews had a chance to answer Tim, the restroom door opened and Officer Withers came out saying...

"*Okay, it's all yours.*"

Deputy Andrews walked Officer Withers down the hall to the small conference room where Sheriff Odem was sitting and eating breakfast.

Going back to wait on Tim to emerge from the restroom, he heard Officer Withers and the Sheriff talking.

Within a few moments Tim came out of the restroom, and Deputy Andrews walked Tim to the conference room, where they all sat eating breakfast.

Tim who at first showed no signs of being hungry, wolfed down the eggs, bacon and toast and said...

"Ok, I'm finished and thanks for the breakfast, but I'm ready to go when everybody else is."

Sheriff Odem, Deputy Andrews and Officer Withers rose from the table and headed down the hall towards the door when Sheriff Odem turned looking at Tim and Officer Withers, saying...

"Now... I got a fax back from your captain, Officer Withers, so you check out, but once we get out there...your friend here stays in the squad car, and only myself, my Deputy and you go inside.

If you don't follow my instructions, I will have no problem with handcuffing you, am I making myself plain?"

Tim acknowledged Sheriff Odem and walked to the squad car waiting to get in the back seat.

Officer Withers got in the squad car and once inside, Deputy Andrews removed the clip from her gun and handed it to her saying...

"Once we get there, if we think you need it we'll give 'em back plus more."

Deputy Andrews positioned himself in the driver's seat as Sheriff Odem turned to the back seat and asked Tim to tell him the entire story again from the beginning to the end.

Deputy Andrews drove the twenty mile stretch to old man Thomas' farm while Tim went through the story to Sheriff Odem.

Sheriff Odem pulled a pad from his shirt pocket and began taking notes, as Tim took him from start to finish.

Officer Withers, had very little to say as she sat looking out the window at the passing landscape.

Officer Withers did not tell the Sheriff nor Deputy Andrews that there were several other law enforcement officers involved in the events, because of the complexity of the situation.

The weather was much calmer than it had been that night. There was hardly a hint of fog, and the rain had reduced itself to a mere drizzle.

Deputy Andrews looked in the rear view mirror at Tim and asked him...

"*Okay Tim, we're turning off onto the drive which leads to old man Thomas' farm, is this where you said you were last night?*"

Tim moved his head around trying to get a clear view of the area saying...

"*Huh yes, I mean it looks like it, but last night there was so much fog and rain...but I think this is it.*"

As Deputy Andrews slowly drove down the driveway, thoughts of Mary and if it was too late to save her and the things which occurred five hours earlier, began flooding his mind.

Deputy Andrews drove up the long gravel driveway and stopped at the front door of Mr. Thomas' house.

Sheriff Odem again turned back to Tim and said...

"*You mind me now, and stay put, if I need you I'll come get you.*"

Tim nodded yes and said...

"*Okay, I get it, I stay in the car, but will you hurry up?*"

Deputy Andrews got out, and opened the rear passenger door and let Officer Withers out, when the front door of Mr. Thomas' house opened.

Emerging and walking with a cane and dragging his left leg Mr. Thomas stood of the front porch and hollered to Sheriff Odem...

"*Okay, hold it right there Sheriff, what you doing out here on my land, I just looked up and seen you coming down the drive?*"

Walking up to the bottom of the steps, Sheriff Odem said...

"*Morning to you Creton. You ought to get you ought to get yourself some dogs, that way you'd know when people are coming. I hate to disturb you, but I got a couple of folks here that say there was some trouble up here last.*"

Mr. Thomas asked the Sheriff to come on up on the porch and turned to sit in the rocking chair saying...

"*Trouble. I don't know what you're talking about. There was a bad rain last night, so I just went on to bed...don't like staying up in a storm...it's the Lord's work, people are supposed to be quiet when the Lord's working.*"

Officer Withers pointed at Mr. Thomas and began approaching the steps when Mr. Thomas shouted...

"I didn't invite no body up here but the Sheriff…now, Sheriff, you know I don't like company, why'd you bring folks up here with you?"

Sheriff Odem signaled for Officer Withers and Deputy Andrews to stay where they were and he sat next to Mr. Thomas saying…

"It's like I was saying Creton, I got these two folks with me, and they say that they were chased by you and a big fella, and some stuff about people over on the next farm being in trouble. Did you hear anything or see anything last night?"

Mr. Thomas began rocking in the chair and suddenly came to a stop, saying…

"Sheriff, I done told you already, I went to bed on account of it was raining pretty hard, and I can hardly walk, let alone chase somebody…you know that."

Sheriff Odem said…

"Look Creton I'm just trying to do my job, do you have any objections if I look around your place a bit, and I promise I won't disturb or take anything?"

Mr. Thomas grabbed hold of his cane with both hands and shakenly stood up saying…

"If you want to look around fine, but what are you going to be looking for?"

Sheriff Odem said…

"Well according to the two folks, they say it was raining, and they were up here last night, and I just want to look and see if there are any tracks….is all."

Mr. Thomas headed to go back inside but turned and told Sheriff Odem, that when he is done looking, to take those people with him and get off of his land.

Sheriff Odem walked over to Officer Withers and asked her…

"Now you say you and your friend there, were inside of this house and you escaped through a window?"

Officer Withers pointed to the other side of the house and saying…

'Yes, we jumped out of the window on that side of the house, so there should be plenty of tracks as well dog paw prints too."

Deputy Andrews, Sheriff Odem and Officer Withers walked to the other side of the house, looking for any evidence of what her and Tim, claims happened, when Officer Withers said to Sheriff Odem…

"*The old man is lying through his dentures. He didn't have a cane last night...Tim and I were in this house, and there were two Rottweilers that were over on the side of the house as well...just wait until you see the tracks!*"

When they arrived on the side of the house, Deputy Andrews turned and said...

"*I don't see any prints at all, human or from animals...are you sure you got the right farm?*"

Officer Withers went ahead of Sheriff Odem to where Deputy Andrews was standing, and couldn't believe her eyes...the mud was fresh and wet, but there were no tracks of any kind.

Officer Withers looked around a minute and said...

"*Somehow somebody has smoothed them over, but there were tracks here...I know it!*"

The three of them walked the entire area of Mr. Thomas' house and then they headed back to the squad car.

Deputy Andrews and Officer Withers went on to the squad car, while Sheriff Odem thanked Mr. Thomas for letting them look around.

When Officer Withers got into the squad car, Tim asked her about what happened and she said...

'*Somebody covered up the tracks...there isn't any proof we were even up here, and the old man is faking his ass off. Last night he was chasing us all over the place and today he is acting as if he can barely walk.*"

Deputy Andrews started the squad car up and was turning around in the driveway when Tim shouted and pointed...

"*Over there...that's where my friend, David Blue's farm is at.*"

Sheriff Odem replied...

"*Now look, we can't just ride up on every piece of property.*"

Tim leaned forward saying...

"*I'm not asking you to go to every property, just this one. It belongs to a friend of mine, and that's where my wife is at...down in the basement.*"

Sheriff Odem lowered his glasses down upon his nose and told Deputy Andrews to make a right and head to the farm.

He also cautioned Tim by saying...

"If we get to this farm and don't find everything as you say it should be…. both of you are going to be in a world of trouble."

Deputy Andrews turned right and a mile up the road made another right onto the driveway which led to David and Deanne's farm.

Heading down the long driveway, Tim kept pointing and saying….

"That's it, right on up there, is an outside door which leads to the basement."

Deputy Andrews drove past the small cabin when Officer Withers said…

"That's the place where me, Tim and my partner held up in last night."

Sheriff Odem turned around saying…

"Your partner…it seems like you two have left a whole lot out of your story, you didn't say anything about a partner being up here with you?"

As Deputy Andrews was pulling up alongside of David and Deanne's farm house, Officer Withers explained…

"I didn't say anything about my partner or the other police officer who is here, because I didn't want you thinking I was as crazy as…"

Tim blurted out…

"You didn't want them thinking that you were as crazy as I am right?"

Officer Withers looked over at Tim saying…

"That's not what I meant."

Tim shouted back at Officer Withers…

"Like hell you didn't…look let's just go get Mary, and we'll walk the hell home…fuck all of you!"

Sheriff Odem shouted out…

"Okay people lets simmer down, there isn't no cause for flying all over the place, and you watch your filthy mouth!"

As Deputy Andrews stopped the squad car at the front walkway to David and Deanne's house, Tim said…

"Just let me out of here, I'll show you where Mary is…let me out of this damn car!"

Sherriff Odem shut the squad door leaving Tim and Officer Withers in the back seat.

Taking their flashlights, Deputy Andrews shone his light through David and Deanne's living room and walked slowly to the side of the house towards the small basement window.

Deputy Andrews crouched down on one knee, calling to Sherriff Odem saying...

"I'll be doggone, will you look at that!"

Sherriff Odem knelt down as Deputy Andrews got out of the way and said...

"Is that what I think it is?"

Sherriff Odem said as they approached the outside basement door...

"Let's check this out a little further."

Sherriff Odem opened the basement door and shining his flashlight around the basement saw, a few boxes stacked against the basement wall, and an old refrigerator, with a foul odor coming from it.

Deputy Andrews meanwhile was walking over to what he saw through the outside window.

Standing next to a table which was close to the window was a 1920 Egyptian made .357 shotgun.

Deputy Andrews picked up the shotgun and examined it, when Sherriff Odem tapped him on the shoulder saying...

"I see it, but put it down, we didn't come up here for that. We're here because fruit loops and his side kick said people were being held and tortured."

After inspecting the entire basement, Sherriff Odem walked up the basement steps into the kitchen and then into the living room.

Tim looked over at Officer Withers saying...

"As soon as they bring Mary out, we're out of here."

Suddenly the rear doors of the squad car were opened, and Sherriff Odem and Deputy Andrews said...

"Both of you want to come with us?"

Entering in through the basement, Sherriff Odem turned to Tim and said...

"Where's this glue and the man that's supposed to be stuck to it?"

Turning on the light switch near the door, Tim said...

"Now wait a minute…they were here. There…right there is where Mary was tied up, and there were four chairs with people strapped to them."

Deputy Andrews and Officer Withers walked over towards the table when Deputy Andrews said…

"There is no blood down here, no chairs, no people tied up, nothing except a few boxes over there."

Sherriff Odem walked over to the steps which lead upstairs and said…

"C'mon folks, I'll show you what we find, and maybe you can clear up a few things for us."

As they all walked into the pantry off of the kitchen Sherriff Odem stopped and pointed down on the floor and up at the back window which had busted out saying…

"For all of the commotion you made last night all we seemed to find up here is evidence of a break in.

A busted window with a brick lying inside on the kitchen floor and cabinet drawers opened."

Deputy Andrews walked up to Tim saying…

"Look pal, all the Sherriff is trying to say is there is no evidence of a crime or any of the things that you were saying, so you two need to come clean about what you are doing up here….and what's really going on."

Officer Withers stood in between Tim and Deputy Andrews saying…

"Look we told you the truth. There were at least five people tied up in the basement, and there was a big man in a ballerina's tutu and a clown's face chasing us along with that old man, but Tim and I got away."

Deputy Andrews said to Tim and Officer Withers as Sherriff Odem walked into the living room…

"They had all night to hide or move the bodies…they probably took them to the barn."

Sherriff Odem returned back to the kitchen where Officer Withers, Tim and Deputy Andrews was standing and said…

"That's enough…we've given you the benefit of the doubt, but we're not about to trance all around on these people's property

without good cause…and from what I see there's not even a clue that anything is going on up here."

Tim stood shaking his head at Sherriff Odem saying…

"So what does that mean, you're not going to do anything?"

Sherriff Odem grabbed a hold of Tim's arm and said…

"What that means is, I'm taking you back to the station and I'm going to find out where the owners are, and in the mean while you two are going to back to your cells until we sort out what's really going on."

Tim tried to jerk away from Sherriff Odem, when Sherriff Odem tightened his grip and said…

"Now look, you can go along peaceably, or I can slap these cuffs on you, but either way you're coming with me."

Tim yanked away again saying…

"But my wife…Mary is up here somewhere and you're not even going to check the barn out!"

Sherriff Odem grabbed his hand cuffs and said to Deputy Andrews…

"Deputy Andrews put these cuffs on him…NOW!"

Deputy Andrews placed Tim in handcuffs, not aware that Officer Withers had backed out of the kitchen and was running out the door towards the barn when Sherriff Odem fired a single shot into the air and said…

"Okay, that's far enough. We've been patient with both of you, but enough is enough!"

Officer Withers stopped in her tracks and turned to Sherriff Odem saying…

"Okay…okay, all we wanted you to do was check out the barn, we're telling you, they're up here…his wife, my partner, and a couple other people…will you please just check out the barn…please?"

Sherriff Odem and Deputy Andrews escorted Tim and Officer Withers to the squad car and as they headed down the driveway towards the barn and the highway, Deputy Andrews slowed down alongside of the barn and said…

"Do you want me to check in there Sherriff?"

Sherriff Odem looked over at Deputy Andrews saying…

"Just go up to the window and see if you see anything or anyone moving around inside."

Deputy Andrews got out of the squad car and walked up to the window and shinned his flash light inside, and then he backed away from the window and hopped back into the squad car.

Sheriff Odem watched Deputy Andrews as he got in the car and quickly shut the door saying...

"Well, did you see anything?"

Deputy Andrews started the car and drove saying...

"No...it's all dark inside and the windows are all boarded up and it looks like no one's been in there for a long time, furniture all covered up and cob webs everywhere."

Tim was wiggling in the back seat saying...

"It's all boarded up, because they don't want you to see what they're doing. Can't you get these damn handcuffs off me?"

Sheriff Odem ignored Tim as they drove off the property heading towards the highway, not aware that Mr. Thomas, was standing on his front porch with the man in the ballerina's tutu observing the Sherriff and his Deputy as they drove away.

Sheriff Odem and the man in the ballerina's tutu walked off his front porch going towards David and Deanne's barn, while the man in the ballerina's tutu went into the house and upstairs to where he tied and hid Deanne's body.

David aroused from being stabbed by the pitch fork, in time to see the tail lights of Sherriff's squad car exiting his property.

David could not cry out for help, because not only would they be unable to hear his cries, but Mr. Thomas and the man in the ballerina's tutu would know exactly where he was.

David limped out of the backdoor of Mr. Thomas's house and down the steps, because he was still weak from the amount of blood he'd lost, and fell off of the last two steps and into the mud.

David tried getting up again and fell onto his back, sitting in the mud trying to gather his senses.

David watched as the man in the ballerina's tutu wearing the clown's mask walked up the front porch steps and into the house.

David knew that he was in no shape to deal with anyone or anything, so he began walking through the woods towards the highway.

Though David was familiar with the area, he was unsure of where he was going, he just knew that he had to keep going, had to find someone to help.

10 miles Outside of Port Clinton, Ohio

Sherriff Odem turned slightly behind him and said to Officer Withers and Tim...

"Look I don't know what kind of game you two are playing but I can tell you that my first thought is to lock you both up, and I got plenty of charges I can hold you on, but I'm going to drop you two off at the bus station."

Tim and Officer Withers said collectively...

"The bus station?"

Sherriff Odem turning completely around and looking at his watch said...

"Yes I said the bus station, there is a bus leaving out for Columbus in about another thirty minutes, and I'm going to make sure you two are on it."

Officer Withers looked up at Sherriff Odem and said...

"Okay fine, but I'm just going to come back up with members from my precinct."

Sherriff Odem laughed and said...

"Oh no, I don't think you will. You see I got a fax from your captain who said to put you on the first bus to Columbus and he'd handle it...so you see, you won't be back up here, and if your friend tries to come back, I will arrest him on the spot."

Tim and Officer Withers sat quietly in the squad car as Deputy Andrews pulled in front of the small bus station.

Sherriff Odem got out of the squad car and walked into the small bus terminal.

Deputy Andrews and Sherriff Odem were inside the bus terminal securing arrangements for Officer Withers and Tim's bus tickets.

Officer Withers leaned into Tim and said...

"Try to keep your damn mouth shut, I'm working on something... okay?"

Tim whispered back at Officer Withers as she noticed them coming out of the bus terminal...

"I know they are going to follow the bus to the edge of town to make sure we are gone, but as soon as that happens, I want you to start getting loud and physical with me...but I swear if, you take the physical part too far I'll let you, Mary and the man in the ballerina's tutu go it alone."

Sheriff Oden and Deputy Andrews came back to the squad car and released Tim out of his hand cuffs and said...

"Okay folks, here you go, you've practically screwed up our plans for a quiet weekend. I can't say, y'all come back' because I don't want to see either one of you back here."

With that said Sherriff Odem and Deputy Andrews watched as the bus pulled off, and just as Officer Withers had said, they trailed they bus until it was at the county line, and then they turned around heading back into town.

The bus crossed the bridge and headed for the interstate when Tim got up out of his seat and began shouting and cursing at Officer Withers and pulling on her clothes.

The bus driver brought the bus to an abrupt stop, when Tim began shouting at the bus driver...

"Keep going, nobody told you to stop this damn bus, keep driving asshole!"

One of the passengers on the bus began screaming at Tim and the bus driver told Tim and Officer Withers...

"Off this bus. I want you and her off of this bus NOW, I don't care what the Sherriff said!"

The doors opened and Tim and Officer Withers exited, and Tim said to Officer Withers...

"Now what. We're off the bus, do...do you mean to tell me that your plan is that we walk over thirty miles back to that farm...back to shit?"

Officer Withers began walking back towards town saying...

"You want to find your wife don't you...and I want to find my partner. Those sick fuckers had hidden everybody, and we're going to find out where."

Tim caught up with Officer Withers saying...

"Okay...now that's what I'm talking about.... but what the hell are we going to do when we get there?'

Officer withers opened her coat and took out a pistol and a box of ammunition when Tim said...

"Where the hell did you get those?"

Officer Withers handed Tim the gun and a handful of bullets and said...

"While that country Deputy was eyeballing my legs and ass, I slipped this from his desk, at times it helps to have a good looking ass and a great pair of legs."

Tim loaded the pistol and said...

"Well I wouldn't know about all that."

Officer Withers said as she and Tim crossed the highway...

"You are such a liar...that's all you been looking since I got here yesterday."

Tim and Officer Withers began walking off of the road on the shoulders to stay out of sight of Deputy Andrews and Sheriff Odem, in case they were patrolling the area.

The walk back to the farm was a good thirty-thirty-five miles, and while the rain and fog wasn't a factor anymore, it was cold and overcast.

Tim suggested that they cut across through the open field in the direction of the farm, the same route they took when they ran from Mr. Thomas's house.

Officer Withers agreed and said...

"Aren't you worried about running into those dogs?"

Tim took the gun from his pocket and said...

"Well this time we're not worried about only having two or three bullets...let 'em come after us, I got something for them."

Officer Withers shook her head and continued walking through the muddy, wet field when she turned around to Tim saying...

"Hey, you want to knock that shit off, this isn't the time to start playing childish games!"

Tim was a good four steps behind Officer Withers when Tim said...

"Playing games about shooting those meat eaters, you lost me."

Officer Withers stopped and as Tim got even with her she said...

"*You know what I'm talking about...I'm talking about you pinching my ass.*"

Tim's head turned slightly to the left and his eye brows arched as he said...

"*Look, you got a nice one...but I promise you that is not on my mind right now, hell I was four of five feet behind you, what are you talking about?*"

Officer Withers grabbed Tim's arm saying...

"*Why don't you just walk right beside me, that way if you do that shit again, I won't have far to reach to knock your ass out.*"

Tim and Officer Withers continued walking through the field when Officer Withers felt something on her behind and screamed...

"*Goddamit Tim, I said...*

Officer Withers ended her thoughts as she looked at Tim who was a step or two in front of her and to her left.

Tim stopped and looked back saying...

"*Okay now what...are you going to start that crap again?*"

Officer Withers whispered at Tim saying...

"*No...I'm telling you something really grabbed my ass, and I know it couldn't have been you, because you've been in over there...I would've seen you, if you had.*"

Officer Withers removed her jacket as both she and Tim inspected it. It was hard to tell just what was on the back of her jacket, when Tim stepped behind her to inspect her back of her pants, saying...

"*I think we better pick up our pace and get the hell out of these woods quickly.*"

Officer Withers put her jacket back on and started walking fast asking Tim several times...

"*Why'd you say that...what was on my pants?*"

Tim kept quiet and refused to answer Officer Withers until she grabbed his arm, and in a curious and upsetting voice said...

"*When you looked at my pants from behind what was on them!*"

Tim stopped and said...

"*I'll tell you when we get to where were going, but not now!*"

Officer Withers opened her jacket and with her left hand felt behind her.

Officer Withers couldn't see anything on her hands as she brought them in front of her face, and again angrily asked Tim...

"What the hell did you see, what's on my pants!"

Tim tried to ignore her and kept walking but Officer Withers jerked Tim's arm saying...

If you don't tell me I swear, I'll shoot you my own damn self!"

Tim looked Officer Withers in the eyes and said...

"All I got to say is...don't freak out! Don't freak out when I tell you."

Officer Withers threw both hands in the air saying...

"C'mon Tim, you're pissing me off not to mention scaring the shit out of me."

Tim looked at Officer Withers saying...

"Just keep walking and I'll tell you. On your left back pocket there is a palm print with only three fingers, and on the right one... are the words help me."

Officer Withers reached back again as they continued walking and wiped her rear pockets, hoping to see a smudge or something, but saw nothing, and said...

"You're sick Tim...out of all that we have to deal with, you're getting off on looking at my ass. Let me say it like this, you and me will never ever happen, so get over it already."

Tim stopped and reached in his pockets for the small case that he kept his marijuana joints in, and lighting up one said to Officer Withers...

"Hold up a sec...look, you're a piece of eye candy no doubt but my only interest lies in my lady who is tied up in the fucking basement.

You asked and I told you what was written on your pants...if you doubt me, take them off and look at them yourself."

Officer Withers motioned for Tim to catch up, saying...

"That was a dumb ass thing to say, I'll just wait until we get to the farm."

The Barn

Steve whispered in the dark...

"Shh...I thought I heard a car coming down the driveway, didn't anybody hear that?"

Reggie shifted the weight of Mary in his arms saying...

"*Hey can we make up our minds... are we going upstairs and are staying down stairs?*"

Just then the lights came on and instantly went back off which made Perry scream, and then everybody began hearing the voices of kids singing and laughing saying...

"La-la-la-la-la-la-la-, la-la-la-la-la-la-la

Teddy Bear Soda Crackers

Teddy in control,

Made the Police, go away

Now, waiting for the rest to come

La-la-la-la-la-la, la-la-la-la-la-la-la."

Everybody looked around to see if they could tell from where the singing was coming from when Reggie whispered...

"*Hold on everybody...it sounds like its coming from upstairs... quiet everybody!*"

Just then every door upstairs began opening and closing.

Det. Horton walked over to Steve and Reggie and said...

'*When you two were up there boarding up the windows, you did check each room didn't you?*"

Reggie laid Mary back over on the sofa saying...

"*Of course we did, we were in all rooms and opened each door except the closet door, and the only reason we didn't check that out, because there's no room for anything...except towels and linen.*"

Steve replied as he walked over to the steps...

"*Well, it's obvious that we need to find out who's up there.*"

Perry walked Kristin back over to the sofa, and after helping her sit down said...

"*Forget what I said about the beds, we're good right here on the sofa.*"

Grabbing the flashlight and double checking the battery, Det. Horton said...

"Well that's all good too, but we're going to have to find out who's up there, we can't just sit down here with this place all boarded up, while something or someone is upstairs."

Reggie kissed Perry on her forehead and whispered in her ear, saying...

"Listen babe, we're going to be right upstairs, if you see anything or if anyone comes through that door, you haul ass up the stairs, okay?"

As the three men walked up the steps, Perry stood up and walked away from the end of the sofa where she was originally sitting and sat at the opposite end closest to Mary and close to the steps.

Mary was trying to talk to Perry, when Perry handed her a tube of lip balm saying...

"I'm sorry about all of this, I think I introduced myself on you earlier when I was helping your friend out...how did you get in all this, and do you know what's going on?"

Mary carefully opened and closed her mouth to ensure that her lips were not going to re-stick, saying...

"Yeah I remembered. My name is Mary, w-where's Tim, have you seen him?"

Perry took a closer look at Mary's lips, lightly touching the swollen areas and said...

"Tim...who's Tim?"

Mary looked over at Kristin and then back at Perry explaining how she and her husband were asked to check up her friend Kristin.

She told Perry, she and Tim were at Kristin's house in Madison, Wisconsin...which is four hundred and twenty miles away from Port Clinton.

She explained to Perry that, one minute they were in Madison and the next minute they were there at the farm in Ohio.

Perry stood up and stretched saying...

"Wow...that's a little hard to believe...I'm not saying that I don't believe you, but if you had told me that yesterday, there's no way I'd believe you."

Both Perry and Mary looked over at Kristin as she was beginning to awaken, when Perry asked...

"*I know this may sound a little messed up, and I'll understand if you don't answer, but what was it like…I mean the whole transporting then…wow, I'm still trying to wrap my head around that?*"

Mary turned and looked at Kristin who was wakening and beginning to cough. Mary reached over and placed her hand on Kristin's arm and said…

"*Oh my God…sh-she's burning up!*"

Perry got up and walked over to feel Kristin's forehead, but as her hand was inches from Kristin's forehead, Perry pulled her hand back saying…

"*No she's not burning up, this poor girl is cooking!*"

Perry jumped up and ran over to the fridge saying…

"*I hope there's ice cubes in the freezer, we got to get her temperature down fast.*"

Perry opened the freezer and pulled out both ice cube trays, one of them was full and the other only had a couple of ice cubes in it.

Perry looked around the living room area and saw a dish towel hanging on the door of the range and emptied the ice cube trays in it and then ran back over to Kristin, empting them in it.

When Perry laid the towel full of ice cubes onto Kristin's forehead she instantly saw water running down her cheeks, when Mary said…

"*What the hell is taking them so long, they should've been back down here by now!*"

Kristin began moaning as Perry rotated the towel from her forehead to her neck and then her chest.

After a few minutes of icing down Kristin, Perry reached to feel her forehead which was slightly cooler and said to Mary…

"*Look, I got to go see what's keeping them, so keep this towel moving from her chest to her head…I'll be back in second.*"

Before taking the towel, Mary tried scooting closer to Kristin. Perry saw what Mary was trying to do, so she helped get her next to Kristin and then went upstairs.

While Mary was moving the towel full of ice all over Kristin, her eyes suddenly popped open.

Mary froze for a second and then moved the towel to Kristin's face when Kristin opened her mouth and began talking in a low voice.

Mary leaned her ear next to Kristin's mouth to hear what she was saying and heard...

"Twisted and dread...twisted and dread

Twisted and dread,

Things are not what they seem

Soon all will be dead

Twisted and dread, twisted and dread."

Mary pulled back from Kristin who was now moaning. Mary placed her hand up on Kristin's forehead and after feeling that she was much cooler, laid the towel onto Kristin's chest.

Mary saw that Kristin was no longer burning up, and sleeping so, Mary pulled one of her legs up to see how bad her feet were.

Instead of seeing a petite pinkish white foot, Mary saw a grotesque, grayish foot, double in size of her normal foot size.

Her foot was disfigured and covered with large pus filled sores, and as she gently touched her foot, she noticed something very wrong.

She was not able to feel herself touching her foot, but instead it was as if she were touching Jell-O which had set too long.

Mary wondered why, if she had no feeling in her feet, why was she unable to walk or stand on her feet, when she placed her foot on the floor and tried to stand, excruciating pain shot up to Mary's head, forcing her to fall back on to the sofa.

Lying on the sofa, Mary felt as if her head was about to explode from the pain in her foot, when Perry appeared at the bottom of the steps.

Perry walked over to Mary with a blank look on her face as Mary said...

"What's wrong, Perry what's wrong?"

Perry just stood there looking as if she'd seen a ghost when Mary tugged on her sleeve and said...

"Perry, are you okay...where are the guys?"

Perry turned and looked down at Mary saying...

"They're not up there...I mean they...are but they're not."

Mary looked up at Perry saying...

"What do you mean, they are but they're not...you're not making any sense."

Mary called upstairs for Steve, but there was no answer from Steve, when Perry sat down and said...

"When I got upstairs, I could hear them talking in one of the bedrooms and when I pushed open the door, there was no one inside... but, I could still hear them talking."

Mary and Perry looked at one another, and Mary was about to tell Perry what had just happened with Kristin when coming through the ceiling vent they both heard...

"Twisted and dread, twisted and dread

Trapped deep in the house they are

Till the other two join us

Then we'll play a new game

Twisted and dread, twisted and dread."

The Woods

I knew the area of Port Clinton pretty well, but with the amount of blood I lost, made it very difficult for me to distinguish if I was going in the right direction.

The morning air was chilly and a light fog covered the entire area as I slowly limped through the woods, leaving Mr. Thomas's farmhouse in the distance.

Looking around as I pushed past some brush and thickets, I came to a clearance, when something very familiar caught my eye.

Standing in the clearance with little to no strength left, as I leaned up against a tree and hugged it saying...

"Damnit...I'm on the west side and heading to my own damn farm...I'm supposed to be miles from here!"

David hadn't made any turns, nor had he changed directions.

He started out walking east away from Mr. Thomas's farm, while his farm was west of Mr. Thomas'.

David glanced all around himself as he leaned against the tree thinking...

"It's starting again, and I might as well walk back to the farm, because no matter which way I walk, I'm going to end up right back here."

David was tired and extremely weak and knew he could not walk too much further when he heard from behind him...

"La-la-la-la-la-la-la-la-, la-la-la-la-la-la-la

Teddy says, you're smart

Says you're smart not to run

Teddy would only have to bring you back!

La-la-la-la-la-la, la-la-la-la-la-la."

I wanted all of this craziness to stop...and I wanted it all to end. Seeing that my barn is in sight, and the fact that no matter which way I walk, I'm going end up here...I might as well just walk through the front fucking front door.

David headed in the direction of the barn until the little girl in the white ragged dress stopped him and said...

"Teddy says come to the house,

Come to the house, not the barn."

I told the little girl...

"I'm too tired to play games...get the hell out of my way!"

The little girl in the white ragged dress walked ahead of me, every few feet she turned and chuckled. The way I was feeling I didn't care anymore, I just wanted to see Deanne one last time.

I could tell I was bleeding badly on the inside as my breathing became more and more difficult and my thirst grew with every step, as I watched the girl mysteriously moving up the path.

Her feet were on the ground but as she moved...she moved in a fast robotic method, ten fast steps then she'd stop and then ten more fast steps. Up ahead I saw that the little girl reached the front porch, when I wondered if I was going to make it.

Standing on the front porch, I could see the man in the ballerina's tutu, and Mr. Thomas and the girl in the white ragged dress.

I reached the top of the stairs and as I passed the girl in the white ragged dress and the man in the ballerina's tutu, Mr. Thomas raised his hand towards the front door, which opened, revealing Deanne lying on the sofa.

I dropped to my knees and crawled up to Deanne, taking her in my arms, when the door slammed shut behind me.

I sat on the floor holding Deanne who was unconscious, when suddenly the door blew open and the outside air rushed in and filled the room with the smell of dead decaying things, as the man in the ballerina's tutu with the clown's face stood in the doorway.

Sitting on top of his shoulders was a medium sized child's Teddy bear and behind him and all around him were six to eight grotesque figures of dead looking kids.

The Teddy bear which sat upon the man in the ballerina's tutu was a regular stuffed teddy bear with plush fir.

Mr. Thomas stepped inside and closed the front door.

Pointing to me Mr. Thomas said...

"I had hoped that the little stick with the pitch fork would have been enough kill you, but it looks like I should've stuck you a couple more times, but that's not going to matter after teddy wakes up."

I looked over at the teddy bear sitting on top of the man in the ballerina's tutu shoulder and, said...

"I don't understand ...why are you doing this?"

Mr. Thomas stood in front of me and said...

"Why? Why not! You all have done nothing but piss on the life you were given...so it's our turn now, and after Teddy awakens the fun will begin."

Mr. Thomas stepped aside as the man in the ballerina's tutu placed the Teddy Bear on the floor while the creepy little kids surrounded it.

The creepy kids pointed their elongated fingers at the Teddy Bear and began singing a creepy tune over and over...

"Teddy Bear Soda Crackers
Teddy, in the night
Twist their souls, heart beat stops
Touch all with pure fright!"

With each chanting of this song, their voices changed from a slow low voiced demonic tone to a high pitched screechy tone, as I covered both of his ears.

I felt Deanne's body moving as she was beginning to come to.

With my hands covering my ears, I looked down at Deanne who was starting to open her eyes, as I leaned over and shielded her.

Deanne began to awaken, pushing me off of her as she caught her breath. I reached down and grabbed one of Deanne's hands, motioning for her to cover her ears.

Deanne lifted up looking around as the creepy kids singing and the man in the ballerina's tutu, and Mr. Thomas swaying from side to side, as they sang...

"Teddy Bear Soda Crackers
Teddy, in the night
Twist their souls, heart beat stops
Kill with your pure fright!"

Deanne started crying and quickly brought her hands up to her ears, covering them as she noticed the Teddy Bear sitting on the floor in the center of the creepy kids.

I felt Deanne getting up, and as she did I looked over at the creepy kids and the man in the ballerina's tutu and Mr. Thomas, which all seemed to ignore her movements.

Just as I was about to get up to join Deanne, I saw something that I'm still trying to wrap me head around.

The Teddy Bear's eyes opened and became a fiery red, as Mr. Thomas, the man in the ballerina tutu and the creepy kids all began chanting and singing, totally ignoring me and Deanne.

The man in the ballerina's tutu and Mr. Thomas were blocking the front door, as Deanne headed towards the back door which led to the walkway. Unable to get up on my own I started crawling after Deanne when she stopped and helped me to my feet.

Deanne and I could have made it easily to the back door, but as the high pitched screechy singing grew louder and louder, and the wind coming through the front door, created a vacuum in the house.

Deanne and I were being tossed and thrown against the walls, and then thrown to the floor.

The vacuum that the wind created again pinned me and Deanne to the wall for a few seconds, and then released us, and that's when Deanne grabbed me and headed towards the back door as fast as we could.

Deanne made it to the kitchen sink which was beside the back door when she screamed.

I was unable to her Deanne's scream because the noise of the wind and the screechy singing was so loud, that I ran into her.

Looking to see why Deanne had stopped running, I could see a small pair of ashen colored hands which had Deanne by the leg.

I took a deep breath and began kicking at the hands holding Deanne as she struggled to get to the door. Seeing the hands letting go of Deanne, she made it to the back door, when all of a sudden... something stood in front of Deanne.

It was the Teddy Bear! With red fiery eyes, twisting and turning its neck in all directions.

I turned around to see if the Teddy Bear was still in the living room and when I looked it was still there.

I grabbed Deanne and pushed her out the door and with a violent move, and went to kick the Teddy Bear, when it disappeared.

I fell through the door and out onto the door as Deanne screamed...
"Oh my God...Blue".

Deanne reached down to and tried to help me up, but the blood loss and the fall w

Had taken its toll on me.

Deanne was kneeling beside me when she whispered...
"O Blue, you're bleeding"

Deanne opened my shirt and saw that I was bleeding from the wounds I suffered from being stabbed by Mr. Thomas.

Deanne knew she couldn't carry me so she said to me...

"Blue...I need you to help me. We got to get out of here, so I'm going to need you to stand."

Deanne's hope was to make it to the walkway, and once there, she was going to help me to the barn, and then down the driveway to the road.

The night's rain had ended, but the morning still revealed dark and ominous clouds overhead.

The moment Deanne and I made it inside the entrance of the walkway, we found it to be cold and dark, a sharp contrast from being inside the house.

Since I had helped construct the walkway, I knew that it literally ran straight for a third of a mile, before reaching the barn entrance...

What I didn't know was...something else was inside the walkway with us.

Deanne took hold of my arm and helped me to my feet and whispered in my ear saying...

"Blue, you're bleeding again...I got to get some help for you, all we have to do is make it to the barn."

I nodded yes to Deanne and tapped her on the shoulder as we began walking through the walkway.

Just a few feet inside the walkway and Deanne jumped and said...

"Something's behind me Blue, something just brushed against my leg."

I replied with labored breaths...

"No matter what, jes-just keep moving forward Deanne...if we get caught, it's all over...cancel Christmas."

I pulled Deanne's arm as I slowly limped in pain unaware that directly behind Deanne was a pair of red fiery eyes, two feet off of the ground following her.

The pair of red fiery eyes which followed after Deanne disappeared as Deanne turned around as Deanne's whispered tone grew louder...

"Oh Blue, damnit... there's something in here with us...shit!"

I stopped and leaned up against the wall, my breaths were becoming more labored as I said...

"*Oh babe, I'm so tired I don't know if I can make it...just let me stay right here and you go one.*"

Deanne stood in front of me kissing my face and lips and then said...

"*BLUE, YOU MOVE YOUR ASS NOW...YOU SAID NOT TO STOP, SO DON'T YOU FUCKING STOP...DON'T YOU QUIT ON ME GODDAMIT!*"

The pair of red fiery eyes suddenly turned into two pair of red fiery eyes, and then three pair, until the entire walkway behind me and Deanne was full of red fiery eyes.

The red fiery eyes seem to keep pace with Deanne and David's steps, not over taking them or catching them.

The shadowy figures and fiery eyes moved along as if they were driving or pushing David and Deanne forward.

David was so weak from the amount of blood that he lost that he fell to the ground.

Deanne screamed and dropped to her knees to help David up and to urged him to keep moving.

Deanne managed to get David to his feet and as she placed his left arm around her neck, she hugged David's waist and helped him the last few feet through the walkway.

Ahead a few feet Deanne whispered in David's ear...

"*A few more feet Blue, just a few more feet.*"

Suddenly Deanne felt a warm breath on the back of her neck and when she turned, from out of the darkness a loud voice screamed....

"฿oo!"

Thomas's farm....

Tim and Officer Withers reached the ravine which bordered Mr. Thomas's farm house, as Tim whispered...

"*Maybe our luck is changing.*"

Officer Withers looked at Tim saying...

"*What makes you say that?*"

Tim was searching his pockets and patting them until he located a small marijuana butt, and lighting it he said...

"Well...for starters, it's not raining, the fog has lifted and two, I don't hear those meat eating dogs."

Officer Withers gave Tim the 'dead-eye' look, and said as he took a big drag of his marijuana roach and snapping his fingers as the fire burned his fingertips...

"Damn Tim, is there ever a time when you're not smoking that shit?"

Tim repositioned the small marijuana roach in between his fingernails of his baby finger and thumb and took a finale drag before letting it fall to the ground saying...

"Yes there is...when I'm asleep I'm not smoking...but I am dreaming about smoking."

Tim began coughing and gagging on the two puffs he had taken when Officer Withers said...

"Okay, the old man's farmhouse is right up there, do we want to bypass it and swing around to the road and head straight to the barn or what?"

Tim stood there looking around in all directions and said...

"Wait a minute...I thought you said that you had a plan?"

Officer Withers pointed up towards the road saying...

"I do have a plan and it was to get us off the bus and back here.... all I'm asking is for a little advice from you, now if you want to give it, fine...if not, fine."

Tim pointed up towards the road agreeing with Officer Withers to head straight to the barn, and bypass the farmhouse.

Tim and Officer Withers were walking through the woods up towards the road when Tim stopped and turned saying...

"Damn...I thought I heard someone behind me."

Officer Withers neither heard nor noticed that Tim had stopped, and when Officer Withers reached the road and looked back seeing that Tim was still in the woods, said...

"Well, you're proving what I've always thought and that s... dope not only slows down the mind, but the whole body as well.

Tim climbed the small grade and walked up on the road, saying...

"Wow those two puffs were killers, I thought for a minute that someone was behind me."

Officer Withers turned and told Tim...

"Perhaps, it's the brain cells that you just killed escaping."

Tim shook his head still coughing and gaging as the two of them walked down the driveway towards the barn, not seeing the figures on either side of the road keeping pace with them.

As they walked down the driveway towards the barn they heard loud, slow, clonking footsteps which sounded as if someone were walking on a hardwood floor instead of a paved driveway.

Tim turned around and looked, and saw nothing. Just then something whispered and then yelled in a low, husky voice:

"YOU SHOULD'VE STAYED AWAY!!!"

Tim screamed like he'd never screamed before.

Once he calmed down Officer withers asked...

"Do you think you can make any more noise...maybe holler to the whole world that we're back in Port Clinton creeping around?"

Tim quickly matched stride with Officer Withers saying...

"Now don't tell me that you didn't hear that...and don't say it was fucking brain cells or no shit like that, because I know you had to have heard that!"

Officer Withers looked at Tim and said irritably...

"Now just what was it that I was supposed to have heard?"

Tim nervously kept walking and turning around and said...

"Never mind...never mind you just wait and see, if something doesn't jump out and grab your ass, then I'm going to pretend like I didn't see anything either."

Officer Withers shook her head in disgust as she pointed to the barn which was only a few feet ahead.

Tim knew that what he heard was not an illusion, or his mind playing tricks on him...the problem was, why Officer Withers didn't hear it as well.

Just then Officer Withers stopped and looked at Tim saying...

"Over there... is it me or do I see a light in the barn?"

Tim strained his eye in the direction of the barn and told Officer Withers...

David Ray

"Kathy, I don't see anything, what are you looking at?"

Tim turned his head from the barn to behind him when Officer Withers tapped his arm, saying...

"Look, there it is again."

This time Tim saw it, it was on for a minute then off and moving from spot to spot.

"It's a flashlight...that's what it is, someone's in there...C'mon!"

Tim and Officer Withers began running alongside the highway until they reached the driveway which leads to the barn.

Thirty feet from the barn, Tim and Officer Withers stopped running. Catching their breaths, Tim said...

"Okay, now that we ran our asses off can you tell me what we're going to do from here? Do we sneak in our bust through the door?"

Officer Withers looked at Tim and said...

"I swear...you watch way too much television, we need to first find out who's in the barn, and once we know that...we'll know how to approach the situation."

Officer Withers and Tim slipped around the side of the barn towards the back door, once they realized that they couldn't see much of anything through the boards nailed to the window.

Officer Withers lowered her head and put her ear to the door and then walked back to Tim saying...

"I think this might be a knocking situation. It doesn't sound like the old man and the man in the ballerina's tutu...I think that I heard a woman's voice but I can't be sure."

Tim looked around and then said...

"This is crazy. We got 'farmer twisted brown' chasing us, meat eating dogs somewhere out here and you want to just go up to the door and knock?"

Officer Withers took the gun from out of her pocket, and eased up to the door, as Tim followed.

Inside the Barn

Perry sat down on the arm of the sofa saying to Mary...

"It's like I told you, I heard them in the far bedroom at the end of the hall and when I peeked inside I could still hear them talking, but nobody was there."

Mary lifted her feet out of the bucket and carefully laid them by her side on the sofa saying...

"Maybe you were just in the wrong bedroom, there are three of them, you know."

Perry began shaking her head and saying...

"No...no, that's impossible, I passed by the bathroom and then the first two bedrooms, looking into each of them, and they were empty...I'm telling you they were in the last bedroom, I heard them but I'm telling you they're not upstairs...they're not anywhere."

Mary opened her mouth to yell for Steve when Perry placed her hand over Mary's mouth saying...

"What if those two psychos hear you yelling?"

Pulling Perry's hand from her mouth Mary said...

"Girlfriend, I think that ship sailed a long time ago, they wanted us all in here, that's why they let us get away."

Perry took her hand away from Mary's mouth and as she did, they heard someone messing with the back door knob, and whispering outside.

Perry was telling Mary to be quiet, as Mary said...

"Maybe it's the guys and they found a way outside, and they've come back for us."

Perry told Mary that she didn't think it was the guys because, all of them would not have left at the same time, and besides, Reggie wouldn't have done something like that."

Perry and Mary continued to hear the back door knob trying to turn as the whispers outside, became audible...

Perry walked over close to the door and bowed her head down to hear, when Mary said...

"Can you hear what they're saying?"

Perry threw up a finger motioning for Mary to be quiet a second, when she turned and said...

"I thought I heard someone at the door name Tim."

For the first time since this whole business began, Mary was excited and a smile crept on her face as she said...

"That's my Tim...he came back for me!"

Perry came back over to Mary and whispered...

"How do we know that for sure? I'm not going to open this door for one of those crazy assholes to come busting in here."

Mary looked at Perry saying...

"What if you're wrong, what if it's Tim and he's bought help and those two psychos catch them?"

Perry walked back over towards the door, and turned and said...

"What do you suggest that I do?"

Mary motioned for Perry to come back over to where she was sitting and told her...

"Go to the door and call his name and ask him what's the first thing he does when he gets up in the morning, if he gives the wrong answer, well then I'll know."

Reluctantly, Perry walked over to the door and did just as Mary suggested. Perry came back over to Mary and said...

"He says the first thing he does in the morning is, he lights up a joint and gulps down a beer."

Mary's heart leaped inside of her as she swung her legs over the side of the sofa saying...

"Let him in, let him in...that's Tim!"

Perry wrestled with removing the board jammed against the floor and braced under the door knob.

Then Perry placed her foot against the side of the board on the floor and pushed and pushed until it began moving.

As the board fell to the floor, Perry very quickly turned the door knob which would not budge, forgetting the lock was on, she unlocked the door and in opening it, standing there was Tim and Officer Withers.

Officer Withers and Tim entered into the barn, and Perry asked Tim to help her place the board back against the door.

Officer Withers walked in and looked around and then went over to Mary who was still sitting on the sofa waiting for Tim and said...

"*Are you Mary?*"

Mary looked up and over towards Tim who was wedging the board in place and then back at Officer Withers and said...

"*Yes—yes, I'm Mary.*"

Officer Withers looked over at Kristin and said to Mary...

"*And who is this...where is everyone else?*"

Tim started making his way over to Mary, when Mary looked back at Officer Withers saying...

"*You're going to have to ask her about all of that...Tim!*"

Tim ran to Mary dropping down on his knees and hugging and kissing her saying...

"*Oh baby, baby, you're alright...I was so worried that something happened to you, but you're alright...c'mon we're going to get out of here.*"

The last time that Tim saw Mary she was tied up and her mouth was sewn shut, but just seeing Mary he had forgotten all about that until Perry knelt down next to Tim and pointed at her feet, saying...

"*Hi, I'm Perry, Reggie's wife. Mary's been through a lot and I'm afraid she's not going to be doing any walking or anything for a while.*"

Tim's eyes followed Perry's as he noticed Mary's feet as she raised them out of the bucket.

"*Oh my God, Mary what did that sick mother...?*"

Mary raised her hand up and placed her finger on Tim's lips, stopping him from finishing his sentence, saying...

"*It's okay baby, I'll be fine, I need to get to a hospital....and I'll be okay.*"

Tim's fingers lightly traced around Mary's lips at the holes where some of the twine was still visible as Perry said...

"*I was able to remove all of the super glue from her lips, and most of the twine, but there's nothing I can do about her feet.*"

Tim carefully picked up one of Mary's feet for a closer look as Officer Withers knelt down saying...

"*This looks bad; can anything be done...we have to be thinking about getting the hell out of here?*"

Perry glanced over to Officer Withers saying...

"She's got severe third degree burns over both entire feet, only a burn unit can deal with it."

Officer Withers stood up and said...

"I'm sorry, I'm Officer Kathy Withers, I came up here with my partner, Det. Fannichuci, who is still up here somewhere, has anybody seen him?"

Perry sat on the arm of the sofa and explained to Tim and Officer Withers How Det. Horton and Reggie helped them escape the man in the ballerina's tutu and Mr. Thomas in the basement, and how they ran into a guy name Steve.

Perry went on to say that, Mr. Thomas and the man in the ballerina's tutu, just simply let them out of the basement and into the barn, as if they wanted them in the barn.

Perry went on to say how Mr. Thomas and the man in the ballerina's tutu spent all night riding around in circles on a tractor.

Tim and Officer Withers looked at each other puzzled as Officer Withers said to Perry...

"So where the hell is Det. Horton, Steve and Reggie, we came up here several hours ago with the Sherriff and his Deputy, and they searched the entire basement, but didn't see anything or anyone."

Perry told Officer Withers, that Steve, Reggie and Det. Horton were boarding the windows shut with boards, and the next thing she knew they were gone.

Looking back over at Tim who was holding Mary, Officer Withers said...

"What do mean they were gone...did they go outside...what?"

Perry stood up and got in Officer Withers' face and said...

"Look, I've had way too much bullshit happening to me, so back the fuck off!"

Tim ran over and separated Officer Withers and Perry saying...

I think everybody needs to knock it down a notch or two, we got other issues to deal with not to mention getting everybody out of here, which might mean one of us going back to the Sherriff's office.

Officer Withers walked away from Perry and said to Tim...

"So that explains why the Sherriff and his Deputy couldn't find anyone...all of you were here...but..."

Mary and Perry looked at Tim and said...

"What...you guys had the police up here, and you didn't think to look here?"

Officer Withers turned saying...

"They did look here, the Sherriff's Deputy was outside with a flashlight and said the place was all boarded up, so they left and put us on a bus for Columbus."

Tim looked over at Perry saying...

"Okay, so where did Steve and the other two guys go?"

Officer Withers walked over to look at Kristin as Perry said...

"They went upstairs to board up the bedroom windows and when they didn't come back down, I went to see what was taking them so long, and when I got up there......they were gone."

Tim and Officer Withers looked at one another when Officer Withers suggested...

"So maybe, they were in another room or something...people don't just disappear."

Perry angrily looked at Officer Withers and with her hands on her hips shouted...

"Fine, if you don't believe me, then you got up there and look for them!"

Officer Withers grabbed her gun from her pocket and said...

"No problem...that's exactly what I'm going to do."

Tim walked in front of Officer Withers and said...

"On second thought...I'll go up there and check, you stay with the women."

Mary held onto the sleeve of Tim's shirt saying...

"You're not going to leave me now...after all of what's happened... let the police woman go and look she has a gun...she's trained to do this kind of stuff."

Officer Withers looked at Tim and said...

"Don't patronize me with that...male macho shit...I hate that stuff, you stay here and I'll go check out upstairs...you still got the piece I gave you?"

Tim reached in his coat pocket and pulled out the gun that Officer Withers gave him earlier saying...

"Right here."

Mary looked up as Tim sat back down next to her and said...

"A gun…you know any other time, I'd be freaking out over either of us having a gun, but just one thing, if that big man gets in here… you blow his damn head off?"

Tim nodded okay, as Officer Withers walked towards the steps saying as she looked back…

"Okay partner, and yes I said partner…so don't let it go to your head, just protect these women…I'll be back in a jiff." ….

Officer Withers began walking up the steps to check on Det. Horton, Steve and Reggie.

The last twelve hours wreaked havoc on everyone in the barn, especially Perry, who was at the verge of mental exhaustion.

Perry had canceled a trip that she had planned at the James Tunnel Survivors Memorial, and came with her husband Reggie, thinking that it was only going to be a few hours.

It was five years ago to the day that Perry was on her way to a conference with twenty other colleagues that she worked with, when a lone madman detonated explosives which caved in the James Tunnel, burying the bus that she was riding on.

Perry was no stranger to disaster, but not the kind that she was experiencing at the farm.

Mary had fallen asleep in Tim's lap, and Kristin was still half in and out of consciousness, moaning every five or ten minutes.

Long before anyone knew it, Perry, Mary and Tim had all fallen sleep, not realizing that it had been an hour since Officer Withers had gone upstairs to look for Steve, Reggie and Det. Horton.

Tim had tied two empty cans together and wrapped them around the back door knob, in the event that someone tried to sneak in.

Reunion

Deanne grabbed tightly onto David's arm and began walking as fast as she could, nearly dragging David every other step.

Suddenly the walkway was filled with voices of kids singing and laughing as Deanne stopped and turned...

"La-la-la-la-la-la-, la-la-la-la-la-la,
Teddy Bear, Soda Crackers
Got you in the dark
First you'll scream, then you'll cry
Till your mind's ripped out...
La-la-la-la-la-la-, la-la-la-la-la-la."

I looked at Deanne and said...
"Babe, I got to lie down...I c-can't go no more."
Deanne grunted as she lifted David up onto her right side and said...
"I don't want to hear that shit Blue, if they get you they're going to have to get me too...so move your ass blue."
All of a sudden...I looked up at Deanne and whispered that something was wrong. I told Deanne that they should be at the barn by now.
I said to Deanne...
"Babe, we've already passed two windows in the walkway, and the last one is right here. From this window to the door is no more than three feet."

Deanne placed left hand at the edge of the window and groped the wall searching for the door.
Somehow and someway, instead of going forward, we were going backwards back towards the house.
I turned my head around to guide Deanne to the barn and whispered...
"Okay this is window number two."
Deanne whispered back to me saying...

"I'm touching window number three right now."

Three feet from the last window and we're at the barn door. I patted my right pocket and whispered to Deanne...

"Deanne, the keys are in this pocket."

Deanne took the keys from my pocket and not knowing that there were already unannounced guests inside the barn, Deanne began searching for the right key.

Deanne tried key after key, but none of the keys she tried would fit the lock. Suddenly, Deanne heard a noise...a thump in the walkway.

Deanne turned to see what it was and all she saw was red eyes in the dark coming her way, along with the laughing and singing of kids.

Turning her attention back to the lock, Deanne suddenly dropped the keys. As Deanne reached down patting the ground and searching in the darkness for the keys, her hand hit something which jingled.

Frantically searching all around Deanne found the keys and cried for David...

"Blue...Blue which key...which key do I use?"

Deanne knew there were only four keys on the ring and she had already tried three...but after dropping the keys she had to start all over again.

David pulled himself up to the door attempting to help Deanne when the door suddenly flew open as I fell through and Deanne screamed!

"Tim!"

When David fell through the door, he landed in Tim's arms who said...

"Dee.... Dee, God am I so glad to see you guys.... get in here, shit what happened to Dave and let me lock this door back."

Tim shouted as he caught me as I slumped against the wall.

Deanne rushed up to David who was unconscious and said to Tim...

"Tim; Blue's hurt I think he's lost too much blood."

Tim looked down and David's shirt at the blood covered shirt saying...

"What in the hell happened, and what's going on up here Dee?"

Deanne explained to Tim that they came up here to check on Mary and that for no reason Mr. Thomas stabbed David.

The excitement of Deanne and David entering the barn woke Perry and Mary as Deanne cried...

"Mary...girl you're okay...oh thank God!"

Deanne ran over to where Mary was sitting and gave her a big hug as Mary said...

"Oh Dee, what in the freak is going on... me and Tim where at Kristin's and then the next thing we know we're here?"

Deanne looked over at Kristin not really paying attention to Mary and noticing her lips and feet.

Deanne asked Mary...

"What's the matter with Kristin?"

Mary looked over towards Perry and told Deanne...

"Deanne this is Perry, she knows more than I do, you ought to ask her."

Perry got up from the recliner and walked over to Deanne saying...

"Hi... I'm Perry Parker, my husband is a police officer from Columbus and..."

Deanne cut Perry off before she could finish saying...

"Your husband's a police officer from Columbus...well what are you two doing up here, and where is he?"

Perry extended her hand and shook Deanne' saying...

"My husband was investigating a case that his partner was working on, and one of the clues his partner had was of this place and an old skeleton key, so we came up her earlier yesterday."

Deanne looked over and then walked to Kristin as she moaned, saying...

"I don't understand it. I don't understand any of this."

Perry took a deep breath and said...

"Anyways when we got here, the old man...huh, Mr. Thomas, showed us where the key was to the house and let us look around, and that's when all of this crazy shit started happening."

Deanne sat down next to Kristin, and put her arms around her and brought Kristin close to her, and looked at Perry saying...

"What happened to my best friend...what happened?"

Perry explained to Deanne all of the events which transpired from the time they arrived at the farm until when Deanne and David came inside the barn.

Then Deanne let out a scream shouting...

"The two people I love in the whole world are..."

Perry put her arms around Deanne as she began crying.

Tim was tending to David's wounds to his back when he suddenly shouted out...

"Hey where's Officer Withers?"

Mary and Perry both cried in unison...

"Oh no...."

Deanne looked up and said...

"Who's Officer Withers?"

Tim told Deanne about Officer Withers, and how she had went upstairs looking for Steve, Reggie and Det. Horton, but never came back downstairs.

Tim forgot to mention that he had fallen asleep and that an hour had passed, but didn't feel it would have a reassuring effect knowing that in the face of danger, he could fall asleep and let something happen.

Deanne looked over at Perry and said...

"So you said that Steve, Det. Horton and your husband went upstairs and they never came back down, and now Tim says someone else went up there and hasn't come down?"

Perry looked up in the direction of the steps saying...

"Yeah, I-I don't think..."

Tim blurted in...

"Nobody else should go upstairs, I think the man in the ballerina tutu with the damn clown's face and that old son of a bitch, wanted us in this fucking barn...they planned all of this shit, that's why they let us get away and come here."

Mary was nodding her head saying...

"Okay, so does that mean that there's something upstairs that'll come down and get us next?"

Tim pushed the recliner over against the stairs and said...

"No, I don't think that there is anyone up there who's going to come down and get us, but I do think there is something up there, a gateway or portal into another world or dimension, or something."

Deanne looked at Tim and said...

"Tim, honestly do you really believe that shit?"

Tim replied as he walked back over to David…

"Yesterday, I would have said hell no…but right now after all the shit we've been through and seen…hell yeah!"

Just then Perry ran to the window and hollered back at everyone…

"Hey over here…, here comes the sick old man on the tractor!"

Tim and Deanne ran to the window in time to see the tractor going around the side of the barn, towards the back.

Just then, Tim yelled…

"I hope he's not doing what I think he's doing."

Deanne ran back to the front window and then turned to Tim saying…

"What's he not supposed to be doing….?"

Tim put his ear to the door and then yelled to Deanne and Perry…

"Hurry…help me push the sofa up against the back door!"

Perry, Tim and Deanne were pushing the sofa up to the back door when Mary screamed…

"LOOK OUT!"

The man in the ballerina's tutu wearing the clown's mask was pulling the boards away from the front window.

During the night when the man in the ballerina tutu was nailing the boards to the outside most of the glass was busted, and now with the boards gone, there would be very little to stop anyone from coming inside.

Tim yelled to Perry and Deanne telling them to push against the sofa, because the old man was going to break down the door with the tractor.

Tim ran to the front window and took the gun that Officer Withers gave him, from his coat.

Standing directly in front of the window, Tim took aim and waited…waited for whoever or whatever was trying to get inside.

Five to six boards were nailed against the windows as Tim thought to himself…

"If this is farmer brown and that ballerina's tutu wearing son of a bitch…he gets every bullet right in the head."

The last board was removed and Tim saw clearly that it was the man in the ballerina's tutu, standing there.

Tim removed the safety and fired nine shots, point blank into the man in the ballerina's tutu' head.

Mary, Deanne and Perry began screaming. The man in the ballerina's tutu fell backwards but not down, as Tim watched him first drop to one knee, and then stand straight up.

Tim looked in amazement as the man in the ballerina tutu was unaffected and walked off towards the back of the barn, holding his face with one hand and pounding along the side of the barn walls with other hand.

Tim started yelling for Deanne to come help him, as he pointed to the ground just below the window, saying...

"Do you see those boards; I need you to grab all three of them. Do you think you can do that?"

Deanne began backing up, crying and shaking her head saying...

"I-I-can't, the man...no I can't do it."

Tim grabbed onto Deanne's arm and said...

"Look if we don't get this window boarded back up the man is going to be on the inside...is that what you want?"

Deanne slowly walked towards the window while Tim was gently guiding her saying...

"That's it, the man is around back. I'm going to hold onto your legs and if I see anything, I'm jerking you back in."

While Deanne was crawling through the opening in the window, she said to Tim...

"Tim, if you let that sick man in the ballerina's tutu get me, I'm going to kick your ass."

Deanne grabbed all three boards and handed them to Tim, as he looked around the room for something to hammer them up with, when Perry shouted...

"Steve and Reggie were using that jack over there on the floor."

Tim nailed the last board up to the window when Perry yelled at Tim...

"Listen, I don't hear the tractor anymore...I think their gone."

Suddenly the man in the ballerina's tutu began pounding on the back door. The entire barn began shaking as if it were in a tornado.

Photos fell from the walls and all of the cabinets in the kitchen opened up and the contents rattled fell to the floor.

Deanne and Perry were huddled in the center of the living room area screaming. Tim rushed over to the sofa where Mary was and held her.

Suddenly the pounding and the screaming stopped. And then it started again, only this time there was a loud rushing wind which was sounded like a freight train.

Slowly the loud wind began dying down when Mary screamed.

On the other end of the sofa, Kristin was slowing getting up. She didn't get up as you would expect someone to, but she was rising straight up about two to three feet off of the floor.

Mary and Perry began crying, and yelling. Deanne stood in the center of the room a few feet from Kristin in shock, softly crying...

"K-Kristin...Kristin."

Kristin's eyes were closed and her head hung down so that her chin touched her chest. Her arms hung limp beside her body, and then her head began moving around and around in a circular motion.

Deanne did not move from the spot she was standing in, all the while softly crying for her best friend in the entire world...

"Oh my God Kristin...no, no, no."

The Kristin's head slowly rolled in a circular motion and then it stopped, and her eyes opened wide.

Deanne stepped back and screamed, because the eyes she was looking at were not Kristin's. Kristin had blue eyes, but these eyes were black and lifeless, much like a doll's eyes.

Slowly Kristin's tongue parted her lips, as she began licking her lips from side to side. Her tongue extended down below her chin.

When Kristin's tongue came out of her mouth...it was long, slender and black and moved much like a snake when it flicks its tongue.

Kristin's tongue slowly went back into her mouth as she opened her mouth wide, and in a mechanical demonic voice said...

"La-la-la-la-la-la-, la-la-la-la-la-la

Teddy Bear Soda Crackers, got you all inside

Watch and see...to this girl

Follow or you'll die

La-la-la-la-la-la-, la-la-la-la-la-la-la

Tim shouted to Deanne as he grabbed hold of her arm pulling her back, saying...

"Get back Dee, get away from her!"

Kristin began floating down and past Deanne and heading up the stairs, her feet still dangling a few inches above the floor.

Tim, Mary, Perry and Deanne watched as Kristin's body slowly ascended up the steps.

At the top of the steps a bright light, almost blue engulfed the entire hallway and stairwell, as Kristin was sucked into it and disappeared.

Deanne turned to Tim crying hysterical saying...

"We got to get out of here... we got to get out of here... we got to get out of here!"

Looking over at Mary who was also crying, Tim said as he checked the gun which was still in his hand...

"EVERYBODY QUIET... we can't get out of here...we can't go outside, and we can't go upstairs...we're trapped."

Tim told Deanne and Perry to help him carry David over to the sofa, so that everybody would be together.

Mary cried out to Tim...

"What are we going to do Tim...what are going to do, the big man and the creepy kids...I-I don't want to die in this shit Tim."

Tim explained that there was only one thing he could think of and that was, someone was going to have to sneak out of the barn and run to Mr. Thomas' house and call the Fire Department.

Perry looked at Tim saying...

"The Fire Department... what good is a Fireman going to do, we need the police or the Sherriff. They are killing us one by one."

Tim told Perry that...

"I already tried the Sherriff once and after he didn't find anything the first time...well he won't believe anything that we told him... we'd be wasting our time.

Perry looked over at Tim and said...

"But what are we going to do?"

Tim stated...

"*We need to get some attention, we're in the middle of nowhere, and the Fire Department would bring a lot of help, maybe even the local news, who knows what else.*"

Deanne stood up shaking and trembling saying...

"*Why don't we pick up Mary and David and all of us get out and start running.*"

Tim walked back to the window, examining the boards which he nailed up and said...

"*Dee, as soon as we start ripping away these boards, farmer brown and that crazy old man will rush right to the front window, and with David and Mary unable to walk...all of us are going to get caught.*"

Mary who was sitting on the sofa with her feet propped up tried to put them down on the floor to show Tim she could walk, when she fell back onto the sofa screaming in pain.

Crying, Mary yelled to Tim...

"*Tim, please don't leave me here...don't leave me Tim... don't leave me.*""

Tim knelt down in front of Mary reassuring her and looking at her feet which were leaking more pus and fluids, as well as bleeding, saying...

"*Baby, I'm not going to leave you...I promise.*"

Perry sat on the arm of the sofa biting her nails saying...

"*Okay, so we either sit here until they get all of us or one of us makes a run to Mr. Thomas' house to call the Fire Department, which means whoever goes will probably get caught...right?*"

Tim and Perry looked at Deanne who was shaking her head and saying...

"*No, don't look at me, I'm not going out there...I don't want to die...I don't want to die.*"

Tim said to Deanne...

"*Dee you and I are the only ones who have been inside that house and knows where the phone is, and Mary, Perry and David will stand a much better chance if I stay and you go.*"

Deanne snapped at Tim as she walked over towards the sofa to be next to David, saying...

"Tim! I hate that macho bullshit...if everybody in here would stand a better chance with you being here instead of me, then why are we trapped inside of this barn scared out of her minds?"

Tim stood there with a guilty look on his face, but also realized that what Deanne said was true, but for the situation they were in.

Mary clutched at Tim's arm crying and said...

"No Tim! You said you weren't going leave me here."

Tim knelt down and kissed Mary saying...

"Baby, I know I said that but we have no choice now. It'll only take me fifteen maybe twenty minutes and I'll be back...I came back before right?"

Mary kissed Tim and said in his ear...

"And what if you don't come back...what am I supposed to do?"

Tim gathered Deanne and Perry in the kitchen and told them as he handed Perry the Jack and Deanne a large pot from the kitchen cabinet...

"Okay, Perry you're going to re-nail the boards back up once I'm out of the window, and Dee, as soon as I get ready to pry the boards away from the window, start banging on the back door with that pot and don't stop until Perry tells you, that I made it."

Deanne was screaming and pounding on the back door with the pot, Tim had pulled two ends off of three boards and was running towards Mr. Thomas' house.

Perry signaled to Deanne to pound louder as she re-nailed the boards back to the window.

Tim had told Mary that fifteen maybe twenty minutes and he'd be back as Mary continued asking Deanne...

"How long has it been, do you see Tim?"

Tim had made it to Mr. Thomas's house and hadn't seen any sign of the old man, nor the dogs that chased him and Officer Withers late last night.

Before going inside, Tim stopped on the side of the house to relieve himself and as he was finishing, he felt something brush past him.

Tim jumped and zipped up his fly quickly and looked all around him, but no one was there.

Tim could see through the light fog the barn and then ran into the house, through the back door and to the phone which he remembered being in the study, where the dogs had chased Officer Withers and himself.

Tim scanned the semi dark house which looked as if not even Mr. Thomas lived in it...his biggest worry being the dogs, which were not inside the house.

There was a coffee cup on the kitchen counter with coffee in it and as soon Tim picked it up, the coffee which was in the cup was no longer liquid, but had more of a molasses consistency to it.

Tim went to sit the coffee cup down on the table which broke when his fingers sat the cup on the saucer.

Tim noticed next to the coffee cup there was a saucer with several cookies on it.

Without thinking and not having anything to eat since early that morning, Tim grabbed two of the cookies and after smelling took a small bite.

Seeing that there was nothing wrong with the cookie... he crammed both cookies in his mouth and began chewing.

Tim headed towards the study when he felt his tongue tingling. The chewed up cookies began burning the inside of his mouth.

The chewed up gooey cookies in his throat made Tim feel as if his throat was swelling.

Tim tried spitting out the chewed up cookies, but because of stuffing three cookies in his mouth at one time, the gooey cookies were stuck in his throat.

Tim ran back into the kitchen and stuck his face underneath the faucet to get some water to wash down the gooey cookies.

When Tim first stuck his mouth under the faucet, there was warm foul tasting water filling Tim's mouth.

The water was almost as if he had sewage water in his mouth, as he tried spitting everything out.

Tim could feel something in his mouth on top of his tongue... panicking, Tim reached up with his thumb and his index finger and grabbed a hold of something large and firm like tar, and began pulling it from his mouth.

Tim had in his fingers a large gooey matter which kept coming until Tim revealed a twelve inch mass of black goo, which he dropped in the kitchen sink.

Tim stood there coughing for a minute and when he looked down into the sink, the large black goo began wiggling, when Tim ran to the study crying...

"Oh God....!"

Tim spotted the telephone on the desk in Mr. Thomas' study and before using it he peeked out the window to make sure Mr. Thomas of the man in the ballerina's tutu hadn't noticed him entering the house.

Feeling safe that his movements went undetected Tim went back to the phone and picked up the receiver and put it to his ear and heard a loud dial tone.

Letting out a sigh of relief Tim took a deep breath and dialed the operator, and after several rings a voice on the other end answered.

Tim stood in the study with a shocked look on his face as he took the phone away from his ear when he heard...

"This is the operator...hold on Tim, I'll ring the Sherriff's office for you."

Tim slowly put the phone back up to his mouth and said...

"Wait a minute...I didn't call for the Sherriff, and how do you know my name?"

The operator's voice got very low and raspy saying...

"Oh Tim we know who you are...we know who everyone is, and you can't get away."

Tim laid the phone down, and as he stood there in disbelief, looking at the phone, and picked it up.

The phone was an old push button phone, and as Tim lifted the phone...there was no wiring connecting the phone.

Just then something out of Tim's right eye caught his attention, something was moving in the darkness.

Tim looked around the musky dark room trying to focus his eyes when, he caught a glimpse of a pair of red eyes in the corner swaying from side to side.

Tim slowly moved in the direction of the back door, keeping the pair of red eyes in view.

With every step that Tim took, the red eyes matched his step, until Tim bolted for the back door slamming it shut and running out of the house.

Tim stood at the corner of the house, panting and trying to figure out what he should do next.

He thought as he stood there...

"I can't leave and go into town, the whole town's in on it...I got to get back to the barn...to Mary...but what if I don't make it."

Tim felt his only recourse was to run as fast as he could back to the barn.

Tim was trying to talk himself into running when he smelled a foul odor behind him and the panting of hot breath on his neck.

Tim turned quickly only to discover there was nothing or no one behind him, and so Tim counted...one, two, three and then he took off running.

Tim's heart was racing as he ran the mile or so to David and Deanne's barn...Tim stopped when he was within ten feet of the barn.

Looking in all directions and checking to see if the man in the ballerina's tutu and Mr. Thomas were nowhere around Tim reached in his pocket for his lighter, and began flicking it hoping to attract Perry's attention, who was at the window watching for Tim.

Slowly and quietly, step by step, Tim approached the front door of the barn, turning every second or so...looking for the man in the ballerina's tutu and Mr. Thomas.

Tim looked behind to see if the red eyes had followed him when he heard a creaking sound and the sound of Deanne pounding on the back door with the pot.

Perry was removing the boards from the window, as Tim ran and began crawling through the opening when something had grabbed his ankles.

Tim tried to turn over and look back to see who it was that had his ankles, but was unable to.

Finally, Tim was able to get inside the barn with Perry pulling his legs, and once inside Perry and Tim began nailing up the boards against the window.

Tim scrambled to his feet and then ran over to Mary saying...

"Whew...It's not good, everybody...I mean the town is in on it."

Perry and Deanne walked over to Tim saying...

"What do you mean the whole town is in on it... is the Fire Department coming or what?"

Tim sat for a moment and then ruffled his hair, trying to regain his composure and said...

"No...no one's coming. I called the operator, and before I said what I wanted she called my name out and said...we can't get away."

Perry looked and Deanne and then at Tim and said...

"Now will you explain what in the hell that means...she called your name?"

Tim explained to Mary, Perry and Deanne what happened when he tried calling the Fire Department, and the operator called his name without Tim saying who he was.

Deanne looked at Tim and said...

"So in other words Tim, we're screwed...right?"

Perry said...

"Yeah, that's what he's saying...we went through all of that, and for what?"

Mary started to cry and said to Deanne...

"Dee Tim tried, why don't you all just lay off of him, he's been through a lot!"

Perry looked over at Mary and said...

"I'm sorry girl...but he isn't getting off that easy, we could've all gotten out of here, but he wanted to call for the damn Fire Department...now look, we're right back where we started... and even worse if the whole town is in on it."

Deanne grabbed Perry's arm and said...

"Hey cool it...we're all in the same crap, so we got to figure out how we're going to get out of here."

Perry snapped...

"Well, we're not listening to boy wonder again...call the Fire Department...oh boy."

Just then the pounding on the back door started up again, only this time, it didn't sound like the man in the ballerina's tutu was beating on the door, because the pounding sounded more like...kid's hands slapping the door.

Suddenly, the sofa which was up against the back door started moving forward, as the back door began opening up.

Mary started screaming and hollering for Tim as Deanne and Perry were sliding on the floor, as they tried pushing the sofa back against the back door.

Tim got up to run over to where Deanne and Perry were when suddenly the remaining front window glass was being busted out.

Tim stopped dead in his tracks trying to decide whether to help Deanne and Perry, or to prevent the entire front window from being smashed all altogether.

When Tim turned back to the window he saw the grotesque little creepy kids coming through the window, climbing on top of one another, as they struggled to get inside.

Tim saw on the table the pot that Deanne used to pound on the back door and hollered for Perry to get it and swap places with him.

Perry ran to the window with the pot and began beating the grotesque creepy kids in the head and hands, until one by one...they started to back out the window.

Tim and Deanne got the sofa back up against the back door when Perry screamed. As Tim turned he saw that one of the grotesque creepy kids had crashed in through the window and was biting Perry on the neck.

Tim raced back over to the window and freed Perry from the grip of the grotesque creepy kid who was biting Perry and threw it to the floor.

Tim and Perry watched as the grotesque creepy kid scrambled across the floor almost like a penguin would walk, and then the grotesque creepy kid started climbing the wall.

Deanne yelled over at Tim saying...

"They're pushing the sofa again...I don't think I can stop them!"

Tim ran over to Deanne saying...

"We don't have a choice we're going to have to get upstairs, they're going to get in here!"

Deanne and Perry picked up Mary by her legs and arms, as Tim ran over to help David stand.

Deanne shouted back to Tim, as he helped David to his feet...

"We're going to the last bedroom on the left...it's the only room that has a door which locks!"

David was nearly unconscious on his feet so Tim bent down and took David's right arm and placed it around his shoulders and shouted for Deanne and Perry to hurry up the steps...

"I think now would be a good time to hurry, they're almost inside!"

Deanne and Perry had carried Mary up the steps, and were on the last step when Deanne turned and saw Tim stagger and fall to the floor as David lost consciousness.

Deanne laid Mary's legs on the floor and told Perry to drag her, because she was going to help Tim.

Deanne and Tim had to literally carry David up the steps, and as they made it upstairs, the back door burst open and Deanne screamed.

Tim and Deanne each grabbed one of David's arms and the drug him down the hallway and into the last bedroom where Perry and Mary were waiting.

Locking the door behind them Deanne ran over to help Perry get Mary onto the bed as her feet began bleeding again, as Mary screamed in pain.

Tim scanned the bedroom which was a nice size bedroom, close to one hundred and twenty square feet.

When Deanne and David had the barn remodeled, the upstairs in particularly the last bedroom on the left was the last one worked on which had very little furniture in it, other than the bed, dresser and a chair.

All of a suddenly Deanne and Perry shouted as they heard scratching sounds and the door knob trying to turn...

"They're at the door!"

Tim went over to the bedroom door and looking at the door's lock, saw that it was a brass rim lock which took a skeleton key, and up top there was a matching chain lock.

When Tim turned, Perry was lightly dabbing Mary's bloody feet with one of the pillow cases from the bed, and Deanne was caressing and holding David's head.

Tim walked over to the window turning around several times to keep an eye on the door, and looked to see if he could see anyone moving about outside.

The scratching sounds coming from the other side of the door were growing loud, followed by laughter and singing...

"La-la-la-la-la-la-, la-la-la-la-la-la,

Teddy Bear soda crackers,

Got you all upstairs,

Take a deep breath, don't you scream

Time to make you wish you were dead

La-la-la-la-la-la-, la-la-la-la-la-la."

Deanne, Perry, Mary and Tim turned to the door, as Deanne shouted and threw one of her shoes at the door, and screamed...

"*What's up with that stupid ass song...I HATE GODDAMN TEDDY BEARS!*"

Immediately, a voice from the other side of the door said...

"...and Teddy Bear hates you too...frito feet!"

Tim turned back and looked at Deanne and noticed something really wrong, saying...

"*Where the hell is Perry?*"

Deanne and Mary looked at one another as Tim scanned the entire bedroom saying again...

"*Where is Perry, she was sitting right there wrapping Mary's feet!*"

Deanne and Mary looked at each other in shock, and then Mary looked down at her feet and said...

"*My feet...what are you talking about, and who in the hell is Perry?*"

Tim walked over to Mary, pointing at her feet saying...

"*Wait a minute...your feet were bleeding and Perry was cleaning up the blood.*"

Deanne got up and laid David's head down gently and looked at Tim saying...

"Tim, that damn marijuana's fried your brain...there's nothing wrong with Mary's feet, who the hell is Perry?"

Tim bent down at Mary's feet and lifted one foot and said...

"Oh shit...Mary, your feet were all messed up and bleeding, and Perry was..."

Mary looked up at Tim as she jerked her foot out of Tim's hand saying...

"As you can see Tim, there isn't a damn thing wrong with my feet and answer the question...who is Perry?"

Tim slid against the wall, shaking his head and saying...

"No-no, wait a minute...Perry, Reggie's wife...she was right there!"

Mary walked up to Tim saying...

"Babe, get a grip, we have a psycho out there trying to kill us, and you're freaking out over some invisible woman...C'mon Tim, back to earth."

Tim stood against the wall with his head lifted and looking into space said...

"Hell no...they're trying to make me think this is just an illusion...no."

Just then the scratching noise started at the door followed by those creepy voices, laughing and singing...

"La-la-la-la-la-la-, la-la-la-la-la-la,

Teddy Bear Soda Crackers

Tim, Tim, Tim...

Ha-ha-ha-ha, he-he-he

Tim's mind is getting soft

La-la-la-la-la-la-, la-la-la-la-la-la."

Tim walked over to the door and balled up his fist and pounded on the door saying...

"Shut up you twisted fucks...if you're going to get us, then come on!"

Deanne walked over to Mary and whispered in her ear, saying...

"Mary, I think Tim's smoked way too much shit, and who in the heck is Perry, do you know who he's talking about?"

Mary walked over with Deanne to check on David saying...

"I've got no ideal Dee...I'm still trying to figure out why he thought my feet were bleeding."

Just then David began moaning and then coughing when Deanne said...

"Hey Perry, will you help me prop Blue up?"

Tim's head popped up as he saw Perry laying the pillow case over Mary's feet and saying...

"Tim, watch Mary for a sec and don't let her move any."

Tim glanced back at Mary who was lying in the bed and said...

"Wait a minute...wait a minute!"

Perry stopped and turned to Tim saying...

"Okay then, you go help Deanne and I'll stay here with Mary."

Tim starred at Deanne as he walked over to Deanne, and once he had knelt down to help prop up David he whispered to Deanne...

"Deanne what just happened?"

Deanne and Tim propped David up against the bedroom wall and said...

"You mean us being locked in here, creepy little big headed things trying to get at us or that twisted fucker in the ballerina's tutu chasing us...take your pick.

Tim looked Deanne in the eye as he grabbed her arms saying...

"Dee, you know what I'm saying...I'm talking about just a second ago Perry wasn't here and Mary's feet were okay...that's what I'm talking about."

Deanne jerked away from Tim saying...

"First of all, get your goddamn hands off of me...NOW!"

Perry stood up and saying...

"You guys alright over there?"

Deanne looked at Perry as she sat down next to David saying...

"Yeah... we're good."

Tim walked away from Deanne and past Perry to the bedroom window, saying...

"No we're not, what we are is screwed...and those things and that fat ass man in the ballerina's tutu are all inside now, and we're locked in bedroom with no way out."

Just then Perry, Deanne and David heard the sounds of a lot of people walking up the steps and down the hallway towards them.

The sounds of laughter, whispers, knocking and dragging, along with multiple over lapping conversations started out loud and then faded as they passed the bedroom door where Tim, Deanne, David, Mary and Perry were holding up.

Perry had her face to the door trying to see out of the key hole, as she waved for Tim to come over to the door.

Tim knelt down next to Perry and asked her...

"You can't see anything can you?"

Perry moved out of the way allowing Tim to look in the skeleton key hole, saying...

"What do you think?"

Tim stood up and called Perry and Deanne over to the middle of the bedroom and said to Deanne...

"I don't know...is there another room pass this one Dee?"

Deanne paused and then said to Tim...

"No there's nothing after you pass this room except a window... why?"

With his back to the door and walking over to the window and seeing a parade of dark figures coming out of the woods, and entering through the barn's back door, Tim said...

"It looks like we're about to have a lot of company!"

Rushing to the window, Perry and Deanne looked out of the window and as they did they saw a parade of figures coming out of the woods through the light fog and towards the barn.

Deanne and Perry looked at one another and then back to Tim who was on the other side of the window, saying...

"Tim...who are all of those people?"

Tim stood watching as they entered the barn saying...

"I don't think they're people...I mean they look like people...but look at them...you can see right through them."

Perry walked back over to the door and got down on her stomach and watching the shadows passing in front of the door, waved at Deanne and Tim whispering...

"Hey, they're all going past the door."

As Tim, Perry and Deanne stood with their eyes glued to the door, suddenly it shook and then burst open.

Tim ran over and tried with all of his might to close the door when Deanne tapped Tim on the shoulder saying...

"Look Tim...Look."

Tim, Deanne and Perry stood as Mary rose up off of the bed, saying...

"Tim...Tim...oh no, what's going on?"

Mary was floating in air in a seated position, as Tim and Perry tried pulling Mary back down on the bed.

Just then a face from one of the figures in the hallway stuck its head in and screamed at Tim and Perry...

"Let her... GO!"

With that, the face opened its mouth wide and began blowing as Perry and Tim were forced back against the wall.

Deanne stood helpless as she watched Mary leaving the bedroom and disappearing into the hallway.

The moment that Mary left the room, the bedroom door began closing and opening, as more and more figures passed by the bedroom.

Tim walked over to the bedroom door when suddenly a ghastly face appeared out of the crowd of figures and stuck its face in Tim's face, fingering for Tim to step closer.

Tim stood at the door as though he was in a trance, not hearing Perry and Deanne's objections...

"No Tim...No!"

Tim looked out the door and as he turned his head to look at the figure, he saw all of them disappearing one by one at the end of the hallway.

Just then Deanne shouted at Tim...

"Tim...where are they going?"

403

Whether Tim was in a trance or in shock, which ever, he still did not hear Deanne shouting, so Perry grabbed Tim's arm saying...

"Hey Tim, Tim...you okay?"

Tim finally snapped to, and backed in to the bedroom saying...

"They-they want us to follow them."

Perry walked away from Tim mumbling...

"Oh brother...here we go again."

Just then Deanne hollered to Tim, saying...

"Tim, what are you talking about...I thought we were supposed to be trying to get away from them!"

Tim sat down on the bed and said to Deanne, Perry...

"Don't ask me how I know...but that thing said we are to follow them or they'll make us...That face, was inside my head and said the crowds of people were those from all over, just like us."

Deanne told Tim...

"Tim I don't know what you're talking about, but me and Blue are not going anywhere with those creepy ass people...you can go if you want to, but I'm staying right here where I belong."

Tim opened his mouth to speak and as he did, the voice which they heard was not Tim's but it was a mechanical one which said...

"This reality is no longer yours!"

Perry and Deanne stood looking in horror at Tim, as the voice continued...

"There is another dimension beside this one...do you think this is the only reality?"

Just then Tim looked around the room at Deanne, Perry, and David saying...

"What...What are you looking at me like that for?"

Deanne walked up to Tim saying...

"Do you have any what you just said?"

Tim looked at Perry first then over to Deanne saying...

"*What are you talking about...I didn't say anything...where's Mary?*"

Perry walked over to the bed and said...

"*Oh yes you did...you were talking in this weird creepy voice telling us some crap about another dimension and some other weird shit like that.*"

Tim stood up with a puzzled look on his face and was about to say something when all of the lights in the house out, as Deanne screamed.

Seconds later, the lights came back on and when they did...David's limp body was floating across the floor towards the door.

Deanne ran over to David and grabbed hold onto his waist and began pulling him yelling...

"*Oh no you don't...help me Tim!*"

Perry started screaming as she saw Deanne and David being dragged across the room towards the door.

Tim made it to Deanne and grabbed Deanne and David trying to stop David from being pulled out the room but their combined strength was no match for whatever was pulling David's body.

As David's body left the bedroom and into the hallway, Tim grabbed hold of Deanne as David's body accelerated and then disappeared, as Deanne cried...

"*BLUE...BLUE!*"

David's body disappeared in the hallway, as Deanne was screaming and crying. Tim dragged Deanne back into the bedroom as the door slammed shut, trying to console her and preventing her from following David.

Tim followed Deanne as she walked over towards the window crying...

"*Oh my God....Blue...Blue.*"

Just then Perry started crying, saying...

"*Oh man, they're taking us one by one...somebody stop this shit!!*"

Tim stood at the doorway crying as the lights went out and Perry screamed.

Just then Tim felt a tug on his shirt sleeve and the sound of Deanne's voice saying...

"*Tim...Tim where are we...where are we?*"

Tim cried out to Deanne saying...

"I don't have a clue where we are."

Just then a man's voice answered Tim, a voice Tim didn't recognize saying...

"We're in some kind of cage."

Deanne held onto Tim as he shouted...

"CAGE! What are you talking about...who are you?"

The man responded...

"The name is not important... as a matter of fact nothing is important anymore.

Several years ago I was on the beach in California walking and the next thing I knew I was here walking around just like you."

Deanne started crying and said to Tim...

"Tim what's he talking about, we can't see anything except darkness how does he know we're in a cage?"

Just then another voice in front of Deanne said...

"Don't worry you'll find out soon enough...when you've been here as long as we have, you'll have a chance to walk all over this place and soon enough, your hands will run into the bars that's holding us prisoner."

As Deanne began screaming, she heard the voice of Mary...

"Dee, Dee is that you?"

Deanne replied to Mary saying...

"Yes Mary it's me, I'm over here, where are you?"

Mary stretched out her arms, and as she did they came into contact with Deanne's back, as she said...

"Dee, is this you?"

Deanne turned around in the darkness feeling the hands which were on her back saying...

"Oh Mary, oh my God...I can't believe what's happening to us, some man said that we were in a cage."

Mary hugged Deanne crying in the darkness as people behind and in front of them bumped into Mary and Deanne saying...

"You can't stop...keep moving; we're supposed to keep moving, not supposed to stop walking."

Mary held onto Deanne as they began walking, when Mary said...

Oh my God Dee, I don't know where we are, or how we're going to get out of here...have you found Tim or Dave?"

Just as Deanne was about answer Mary, an arm touched Mary and said...

"Mar...oh my God Mar...it's me Tim."

Mary began crying tears of joy that Tim was with her and said...

Oh Tim, how did we get here and who are all of these people?"

As they aimlessly walked, the heard multiple conversations and people moaning and crying when the man who spoke to Tim said...

"Everyone in here are people from different places all over the world. We were in our homes and on our jobs when suddenly we came to a farm and then awakened in this place."

As soon as the man stopped talking another man whispered...

"We have been here for years, just walking never stopping, with no food or water. The odd thing is we never seem to be hungry or thirsty."

Deanne started crying and began shouting...

"Blue...Blue where are you, are you in here...Blue...Blue!"

Mary asked the man who spoke to them saying...

"Is this hell...do you think we're in hell?"

Just then the same mechanical voice shouted laughing...

"Where you are and where you are heading is far worse than hell...
Ha-ha-ha-ha-ha...aha-ha-ha-ha-ha."

Suddenly people were screaming as the mechanical voice shouted...

"Tick-Tock, Tick-Tock,
None of you shall leave until Teddy Bear's
Gathering is through...
Tick-Tock, Tick-Tock, Tick-Tock."

Just then, a dim light shone in the place where they walked, and instead of it being pitch black...a milky mist filled the place.

407

Tim, Mary, Perry and Deanne were finally able to see where they were. It was a large tunnel full of people pushing and shoving one another.

People of all ages, races, young and old, men and women, boys and girls, going in all directions, with bars surrounding them on all sides.

As they walked through this tunnel, and in no discernable order people were screaming as they were being plucked out.

Tim shouted to Mary, Deanne and Perry...

"Everybody hold on to one another."

Just then Mary screamed...

"TIM!"

"Teddy Bear Soda Crackers, Teddy Bear says,

Watch where you are and what you do,

Teddy says he'll see you, if not tonight real.......

Soon!"

BOO!

Printed in the United States
By Bookmasters